Our
Shadows
Have
Claws

Our Shadows Have Claws

15 Latin American Monster Stories

edited by Yamile Saied Méndez
and Amparo Ortiz

illustrations by Ricardo López Ortiz

ALGONQUIN 2022

Published by Algonquin Young Readers
an imprint of Algonquin Books of Chapel Hill
Post Office Box 2225
Chapel Hill, North Carolina 27515-2225

a division of Workman Publishing
225 Varick Street
New York, New York 10014

Library of Congress Cataloging-in-Publication Data
Names: Méndez, Yamile Saied, editor. | Ortiz, Amparo, editor.
Title: Our shadows have claws : 15 Latin American monster stories /
edited by Yamile Saied Méndez and Amparo Ortiz.
Description: First edition. | Chapel Hill, North Carolina : Algonquin, 2022. |
Audience: Ages 14 and up. | Audience: Grades 10-12. |
Summary: "Fifteen original short stories from YA superstars featuring the
monsters of Latine myths and legends"—Provided by publisher.
Identifiers: LCCN 2022011320 | ISBN 9781643751832 (hardcover) |
ISBN 9781643753331 (ebook)
Subjects: LCSH: Children's stories, American. | CYAC: Monsters—Fiction. | Animals,
Mythical—Fiction. | Short stories. | LCGFT: Short stories. | Mythological fiction.
Classification: LCC PZ5 .O9345 2022 | DDC [Fic]—dc23
LC record available at https://lccn.loc.gov/2022011320

10 9 8 7 6 5 4 3 2 1
First Edition

Para mi hermano Damián Omar Saied
—Y.S.M.

En honor a mi gran amiga, Maritza Cardona
—A. O.

Contents

Our Shadows Have Claws

The Nightingale
and the Lark

Chantel Acevedo

They say our myths are born in the rivers and valleys, in the mist-cloaked mogotes of Viñales and the cold caves of Matanzas.

They say our myths are open-mouthed screams, rows of jagged teeth, fiery balls of light, and mothers in mourning.

Our myths are also this: A whispered "Te veo," when nobody is around. A giggle in the night. A dirty rag around your throat.

Whatever the campesinos tell you about our myths, you'd better believe them, for they are formed of blood and sacrifice, torment and star-crossed love.

But be warned, this story is both a lesson and a curse. Most stories are.

Pebbles struck the window. My heart flickered like a flame at the sound.

I checked the door to my bedroom, making sure it was still locked. Outside, I could hear the noise of relatives gathered to celebrate both my fifteenth birthday and my first hunt. I'd told them I was still getting ready, and they'd left me alone for a few blessed moments. Just enough time for . . .

Tap, tap, tap.

The window again. Julio.

Julio Capó was here, and I could not ask for a better birthday present.

I opened the window quietly, slowly. There he stood in a shaft of moonlight, like a dream. Julio's dark hair was slicked back and stylish. He looked like a Cuban James Dean, and he'd chosen me, *me*, as his novia. It was a cold night, probably the chilliest of the year. Julio's breath came out in little clouds.

"Buenas noches, caballero," I whispered. He put his hand over his heart and sighed. I laughed at the dramatic gesture.

"I like when you laugh, Rosa." He shoved his hands in his pockets. "Have you thought what your birthday wish might be?"

I rested my elbow on the windowsill, set my chin on my hand. "If only birthday wishes really came true, I'd wish for Papá to let you come inside."

"He really doesn't like me." It was an understatement. The first time I'd invited Julio over, Papá had clapped him on the shoulder and taken him outside "for a talk." When they returned, Julio left without another word.

"It's not you," I said. "Not really."

Julio nodded. The Capós and the Monteagudos had never gotten along. The feud went back nearly a century, when Cuba had gone to war with Spain for its independence. The years of war had changed the island. By day, the Spanish butchers fought the rebels, the force of an empire coming down on our island. By night, other forces lurked, feeding off our suffering.

"Where there is war," Papá always said, "there are monsters. They are drawn to the violence, seduced by the evil on display in humans. And when monsters slip into a place, they never go away."

During the war, the Monteagudos became monster hunters, while the Capós sheltered the ones they could find. They argued that the vampires, werewolves, cagüeiros—all of them—were people in pain, people who could be rescued, made good again. The specifics of our families' ancient grudge were lost to time. Papá always told me that the Capós had once sheltered a vampire so vicious that it had killed every man, woman, and child in the entire village of Santa Damiana. The Capós claimed no such being ever existed, though it was true that even today, Santa Damiana is a village ringed like a fortress by sharpened stakes and festooned with garlic wreaths on every door. Meanwhile, the Capós said that the Monteagudos had once shot every animal in the Valle del Silencio for fear that the valley was overrun with cagüeiros. We vowed we didn't, but the valley remains eerily silent, bereft of birdsong or the whistling of jutías in the treetops. Whatever the truth was, somehow everything came to a head between the families, and a pact was made. Monteagudos could not step on Capó property, and the monsters the Capós were trying to rehabilitate were only safe within the bounds of Capó territory.

As far as I knew, the pact had never been broken by either side, but tensions lingered. Capós and Monteagudos didn't socialize, didn't meet one another's gaze in the street. They attended different churches, shopped in different stores, and they absolutely, definitely did not fall in love with each other.

Yet somehow, against the odds, Julio was here at my window.

Except, he wasn't quite himself the night of my birthday. His eyes were as they always had been—brown with pools of green in them, like swirling galaxies—but there were dark circles beneath them and the corners of his mouth were turned down. I suspected the reason. "How's Marcelo?" I asked. His brother, who was two years older than Julio, had been ill.

"Better," he said. "Sleeping less than before."

"Ah, that's good."

"One day you'll meet him," Julio said, brightening. "He's funny and brave. More handsome than I am, too." He stopped and his lip curled in that delicious smirk I so loved. "Never mind. You'll fall in love with him and leave me behind. Pretend I don't have a brother."

I muffled my laughter behind my hands. I wanted to tell Julio that what he'd described could never be. That there was only one person for me, and he was it. But I wasn't brave enough to do that just yet. "I wish I had a brother or sister," I said instead. "Maybe then my parents wouldn't ask so much of me. I could be their lazy, useless child."

"You could never be that, Rosa. You always give everything your all."

Before I knew it, the words had left my mouth: "I'd give you my all."

Time stopped. I wished it would go in reverse, wished I could take the words back even if they were true. But Julio only blushed.

Good Julio, kind and gentle Julio, oh!

"You're going to go hunting tonight, aren't you?" he asked. He crept closer as he spoke, making me feel like *I* was being hunted. My stomach flipped in anticipation.

4

"I am," I said, not hiding the pride in my voice. I'd trained all my life for my first hunt. I wasn't ashamed, even if it was Julio, a Capó full of Capó convictions and self-righteousness, looking at me like that. Monsters were monsters, and the people of Dos Ríos depended on my family to keep them safe.

"Do you know your target?" Julio asked. He spoke very slowly, and I know he was trying to keep an edge of criticism out of his tone.

I shook my head. "Vampire, maybe? Chupacabra perhaps. I know someone reported a horse on Calle Maestra drained of blood and still attached to a wagon."

Julio took a very deep breath. He stepped closer. "Promise me you'll be careful, Rosa."

"I promise," I whispered. "And you be careful, too." Julio frowned at that but didn't argue with me. Whenever the papers printed an obituary for a member of the Capó family, everyone just assumed they'd died violently, betrayed by the monsters they were trying to help.

My family was getting louder on the other side of my bedroom door. Soon, they'd knock, demanding I come out for cake and presents.

"My rose. My sweet-smelling rose," Julio whispered, urgency driving him to my window, his elbows crowding mine on the sill. He pulled my hand out from under my chin. His breath was on my face. "Promise me you'll be merciful."

I swallowed. I wasn't trained to be merciful. I was trained to be brutal and quick. Perhaps that's the humane way to do it, but it wasn't mercy.

"Rosa! Come out!" my mother called.

"Ya voy, ya voy," I shouted in return. "Julio. I have to go."

"You didn't promise," he insisted.

"I can't promise that."

"Then promise you'll look them in the eyes before you kill them, Rosa." He swallowed hard, and my heart felt like it was shattering in pieces.

"I swear it. I swear by the moon above."

Julio's left eyebrow went up. "The moon? She's a fickle thing to swear by."

Outside, my relatives were chanting my name, "Rosa! Rosa! Rosa!" I know they were only teasing, insisting that I come out and join the party, but it felt like they were cheering me on.

Julio laughed softly. "Rosa, Rosa," he whispered, mimicking them.

Impulsively, I leaned over and kissed him. I tried to capture all of the sensations at once—the press of his lips, the sweetness of his breath, the way the stubble on his cheek felt under my hand. Our mouths parted and then everything fell away and I thought for one wild moment that we would be able to do this one thing forever and ever.

A snapping sound behind Julio startled us both. The top of my head banged against the window, rattling the frame. I turned toward the source of the sound. Julio gripped one of my hands fiercely. For a second, we stared into the night. I knew where Papá kept his machete and his gun. The muscles in my legs tensed, ready to run for the weapons if needed. We watched for a few moments before a calico cat jumped out of the avocado tree in my yard. It peered at us intently. A star-shaped patch of fur was set over its eyes. It meowed loudly, then leaped away.

"Maldito gato," we both swore at the same time.

Relief made me giggle, but Julio was still staring out into the darkness. Gently, I turned his face so that we were looking at one another again. But he was distracted, his eyes darting behind me, watching the door to my bedroom.

"Julio, stay with me." I meant in the moment. I meant to focus on us. But if he'd misunderstood, if he'd crawled through the window to hide under my bed until I returned, I wouldn't have protested.

"How's your head?"

"Fine," I said. "Stay with me."

"I'll come tomorrow after dark."

"ROSA! Por Dios!" my mother shouted, right at my door.

"Coming!" I said. Our time was up, and it felt like being robbed.

Julio squeezed my hand again and gave it one last kiss, then he was gone.

My relatives cheered when I finally left my bedroom and entered the living room. "Al fin" and "Felicidades," they said, wishing me all manner of good things.

"Tan linda," my cousin Berto said as he took my hand and gave me a twirl. My dress whirled around me. It had been sewn by my abuela Aris. She made it of turquoise taffeta and my shoes were dyed to match. Mamá played records while the family chatted. The Big Bopper and Richie Valens sang for a while, and then Mamá switched it out to a Sonora Matancera record, and everyone danced to the rumbas and Celia's soaring voice. Every so often, a relative would pull me aside to give me a gift, urging me to open it at once. I received a second dress made by Abuela, this time in pink, a pair of saddle shoes from my tío Ernesto, and from my parents, tiny ruby earrings that glinted like drops of blood. There were other gifts, too—a necklace with an azabache to ward off evil, a knife with a mother-of-pearl handle, and the fang of a madre de aguas monster dangling from a chain.

It was tradition to display one's gifts on their bed so that relatives might come in and admire them. I took a moment to lay them all out, the earrings beside the knife, the fang and azabache on their chains draped over the dress. Mamá came in to see how I was doing.

"My girl is getting so grown," she said, and kissed the top of my head. Then she noticed my window. "You know better than to leave this open." She latched it closed again. "Unspeakable things lurk in the night."

I felt my cheeks burning. What would Mamá say if she knew Julio had been at my window earlier in the evening? What would she think if she could read the contents of my heart? All my life, I'd been told that the Capós were idiots, that their softness made them treacherous. Meanwhile, Julio had been taught that the Monteagudos were the real monsters in the story of our island. That we were bloodthirsty, battle-obsessed, and hard of heart.

I'd believed it, too, until the night of Asela Monteagudo's wedding. The reception was held in a courtyard lit by paper lanterns. Guests were given paper masks to wear. The elders objected to the masks, saying that any stranger could hide behind them, but stylish Asela insisted. I was dancing to a bolero with a cousin of the groom's, a boy named Tomás Robaina, who stepped on my shoes the whole time. Then Julio came along.

"I thought I knew what beauty was but then I saw you," he said to me right over Tomás's shoulder, bold as anything.

I stopped dancing. My heart hammered in my chest.

Tomás sputtered, but I gave him a small smile and slipped my hand out of his sweaty palm midsong, grateful for the excuse to get away. "You flirt by the book," I told Julio once my former dance partner was out of earshot. He laughed. I liked the way his eyes crinkled closed. That was the start of everything. We only danced the one song together, and I wish that I remembered which song it was. The moment I saw those celestial eyes, I knew I was happily doomed.

I wished I could say all of this to Mamá.

Mamá ran her hands over my hair, smoothing it down. She arranged the ribbon in my ponytail so that the loops were even. "I'm so proud of you, Rosa," she said when she was finished, leaning forward and touching the tip of her nose to mine. Her eyes watered. "Your first hunt. I can't believe the night is already here."

"I've worked hard, Mamá," I said, worry in my stomach as I thought about the grisly work to come.

"I know. But you are a Monteagudo and you, mi vida, are ready. Are you scared?"

"A Monteagudo is never scared," I said as bravely as I could manage, though I couldn't help the hitch in my voice.

My mother smiled and kissed my cheek. "Así es. Let's go, quinceañera. Wait until you see the cake your tía Carmen made!" We linked arms and returned to the party.

The party lasted long into the night. I'd gossiped with my cousins and posed for photographs with every member of the family behind the cake table. My tía Carmen had, indeed, baked a beautiful three-tiered cake and frosted it with lemon-yellow icing. On the back patio, the men played dominó while the women chatted inside. My little cousins wanted to dance with me, and I twirled them around like princesses.

And I endured the question "¿Tienes novio?" from everyone, only smiling demurely in response.

After midnight, once the last of the cousins had left and my house was quiet again, I sat on the couch and tugged my satin pumps off my swollen feet. Leaning back on the cushions and closing my eyes, I thought of Julio. He was there always, seared in my imagination. I envisioned him in my room, the two of us together at last. In my dreams, whenever the morning came, and the lark cried out, he would rise to leave, and I would urge him to stay, saying, "No, Julio, it is the nightingale you hear. The moon is still young in the sky."

And Julio would loom over me, a smile turning his countenance into a blinding light, and he would stay.

Suddenly, I felt the sofa shift and I startled awake. Papá was sitting beside me.

"Happy birthday, sleepyhead," he said, his voice a deep, gravelly thing. I leaned my head on his shoulder.

Papá. My strong, stubborn, Papá. Oh.

"¿Lista?" he asked.

The piece of cake I'd eaten was still sweet in my mouth and the dream in my head lingered, so real it felt I might reach out and touch it. "Yes, Papá."

That was all he needed to hear. He shoved his hand into his pocket and leaned forward. "This is how you prepare the bala," Papá instructed, holding a bullet up for me to see. He brought it to his mouth, placed it between his incisors and bit it hard, leaving a mark. Then he turned la bala and bit again, so that the second mark formed a cross on the metal. "You need silver bullets to kill a werewolf, but any kind will do for a cagüeiro as long as it's marked with a cross. Here," he said, and handed me another one from his pocket.

"We're hunting cagüeiro tonight?"

Papá nodded. "There's been one spotted near the Ortiz family's finca."

I put the bullet in my mouth and bit hard, feeling the metal give way under my teeth. It tasted coppery, like blood. So we proceeded, taking turns marking the bullets until Papá's gun was loaded. With each bite, I thought of the promise I'd made to Julio—to try to remember that the monsters were human underneath. The truth was I didn't know if I could do it.

I'd been preparing for this night since I could walk. As a little girl, I had practiced handling the machete against the thick trunk of a flamboyán in our backyard; I understood the mechanics of a gun; I knew how to get bloodstains out of fabric. For years, I'd sat and listened to the campesinos and their monster stories, unafraid. Only one monster frightened me. The cagüeiro. The cagüeiro always wrapped a rag around its neck, a trapo, one the monster knotted tightly against its throat, which gave it the ability to transform. A cagüeiro could be anyone or anything—a rat, a hound, a panther—and then it would do the devil's work. The worst of them would change into a different person, resembling somebody's abuelo, or little sister, or mamá. Once, Papá had a killed a cagüeiro in Santiago who had shifted into his estranged wife's mother and stabbed her when they embraced. The cagüeiro had told my father, "Tempt not a desperate man," and then shifted into Papá. When my father fired the bullet that killed the monster, he had seen his own death played out before him. Some nights, Papá wakes up in a cold sweat, dreaming of that moment. Mamá always makes him some tilo and stays up with him until the terror passes.

Because the cagüeiros are capable of such deception, our family had a code to prove our identity when in doubt. When we answered the door, we greeted each other with, "Tempt not a desperate man" as a reminder of how dangerous cagüeiros could be.

Cagüeiros weren't unlucky victims of a bite, like werewolves and vampires. They weren't ghosts who had been betrayed in life, or zombies infected by a disease that couldn't be helped. Cagüeiros could not be forced to wear their trapo. They elected to wear them. At best, the creatures were thieves, using their powers to steal from the campesinos, many of whom had very little to begin with. At worst, they were murderers. Either way, as long as cagüeiros were around, every creature out there could be one.

"Why would a person choose this life?" I'd asked my father once, and he told me that wickedness calls to certain hearts, but that the Monteagudo family exists to stamp it out. Papá and I were the latest in a long line of cagüeiro hunters, and we would do what needed to be done to keep Dos Ríos safe from monsters.

Of course, my first hunt would be a cagüeiro.

The night was cold, bitterly so for a Cuban winter, and Mamá had made me wear a bufanda wrapped three times around my neck. "Like a little cagüeiro," she'd joked, and Papá had sucked his teeth in disapproval. The scarf didn't help. My nose ran as we tracked the creature, and I couldn't feel my lips. We tramped through the Ortiz finca, where it had last been seen in the shape of an enormous land crab, stealing bottles of milk.

"Just a few days ago," Papá explained, "the cagüeiro we are hunting was spotted in the sky transformed as a wyvern. It was setting the roof of the Avilas' house on fire."

"Was everyone okay?"

"Yes, but Leticia Avila is still coughing up smoke. Pay attention, Rosa. The cagüeiro always escapes," Papá whispered. "That is, unless he's facing off with a member of the Monteagudo family. Then the beast is ours." It was his way of bolstering my confidence. A crackling noise behind a wooden shed caught our attention. Creeping silently, we walked past an oak that had been lightning-splintered. Our breath puffed out before us, faster now that we could hear a rustling ahead.

We rounded the shed and spotted the cagüeiro in the moment of transformation, shifting into a man. He had his back to us, but I watched as his limbs shortened, his fur fell away, his tail disappeared. He was a young man with dark hair, with a trapo hung around his neck. He held a small torch. The cagüeiro was unclothed, and he shivered so hard I thought his flame would go out. As we snuck forward, I stepped on a branch, snapping it. The cagüeiro must have heard us because he quickly began to retie the trapo.

"¡Diablo!" Papá cried, rushing forward to snatch the creature. I followed right behind my father, my hand on my machete, still in its sheath. Every muscle in my body tensed. I was clenching my back teeth together so hard my jaw ached.

This was the moment I had trained for. "Te tengo," Papá said, grabbing the cagüeiro just as it transformed back into a thrashing calico cat.

The cat's squeals pierced my ears. Had this been the same cat that had spied on me and Julio? I drew closer. It was! I recognized the star-shaped patch over its eyes. Julio and I had been spied on by a cagüeiro. My hands tingled and I felt cold all over. What did it want? In that moment, I remembered my promise. I had to look at the cagüeiro in its eyes. "Stop, Papá!"

My father threw the cat on the ground and quickly stepped on its back, avoiding the claws. Looking up at me, he smiled. "That's my girl," he said, and handed me the gun with the marked bullets.

I took it shakily in hand as I drew closer.

"Cuidado, Rosa," Papá warned.

The cat was mewling now, his limbs weakening, striking my father's legs without effect. I knelt down and peered into its eyes, wondering what it was Julio hoped I'd see.

The gun fell from my hand.

I stumbled back.

Faster and faster I fled, never losing sight of the cat, until I lost my footing and was on the ground, too.

Galaxies. Galaxies in its eyes.

It couldn't be. It couldn't.

The crack of gunfire snapped me back to myself. My father held fast to the smoking gun still pointed at the cat, though the creature was finally motionless. Beside him, a small fire grew where the cagüeiro had dropped the torch. My father stomped it out with his foot.

"Tears, Rosa? For a cagüeiro?" my father sneered.

Julio. It was Julio's eyes I'd seen. The cat in the tree! Julio must have remembered that moment with me as he transformed. Dios mío, his last thoughts were of us! Of *us*! And my father had just murdered him! Smoke swirled around my father's ankles, and the world felt like it was tilting beneath me.

"I think he was just cold, Papá," I said, trying to compose myself even as it felt as if the world were crushing me down to nothing.

"La cabeza," Papá said softly, indicating the cagüeiro's head. He unsheathed his machete and tried to hand it to me, but I shook all over.

My brain felt like it was stretching, tearing. *Julio, ¡un cagüeiro!* my mind screamed at me, but I kept drawing a blank, forgetting where I was, or what was happening, unable to complete the thought.

Julio. Dead.

The odor of gunfire, sulfurous and rotten, filled the air between Papá and me and what was left of the cagüeiro. I watched in horror as my father squared his shoulders and held his machete firmly in both hands. Papá pointed to the cat's slender neck, and without wanting to, I calculated how much force one would need to cut through the muscle and bone, severing the head from its body.

Papá counted off. "Uno, dos . . ."

I closed my eyes and screamed, so I couldn't hear the sick crunch.

"Weak. Like a Capó," I heard my father mutter under his breath as he watched me cry. His words sliced through me, and my stomach twisted in revolt. How I wished I'd been a Capó then! Julio might have looked at me as a cousin or a sister and left me alone. Then his lost face wouldn't be swimming before my eyes, making me want to hurl myself against a tree and forget everything.

"Next time, you'll do better," Papá said after I'd gone quiet. "Get the trapo."

I crawled over to where the cagüeiro—no, *Julio*—lay. Trembling, I petted the soft fur. "Perdóname," I begged, then I picked up the trapo and held it to my heart.

"I don't know what's wrong with her," I could hear Papá saying from the other side of my bedroom door. My mother was sweeping the house, taking down birthday decorations, while my abuela snored on her rocking chair, a duster still in her hand. I ran to my bedroom, locked the door, and opened the window. I could hear the River Cauto in the distance, crying out on my behalf because I couldn't bear to make any sound at all.

Galaxies had once swirled in my beloved's eyes.

I saw them in my head all night long.

Papá knocked on my door just before dawn. "Mi niña," he said softly. "Talk to me. Tell me what happened."

But I couldn't tell him because he wouldn't understand. Not now. Not anymore. Once, when I was seven years old, I had a run-in with a baby chupacabra. The pup, cornered against a fence in our yard, had snapped at me when I tried to capture it. I cried all day, thinking that maybe I wasn't cut out to be a Monteagudo after all. It was Papá who had consoled me, who had said, "No importa, Rosa. We all grow and learn every day. And you grow best when challenged. I am so proud of you."

But would he say these things to me if he knew how I felt about Julio Capó, protector of our enemies?

"I want to be alone, Papá," I told my father when he knocked on the door again. He left in silence.

For all of the next day I remained in bed, leaving my room only to use the toilet. Papá asked me for the trapo so that he could destroy it, and I handed him an old strip of a blanket I once used to swaddle my dolls when I was little.

He couldn't tell the difference.

Moments later, I could smell the fire and hear Papá's prayers above the crackling flames. Julio's trapo, meanwhile, lay under my pillow, feeding me nightmares when I slept. The day rolled on, and thankfully, my parents left me alone.

"Perhaps she's not meant to hunt," I heard my father tell my mother, and then listened as my mother comforted my father, "No llores, Antonio. It'll be all right."

My father was shattered, but I would never hunt again. If Julio had been a monster, then we Monteagudos had been utterly mistaken. The Capós had been right all along.

Later that night, a rain of pebbles flew into my room from the open window, interrupting my thought.

"¡Coño!" I heard a voice cursing outside. "I didn't realize it was open!"

It couldn't be!

Flying to my window (I flew, I *must* have flown!), I leaned out to see him, Julio, whole y sano, looking sadly up at me in the dark. I reach out my hand and he took it, dropping a long kiss on my knuckles. He was real! And alive!

"Come in," I urged him, but Julio looked uneasy.

"Your father will kill me."

I laughed involuntarily. "He'll have to kill me first."

Julio narrowed his eyes at me, those eyes swirling with planets and worlds beyond. Then he climbed into my room.

I threw my arms around him, kissing his mouth, his cheeks, his chin, his eyelids, until he said, "Oye, oye, slow down."

We sat on my bed, and I said, "You're here. You're okay."

"I've been better."

Things really did slow down then. The air between us stopped burning for a moment. "What happened?" I asked.

Julio ran his hand through his hair. "My brother, Marcelo, he didn't come home last night. He's been ill, you know? It's—it's not safe for him to leave the house. He's a good kid. Really, he is. I need you to understand certain things about Marcelo, you see. It's just that . . ."

We have a saying in Cuba that we use whenever someone realizes something a little too late—"I fell out of a tree"—and it refers to the shock of falling, of learning a difficult lesson. And the more Julio talked about Marcelo the more it felt like I was falling.

I didn't want to ask him about his brother, and I didn't want to tell Julio about the cagüeiro my father had killed. Part of me thought, wildly, that this was a secret I could keep. That Julio and I could plan a future together, and the mystery of his missing brother would stay a mystery for the rest of our lives. But the other part of me knew that the secret would eat us alive.

"Julio," I asked, interrupting his nervous chatter. "Does Marcelo have eyes like yours?"

When he looked at me, the universe in his gaze, he knew. He *knew*. He chewed his bottom lip and his nostrils flared. Swallowing thickly, Julio said, "Rosa. Oh no, Rosa," while I slipped my hand beneath my pillow and pulled out the trapo that had surely been Marcelo's.

Julio wasn't a cagüeiro, but the sound he made at the proof of his brother's murder was that of a wounded animal.

"Shh, shh," I urged, worried my parents might hear him.

"You promised," he whispered, clutching the trapo as if it were hurting him.

"I'm sorry. It wasn't me. I couldn't. I would never," I said through tears. "I looked into his eyes, Julio. But I panicked. I couldn't stop my father."

Julio was on his feet, wrapping the trapo around his wrist again and again, leaving his skin raw. "My brother became a shape-shifter to help others. We've saved many cagüeiros this way." Julio stopped, sobbed into his hands.

"Por favor, I'm—"

"Enough, Rosa. You don't understand," he insisted. "Marcelo, my brother." Julio stopped, caught his breath. "Marcelo, my brother whom you murdered—" He stopped, the phrase unfinished.

"No, please," I whimpered and dropped to the floor as if the bones in my legs had disappeared.

Julio sniffed and when I looked up at him, his eyes were brimming with tears. "You can't understand the many reasons why people choose the trapo," Julio whispered. "The man you murdered has saved more people than you can imagine. He finds them, cagüeiros, transformed into creatures like jutías, eating insects to survive, and he joins them and helps them see there can be a safe world for them. He convinces them to give up the trapo. Did you know that was even possible? There's one out there now he'd been tracking. Just a little girl stealing milk and playing with fire. That's why he's been—" Julio shook his head and when he spoke again his voice sounded like it had been stretched too thin. "He *had* been so tired and sick. He was wearing himself out trying to save her." Julio breathed hard, in and out, and I could only watch as he tried to hold himself together. Shock gave way to anger. It twisted his features into something I did not recognize. He held up the rag in his fist. "You can't understand it, can you? With your birthday parties and your happy cousins." He stopped again before adding, "You hate what confounds you."

Through all of it, he'd whispered, protecting me from my parents on the other side of my bedroom door. Even then, he was looking out for me.

"Forgive me," I pleaded.

Julio only shook his head. Then I watched as he held the trapo that had been Marcelo's, weighing it in his hands. Of course, I knew what he meant to do, what he felt he had to do.

"No, Julio."

He wouldn't look at me. My eyes would never again meet the stars in his. Slowly, he wrapped the trapo around his neck. Immediately, his face began to change. First, Julio's long nose flattened until two slits remained of his nostrils. Then every bone cracking into a new place, his arms and legs withered and were sucked into his body, which grew longer by the moment. Julio grunted painfully through it all. I reached out with a trembling hand but dared not touch him. Before I knew it, Julio had transformed into a black snake, enormous and shiny. He slithered out of my room through the window and left me there, shaking in horror.

Dark days followed with no word from Julio. Mamá could not understand why I'd lost my appetite, and Papá only spoke to me about cosas de la casa—asking if I could iron his shirt or fry up an egg for his breakfast. I didn't train with him anymore, and conversations he had about the hunt with my cousins were held out of my earshot.

Each evening, when I said goodnight to my parents, I begged my father to stay home.

"Por favor, Papá," I would plead. "You don't understand the pain you're causing."

"You've forgotten yourself, Rosa Monteagudo," my father reprimanded at last one night, having decided that he'd given me enough time to heal from the shock of my first hunt.

A firmness took hold in my mind at that. I would make amends with Julio somehow.

From my bedroom, I listened as my father prepared to hunt. I'd overheard him talking about a cagüeiro that was slipping into homes and raiding refrigerators. I thought of what Julio told me, of how there was a little girl shape-shifting to survive. And I knew Julio was out there, too, picking up where his brother had left off, trying to rescue her. I looked around my room, at my closet full of dresses and the framed quinceañera portrait I'd taken earlier that month, at the weapons I'd once polished with such pride, gleaming on a shelf.

How foolish it all seemed compared to going hungry, to running scared and alone, to turning into a monster in order to live.

I slipped on a pair of black pedal pushers and a black button-up shirt. Silent in my room, I listened for my father's departure, then counted to ten before slowly opening my window and crawling out into the night. I tracked my father the way I'd been taught to track monsters—silently, on alert, like a woodland creature. I could smell his aftershave, hear the faint crackling sound his left ankle made every few steps, spot the places on the earth where he'd knelt down.

It was entirely possible that Papá knew I was tracking him, that he was keeping an eye on me, too. But I persisted anyway.

We were getting closer to the River Cauto with each step. The air was damp and smelled fishy. Once, on the banks of the river, I'd helped my father dispose of a madre de aguas monster, separating the tough flesh from the bones, which we burned in a fire. The stench had seared itself in my memory, and I could almost smell it again now.

Stepping into a clearing, I watched as my father froze, crouching. "Rosa," he whispered without turning around. "I knew you'd find your courage again someday. Mi hijita, ven." He gestured for me to come closer, so I did. Papá pointed to the river's edge. There, a girl dressed in rags was rooting inside a leather purse. She'd dumped half of the contents onto the ground and picked out coins from among the lipsticks, pencils, and receipts. She looked about eleven years old.

"I have her now," my father said, taking aim with his gun.

Horror coursed through me. "She's a little girl!" I hissed, laying my hand on top of Papá's pistol and forcing it down.

My father stared at me, understanding dawning. "You came to stop me? If you weren't sulking in your room all day and night, you'd know that Dr. Méndez, the very man who delivered you and every baby in Dos Ríos, says that his wife is no longer who she once was, that she eyes him with hatred lately, and he suspects a cagüeiro has taken her form and done who-knows-what with the real Señora Méndez!" He pointed at the little girl in the distance, as if proving a point.

"She's probably grown tired of him, that's all. Not every bad thing that happens in Dos Ríos can be blamed on monsters."

Papá nodded, his mouth twisting in disappointment. "That child you see over there? Yesterday, I watched as she transformed into a venomous spider and crawled right into the Amador barn. I couldn't stop her. Juan Amador is now in a hospital in Santiago, fighting for his life. *That* little girl is a monster, but you, *little girl*, are a coward."

"Can't you imagine her fear, Papá? I would bite Juan Amador, too!"

My father's eyes widened and he pointed his pistol at me. "The phrase, Rosa. Tell me the phrase or so help me—" His voice wobbled and tears sprung into his eyes.

"T-tempt not a desperate m-man!" I shouted, then stood there looking at him, blinking through my tears. It felt as if a black cloud had settled over me, blotting out everything I once knew to be true. I couldn't tell what was worse. Losing myself or losing the love of my papá.

But his arms were around me at once, holding me tight. "Mi hijita. Mi hijita," he kept saying. "Forgive me," he whispered.

"Of course," I said at once. I could feel the fear that made his shoulders tremble. Maybe everything would be different now.

Papá and I would go home and talk things through. Perhaps a new pact could be made with the Capós. We could join their efforts to help rehabilitate the monsters, and those who could not be helped, those who clung to evil no matter what, well, the Monteagudos had skills for that.

But I heard Papá gasp suddenly, and when I looked up, there was Julio crouching in front of the little girl, his hand outstretched, talking calmly with her.

"Ju—" I started to call out, but my father clamped a hand over my mouth.

"A Capó," my father said. He started to lower his gun when Julio pulled a trapo from his pocket. He was showing it to the girl and then slowly placing it around his neck. "What is he doing?" Papá wondered aloud, but I knew.

Julio tied the knot in one swift movement, and he became a nightingale, dusky brown with a gleaming white chest. He hopped around the girl, who giggled into her hands.

"Capó or not," I heard Papá say as he moved slowly, releasing me from his grip. He raised his pistol to take aim.

I ran. I ran faster than I ever had, as if I could speed past a bullet. The girl screamed, and Julio fluttered into the sky, dropping down again a few feet away and hopping up and down in distress.

"Get out of the way, Rosa!" my father shouted, anguish lacing his voice.

As for the little girl, she desperately tried to tie her own trapo, her eyes darting to the river. "Stop," I said and held her hands. "Let me help you. Dámelo, please." I gestured toward the rag around her throat.

My father stepped onto the shoreline and approached us

with his gun held up. Julio took flight again and scratched at the top of my father's head with his tiny, sharp claws.

"Julio, no!" I said, then turned back to the girl. "Give it to me, please. We don't have time!"

"It's all I have," she said, gripping the ends of her trapo. "How else will I survive? I don't have anyone."

"I know a place," I told her, keeping my voice low. Julio alighted at her feet and seemed to nod. I picked up one of the fallen receipts and a pencil and jotted down directions to the Capó home. "Here. They'll help you. I promise." I looked in her eyes. They were a deep brown, like wood that has been polished into something priceless.

All the while my father was yelling at me to get away, to allow him a clear shot. "Rosa, please," he cried desperately.

The girl clutched my arms in fear. "Go. I'll keep you safe," I told her, and she finally relented. She packed the contents of the purse, slung it over her shoulder, and with a solemn look at it, handed me the trapo. Then she ran off into the woods, light on her feet.

As for Julio, he'd flown up to my shoulder and chirped in my ear. In it I heard a promise. I heard forgiveness. I heard sacrifice.

I took one last look at my father, who had lowered his gun and was openly crying now. "Mi hija, come home. I won't speak of what happened tonight. Give me the trapo and together we can burn it and do our duty."

Duty. I had a new definition of it now. I couldn't go back to being a Monteagudo, not when I knew the truth. I could only hope my father could learn this lesson, too. Until then, there was one way I could keep the other cagüeiros out there, the ones who were good and scared for their lives, safe from him forever.

I placed the girl's trapo against my neck. It vibrated there, growing warmer by the second. "I must be gone and live, Papá, or stay and die."

"Por favor, no, Rosa," Papá pleaded.

Julio trilled in my ear, giving me strength. "Tell Mamá that I love her. And Abuela. And you, too, Papá. I'll come home if you let me, when the time is right. But for now, every cagüeiro you meet is me. They are all me, and you will have to look in their eyes before you raise your pistol or draw your machete."

I wrapped the trapo around my neck and tied the knot.

The pain was blinding but brief, here and gone like a flash of lightning.

I stretched my wings, testing them out. Chirruped at first, then sang a lark's call to the nightingale, who responded in kind.

Together, Julio and I took flight.

¿Dónde Está el Duende?

Jenny Torres Sanchez

I tell Mamá about it in the morning, after breakfast, after Tía Susanna has taken Papá outside to show him the garden in the backyard of her new home and my cousin Daniel has quietly excused himself from the table.

"Scratching? What kind of scratching?" Mamá asks. She's washing dishes in the tiny kitchen, staring out at the backyard through the window above the sink. I take my plate over to her and look out at Tía and Papá talking to each other over some ripped up tomato and green bean and pea plants, surrounded by the swampy forest that creeps right up to the edge of Tía's property.

The scratching sound had kept me awake all night though I was tired from our long drive from New Mexico. I even tried to convince myself I was hallucinating, my mind suffering from the aftereffects of listening to our tires drone on thousands of miles of highway, from the warmth inside our truck as the air conditioning desperately groaned on, from the constant motion as we drove through Texas, Louisiana, Mississippi, Alabama, Georgia, before finally arriving at my tia's new house in Florida. With each sharp scratch I heard, my mind ran wild. *Rats in the ceiling. Or a rabid raccoon! Maybe that's what got to Daniel. That's why he looks so sick, so feral.* Or maybe the sound had been someone outside trying to get Daniel's attention.

All night I wondered if Daniel had fallen in with the wrong crowd here. Was it possible he'd started using drugs? Is that why he looks this way? Images of my cousin shooting up somewhere, surrounded by people who don't care about him—people who only saw a sad new kid—floated in and out of my mind to the rhythm of the scratching. That could explain it. And maybe it was what we were all thinking but not saying.

Go to sleep, I told myself, as my worry and paranoia made my ears tune in more to the sound of Daniel's breathing as he slept on an air mattress on the floor below, the sound of Papá's snoring from the pull-out couch in the living room, the sounds of insects and frogs just outside Daniel's window. *You're just imagining things,* I told myself as the scraping sound gently cut through it all.

"Miranda?" Mamá says now, "I asked what kind of scratching?"

"Just . . . a weird sound." Now, in the light of day, away from my worry, it seems ridiculous. I shake my head, hoping she'll dismiss it.

"It's because you're in a new place. Our senses get heightened," Mamá says as she rinses out cup after cup. She stares out the window. "I'm glad your tía is gardening. Even if the animals tear up her plants, it doesn't matter. It's therapeutic. Just look at her, she's been through so much. Both of them have." Mamá's voice fades as she looks out with knitted brow at my tía.

There'd been a hush last night as soon as we saw Daniel. He was so emaciated Mamá had barely kissed his cheek as if she was afraid she'd break him. And Papá, instead of giving him a hard handshake and slap on the shoulder or cracking a joke about how Tía must not be feeding him, gave him a silent, gentle hug. And I stood there, hoping for the warm smile Daniel always had for me. But instead, I got a cold nod that splintered my heart.

Out the window, Papá embraces his sister, and she wipes away tears.

She'd been calling Papá repeatedly over the past six months, trying to convince him to visit Florida for the first time. "It's gorgeous!" she told him. "Such a nice change from all that dust! I tell you, once you set foot here, you'll never go back to New Mexico. I know I never will." Tía had developed a deep grudge against the Southwest when it took her husband away from her. Tío Félix had a heart attack one day while working outside and after that, Tía Susanna never wanted to see dust or mountain or desert ever again.

"Come visit! Please. We'll take Miranda and Daniel to Disney before they don't want anything to do with their viejos."

"Disney! You're out of your mind. ¿Con qué pisto?"

Papá recounted every call to Mamá while I quietly listened, hoping we would go. At first because I hoped maybe somehow we'd be able to afford to go to Disney. Then because that wasn't possible, I imagined immersing myself in the shimmering waters of the ocean. And then because after he ignored countless texts and phone calls, my anger at Daniel had finally given way to worry.

Tía's calls had already become more frequent. More frantic. Until finally one day in late July, we were loading Papá's truck and heading out to the swamps of Florida, Papá telling Mamá that we should have gone sooner.

After the breakfast dishes are washed and Tía and Papá have come back inside, it is decided we will all go to the beach. Mamá and Tía immediately begin preparing and packing food. Papá fills a cooler with ice and sodas. And after the commotion of preparations are done, Tía coaxes Daniel out of his room. I notice a small smudge of dirt on his face but say nothing as we all climb into Papá's truck.

The whole ride, Mamá and Tía blare their favorite cumbias and shout over the steady rhythm, laughing and reminiscing about days before Daniel and I were even born. I laugh listening to their stories and it almost feels normal— all of us together again. And when we arrive at the beach I lie on the sand, relaxing beneath an umbrella with my eyes closed and only the lulling sound of the ocean and Mamá, Papá, and Tía in the background. For a while, I can almost fool myself into thinking that everything is fine. That Daniel is fine.

Except I don't hear *him*. Not a word. And when I open my eyes and see him sitting on the edge of the blanket, staring out at the immense sea, he looks even smaller and frailer than he does at the house. A wave of sadness rushes over me. Daniel and I had still hardly said a word to each other. He'd had his earbuds in the whole drive here, and I couldn't help but feel like he was trying to avoid me. It was like he'd forgotten we'd once been so close.

"You're pale, cuz." My voice sounds weak against the sound of the ocean. I sit up and catch sight of his legs—I can see the spidery faint blue web of his veins underneath his skin. Back in New Mexico, Daniel had loved being outside. His brown skin had always been dusted with the orange of the southwest dirt and sun. But now, a sickly green hue sticks to him. "How's this kind of paleness even possible in Florida?" I tease gently, hoping he will read between the lines. He reminds me of something delicate, something fragile that cannot be pushed too much.

Talk to me, Daniel. Tell me what is wrong.

As if hearing my silent pleas, he turns and stares at me—the most reaction I'd gotten out of him since arriving. But his look is distant. "I don't go out much," he says.

"With the ocean so close, I'd beg to come here every day." I wait to see if he'll say anything more, but he doesn't. So I stare at the water.

"Remember when Tía would fill up that tiny inflatable pool for us at your old house and tell us we were going to la playa?" I ask. Tía would tell us we were at the beach as she handed us plastic pails and shovels and set up an umbrella. "So funny, right? And a little mean, too, because I *actually* thought we were going to the beach!" I laugh. "You remember?" I think back to us as little desert kids, sitting in that blue five-dollar pool from Walmart while Tía sprayed us with the hose.

Daniel looks at me, says nothing.

"Do you?" I ask again.

He puts his earbuds back in and lies down, his arm over his eyes as if he's blocking out the world. I stare at his dirt-encrusted fingernails.

And in that sweltering heat, a shiver runs down my spine.

Tía comes into Daniel's room that night and apologizes again because I don't have a room to myself. "I'm sorry, hija. This house is so small. I knew you wouldn't mind. Not our sweet Miranda," she says, caressing my long hair as I settle into bed. Daniel is on the air mattress watching the television set up on his dresser.

"No se preocupe, Tía." I smile, trying to reassure her. I don't want her to worry any more than she's obviously been worrying. Her fingertips graze my neck ever so gently and something compels me to reach for her hand, hold it. And when I do, I feel an unmistakable shakiness in it. She pulls her hand away.

"Anyway, I figure this way, you and Daniel can catch up without your viejos around. Tell each other what you've really been up to, ¿verdad?" Her eyes look shiny like she's been crying but unsettlingly hopeful. Like maybe Daniel and I will stay up all night digging up our old memories, confiding in each other like we used to.

Pobre Tía.

I nod and turn my attention to my phone, not wanting to look at that hope in her eyes. Tía lets out a deep breath. "It's like the old days, right? When you two were little and we had sleepovers? Those were good times, weren't they?"

I feel another jab to my heart.

"The best," I say.

She nods, leans down, and kisses me goodnight on the forehead like when I was little. "Ay, hija. I'm sorry. I know you understand," she whispers. And I want to tell her she doesn't need to keep apologizing about the room. But then, I wonder if she's apologizing for how Daniel is now. Daniel who doesn't even look at her when she softly says, "Goodnight, hijo. Te quiero."

Tia closes the door as she leaves, and my heart finally collapses in on itself.

I try to be understanding like Tía thinks I am. I try to act normal as I scroll through my phone and Daniel mindlessly watches television. But with each flick of my thumb, each additional minute of silence, my patience wears thinner and thinner.

"You shouldn't be like that, you know. With your mom. Or . . . with any of us," I mumble.

Daniel doesn't move or acknowledge me. The anger I'd felt in New Mexico as Daniel ignored each of my texts, each of my calls, slowly starts bubbling back, replacing the sympathy I'd felt when I first saw him. I push it away and try again.

"Wanna watch a movie?" I grab the remote and search for one we used to watch back home. Finally, I find our favorite.

"Nachoooooooooo," I say, laughing as Jack Black, dressed as a monk, fills the screen. "Come on, cuz! Do Esqueleto, okay?" I tell him. Daniel shrugs but stares at the screen. I offer the same commentary as I always do, wait for him to jump in and repeat the lines that have become our own jokes. But nothing. The anger and hurt I'd been carrying for months and miles bubbles to the surface again, this time spilling over.

"Man, what's up with you?" I ask. "Like seriously, what's your problem? You know you can tell me, right? No matter what, Daniel. You can tell me. Why don't you trust me anymore?"

He keeps his eyes on the screen, not even bothering to look at me. It's too much and before I can stop myself, I throw the remote at him, hitting him hard on his back.

Slowly he turns his face up toward mine and his dark eyes—bright and reflecting the light of the television screen but still somehow vacant—lock with mine.

"I'm . . . I'm sorry, Daniel," I start. "I didn't mean—"

"Who even *are* you?" he asks. *Who are* you? I want to ask him, this stranger who is nothing like the Daniel I knew. But before I can say anything, he turns away, tucking the blanket around himself like a small child.

I sit motionless on the bed, torn between rushing to Daniel and shaking sense into him and running out of the room to talk to Mamá.

But looking at Daniel so small and fragile, so completely transformed by grief, another wave of sympathy overwhelms me. How hard Tío Félix's death has been on him. How close he and his dad were. Just thinking about those times, about my tío, his kindness, how much he loved Daniel, how much he loved all of us, makes me want to sob. My mind rushes with memories of the way Tío Félix would chase us, his laughter, his gruff and gentle way, the view of the mountains from their little house where I spent so many days. Maybe this is just Daniel's way of dealing with it all, maybe turning off his feelings, his memories of New Mexico, of all of us, of even *me* is the only way he's been able to go on.

Of course Daniel isn't himself. He will never be himself again.

More memories come. And then more. I curl up in bed and shed quiet tears until I begin to fall asleep.

From somewhere faraway, I think I hear the creak of a bedroom door and the flick of the light switching off. The scent of Tía's perfume reaches me as my memories intertwine with my dreams. Until I am floating between the bright blaze of New Mexico's sun and Daniel's dark room now, eerily illuminated only by the television. And from somewhere, here or there, it comes again.

The scratching.

I wake trying to hold on to a fleeting dream. I'm still trying to recall it when I walk into the kitchen and Tía says, "¿Y cómo durmió mi sobrina favorita?"

"Okay, Tía," I answer, the last fragments of my dream falling away.

"So glad," Tía says. "I made platanitos. They remind me of home. El Salvador," she clarifies. I nod as Papá agrees and Mamá sets a plate of sweet plantains in front of me. My mother being from northern Mexico never cooks sweet plantains so I always love it when Tía does. And how she describes the different ways she and Papá would eat them growing up. Con *frijolitos*. Con *crema*. Con *azúcar*.

"Mi querido El Salvador," Papá says, the way he always does when his home country is mentioned. "How I wish I could show you jóvenes the beauty of mi tierra." He looks at Daniel and me.

"Ah, you have such romantic notions of it," Tía says.

"El Salvador is beautiful, Susanna!" Papá says. "Be good or I'll get el duende to come get you!"

Tía drops the spoon she was using for the black beans onto the floor. "¡Ay, por favor, hermano! Don't start with those nonsense stories. I don't believe in any of them," she says, rushing to wash the spoon and clean the mess.

"What's a duende?" I ask.

"El duende," Papá begins over mouthfuls of plátanos, "is a strange little green elf that lives deep in the bosques of Central America." Papá laughs.

"No, no," Mamá cuts in. "El duende lives in the walls of children's rooms and eats their toes if they're bad!"

Papa shakes his head. "No, it loves the forest, isn't it? And it lures kids with a whistle to make them lose their way there. Or wait, maybe it helps them find their way if they're lost? Dios, I don't remember exactly," Papa says. "All I know is I was scared of it as a kid when my mamá would tell us stories. I always got the feeling el duende was one baaaaad dude." Papa shoves another plátano in his mouth and winks at Mamá.

Mamá laughs. "¡El duende, un enigma!"

"No más, no más," Tía says, shutting down the conversation as she spoons black beans and then cream on my plate. "There you go, Miranda. Your favorite way." She smiles at me, then looks over at Daniel and carefully offers him the sugar bowl. A slight gasp of disbelief escapes Tía's lips as he takes it and sprinkles sugar over his plantains.

"I'm so hungry," he says as he digs into them.

Tía stares at him. Then looks over at Papá and Mamá. The sweet plantains on Daniel's plate are gone within minutes.

"Are there more?" he asks.

"Of course, of course!" Tía says, hurrying to the stove. "It'll just be a minute!"

This is the most animated Daniel has been since we got here, and even though I'm glad, it annoys me that Tía is running around for him after he's been such a jerk. He looks my way, but I turn my gaze to my plate and take a small bite of my own food. The plátanos taste burnt and treacly. I push them around on my plate and listen as Papá and Mamá talk to Daniel, cautiously at first, and then with more enthusiasm as he actually engages in conversation with them. By the time Tía has another batch of plátanos ready for Daniel, everyone is laughing and making plans for the day. But all of it—their voices, the smell of food, the laughter—grates on my nerves. Like nails on a chalkboard. I try to ignore them and look out the kitchen window to Tía's yard, suddenly hungry and yearning for something I can't explain.

Tía announces that she's been wanting to go to a popular botanical garden nearby. "They have all kinds of flowers in bloom. And well, I know it's not the theme parks, but you'll see. We'll have a good time!" she says.

"Sounds boring," Daniel says, but he smiles and Tía playfully slaps his shoulder.

"I think maybe I'll stay behind," I say, surprising myself and everyone. "I just . . . I think maybe I didn't sleep well last night."

"Como qué you're going to stay behind?" Tía says. "I want you to see this place. I just know you'll love it, okay?"

I nod and an hour later, we are all getting into Papá's truck and heading to a place called Leu Gardens. The drive isn't long, but still, I find myself drifting off while everyone is talking and laughing.

"You okay, m'ija?" Mamá whispers as I lean my head on her shoulder.

"I'm fine," I tell her. And really, by the time we are strolling through the paths of the garden, my agitation and tiredness have disappeared. I feel oddly invigorated, even in the overwhelming humidity.

"It's too hot to be doing this," Daniel complains to Tía. And from the looks on Mamá's and Papá's faces, I can tell they agree with him. But Tía looks at me with curiosity as she fingers the leaves of a tree. "What about you, Miranda? What do you think?"

"I think it's *beautiful*," I tell her. But it's not the flowers I love. It's the trees, the hanging Spanish moss, the lushness everywhere. The temptation to walk into all that foliage is almost too great. I want to feel the trees crowded around me. I want to feel the waxiness of the leaves on my skin, pressed against my face. The smell of them—a mixture of water, dirt, and *green*—fills my nose.

"¡Ya ven!" Tía yells. "I knew Miranda would appreciate it."

We continue, Tía pointing out every plant and tree we encounter until Papá finally says, "Okay ya, Susanna, por favor! Let's go get some ice cream."

Mamá quickly agrees and Tía laughs, giving in.

"Fine, you all look like wet rats, anyway," she says. "Except you, Miranda. Florida is good for you. Look at your bright eyes— you're radiant!" She wraps her arm around my waist as we head to the car.

"Remember the time we went to City of Rocks?" Daniel asks that night. I'm too tired to talk, but I try to make an effort. *City of Rocks*. The words, empty of any memory, get stuck in my head that aches and feels gelatinous from the heat of the day.

"Yeah," I lie, trying again. But I don't feel like reminiscing with Daniel.

The overhead light is so bright that it makes my head throb more. "But turn that light out, will you? It's killing me."

I hear Daniel get up and flick the switch. "Sorry," he says. "I thought we'd talk. I guess I've been checked out since you got here. Honestly, it's like I looked up and you were suddenly here. But I don't remember . . ."

His voice continues in the dark but gets farther away as I fall asleep. I don't know how much time has passed when I suddenly sense something else in the room. A heavy, threatening presence that thickens the air and makes my mind feel muggy. Some part of me tries to scream, but my mouth won't open. My voice won't work. And an invisible force holds me down, making even the smallest movement impossible.

The room fills with the unmistakable leaf scent I found so intoxicating earlier today in the gardens, but now it is putrid and rotten. And from half-closed eyelids that refuse to open fully, I see a greenish glow radiating from the wall behind me.

It's just a nightmare! I tell myself, even as my body fills with terror and the smell becomes so strong it burns my nostrils. Even as all the walls seem to pulse in sync with the throbbing that has begun in my head. Even as I watch two terrible hands—disproportionately long and clawlike with sharp black nails—appear on either side of me attached to dirt-streaked arms reaching out from behind the wall. They extend farther and fiercely grasp my head.

Noooooooo! I feel the sharp claws pierce my skin at my temples. And then I feel those hands *inside* my head, caressing my brain, those nails scratching at its surface. A strange grating voice sings a distorted lullaby.

¿Dónde está, dónde está, dónde está el duende?
En el bosque, en tu pared, en tu cabeza,
Allí es que vive el duende.
¿Y qué hace, y qué hace, y qué hace el duende?
Roba las memorias de los niños
Porque de eso vive el duende.

The nails rake my brain. My head fills with hundreds of memories; each scrape feels like they are being turned over like dirt. I feel a strange pulling, hear a strange suctioning sound, and realize my memories are being siphoned out of my head.

I try to *scream*.

But nothing comes out.

"Good morning, ¡preciosa!" Tía Susanna exclaims as soon as I enter the kitchen. Already the stink of food fills the air. My stomach clenches. "How did you sleep last night?"

I sit down at the table without answering. My mind gets stuck on the words *last night*. They turn in my head and a sense of terror fills me. *What happened last night?*

I try to remember as I stare at the heaping plate of eggs with onions and tomatoes. At a bowl full of beans and a stack of tortillas. Tía spoons food onto a plate and sets it down in front of me. I'm nauseated by the smell and sight of it.

Mamá and Papá are talking about maybe fishing at the Cocoa Beach pier, or maybe shopping for some souvenirs. But above this, all I hear is the sound of them eating. Of the food being masticated and turned to mush in their mouth, the smacking of their tongues, the oiliness of their lips. I push my plate away.

"¿Qué te pasa, Miranda?" Mamá asks.

"I don't feel well," I tell her. Mamá puts her hand on my head, and I fight the urge to push it away.

"Ay, no . . . don't tell me you're getting sick!" Tía says, rushing over to me. Her voice booms in the small house. I wish I could hold my hands over my ears and tune it out.

"You don't look too good," Papa says.

"We'll go to the pier tomorrow," Tía decides. "Let Miranda rest some more in Daniel's room today. Maybe we go to pick up some souvenirs at the dollar store?"

"If Gerardo stays here, I guess we can go for a quick trip. But I don't know," Mamá says, looking closely at me again.

"Go, go," Papá says.

"I'll keep an eye on her, too," Daniel says.

"Go, Mamá. I just need some sleep," I tell her, getting up from the table and heading back to bed. I slip back under the covers and feel myself falling as soon as my head hits the pillow.

I wake to Daniel coming into the room, a teacup in his hands. "Our moms went to the store, but they made this before they went. Told me to make sure you drink it."

My head feels tender and bruised. "I don't want it," I tell him. "Please, just go away."

A heavy silence fills the air. "No, sit up. Smell it," he says, bringing it closer to my nose. I'm about to smack it away when I catch whiff of the hierba buena. The smell is wonderful, and I reach for the cup and snatch it out of his hand so fast, it sloshes onto the bed.

"I . . . I put some fresh mint leaves in there for you. Lots of them . . ." he says.

I dig into the cup with my fingers and pull out more and more leaves, gnashing them between my teeth, letting their earthiness fill my mouth.

Daniel stares at me, his eyes wide and frightened but knowing. "I knew you'd like this, cuz," he whispers. His voice is urgent. "I'm sorry it got to you, Miranda. I don't know what it is. But just give it your memories. It feeds on memories. And these." He pulls a folded paper towel from his pocket and hands it to me.

I can smell it. The *green*.

I quickly unfold it and shove the clump of plant leaves still sprinkled with dirt into my mouth as Daniel watches.

"Thank you for saving me," he whispers, on the verge of tears. But I don't care. All I care about are the leaves.

They taste amazing.

That night the hands come out of the wall again, the claws rake my brain again. It happens every night, until my head feels numb. The only thing that matters are the leaves the boy keeps bringing me.

"We have to go, Susanna," the woman says one evening at the kitchen table.

"Ay, no, don't say that. We'll take her to the doctor."

"No, no, I'm sorry, but . . . we have to go. We have to leave this house, Susanna. And I think you should, too. As soon as possible."

"What are you saying?"

"Something is very wrong here! It got to Daniel. And now, look at my Miranda."

"Are you . . . are you blaming me for Miranda getting sick?"

Some sort of understanding flashes on the face of the woman not named Susanna. "Why did you keep inviting us here? Why did you put her in Daniel's room?"

Susanna shakes her head and stares at her hands, before finally saying, "If you want to leave, then leave." Then quietly, she gets up from the table and walks out of the kitchen.

Within moments the man and woman are shoving suitcases out of the house and leading me to the car. I look out the truck window as we pull away, wondering why the boy waving good-bye looks so sad.

Nighttime comes quick as we travel in the glow of orange highway lights. Cars speed next to us and past us.

I stare at the man and woman in the front seat. At the way they keep looking back at me. I know them. But I can't remember them. I close my eyes and try to coax who they are from my memory, but it's a blur of too many strange and unfamiliar faces.

When I open my eyes, it is daytime again and the woman is staring at me. There's something familiar about her, but in seconds the feeling is gone.

We drive. Each mile we travel makes my head ache until it is flashing with pain. It travels throughout my whole body, until it feels like I'm being torn from limb to limb, like I'm being torn away from *myself*. I groan and cry.

When I open my eyes this time, I can barely make out the man sitting in the passenger's seat, and the woman is driving. I open my mouth to ask them who they are, where are we going, but I can't. The pain inside my head is so fierce, the stretching and pulling through my body so severe, I can't even cry anymore. Bright streaks of color burst and separate in my mind, revealing a place that feels familiar.

I remember being there, hidden in the woods. I remember the house with that garden in the back. How in darkness, I moved from the trees into the walls of that house.

I remember all the children in that room. Watching, waiting for sleep to come, to dig their memories. Nourishing me. Giving me life! How they became me and I became them.

"Take me back!" I screech. The voice that comes out of me is a collection of all their voices, an ear-splitting cacophony of all those children. I shiver with the sound of their screaming, crying, laughing, whispering captured in unison in my throat.

"Miranda!" the woman screams as I lunge for the wheel. I *need my green forest.* But the man pushes me, and I fall back easily, no strength to fight him.

"She's convulsing!" he yells. "Pull over, pull over!"

My mind flashes green and hot and lush. Full of so many faces, so many memories, too many to hold in this human body.

I feel the car pulling over. I feel myself being pulled out, dragged over dirt and rocks and dust. My eyes search for trees, for forest, for *my color.* But there is only desert here. Only brown and desolate land.

"Her eyes! Why are they glowing like that, Gerardo? ¿Qué le pasa a nuestra hija?" the woman yells. The taste of sulfur fills my mouth, and then I am gagging.

"¡Diosito santo!" the man yells. "What is that?"

A stream of bright, hot green escapes my mouth. Liquid that tastes like putrid leaves spills from my lips and onto the ground. My throat and nostrils burn as more and more comes out. The smell of rot surrounds us.

"What is it?" I mumble as the pool of sick rises, filling the dark night with a verdant glow. They hold me up as I choke out one last drop.

The luminous cloud swirls in the black sky, taking shape of a ghostly man with a large hat. The silent desert suddenly fills with the shrieking sound of children's voices.

The figure tips his hat to us and rushes in the direction of the last town we passed through. Mamá and Papá hold me tighter as we watch the glowing green dim, as the scent of sulfur dissipates, as the sound of the children's voices grows fainter.

But I still hear them, in the distance, singing el duende's lullaby.

And somewhere in all of them, I recognize my own voice.

Far, far away.

El Viejo de
la Bolsa

Alexandra Villasante

Marta was late.

July in Montevideo was cold and the sun set early. With the light fading, the vendors of la feria de Tristán Narvaja packed up their fruit and vegetables, their bronze souvenirs, their skeins of wool and salvaged machine parts (a tray of metal letters from a broken printing press), and a set of colorful quilted bags. Esther Mautones picked up a little drawstring bag, patchworked in velvet and green satin and inset with mirror spangles.

"Those bags are from India," the vendor said, keeping an eye on Esther as she packed up the rest of her wares. "Very cheap for you, gurisa." It *was* cheap, which meant it must not have come from much farther than the border town of El Chuy. But it was pretty. And Marta liked pretty things.

"Gracias, señora, but not today," Esther said, turning away.

She took advantage of the late hour, buying the last of the homemade food—cheap— from vendors who wanted to get out of the cold and go home. Like the vendors, Esther wished she could get home. Instead, she lingered, shivering in her father's wool-lined chaqueta until the street had emptied.

Marta wasn't coming.

She made her way to the little one-bedroom apartment in San Martín, which was as much her home now as any other place.

The apartment of Doña Pereira had no windows. Instead, where the ceiling over the sala should have been, a gargantuan structure of welded iron and glass panes capped the apartment like a terrarium, providing a view, though smudged by soot, of the azure twilight sky above.

When Esther entered with the end-of-day food from the fair, she saw that the makeshift Pereira family had gained another lost child. A little girl—too thin in her sagging tights and corduroy skirt—held tight to Doña Pereira's sweater. Her name was Carolina. With a look heavenward and an impatient shrug of her massive shoulders, la doña let Esther know it was up to her to convince the new girl that this house wasn't a prison.

"Mira, gurisa, want to see a magic trick? Come." Esther's outstretched hand was a slow magnet, pulling Carolina away from la doña's skirts.

"See the window?" Esther said, pointing up.

Carolina took the few steps to Esther's side, transferring her fierce grip to her waist. "Sí, but it's a little dirty," she said shyly.

"It's called a claraboya, and it doesn't matter that it's dirty, because . . ." Esther turned the metal crank embedded in the plaster wall. The crankshaft rose up the wall into a box of machinery at the base of the skylight. With a screech that made Esther wish she'd gone up on the roof to oil the gears, the rectangle of glass began to move.

"¡Ay!" said Carolina. Susana and Pablo, who had seen the minor miracle before, stopped arguing with each other and looked up. Even la doña paused her folding of endless laundry.

The glass top moved on a track, making its noisy way across the flat roof, finally exposing the ink blue of a new July evening. Turning the crank one-handed took effort, but Esther didn't want to let Carolina go. She could feel the little girl relaxing her grip around Esther's waist as she stared at the sky.

Once it was completely open and Esther had allowed the little girl a moment of wonder, she decided she couldn't test Doña Pereira's patience anymore. She took the basket of laundry and led Carolina out of the apartment, down an outside hallway and to the steps leading to the roof. She frowned and moved little Carolina to the inside of la escalera, since there was no banister here. She added to her list: Ask el flaco to find and install una reja, so the little kids didn't fall off the stairs and break their necks. After all, they were supposed to be at Doña Pereira's to be safe. But safety was a relative thing.

When Carolina and Esther had hung all the laundry on the rooftop clotheslines, they came down to the comparative warmth of the kitchen to eat. The claraboya had been cranked almost closed; a space of about a foot left open to let the smoke from whatever la doña was burning escape.

Carolina got hot milk with honey while the older kids passed around a mate sweetened with sugar.

There were day-old bizcochos, softened in milk, as well as hard cheese, tongue a la vinagreta, matambre, and ensalada rusa.

Carolina stared at the tongue like it was still attached to the cow and pushed her plate away. Nothing on this earth was more guaranteed to throw Doña Pereira into a frenzy than a child refusing to eat. But before she could gather her breath to yell, Esther had poured a neat shot of caña and placed it in front of la doña.

"You know what happens when kids don't eat, right, Carolina?" Esther asked casually.

"No," the girl said, wary.

"Well, the old man comes. El viejo de la bolsa."

"Yeah," said Pablo, "he comes and we feed him this garbage." He laughed. La doña, who'd downed the first shot and was pouring herself another, slapped his ear without much enthusiasm.

"No, that's not what happens," Susana said. Esther knew she relished telling this story; their parents were colleagues and friends and she used to babysit Susana. Soon after Esther's parents had been accused of being revolutionary Tupamaros and disappeared on their way to the university, Susana's parents had disappeared, too—a few blocks from this apartment in San Martín. Doña Pereira had cleaned house for both families; now she took care of their children.

"What happens," Susana continued, "is that he creeps into your bedroom."

"If you have your own bedroom," Pablo huffed.

"With his filthy cloth bag, dressed in rags," Susana said.

"The cast-off clothes of his victims," Pablo added, deciding that, if he couldn't be the center of attention, he'd take on the role of gruesome embellisher of tales.

"And when you least expect it," the older girl said, moving her fingers across the table like a spider, as Carolina watched with horror and anticipation. "He snatches you!" She grabbed Carolina's thin wrist and yanked. "And stuffs you into his bag!"

Before Carolina's terrified shriek had faded, Doña Pereira

had taken the bottle of caña and moved to the sofa under the claraboya.

"What does he do then?" Carolina asked, unable to stop herself.

"He drags you, kicking and screaming, to the Cementerio del Buceo, where the dead sit. Then he eats you, clean to the bone," Pablo said, wiggling a slice of tongue in front of her, before dropping the meat onto her plate with a look of disgust.

"Does he, indeed?" Susana asked, turning to Pablo with an academic attitude she must have copied from her parents. "And what proof do you have for that?"

"Don't need proof. It's a fact. That's why his bolsa is so stained. Blood of his victims. He eats them out of the bag."

"Why does he take you to el Cementerio del Buceo?"

"So your bones get mixed with the bones of others. Hide the evidence."

"That doesn't make sense."

"Oh, that's what doesn't make sense?"

Esther, who had been about to start washing the dishes, instead went to the large radio in el living and turned it on. A detailed and gruesome argument about a bogeyman was the last thing she wanted; she wanted the kids in bed, Doña Pereira lazy and tranquil. That way she could sneak out and find Marta.

She tuned to Radio Sarandí, where a warbling tango was playing. She turned the dial until the music overcame the static. The radio, like the newspapers, was often full of lies. Cheerful, soothing lies that Esther wished she could believe. If she hadn't lost her parents inexplicably and completely, maybe she could believe that Montevideo in the year of our Lord 1977 was a beautiful place.

"Carlos Gardel is the greatest tango singer in the world!" Pablo declared, strutting across the worn rug in front of the radio cabinet like he was giving a dancing demonstration in Plaza Independencia.

Susana lay on her stomach, leafing through a magazine she must have memorized by now. "I hate tango," she said. "I hate old people music."

"What do you *like?*" Carolina asked from the depth of an armchair that Esther knew was cozy and smelled only slightly of camphor.

"I like the Beatles and Jaime Roos. And I like Mercedes Sosa. Esther, can't we play something better than this?"

"Not tonight, querida," Esther said. Sometimes, she would play records on her mother's powder-blue portable player. She had managed to salvage three LPs from home: *Mujeres Argentinas*, *Abbey Road*, and *La Traviata*. If the kids tolerated it, and she was in a particularly somber mood, Esther would listen to "Alfonsina y el mar" over and over again, barely waiting for the last note to die away on the tiny, built-in speakers before lifting the needle and moving it back to the beginning of the song.

"Ugh," Pablo groaned. "I don't want to hear about Alfonsina la torpe idiota again!"

Susana stood up, towering over Pablo in a way he hated. "You have no culture! That song is a beautiful masterpiece. Mercedes Sosa is Argentina's treasure."

Pablo put his fists at his waist. "Pero we're not in Argentina, so can we listen to something less depressing?"

"Okay, okay, let's see if we can find something you both like," Esther said, tuning the dial to Radio Colonia in time to hear the lottery numbers and las noticias. Half an hour later, "Mi Buenos Aires querido"—another tango—threatened to restart their fight. A loud snore, like a car engine failing to turn over, pulled all their attention to the sofa and Doña Pereira. But the sound came from tiny Carolina curled up and asleep in the armchair. With a look, Esther managed to motivate Susana and Pablo to get ready for bed. She picked Carolina up and moved her to the bedroom, where the others would soon join her in sleep. She was good at getting the kids to do what she wanted. Why couldn't she control anything else in her life?

At nine thirty, Esther was electric with anxiety. La doña was passed out on the sofa—a nightly occurrence—where she would reliably sleep until dawn. Esther usually slept in la doña's bed, but not tonight. She needed to find Marta. She needed to know what had happened. After putting a blanket over la doña's sleeping form, she checked to make sure the kids were asleep.

Pablo and Susana were asleep, but between them, sitting bolt upright, Carolina stared at the walls in terror.

"¿Qué pasó?" Esther whispered as she entered the room.

"El viejo. I saw him. I saw the old man coming and he's going to eat me."

With a desperate hug, she buried her head against Esther's neck.

"No, of course not. You ate the matambre, remember?"

"But Pablo said because I didn't eat the tongue, el viejo will be mad."

Pablo is a pain in the traste, Esther thought.

"Pablo is wrong about so many things, Carola," she said, gently wiping her face of tears. "He just does a really good job of sounding like he's right."

"He's so much older than me, and he knows so much. He told me."

"He's twelve and when he got here six months ago, he still wet the bed." As soon as she'd said the words, Esther felt bad. Pablo had been a wreck when he'd arrived. Afraid to get up and make noise in the strange house, he'd peed on a corner of the mattress and hoped la doña wouldn't notice. Esther had cleaned it up and made sure she never knew.

"But you can't tease him about it or tell him you know. Keep it secret in your heart, like a little piece of knowledge—a fact—that tells you that even big Pablo was afraid of something. There's no shame in being afraid, okay?"

"But I don't want to be afraid of el viejo de la bolsa. I want him never to catch and eat me."

"He won't."

"How do you know?"

"Because he's not real. He's an old fairy tale that padres tell their children to make them eat and not be wasteful. Kids don't disappear because they don't eat food, honest."

"But grown-ups disappear. Does the viejo de la bolsa take them?"

"No, there's no viejo de la bolsa, te lo juro."

I swear. Esther gave Carolina her own stuffed bear from her niñez, Oso, and tucked her back into bed.

"Will you stay here?"

"Boba, I sleep here. Where else will I go?" Esther said.

"No, here, next to me. Stay with me?"

"Okay."

Carolina didn't look convinced, and time was pressing uneasily on Esther. *Marta, where are you?*

"Yes. I'll stay with you. I promise," she said, and watched Carolina fall asleep with nearly superhuman patience before slipping out of the quiet apartment and on to Avenida General San Martín.

Los milicos were stationed at the corner of Fructuoso and Morales, six of them in a show of military force that looked simultaneously menacing and ridiculous on the mostly empty streets. Esther doubled back until she got to Millán and the little park that ran next to the Hospital Vilardebó. The stories she'd heard about the mental hospital, along with the faded, peeling lemon-colored paint, never failed to give Esther the creeps.

Behind her, she heard shouting and ducked away from the light of the streetlamp, against the shuttered gate of a hairdresser. It might be a boliche, letting some of the drunken patrons out into the street, or it could be the milicos she saw earlier beating the hell out of someone—or worse, dragging them off into una chanchita, the blue vans of the military police.

Esther waited and the shouting started again—definitely not drunken revelry—and then most horrifying of all, pounding footsteps. She grabbed the top of the ornamental iron fence and hauled herself up and over, running through the grounds of the Hospital Vilardebó.

In the shadow of the crumbling building, dried leaves and pieces of bark swirled in the bitter wind. Esther cursed herself for being an idiot. No one was looking for her. She had her carné de identidad in her pocket and a story ready for why she needed to be out in the streets so late. With her short dark hair and her father's chaqueta, she might be mistaken for a man if she kept to the dark. At least walking through the Hospital Vilardebó would be a shortcut to Marta's.

Marta and her parents lived above the almacén they owned, which sold everything from bombillas y mate, milk, and cookies, golosinas, lottery tickets, and mousetraps. It also had the only residential telephone for blocks. People would knock at the back door, even when the store was closed, to call loved ones, the police, lawyers. They'd leave pesos in a jar next to the phone to cover the cost of the calls, and they'd always remember to wipe their feet before entering. If anyone asked, Esther would say she needed the telephone.

"Marta!" Esther's frantic whisper came out like a hiss as she scanned the narrow alley that ran behind the almacén. Marta hadn't been at la feria, and she hadn't responded to any of her letters. Fear suffused the air in Esther's lungs. If Marta had been taken; if something had happened to her—

From the ground floor window of the tiny storeroom where Marta and Esther had kissed and laughed and dreamed, Marta's voice called, "I'm here."

Esther ran to the window, holding out her hand. But Marta did not reach for her.

"Where were you?" It sounded more accusatory than Esther wanted.

"I'm grounded," Marta responded dully.

"Why? What happened?"

"Mamá found your notes."

If it hadn't been so dark in the alley, Esther's tan face would have burned fuchsia.

"I'm being sent to Tacuarembó tomorrow, to stay with my abuelos."

Esther felt herself absorb the blow through her body. Tacuarembó was deep in the Uruguayan countryside, hundreds of kilometers away. No Marta. No laughing or kissing or dreaming.

"It'll be okay," she said as much to herself as to Marta. "You'll be back soon. We can still write."

"No, Esther. I can't do it anymore." Marta was crying, but Esther couldn't summon a single tear, even as her heart slowly dissolved and her world crumbled. Marta cried beautifully, at all the appropriate times, showing exactly the right amount of emotion. Then, after the storm was over, she would forget all about it. Esther didn't forget anything.

"You love me," Esther said hopelessly.

"Sí. Como una amiga, una hermana."

"No. Not like a sister. Tú me amas. I know you do."

"It doesn't matter."

"You don't mean that, amor," Esther reached out a hand again—to try to comfort, to try to stop what she knew was unstoppable.

Marta ignored her offered hand. "I'm tired! I'm tired of working at the almacén all the time, and I'm not smart like you, I'm not going to la universidad."

"You are smart; you could go."

"I don't want it to be so hard, like it is for my parents." She crossed her arms around her like her stomach hurt. "I will find a man to take care of me. Someone like Daniel."

Esther's mind was a stunned animal; she had no words. Daniel lived next to Marta's abuelos. He was big and smiley and tan creído, he acted like he was God's gift. He cheered for Nacional and worked for the disintegrating railroad like his father and brothers before him. He'd want a wife who cried beautifully.

Marta tossed something from the window, and Esther caught it involuntarily. It was the keys to their moto. They'd pooled their money together to buy a third-hand motocicleta. All summer they'd gone to the beaches in Atlántida, once to Piriápolis. Esther had been saving money to surprise Marta with a winter trip to las termas in Minas, a vacation to the thermal springs to keep themselves warm, keep themselves wrapped up in each other.

Because, if she'd been honest, Esther had felt Marta pulling away from her, as if letting go of her hand, finger by finger.

Esther stared at the keys in her hand, unable to look at Marta.

"I had Papá take la moto to your house. It's in the back. I'm sorry, I didn't have a chain to lock it."

"That's what you're sorry about?"

"Esther," she whispered with just enough longing to make her tears believable.

The one thing Esther could do was not beg. She could turn around, leaving the girl she loved weeping like the heroine of a romance that Esther was no longer part of. She made herself do it, without a backward glance. By the time she'd reached the apartment in San Martín she was sure she didn't have a heart to break.

Past midnight and she would catch hell if anyone in the apartment was awake, but she couldn't go in, not yet. She went to the back to check on la moto—they'd christened her Pólvora because she was temperamental like gunpowder, sometimes starting with a bang, other times not starting at all. The three of them had spent the summer together, glorious when the sun shone and kissed their skin, glorious when Pólvora wouldn't start and they had to walk her to the nearest gas station. Every moment was an adventure; now it was over.

Marta's father had left Pólvora leaning against the stairs. Esther told herself that she would go to bed after sneaking a well-deserved cigarette and climbed up to the roof. She always had at least one pucho in her pocket, usually a few, even though her father had been fervently against smoking. He wasn't here, and now she didn't have anything left to care about. A single cigarette would not make a difference one way or the other. As long as la doña didn't find her.

Esther lit the pucho, inhaled deeply and coughed. Maybe it had gone stale, or maybe it had been too long since she'd smoked. The taste was bitter in a way that made Esther more miserable than she thought she could be. She felt bodiless, as if the last string tying her to the ground had been cut. Her parents. Her home. Her love. Without them, she didn't know who she was.

Through the opening of the claraboya, the thin strains of yet another tango drifted up to where Esther stood. Someone had turned the radio on after she left. Either that or she was hearing "Por una cabeza" in her mind. She flicked the half-smoked pucho off the roof and turned to climb down when a sound caught her attention.

A truncated, stifled sound, like a hand over a mouth or a halted exclamation. She told herself to leave whatever new trouble this was far behind her. Not to turn around, like she'd left Marta.

But she turned back anyway, in time to see a hunched figure illuminated by the light from the claraboya, a mass of rags fluttering in the wind. Over its shoulder hung a greasy-looking bag, a tiny hand reaching out of it.

She stepped toward the figure, but it seemed to take forever. In the moments, years, decades that must have elapsed before her feet obeyed her, she heard Carolina's muffled scream again, and the viejo and his bag disappeared over the edge of the roof. Esther ran to the edge, nearly toppling off into the calle below. There was no one. Not an old man dragging a sack, not a drunk, not even a dog. All of Montevideo seemed eerily quiet.

Esther felt nauseous, wavering between belief and doubt. Had she seen the fluttering bag, the small white hand? Had she heard Carolina's cry? What was real? She couldn't make up her mind. But she knew she could choose to *not* believe. She could go down the steps, into la doña's house, slip into bed and sleep. She could pretend she hadn't seen the little girl's hand, heard her fragile cry. In the morning, when Pablo and Susana and Doña Pereira wondered what had happened to little Carolina, Esther could be just as bewildered and surprised as they were. She had seen others do it. Her neighbors, refusing to meet her eyes after her parents had been taken, were the same neighbors who closed their curtains and turned off lights at the sounds of los milicos in the street. Her teachers had done it, telling her she was una histérica, making too much of everything. Making people disappear is like balancing an equation; one half is the taking of a person, the other half is pretending not to see.

Esther raced down the back stairs, tripping on the last two and nearly falling against Pólvora, la moto. She prayed like she'd never prayed before that the little red Zeus Puma would start and she did, with a roar. A moment, a beat, to tell her chaotic brain to *Think, carajo, where was she even going?* She was all adrenaline with no direction, until she remembered Pablo's words, "He drags you, kicking and screaming, to the Cementerio del Buceo." She pushed Pólvora as hard as she could down Avenida General San Martín, turning a sharp right onto Boulevard José Batlle y Ordóñez, heading straight for el barrio Buceo.

The entrance to the cemetery at Buceo was ornate stone and iron. The main entrance closed at five, a large chain secured with a padlock kept the homeless, lovers, and thieves away. But tonight, the gate was wide open; the lock and chain discarded on the ground. Esther wished there was more than a half moon, anything that would make the night seem a little bit brighter. She leaned Pólvora against the wall, wrapping the chain from the gate around la moto—at least to give the impression that she was protected—and walked into the cemetery.

Adrenaline made Esther slightly nauseous, or it was the night, or it was the memory of the tiny hand reaching out of a greasy bag. She pushed that feeling away, along with the voice that told her she was una idiota for believing in cuentos de hadas, believing in a myth like el viejo.

On either side of the wide pathways, the palm trees looked arid and leached of color. Somewhere a cat was mewling. An occasional streetlight cast a cone of warmth and clarity where Esther could make out ancient marble crypts and statues of poured concrete. But in the dark those same shapes turned into sleeping giants and gardens for monsters.

When Esther was little, her parents had brought her to el Cementerio del Buceo on a picnic to look at the famous people buried here and the beautiful sculptures of angels and Madonnas, heads of state and weeping men. She had mistaken the mausoleums with the bronze plaques of family names for tiny houses, just her size.

"I'll buy you one of those houses, Mamá, and the three of us can live inside," she'd said, and her parents had laughed. The tiny houses mocked her now, filled as they were with families and bones and perfect silence.

There was one sculpture that used to fascinate her. Papá called it her little friend, and in Esther's mind, he *was* her friend. A boy, not much older than nine years, slept under a weeping willow, his rounded cheek pillowed on his arm, one leg straight, the other bent. She would stare at the boy's stone chest as if, any moment, she would see it rise and fall in gentle waves. When she'd been hot from the sun and tired of hiding from Mamá between the graves, she would sit with the statue, keeping him company until he woke up.

Suddenly, Esther knew where el viejo had Carolina.

On the other side of the wall, the bluff overlooked la rambla, the road that wound against the shoreline where the Río de la Plata met the Atlantic Ocean. Out of the corner of her eye, Esther could see twinkling lights of the wealthy neighborhood below. But her attention was entirely on the hunched figure in front of the statue of the boy. As she watched, the figure straightened and lengthened. Like an actor stepping out of character, he stepped out of a carapace of rags, bundles of bloodied clothes behind him. He'd shucked years off his face and body, too, for the old man with the bag was now a young man in jeans and a leather jacket.

"Hola, Esther."

"You know me," she said, not bothering to make it a question.

"Not you, but your parents."

"My—" She couldn't even say the words. Mis padres. Amá y Papá, who were supposed to be here, protecting her, and had not even been able to protect themselves.

"I know all the lost people, querida. It's my job."

In the same liquid way that el viejo had turned into a young man, his hair lengthened, his chest broadened, and his voice turned crystal. The young man became a young woman.

"I'm with them when you cannot be," she purred, silk and velvet in her voice.

"I want to be with them," Esther stammered, forgetting for a moment what she was here for, what she was arguing for.

The young woman floated closer to Esther. She was beautiful: dark haired, dark eyed, brown skinned like her papá's family.

Everything about the woman was comforting, and Esther would give her whatever she wanted.

"Do you, Estercita? Do you want to be with your parents? Little Carolina wants to be with her parents. That's why she's here."

Where the greasy rag sack used to be, a rectangle of gold cloth had been set down on the grass. It looked like one of the displays she'd seen this afternoon at Tristán Narvaja; fresh cut flowers, bronze plaques depicting historical moments, and beautiful wooden dolls, no more than a foot high and so life-like that Esther was entranced by them.

"Care to take a closer look?" the woman asked, only she was the young man again, his hair shorter but still fashionably long. Esther sensed the viejo—she had to call him something—shifting like water within whatever shell he chose. Young or old, male or female, he spilled from container to container as if all of them, and none of them, were the right fit.

Esther picked up the first doll. She felt the grain of the unpainted wood beneath her fingers, but in all other ways, the doll was perfectly realistic. A young girl in a sundress and sandals, a bow tied around her head. The expression on the little doll, or maybe it was better to say, the escultura, was uncertain, tinged with small worry that would inevitably grow.

"Who is she?"

"Her name is Carmen, and she was unhappy but only a little."

Esther set Carmen down gently, and even then, the wooden doll wobbled slightly on her carved pedestal. The next doll was a young boy, almost a baby. He, too, looked caught in a moment of transition, when the realization creeps in that something wonderful is over. The way the wood was sculpted, the roundness of cheek and limbs made her think of her stone boy. How could carbon and minerals and inanimate materials soften as if with moisture, breathe as if with life?

Because they are alive, thought Esther suddenly, and nearly dropped the precious wooden little boy.

El viejo, back in his female aspect, smiled fondly. "That little gurí is a charmer. His name is Alejandro, and he loves ice cream so much, having it can make the difference between happiness and sorrow. Aren't children the most wonderful creatures?"

"Give me Carolina and I'll leave you alone."

El viejo laughed, loud as a crack of a bell, the sound rebotando through the cemetery, repeating like thunder.

"You don't want to leave me alone, Esther. You came here because you want something. Something only I can give you."

Esther couldn't put Alejandro's wooden figure down, but she scanned the others, looking for Carolina's face, her too-big corduroy skirt.

"I don't want anything from you." *Except my life, except her life, except their lives.*

El viejo was once again dressed in rags, but his face was the young man's face, and his spine was straight and strong. Each of el viejo's faces were faces that Esther knew she could love, human faces, full of curiosity and flaws and fierce wanting. What could be more attractive in a person than them wanting you above all other things?

"I'm not a common seller of secondhand goods like you see in las ferias. None of these children are stolen. They've come to me so I can keep them safe."

"You keep them away from their families. You steal them away and leave us—them—brokenhearted."

El viejo lifted a hand and the slab of marble behind the statue parted with the grinding sound of stone against stone. Esther thought of her church lessons, of the boulder at the entrance of Christ's tomb rolling away, a miracle. She almost ran. All her courage evaporated as hands from inside the crack in the monument pushed the opening wider. But then she heard her name.

"Esther?"

No one can forget their mother's voice, not really. There is a cadence and a message in every syllable used to call your name. You may never want to hear her voice again, or miss it with an unbearable ache, but you cannot mistake your mother saying your name.

"Mamá."

Señora Mautones stepped from the stone boy's monument wearing the same clothes she'd worn on the day she disappeared; her smart suit of pieced suede and what she called her teaching shoes, low heeled and square toed. Her expression was one of mild confusion as she took in her surroundings.

She's not dead, thought Esther, who had feared the worst for over a year. Then: *She must be dead.* There was no other way.

"I know you want to join them," el viejo said. "And I will let you. That is my job."

"You stole them? You stole my parents."

"Oh no. I don't take adults! Don't you know anything about el viejo de la bolsa? The bag is only big enough, believable enough, to fit children. I *do* take children—not to eat them like they say, what a disgusting thought."

"Then why take them?"

"To reunite them with their families, of course. The world is cruel, Esther. All these children and thousands more have lost their parents. They cry and grow thin because they cannot eat, their sadness sits in their bellies like spoiled meat. I bring them here and reunite them with their mamás y papás."

Esther looked at the line of dolls, lined up like soldiers, so delicate and breakable; five in all with Alejandro still in her hand. With a start, Esther saw a sixth doll, tucked under the edge of the gold cloth; Carolina's braids, her expression of warring hope and fear perfectly captured in wood. Behind el viejo, her mother contemplated her with calm expectancy. *Well, Esther, mi vida, what will you choose?*

"You are my biggest prize, I have to admit," el viejo said with an enormous smile and his perfect white teeth. "You would never have fit in my bolsa, querida."

"Where is mi papá?"

El viejo's smile dimmed. "You want to see your papá? I thought you were a mama's girl, but I understand. You want to make sure you are getting a bargain." El viejo turned to Esther's mother. "Florencia, bring your marido, please. Your daughter is just as stubborn as you said she was."

El viejo watched Esther's mother stand, smooth down her skirt, then pick her way to the opening in the monument. She slipped a bit and then stepped more carefully with her heeled shoes over the broken pieces of marble and masonry. Esther had a single moment, not longer than a second, to see her mother's face and unleash a tidal wave of longing—an urge to let go and stop fighting—that almost washed her away, into that crack in the monument, over the wall of the cemetery, mixing with the sweet brown waters of el Río de la Plata and the salt blue waters of the Atlantic.

The next second, Esther grabbed the cloth of gold, making

a bundle of the flowers, the dolls, the dull-edged souvenirs, and threw it over her shoulder like una bolsa.

She ran.

At the gate she threw the chain off of Pólvora and climbed on—taking a second to tie the bundle around her back. Pólvora's engine ground but didn't catch, and Esther cried, "Please, Pólvora, I just don't want any more lost people." Finally, the engine caught, sputtered, and steadied. She stole a look behind her and saw el viejo de la bolsa at the gate, looking again like any young man she might pass on the street.

He gave her a little bow. "I'm here for you, if you need me."

Even though Esther was afraid Pólvora might make like her namesake and explode, she pushed la moto to her limit. Esther refused to stop, refused to think, until she made it to the little apartment in San Martín.

There was no point in trying to sneak in, it would be impossible. She rang the doorbell three times, knowing that even if la doña was too drunk to wake up, Pablo was a light sleeper.

But it was Susana who opened the door, an expression of worry and fear on her face. Behind her, Pablo struggled to hold la doña's heavy frying pan over his head as a makeshift weapon.

"Esther? What are you doing out?"

Esther pushed the door wide so that Alejandro, no more than two, could come inside. He pulled his sister, Carmen, by the hand behind him like a deflated balloon. She shivered in her orange sundress, bewildered and blinking in the light from the kitchen. Behind her, a girl of eleven, Paolina and her nine-year-old cousin, Marco, staggered, dream-children, trying to adjust to reality. Carolina held on to Esther's waist, tighter than ever. Esther shepherded all the children into Doña Pereira's apartment of no windows and a magical glass roof, the now empty gold cloth slung over her shoulder. Tomorrow she'd burn the thing.

Esther hugged her back. "Vamos, gurisa. It's time for bed," she said. "I'll stay with you."

Esther didn't think she would be able to fall asleep, but a sound like her mother's voice woke her from a heavy, tiring dream. She sat up, looking to the other bed, the blankets on the floor, and tried to make out the bundled shapes there. Carmen was curled around Alejandro like a protective shell. Paolina had put Marco between herself and the door, and he was hogging the blanket. On the far side of the bed, Esther heard Susana's fluttering sighs but not Pablo's light snores. But next to her, in la doña's bed, Carolina was gone.

Esther pulled out the iron meat tenderizer—a square mallet with spikes on each side—which she'd placed under the bed, and slipped from the room. The radio was off, but she heard faint music from somewhere. La doña slept on, under la claraboya, as she had all night, undisturbed. At the kitchen table Pablo and Carolina were eating. Esther set the tenderizer on the floor, her shoulders sagging.

The tin garbage pail had been upturned onto the table, the food scraps separated from the empty bag of yerba mate and the grease-paper packaging from la panadería. On Carolina's plate were the last tough pieces of tongue from dinner; on Pablo's plate was the sodden mess of the milk-softened bread. Esther's powder-blue record player turned lazily, the Mercedes Sosa record playing so low that Esther remembered the lyrics more than she heard them.

Esther had no words for these little children, dutifully filling their mouths with garbage, as they listened to a song about a woman who walked into the ocean and did not come back.

When Pablo saw her, he smiled. "No need to worry, Esther. El viejo won't get us now."

Beware the Empty Subway Car

Maika Moulite and Maritza Moulite

Today you are a beggar, your preferred disguise during the wintertime. You are curled into a ball but still stretch across two seats at the far end of the subway car. Your hands are buried in your pockets, and you caress the tattered photo hidden in its depths. You are alone. But not for long.

Stand clear of the closing doors, please.

"Hurry! There's no one in this one!"

You hear before you see, smell them before that. The wheels of an overly stuffed suitcase spin rapidly across the dirty rubber floor. There are two of them. One much heavier than the other.

"Don't they say you should avoid empty subway cars?" one of the travelers asks, a man if you had to guess. Barely contained mirth creeps into the edges of his voice, laughter from an earlier joke you hadn't heard clings to each word. He and his companion flop down into their seats.

"And who is 'they' exactly?" the second person purrs. The woman's pitch is low, the warm timbre of her voice enveloping them in a cocoon of intimacy. There's a rustle of heavy winter coats as they presumably slide closer to each other.

Lovers.

You know what they are now, so you sit up in your seat, your tightly coiled, gravity-defying curls reaching toward the fluorescent lights overhead. To their eyes, it will seem as if you've appeared out of nowhere. One moment they are alone on the D train, riding express to 59th Street-Columbus Circle during the wee hours of the morning. And the next, their heavy petting will abruptly come to a stop. Not because they care about other passengers but because seeing a dark-skinned girl of no more than sixteen years, dressed in stained winter clothing, riding alone in the night, stabs a tiny hole in their balloon of fun.

All types of people ride on the subway car: single commuters, groups of teenage students, mothers with their newborn babies swaddled in their arms. But it's the couples who draw your eye. You have your aunt to thank for that. Each pair of lovers is different, but there are a few who are the same. There are the new lovebirds who huddle close like moths drawn to a blaze. Or the more established ones who sit together comfortably in companionable silence. The two who are on the brink of a breakup, stuck beside each other out of a sense of obligation. Or spite. Conversely, there are the couples who are charcoal and matches waiting to combust. The most difficult to handle are the pairs who crave a child of their own, who see an underage girl with no apparent guardian to care for her as a chance to demonstrate to the universe their willingness to parent. Their heartstrings are drawn tight, compelling them to ask about the last time you ate.

The easiest are the people who never look you in the face. Locals and visitors alike who avert their eyes when confronted with even an ounce of proof that the American dream is more nightmare for some. No need to have their alcohol-softened realities pulled sharply into focus when they'd rather lose themselves to the city that never sleeps. They forget that without slumber there is nowhere for unshakeable fears, let alone great hopes, to take root.

This couple is on the brink of igniting. You know how to handle them, so you stand without delay. You feel the vibrations of the train's wheels spinning rapidly beneath your feet as you creep toward them. Their heads are bowed together, whispering.

"Oh God. I hope she isn't coming over here to ask for money."

"I know. Try to avoid eye contact. They usually leave you alone if you do."

You see some of your country folk in their faces, though they look nothing alike. But the haves and the have-nots have similar sensibilities whether in Port-au-Prince or Manhattan. Besides, it's only been a year since you left your island so you can't help but draw comparisons and contradictions. In your village, mostly everyone is suffering, so no one is able to spare you a glance. But here? The people don't look at you because it's the easy thing to do. You do not mind. Their downcast eyes prevent them from noticing how you shed your clothing as you move closer. Closer, still.

First glove.

The second.

Your winter cap.

Loosened scarf.

Outer jacket.

Each item falls silently to the floor. This is purely for your own dramatics as they are determined not to look at you. If they did, every article of clothing would be a red flag. Maybe they'd be able to fight back. At home, everyone was always on alert for lougarou like you. There was no catching them off guard unless they were foolish. But everyone is a fool here. You tell yourself, *If they look up, I will let them go.*

They never do.

You choose a snake today. There is no mess when a snake eats.

Tati's voice rings in your ears, as clear as if a tiny version of her were standing on your shoulder. "And what do you do when you see a couple?" she asks.

You sigh deeply and then recite what she's taught you about the hunt. "It's harder to corner a pair, but if you do, you will be fed for weeks."

There is no denying the truth of what your aunt has taught you: More people bring more sustenance. Yet you spend your childhood wondering why she singles out lovers in her training. Is it the thrill? The chance to demonstrate her power? While these questions may bring you close to the truth of why, they don't fit your understanding of who Tati is.

You and Tati crouch down now, obscured by an asosi bush. During a hunt, Tati's instructions are to be followed exactly. Always keep your focus on your meal. One moment of distraction can mean the difference between a full belly and capture. But for once you defy her and your disobedience is rewarded with knowledge. It happens by chance. A furtive glance to your right brings Tati into focus as she continues to squat beside you. Her fingers curl into the dirt, her grasp so tight you can see all the fine bones in her hands. As you gaze into her face, her eyes fixed on the young couple lying intertwined in each other's arms, it becomes clear. Tati's heart is broken. It is an old wound, but the fragments of her shattered love are still sharp, jagged edges of misery etched into her forehead, skin pulled tightly around her mouth in a scowl. But it's her eyes that startle you most. They shine brightly with unshed tears. It's the closest Tati's ever come to crying in your presence.

You avert your gaze just as Tati glances over at you. Good thing. Tati is not one to accept disobedience. She doesn't have time for meaningless questions or defiance from anyone, let alone a parentless girl like you. These are her words. Though Tati watches over you diligently, it is only because of fealty to her sister, your mother, and not her responsibility as your aunt.

"I know you think me uncaring, child," Tati says interrupting your thoughts. "But I swore an oath to my beloved sister the day I held you in my arms. I promised to prepare you for the cruelty you would meet in this world so that you might have a fate different than hers."

Hours later, you and Tati are seated in front of the tiny television set in the small one-bedroom shack you call home. Your appetite is finally sated, and you try hard not to doze off as you sit atop a cushion on the hard-packed dirt floor, positioned between Tati's legs with a large towel stretched out beneath you. Tati braids your hair into cornrows. Each dab of her castor-oil-soaked fingers across your scalp makes you shudder awake.

It's the first time in weeks that the electricity has been on for more than two hours at a time. The television plays softly in the background, an American cartoon about silly underwater creatures. The silence between you and Tati is a familiar one. Each of you sits quietly together but are lost in your own worlds. Your thoughts drift to the look you saw on Tati's face earlier. You wonder briefly if you should bring it up but decide against it. Though it's been years since Tati lost your mother, her presence looms still. You know it is an ache that will never leave her, yet you can't help but wish you could've had the chance to make memories of her to miss, too. All you have is a photo that you sneak glances at when Tati isn't looking. It's your most prized possession.

The characters on the television let out a squeal, and your attention turns to the screen. Watching the English-speaking animations and dramas that are broadcast on the island allows you to practice the foreign language. The words sound stuffy on your tongue, smothered in a layer of Creole when you do. The cartoons have just gotten off a sea bus and are traipsing through an underwater version of New York City. While Tati doesn't speak often about your mother, there's one story she loves to share, no matter how often you ask her.

"Tell me about the time that you and my mother went to New York," you ask sleepily.

You can hear the smile in Tati's voice as she says, "You never tire of this memory?"

You shake your head and feel the swift thwack of the comb on the back of your neck to sit still.

"I've only left the island once," Tati begins. "And as luck would have it, it was all thanks to your coward father. You will have your chance to leave, too, one day. I'll make sure of it."

Tati doesn't skip any details about her long-ago trip. Each of the few stories Tati tells about your mother falls into one of two buckets: before your mother met your father or after. The trip to the states was your father's attempt to go away with your mother but since they weren't married, Tati only agreed to allow it if she went along as a chaperone.

You can see everything from the preparation of their trip to the commotion of the city in your aunt's words. She even explains the minute details of preparing her passport, securing her ticket, packing her bags, going through the airport, buzzing through subway cars. You listen attentively even though you've memorized every part of Tati's tale. She's made sure that you can make the entire trip on your own when it's necessary.

Tati finishes with what is clearly her least favorite part of the story, "On the last day, we went to visit Madame Charles, an old friend who left Haiti many years ago. She's like us, you know?" You start to nod but quickly stop yourself.

Tati continues, "As I gathered my things to leave, I realized that your mother and father were nowhere to be found. We searched the entire house. Just when I was ready to pass out from worry, we heard a noise. And what do you know? They'd gone into the coat closet to hide away and somehow had locked themselves inside." You sit quietly as you imagine the moment your aunt found your mother, relief mixed with a twinge of annoyance.

"Do you think he ever loved her?" you ask.

"There is no love for women like us."

He is beautiful, unintimidatingly handsome. His brown skin is so smooth you know God must have painted him with special care. His top row of teeth are slightly crooked, a feeble attempt at keeping this young man humble, but all it does is add to his approachability. He sits perched at the end of his seat, with a paper bag in his lap. He must be around your age, though his anxious expression makes him look older. He taps his foot nervously, bouncing to a rhythm only he knows. A girl in a high school uniform watches him from a few seats away.

"No way! Are you serious?" She tosses her hair to the side as she speaks loudly on the phone, swinging her head as though partly decapitated. You both steal furtive glances in the boy's direction. But he is swimming alone in a pool of his own thoughts.

A flash of vindication warms the pit of your gut as you sit huddled in your corner, covered in all your layers and dirt. Ignoring you is a matter of course, but at least he isn't so easily swayed by the preening girl clamoring for his attention. You debate whether you should change your appearance to something more pleasing to what a person like him might be drawn to. Dimples. Smooth skin. This internal monologue makes you uncomfortable. You've never wanted to be *pretty* before. Prettiness is lies you tell yourself . . . as you resist the urge to make eye contact. It is a veneer for the unloveliness within us all . . . No need to create a song from the rhythm he taps out with his feet. Beauty is simply an unnecessary coating to crack through as you suck in a soul . . .

But his eyes look so kind.

What would it hurt if you grew the coils on your head out a bit more? Who would notice if your knuckle hair disappeared? It would just be a redistribution of assets you already have. It would still be *you*, even if you chose not to hide in plain sight as a beggar today. Just for a change.

You wish it could be that simple.

No.

You do not fight the voice in your head that tells you to reject this sudden desire to be noticed. To be seen. To be beautiful.

This is a Bronx-bound D train. The next stop is One Hundred Twenty-Fifth Street. Stand clear of the closing doors, please.

As you reach this uneasy conclusion, it is for nothing. He exits the train car.

It is a pleasant surprise when you see him again a few weeks later. You didn't forget his face, the thick eyebrows framing his glasses. You wonder now, as you did then, how good his vision is when he takes them off. Would his other senses sharpen if you crept near him, alerted to the threat of danger? The pierced lobe in his left ear is bereft of an earring. Perhaps he is trying to close the hole.

You are not hunting now. Not for food. Seeing him reminded you why you left.

"Why must we be the ones to hide?" you have asked since you were a child, confusion twisting into frustration until, eventually, begrudging acceptance closes the loop. You dig your toes into the warm sand and feel tiny pieces of rock slip under your sharp nails. It is dark. The glow of the full moon bounces on the surface of the sea and allows you to just make out Tati's profile.

She sucks her teeth. "Aha. You don't get tired of asking the same thing over and over again?"

"Don't you?" you retort.

Tati smiles. Her tongue lazily slides over her teeth and pauses to press into a fang. "You are smart, manmzèl," she says. "You know this. I know this. So I don't understand why *you* don't understand why we should stay in the shadows. Think of—"

"Manman m," you say flatly.

"Yes. Manman ou."

You don't say anything else as you stare out at the inky black waters, nor does Tati try to fill the silence. What is there to say? Manman thought she could tell your father who she was. What she was. He had already seen all the ugly parts of her. He'd shared his own dark truths with the callousness of a man with no shame. Surely he would love her still. As they lay wrapped in each other's arms in the discarded boxcar that sits on the far edge of your village forest, spent from a night of loving, Manman had whispered who she was. What she was. The man who they call your father fled without a backward glance. He ran and he ran. And didn't stop until he'd found an officer.

"She's a lougarou!" he'd yelled. "She tried to trap me!"

They didn't wait until morning to find her. Threw her in jail without a key and without a care. While imprisoned, doctors discovered your mother was expecting. Each checkup was met with derision. The nurses prayed that she would not carry to term.

"It would be a mercy on the child's soul," they'd said.

It's been a week since your subway car was last empty. It's the time of year when people throw holiday parties to celebrate their love for family and friends, all while wishing their guests would hurry up and leave their homes. Normally you'd search until you found another train car, one less crowded, but you stay. You don't want to admit to yourself that you're hoping to catch another glimpse of the handsome boy. It seems a fruitless wish, to see someone three times on the same subway car in a city of millions. Your hands fiddle in your lap, pulling and stretching a long thread dangling off the edge of your jacket.

Stand clear of the closing doors, please.

You look up. And there he is. Did you conjure him? No, no, that's not one of your talents. But would it be too much to hope that he would throw a glance your way? He hasn't moved from his spot in front of the subway doors. He looks slowly through the car. For the perfect seat perhaps? His eyes continue to scan the mostly empty vehicle and then it happens. He sees you. Looks directly into your eyes.

You freeze.

This is what you wanted but when the moment presents itself you are a sewer rat caught in the gleam of a maintenance man's flashlight. He sees you and all you can think about is how you wish you would've changed your hair, cleaned your face, straightened your clothes. There's nowhere to hide.

But wasn't this your desire? To be seen. Perceived. To no longer have to scurry into the shadows because of who you are. You remember yourself now. Your spine elongates, a sugarcane stalk stretching gracefully toward the sun. Your chin juts forward. Haughty. Proud. He should be so lucky to gaze upon your face. He must know it because he smiles, a slight tilting up of the right side of his wind-chapped lips.

He settles into the hard plastic bench across from you. He's found his seat at last.

You stand in front of a white backdrop as Tati uses a borrowed camera to take pictures of you. You open your mouth to ask what this is for, but the look on Tati's face freezes the question on your lips.

Now you sit in a low rattan chair across from the owner of the borrowed camera.

"Let me see your hand, child," the bokor says in his smoke-scratched voice. You hesitate even given the fact that he's just done an unnamed favor for your aunt. Although your gifts as a lougarou are formidable, you are not ignorant of the talents that bokor can have. Sometimes the witch doctors are tricksters. Other times they forego the distraction of riddles altogether and are predators outright. They can sniff out the secrets buried deep within your core, the scents of each one racing straight into their greedy nostrils.

You wonder how he pounced once your mother disclosed her hidden longings.

"Do you have a potion to ensure you never lose your love's affection?"

"But of course . . . if you promise yourself and unborn child to become lougarou and to never reveal your true nature to this love."

Once they've caught a whiff of veiled desires, there's no denying their offer. You will pay the cost, no matter the price.

The bokor takes a puff from his corn cob pipe. "She is stubborn." He says this to Tati but looks at you as he does.

"I can slap it out of her," Tati says darkly through clenched teeth. She does not like to be embarrassed. You can almost feel the sting of her hand against your face, so you stretch out your own toward the man.

He puts down his pipe carefully, taking his time. You made him wait, so he will return the favor. He holds your upturned hand firmly in his left, the fingers of his right tracing along the lines fate has etched into your palm.

"You know loss, don't you, child?"

"That is no secret," I say. The whole village knows that you are your mother's daughter. Though lougarou are not passed down through the blood, there are whispers of exceptions. People who submit their children as offerings to attain the yearnings of their own selfish hearts. The old wives' tales say that in these instances, a lougarou must feed before giving birth to another lougarou or the ancestors will call one of them home. The day you were born, your mother screamed for her pain to end, and you entered the world just as she left it. The authorities went to call Tati, but she was already outside of the jail, waiting for them to let her in. When they asked her how she knew to come, she said simply, "I felt it in my bones." Her quick arrival ensured that no one ever saw the lougarou in you. As your mother's only living relative, the officials did not hesitate to put you in her custody, for your aunt to start to raise you just as she lowered her sister into the ground.

"This is true," the bokor says as though he hears your thoughts. "You are lucky to have an aunt who cares for you so. One who would become a lougarou so that you would not be alone." You've heard this story before, from your aunt.

The bokor picks up his pipe in one hand, using the other to tilt your palm this way and that. Finally, he lets go. A chill runs through you as the contact ends. The ramshackle home that you sit in is humid, and sweat pools at the small of your back, but you don't resist the urge to rub your hands up and down your arms to chase away the goose bumps that have risen there.

"You have seen me fifteen years now, thanks to your mother's transgressions," the bokor says as he puffs. "Tell me, have you ever been in love?"

"You should know," you say.

He chuckles again. "You have not."

Tati fans herself beside you and casts another hard look. Though she's never wanted children and has not hidden that truth from you, she wields that sharp gaze with parental precision.

"You have not known love," the bokor repeats. "But you will. It will be swift, a tie that pulls you to one another. But it will not last."

"And why is that?" you ask.

"You will ruin it," he says simply.

"Oh."

"It cannot be helped. You are your mother's child; it is in your nature. Nothing that comes into your life will stay. And the things that do, well, it might be better that they didn't."

"What can I do to change my fate?" you ask.

The bokor puffs thoughtfully on his pipe. Closes his eyes to savor the tobacco.

"There is fate and there is choice. Whichever prevails is up to you."

You and the boy now have a ritual. He's ridden in your subway car for four consecutive days. Each time, he sits across from you and says not a word. At times he reads a paper book with illustrations all over it. Cartoons? When he's not staring at you, he focuses his attention on the colorful pages in his hands. He relishes each image, each word that is written. You wonder if he is an artist. Or a writer. Maybe he simply loves to read paper books with pretty pictures. It is a comforting rhythm.

On the fifth day he is late. You think maybe he's gotten bored of you. You try not to sulk in your corner and look out the window as the underground tunnel walls race by in a blur. The view alternates between blinking yellow lights and pitch-black darkness until, finally, the train slows to a stop.

Stand clear of the closing doors, please.

You can hear the shuffle of passengers exiting the car and then the footsteps of someone who has entered. It's been days since you've last eaten a proper meal because you've lost yourself in the ritual of comforting silence with a perfect stranger. The seat across from you creaks as someone sits down. It is him.

"Look at our fortune," Tati says as she looks down at the man whimpering at her feet. He's frozen in place and unable to move, though his eyes still frantically look for an escape. You can smell the alcohol oozing from the man's pores. He must've tried to drown his sorrows in a bottle of clairin and passed out at the foot of a banyan tree with pitifully sparse leaves. Tati had become a tarantula, two swift bites fortified by her power to ensure he wouldn't run away.

"There is no strength like that of a drunk man," Tati'd explained right before she'd bitten the man, even though he already lay sprawled on the ground.

Tati settles down in front of him. His eyes are blurry with her poison and alcohol coursing through his veins, but even still, the windows to his soul show his awareness that he is not long for this world. "Go fetch us some water," Tati says. "We will need to wash him down with something so we are not drunk for too long."

You make your way back to the throng of people in the makeshift tents that mark the center of your village, looking for something to use as a bucket. There's a discarded calabash bowl at the side of the road. The rim is cracked and jagged, but it should hold enough water for you and Tati. *Fortune is truly on our side*, you think as you make your way through the crowds of stinking people and wait at the water pump. The line is long but moves swiftly. There's been talk of a lougarou discovered on the edge of town, so the villagers have been on alert. There's no way to know whether or not the stories are true, but it's meant two weeks of no hunting to be careful. When it is finally your turn, you waste no time filling the bowl.

As you walk back, you start to fantasize about your feast. You've never been drunk, so you wonder what it will be like. In the distance you can see the tree where you left Tati and the man but immediately you sense that something is not right. You can hear Tati's clipped tones as you step nearer. It is the deep baritone of a man that makes you freeze. But it cannot be the drunken one, the poison would be almost done with him by now. You hide behind a tree, still holding the calabash carefully to not spill any water.

"What is going on here?" the man asks in a frightened voice.

"I told you," Tati answers. "I found this man here bleeding and wanted to get him help. But I couldn't leave him here, alone, in his final moments."

"But you are covered in blood . . ." the man says tentatively.

"I was cradling him, singing a final hymn," Tati replies. You can tell she is trying to sound like a proper, devout churchgoer.

The man scoffs loudly. He does not believe her piety. "He looks like he's been devoured by a beast," the man says, his voice rising.

"And that is how I found him," Tati tries to explain.

"Ase!" The man says. "I know you are a lougarou. Look what became of your sister."

"We all know that it is not passed through the blood," Tati hedges.

The man ignores her, his voice rising. "Your secret is out now, and I have the proof! Where is your niece? We'll take all of you wicked women into custody."

"Custody?" Tati says in exclamation. "For what? I tell you that I comforted this man as he left this world, and you accuse me of such a crime?"

The man has had enough. You can see through the leaves when he lunges at Tati. When did he pick up such a large rock? He swings his arm and though you cannot hear the crunch as it slams into the side of Tati's face, you watch her crumple like an empty potato sack.

"Where is your niece?" The man shouts as he stands over Tati.

The calabash you had in your hand is now tossed to the ground. Your feet carry you away as you shift. A wild boar. They are endangered on the island, but a few still remain. No one should think twice if they see you racing by.

You can just make out Tati's voice as she answers, "I ate her."

Your cries of agony blend nicely into the squeals of a pig. You run.

"The train is running late today," the boy says. These are his first words to you. You open your mouth to answer but decide against it. In private moments you continue to try and mold the harsh angles of this language around your tongue, but they do not always fit. Instead, you nod.

"Are you hungry?" he asks. There's a covered plate in his hands. When he lifts the lid, there are four slices of pizza inside.

"Two for you, two for me." He extends the platter toward you for you to take.

You look at him. He is smiling, encouragement shining in his eyes. You reach forward and take your share. You can eat this food, though it does not fill you the way a proper meal would. As he shifts back in his seat to eat a slice, his scent meets your nostrils. He smells sweet but not sickly so. Your mouth waters. You take a bite of pizza and try not to wonder what it would be like to do the same to him.

It's been a month since Tati was discovered. You dare not visit the jail because you know what fate awaits you if you do. There is a small hope inside you, praying that if anyone can find a way out, it would be Tati. But as each day fades into night, you know that it is senseless to hope for the impossible. Tati is bound just as your mother was before her. To be imprisoned as a lougarou is a death sentence. And the entire village is looking for one on the loose. You.

You've been forced to spend your days as a small dog, relying on the kindness of strangers for both scraps of food and information. People's lips are loose when they think you are nothing more than a beast.

"Yes, they say she ate the man and her own niece the same night. She lost control of herself!"

"No, they say the niece is alive, waiting for the best moment to get her revenge."

"I saw the niece just the other evening. She was fat from all the people she had devoured but swift as a lion. That's the only reason why I didn't catch her myself."

Each tale is taller than the last, tiny bits of truth baked into the center of an entrée of lies.

You spend your nights in the empty boxcar that once belonged to your mother and the man they call your father. No one knows how it ended up at the edge of the forest, but most believe it to be cursed. Fear of the unknown acts as a powerful repellent and no one comes near. You embrace the time to reflect, the photo of your mother your sole companion.

You try to envision what your life could be, but it's hard to imagine a new tomorrow when every day is the same. So your only goal is to survive. You think back to your recurring conversation with Tati, thinking about why you must hide. If she had said "Because if we don't, we'll die," would it have changed your desire to be seen?

It is a new day and unless you find something to eat soon, it may be one of your last. You venture from your boxcar and head over to the village. Your ribs are on display through your matted fur. You come across a pile of garbage and burrow your head into its depths to see if you may find something to eat. As you search, you hear a woman speak.

"Yes, he says he's come back for his daughter. Just got into the village today."

You don't know why you stop, but you do. You listen.

"Did you tell him that no one's seen her? She could be dead for all we know." A man.

"I did," the woman replies. "But he said that he will not stop until he's laid his eyes on her himself."

"What's a Christian man to do with a lougarou like that? He should let the spirits do with her whatever they desire and consider himself blessed for having had nothing to do with her."

If you had strength, you would nip at their heels. But you do not. So you crawl back to your boxcar to wait for fate to find you.

The boy is nervous. You can tell by the way each word tumbles quickly out of his mouth. He is an artist, after all. The cartoon books he reads are called comics. He wants to learn to make his own, so he studies the best for inspiration.

He leans over to show you his favorite story so far and then he looks at you intently. He wants to ask you something but hesitates. Finally, he says, "That cool? If I sit right there so you can see better?"

All you can do is nod. He moves into the seat beside you and you try unsuccessfully to focus on his words. You can't figure out why he decided today would be the day to approach you, but you are glad. Now that he's closer, you can make out the sweet smell of his essence. There is a rawness to it, too, like a cake that hasn't baked long enough for the center to firm. The heat of the world beats down on your back until you present what they want to see, but the inside of you, your core, is still tender and unformed. You know what that is like.

As you enter the boxcar, you can see someone huddled in the farthest corner, leaned back against a black bag. The man they call your father steps forward, now adjusting the bag over his right shoulder. He is tall and thin with a reedy voice to match his frame.

"I knew it was just a matter of time before you arrived," he says.

You stare at each other until finally he speaks again.

"I heard about your aunt." He does not wait for you to respond. "And I have come to collect you." To collect you. Like when your credit at the market has run out and the merchant sends authorities to get her due.

"I was afraid," he continues. "When your mother told me what she was, I was afraid. I did not know about you until I was already away. Your aunt called me the day you were born, the day your mother died. She said that she would send me a copy of your birth certificate because I was the only parent you had now. When it arrived, I felt so much shame. I called your aunt and told her not to contact me again."

You don't want to ask but you do, "Then why are you here?"

"I received a letter from your aunt." He notices the flash of hope that shines across your face and shakes his head. "She sent it a month ago, when she was first imprisoned. She told me that her days were numbered and that you were in hiding. She told me . . ." His voice catches as he collects himself. "She told me that if I ever loved your mother, then I needed to do my part and take care of you. She'd included two pictures of you with her letter so that I could get a passport made. I've been living with this shame for fifteen years. And now I have a chance to make it right."

You try to imagine what it must've been like for this man, to learn that the beasts from nightmares existed in the woman with whom he had made a child. Although that isn't quite true. The beasts from nightmares did exist. But they live in the men and women who fear without understanding, who condemn the people to whom they say *I love you* in one breath and *burn in hell* the next.

The man who calls himself your father speaks without end, as if his chattering can make up for the years he spent away. In fear. In shame. He says that he cannot leave you here alone and that he has a new home for you in New York. He paid a hefty fee to expedite your documents, bought two plane tickets, one for you and one for him. Fresh clothes for the four-hour flight that will carry you into a new life. All stuffed into the duffle bag he adjusts on his shoulder.

"How funny I would find a home in the city that never sleeps, filled with subway cars that can take you anywhere, any time of day." He glances around the boxcar and says, "It kind of reminds me of this place. Though the empty ones are never a good sign."

The man settles against the train car's wall farthest from you. He says you both will make your way to the airport tomorrow and talks until sleep finds him. You crawl closer and take in his face. You see nothing of yourself there and that is a small comfort. As you watch him sleep, your aunt's voice rings in your ears. And finally, fate has found you. You pull out your cherished photo and study it silently. You shift into your mother. You do what she should have done all those years ago.

The boy is reading to you now. You don't care for the story, but he's so enthralled that his excitement echoes in your chest. You place a hand on his and he stops the tale to look at you.

"Do I frighten you?" you ask.

"No," he says without hesitation.

"Do you believe in fate or choice?"

He considers your question carefully. Finally, "A bit of both, I think."

You smile at him and nod. He smiles back. His sweet, sweet scent tickles the fine hairs in your nose as he gazes into your eyes. You hold his hand and squeeze, taking another sniff.

Stand clear of the closing doors, please.

You make your choice.

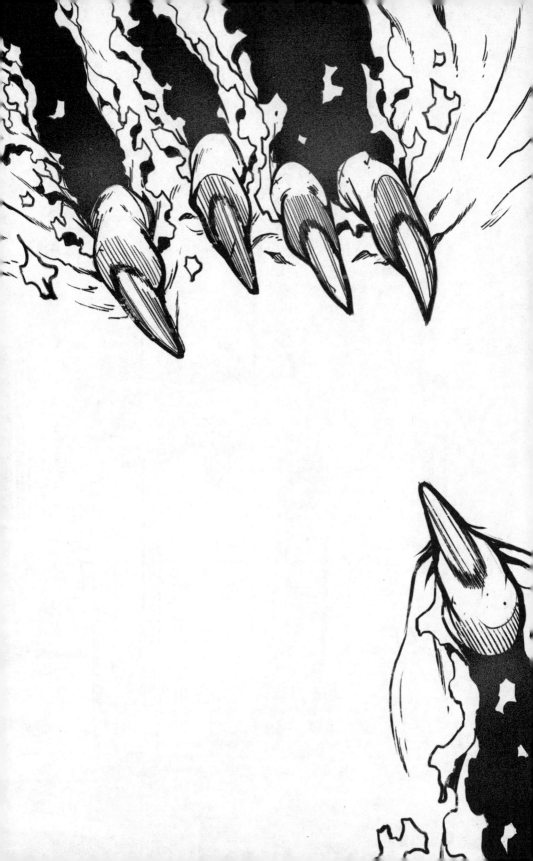

Dismembered

Ann Dávila Cardinal

I hadn't expected to spend half of my eighteenth birthday in a lawyer's office in Lajas, Puerto Rico, talking about my dead grandmother, but there I was. First thing that morning, I'd driven my shitty stepmother to the San Juan Airport so she could escape as soon as she was legally free of me. Good riddance, Karen.

I'd never been to a law office, but it was pretty much exactly the way I pictured it. Serious adults in suits; lots of shiny wood; offers of water, coffee, and tissues. I had been summoned there to go over my grandmother's "estate and holdings," whatever they were. I imagined it would be a room full of long-lost cousins, whom I might or might not have met over the years, and a lot of whispered adult talk. But there couldn't be much left to me, or my stepmother would still be here, trying to take it.

I was shown to an empty conference room, and two lawyers followed me in and closed the door behind me.

"Where is everyone else?" I asked, confused.

"There is no one else," said one of the lawyers. She had a

kind face and perfect makeup, and gestured to a chair at the long table.

I had no idea what was going on, but I sat down. A frosty glass of water was placed in front of me, and I folded my hands in my lap to stop their shaking as I waited. "My stepmother flew out earlier this morning," I reminded them, even though their office had arranged her flights, the hotel, and rental car.

"Yes, we know," said the other lawyer, who looked like a cranky-ass Oscar Isaac in a blue suit. "Your grandmother specified that we were not to discuss this with your stepmother, nor have this meeting until after your eighteenth birthday."

Huh?

My confusion must have been apparent, since he kept going. "When she prepared her will this past winter, she was concerned that your stepmother would try to take control of your inheritance."

Inheritance? Winter? "She died in a car accident. She couldn't have known that—"

The woman lawyer put her hand over mine. "Your abuela was sick, Raquel. Stage four lymphoma. The doctors told her she didn't have much time."

No. She couldn't have been sick. Abuela would have told me she was sick. Right?

The Oscar Isaac lawyer shuffled papers and manila folders. "So," he continued, "she left you the house on Route One Sixteen."

"The house?" I knew she was close with her late husband's children. I had dozens of cousins I only saw at big parties every summer, but she spent a lot of time with them. She left *me* the house?

"Of course, the Nissan was totaled. That's why the trust got you a rental car until you can procure a new one."

Procure? Trust? I had exactly twenty-three dollars and thirty-two cents in my wallet. I wouldn't be procuring shit. Then my brain caught up with what he had said. "Totaled? Wait, how bad *was* this accident? I mean, I wondered about the closed casket, but . . ."

The two lawyers looked at each other.

Oh Jesus. It was bad. My throat was suddenly bone dry.

The woman put her manicured hand over mine again. "It's just . . . Raquel, it was rather . . . terrible."

I pulled my hand out from under hers and sat up straight. "*How* terrible?" They'd treated me like an adult from the minute I walked in the office, now they were going to baby me? "Please. I need to know."

"What does it matter, m'ija? You really don't want—"

"How. Terrible?"

"Señorita Smith, your grandmother was pinned at her legs, and she was . . . decapitated by the windshield."

My mouth started watering, and I knew I was going to throw up. I grabbed the recycling bin behind me and vomited on a half dozen empty Diet Coke cans. But my head . . . my head was spinning . . . and I couldn't stop it. I put my forehead on the cool surface of the table and watched my breath frost up the glass.

Decapitated.

The kind lawyer came over and rubbed my back, calling to the secretary for a ginger ale. I couldn't get the image of my grandmother's headless body out of my mind. Why had I asked? Why had I pushed? I always push and I'm always sorry. They waited quietly for a while, but then their assistant came in and whispered that their next appointment was waiting. I couldn't stay there forever, but I couldn't imagine going on with my life either.

"Señorita Smith, there's more."

I sat up. "More? More what?" I couldn't handle any *more*.

Another stack of papers shoved at me.

"She also left you the bulk of her estate, dividing the rest among her stepchildren."

"Estate?" Individual words weren't making sense anymore.

"Yes, she had financial holdings in excess of two and a half million dollars."

I stared at them with my mouth open, gasping for air like a fish.

"There was also a piece of jewelry she was very specific that you should get." He shuffled through the papers. "Something she got in Fátima, Portugal, and said she wore all the time . . ." More shuffling.

I saw it clearly in my mind. "Her silver rosary."

"Yes, that's it."

I looked around the table, but all I saw were piles of paper. "Where is it?"

The woman answered. "They couldn't find it at the scene of the accident."

What? Suddenly, all I wanted was that rosary. If I could just put it around my neck, she wouldn't be gone. Not entirely, anyway. I felt anger build in my chest. But it wasn't their fault, or anyone's really. There must have been a mess at the accident site. I swallowed hard, trying to keep the tears at bay.

We went on to signing dozens of pages on dozens of documents. It got to the point where my signature seemed like

someone else's. It kind of was, because in Puerto Rico I was
Raquel Smith Cortez. I liked that on the island you got to keep
your mother's name, too. As I looked down at the last document
I signed, I decided that if I truly were an adult as of that day, I
was going to change my name legally to Cortez, forever tying
me to Abuela.

They gave me a packet of documents to keep and wished
me well. They were nice to me, but I can imagine they were
also relieved to see my vomiting, crying ass gone. After the door
clicked closed behind me, sucking the last of the cool, condi-
tioned air back inside, I stumbled down the sidewalk. The mid-
day sun beat on my head, and the world as I knew it continued
to buck and crumble. I dropped to a bench in the town square,
documents clutched to my chest, just staring at the sidewalk.

What had just happened? I don't know how long I sat there,
but the sun was lower in the horizon when someone stood in
front of me.

"Hey, are you okay?"

I looked up, but the light behind her hid the woman's face.

"Raquel? Is that you?"

I shaded my eyes with my hand until I could make out a
black-haired, punky girl with many earrings. She was older, we
both were, but I would recognize her anywhere.

"Luna?"

I jumped up, dropping the folder on the bench, and grabbed
her, holding tight, then sobbing on her shoulder. She was
Abuela's next-door neighbor's daughter, the girl I used to play
with before she moved away.

"Raquel, amiga, what's the matter?" She pulled back and looked
into my snot-smeared face, tears streaming down my cheeks.

"Abuela, she—" But I couldn't finish.

Luna nodded and then pulled me back into a hug.

"I was so sorry to hear about your abuela. Especially given how hard it has always been for you at home."

"I . . . I can't believe you remember that."

She shook her head. "How could I forget?" She paused and looked into my face again. "Hey, you want to get a coffee? I'm on a break from work"—she pointed to the new bookstore on the other corner—"and we could get something."

"No, thanks. I . . . have to get over to Ab—the house, I haven't been there yet, and—" I didn't finish my sentence, just grabbed the file, clutched it to my chest, and took off toward the car. I could feel Luna staring at my back as I scurried away, but I was too freaked out to care.

As I pulled into the gravel driveway, I caught the first glimpse of the house. For a moment, I expected Abuela to come out and greet me wearing a cotton dress and a big smile, dirt from the garden still under her fingernails. She would coo at me as if I were an infant, then grab my cheek and twist, like a lump of bread dough that required pinching. I could almost feel it, the ghostly echo of her fierce love. Grief tightened around my chest like a tourniquet, and I turned the car off and just stared at the house. I'd never stayed there without her, never even imagined staying there without her.

I swallowed hard, got my suitcase from the trunk, and let myself in the front door. Once it was closed behind me, I flipped on the lights and looked around. I'd been coming here for summers my whole life, and this house had always been so . . . alive. Abuela brought life to everything. From her wild hair to her fast gait, she was the most alive person I've ever known. I walked around and opened all the shutters, the afternoon sun reaching in with golden fingers, the sound of birdsong and rustling leaves riding in on the hot afternoon air. Once it was all opened, it started to feel a bit more like it used to. Like home.

I thought about going to Amigo supermarket, but when I opened the fridge, I found it was still stocked with her usual staples: eggs, butter, bread, milk, all the essentials. When I saw the half empty bottle of artisan guava jelly she always got, I picked it up and smiled. Abuela could pinch a penny with the best of them, but this was her one indulgence. Actually, having learned what she really had in the bank, her frugality was completely unnecessary, but somehow still made sense for who she was. My smile quickly devolved into a frown, and I ended up sitting in front of the open fridge, grasping that jelly jar to my chest, sobbing.

Eventually, I pulled myself together enough to make a peanut butter and guava jelly sandwich in her honor and ate it standing at the kitchen counter. I couldn't sit at the table by myself. God, the house felt empty. Like a huge chunk of it had been bitten off and spat out. Had it ever been this quiet? I remember it filled with sound and purposeful movement, salsa playing softly from the radio, and the starchy, golden smell of plantains and garlic frying. Abuela tried to teach me how to cook every summer, but I was always so desperate to get outside, play in the sun, go to the water. I would act all grumpy and uninterested until she cut me loose and I ran out of the house at top speed to play with Luna and her brothers. Even after Luna and her family moved away, I never did let Abuela teach me. I would give anything for one of her cooking lessons now.

I was crying again, though I'd thought there were no more tears to be had.

I should have been an expert in death and loss. My mother died when I was two. My father, just over a year before Abuela. A father who had, by the way, left me with the evil woman he married eight months after Mom's death, replacing her like she was a broken toaster. Abuela was all I had. I looked around the house I knew so well, and it looked different to me knowing it was now mine.

I couldn't continue that thought. The power of it pushed down on my shoulders and was going to shove me to the floor until I was nothing more than a puddle of sadness. I took a shower in the hopes of washing it away. It helped. A bit.

I settled on the couch to lose myself in movies on my iPad and must have fallen asleep, because I woke just before midnight to the sound of barking dogs. Lots of barking dogs. Even the coquíes, the tiny tree frogs whose song always filled the night, were shocked into silence. I remember summers where I woke up once or twice to the sound of barking, late at night. For some reason, it seemed to make Abuela nervous. Each time she would close all the shutters, double check the locks, and make the sign of the cross. I didn't understand why. I still don't, but I go through the same precautions anyway, topping it off with a sign of the cross. Just in case.

I was heading to my room, trying not to think about the fact that I was alone in the house, when I heard a dragging sound outside the front windows. Like someone was hauling a full garbage bag across the gravel with long, scritching noises.

I peered out but saw nothing. The motion-sensor light hadn't kicked on. After a few minutes of silence, my breath slowed. Probably just an iguana. I yawned and straightened the couch cushions, already fantasizing about dropping into the guest room's familiar bed.

BANG! BANG! BANG!

Someone was at the front door.

I froze. *Who the hell is that?* I tiptoed over, stopped, and listened. When it came again, I jumped a foot in the air.

BANG! BANG! BANG!

It was coming from low on the door, like three feet from the ground. I put my ear against the wood. Silence again. Had I imagined it?

BANG! BANG! BANG!

No freaking way was I going to open that door, I didn't care who was there. I frantically looked around and spotted my phone on the coffee table. I rushed over, grabbed it, and then just stared at the glowing screen in my shaking hand. Who could I even call? The police about a knocking on the door? They'd probably laugh at me. The law office? At midnight? I could feel my heart knocking in my chest like an echo of the terrifying sound.

I stepped back to the door and pressed my ear against the cool surface once more.

Nothing but some barking from off in the distance.

For a second, I heard that scritching sound again, but this time it was moving away from the house.

The barking stopped. The coquíes resumed their song.

I let out a huge breath. "Jesus Christ!" I whispered, and immediately felt bad. I could hear my pious grandmother's voice. *Do not use the Lord's name in vain, Raquel. You never know when you will need him.*

I stood there for a long while, making sure it was over. Eventually, I made my way to the bedroom, though it felt like forever before I fell asleep.

I woke to the morning sun painting the floor of my bedroom in golden stripes, the early summer air already heavy. I was halfway to the bathroom when I remembered:

Abuela was dead.

And last night there was some scary-ass banging on the door, which I might or might not have imagined.

I tried to do normal morning things, things I used to see Abuela do. Sweeping off the patio, wiping down the kitchen counters, but I was just going through the motions, playing house. There was nothing about the situation that was normal, and I eventually gave up.

"What do I do now?" I said, my voice loud in the silence.

A walk, maybe that would help. I grabbed my keys, locked the front door, and rushed down the path, feeling calmer the farther I got away from the house. It used to be the safest place in the world for me, but without Abuela, it was an empty husk.

Everywhere was. As I reached the edge of town, everything I passed reminded me of her. Rosa's Beauty, the salon that she dragged me to, where they styled my hair big and poufy like I'd been time-warped to the 1980s. The gas station with the middle-age owner she'd known since he was in diapers who called her la doña and gave her homemade cassava bread.

She was everywhere. And nowhere.

I headed toward the town square though I didn't know why, walking in a complete daze, my body pulling forward of its own accord. When I got there, I looked around and noticed the bench where I'd sat the day before. Was it only the day before? It felt like years.

Luna'd said she worked at the bookstore. I crossed the street, grateful for the bright, cheery window filled with bestsellers and brightly colored children's books.

The bell on the door chimed like it was oh-so-glad to see me, and the air-conditioning hit me with a shudder. I could see Luna's head of dark hair behind the counter, but she was talking to a customer, a guy with a small kid in his arms. I perused a rack of books about the island and chose one about life after Hurricane Maria as I waited. I flipped the pages and looked at the photos of the devastation, roofs torn off houses, mile-long lines for gasoline, all stark in black and white. I had seen images online, had reposted articles on Facebook, but seeing them printed across the pages of a book made them history. It was heartbreaking.

The father brushed by and I heard her voice next to me.

"Scary as hell, right?" Luna said, gesturing to the page I had open.

I put it back on the shelf and turned. "Yeah. It took me three days to reach her, but when I did, Abuela tried to play it down. I had a feeling it was worse than she was saying, though."

She smiled. "That was classic for her. She was a total badass. You staying at CasAbuela?"

I chuckled. "I'd forgotten we called it that!"

"That was how you used to say it, like it was one word."

The memory was sweet, but sad also, like the taste of a fallen ice cream cone that lingers on your tongue. The tears started again. Luna put her hand on my shoulder.

"Hey, have you eaten lunch?"

I shook my head.

She called over to a coworker that she was taking a break, then took me by the arm. "Let's get you some food and catch up."

And then she was leading me down the street. She had this way of talking, so musical but also straight to the point, a symphony that pulled no punches. We walked as if there were no hurry, and she chattered on, but I stayed quiet. We hadn't seen each other in more than four years, but we'd been close during those summers and being with her felt familiar.

We settled into a booth at the local café, and after we ordered, I took a deep breath and sat back.

"So . . . are you staying at the house with the evil stepmother?"

"Nah, she went back to Queens yesterday."

"Good." See, no punches pulled. "Wait, you're not staying there alone, are you?"

I nodded. "Yeah, but I think it's good for me. Except . . . last night something weird happened."

"Weird? Like what?" Luna asked as the waitress, an older woman, arrived at the table and began to set sandwiches and drinks down in front of us.

"At about midnight, there was this scary banging on my door. Seemed to go on forever."

"Well, that's creepy as shit! Who was it?"

"I don't know. But just before all the dogs started barking. I mean *all* the dogs."

When I said this, the waitress froze, holding Luna's coffee in her now quivering hands. After a second she put it down, did the sign of the cross, and scurried away.

I watched her go. "What was that about?"

Luna gave a wry smile. "People around here are superstitious." She took a sip of her iced coffee.

"But what did I say that scared her?"

"It sounded like los desmembrados."

"Los what?"

Luna rolled her eyes. "A ridiculous local legend about Route One Sixteen."

"Our street?" Abuela's house and Luna's old house were on Route 116.

Another shrug and she took a bite of her sandwich.

I wasn't interested in food anymore. "But what is the legend?"

Luna looked at me through narrowed eyes. "Are you sure you want to know?"

"Why is everyone asking me that?"

Another shrug. "Okay. The legend says that the dismembered body parts of the people killed on Route One Sixteen walk around late at night. 'The dismembered,' that's what it means. Supposedly it starts with dogs barking."

I gasped.

"Oh, Raquel, it's just a crazy old wives' tale they came up with it to justify all the accidents. Hundreds of people go down to party at the waterfront each night and drive back on that winding road, drunk. No wonder they—" I could tell by the look on her face that she had just remembered how my grandmother died. "Oh, amiga, I'm so sorry. It's just a silly legend. I mean, this is the town where the mayor built an actual airport for aliens!"

"True." We went to visit that "airport" one year. It's just a road sign and a grown-over "landing strip." Abuela laughed so hard she cried. I swallowed and changed the subject. "What have you been up to? I have no idea what happened to you after you moved away." There was a hurt edge to my question, but I couldn't help it.

"Was dragged away, you mean." She shrugged. "High school in Florida sucked. And I only lasted a semester in college. Just not my thing. So I worked all spring to save up my money and come back here."

"Why did you come back?"

"This is the only place I really feel like I belong, you know? I was always considered weird here, too, but that was okay. Even though my parents and bros are still in Miami, this feels more like home."

I remember Luna struggling a bit with being edgier than our peers. Not interested in boys, listening to vintage punk rock music, wearing nothing but black. But she was still a local, and it was okay. "I get that. Coming here was the only time I felt comfortable and welcome. But that was just Abuela."

Luna put her hand over mine. "This will always be home for you, too, amiga." She squeezed, then let go and took another sip of coffee. "And don't worry about the banging. I'm sure it was just some kids messing with you."

I looked at her for a breath, then got an idea. "Hey, what are you doing now?"

"I'm supposed to go back to work at the bookstore, why?"

"When you're done, would you go do something with me? On Route One Sixteen? Something of Abuela's was lost, and I want to see if I can find it. I just need to figure out exactly where the crash was."

"I know where it was." She looks at me. "Tell me you plan on doing this in the daylight."

"Of course! I'm not stupid."

"Then sure. I love a post-work adventure!" She drank the last dregs of her coffee and stood up. "I'll pick you up at six."

If she didn't believe the legend, why did she look so nervous?

On the short drive from the house to the crash site we reminisced about late nights and made-up games from our childhood summers. It was so fun I almost forgot where we were going and why, but as Luna pulled her car to a stop on the side of the road and put her hazard lights on, I wasn't sure I could even get out of the car.

Luna noticed. "What are we looking for exactly?" she asked, her voice quiet.

"Her rosary. The lawyers said the emergency responders didn't come across it at the crash site. But I can't imagine they were looking too hard. It was never far from her."

"I remember it. She took it off at church every Sunday and worked it one bead at a time. My grandmother has one made of olivewood from Jerusalem."

"This one is silver from Fátima."

"Well, silver should be easier to find." She put her hand on my shoulder. "Let's do this together, okay?"

I nodded, took a deep breath, and pushed open the car door.

The early evening sun was just below the tree line, but its light dappled through the palm fronds, drawing crisscrosses along the thick greenery on the side of the road. It was a windy road, with hairpin turns. No wonder it's so dangerous. Cars whipped by us, but the shoulder was larger there, the plants beaten down, probably because of the crash. "So, this is where she died?" I looked around at the ordinary roadside, where a few discarded cans and cigarette butts peppered the dirt. I half expected this place to have sharp teeth and a gaping mouth since it had swallowed all that mattered to me in the world.

"Yes." She paused searching to look over at me. "You know, I can come back and do this for you. You don't have to."

"No. I want to." And we both went back to parting the grass, moving rocks, scaring lizards.

After an hour or so, we found nothing but a ragged cellphone cord and a headless doll with one arm, her chest smeared with dirt. On the drive back, Luna stopped at a food truck and picked up some dinner, though I couldn't imagine eating.

When we got to the house, I closed the door behind us.

Luna looked around, balancing the greasy brown paper bag in her arms. "Oh . . . it looks the same! I missed this house."

I smiled.

Luna gave me a one-armed hug, then made herself comfortable in the kitchen, filling two dishes with piping hot food, the smell of garlic, oil, and golden starchy plantain heavy in the air. I was salivating by the time she set a plate and a frosty bottle of Medalla beer in front of me.

"Oh . . . I'm not twenty-one—"

Dismissive wave. "Girl, remember? The drinking age is eighteen here, and even that is more of a suggestion than a rule."

"Well, then it's legal! I'm eighteen as of yesterday." I held up my beer.

"¡Feliz cumpleaños, hermana!" She lifted her bottle to mine, and we tapped them, sloshing a bit of beer on the table. She settled into a bamboo chair across from me.

We tucked into the food and talked. Luna had moved in with her aunt while she figured out what was next. She was single, though there was a girl at her work who she found super cute. By the time I shoved the last piece of flaky cod fritter into my mouth, I realized all my anxiety from the last few days was gone.

"Wow. That was the best meal I've had in a while."

She raised her eyebrows. "Really? Don't you eat Puerto Rican food in New York? I mean, there are more Puerto Ricans there than here!"

"Nah. I ate whatever was in the house. Karen took most of the money I earned."

"What?" She slammed the bottle down on the table. "God, I wish I could punch that woman."

"You and me both. But my abuela left me some money, so I won't need to take Karen's 'charity' anymore." I decided to keep the details of just how much money to myself. I didn't want her to treat me differently.

"Hey, there's a *Bachelor* marathon on tonight!"

I smiled. We used to watch it in reruns religiously all summer.

And for the next several hours, we lost ourselves in mindless television. Making snarky comments about the basic girls, about the bland white Ken doll guy, and we laughed late into the evening just like when we were kids. My grandmother always gave us our space on those nights, staying in her room and reading, occasionally coming out to check on us. There was no one to check on us tonight, but every couple of hours, I'd listen for the sounds of her shuffling through the house and feel a pang. Eventually, the one and a half beers made me sleepy, and I settled into the corner of the couch. Luna had just leaned back and put her feet on the coffee table when it started.

Dogs barking.

So many dogs.

We both sat bolt up and looked at each other. Luna was about to say something when we heard the dragging sound across the gravel, heading toward the front door. She reached out and took my hand. We both ducked behind the couch. There was only the sound of our breathing when the banging came again.

BANG! BANG! BANG!

"Jesus Christ! What the hell is that?" Luna whisper-yelled at me, her eyes wide.

"*You* told me it was nothing to worry about! Just kids playing a prank, right?"

"I had no idea it was that loud! That does *not* sound like kids!"

"I know!"

BANG! BANG! BANG!

I put my hands over my ears, but then Luna touched my arm.

"Raquel, what's that other sound?"

I listened and heard the rattling of metal. Then the unmistakable sound of the doorknob turning.

Oh my God. Had I forgotten to lock the door?

Then, as if in answer, the slow squeal of hinges.

I was about to scream when Luna put her hand over my mouth, making a *shhh* gesture with her other hand.

Whatever it was, it was dragging across the tiles, coming deeper into the house. A smell reached me, rot but with the metallic scent of turned earth. It paused, then resumed, heading in our direction. We scuttled backward on our hands and knees as it dragged itself around the corner of the couch and slowly into a shaft of moonlight. I felt my stomach lurch.

A headless torso used its arms to drag its legless body across the floor.

Luna screamed, the sound echoing around the room. We backed up faster, until our feet hit the wall and we were trapped. The thing dragged itself toward us, drawn by . . . what? It couldn't see, or hear, or even smell, but it seemed to know exactly where we were. It wore the tatters of a dress, the pearlized buttons still glinting in the moonlight. There was no blood, thank God, though the skin on her neck looked like torn fabric. I knew it had been a woman, but I was having trouble associating the thing in front of me with a complete human.

Wait.

That dress looked familiar . . . and something glinted around her neck . . .

The gasp seemed to freeze my heart in my chest.

"It's Abuela!" I cried, my mind hamster-wheeling to try to understand. This couldn't be Abuela. No. This was a monster, crawling straight from my nightmares or a late-night horror movie. Not my bursting-with-life grandmother. I pointed with my shaking hand, but it felt like someone else's, like I'd left my body and it was moving on its own. "The rosary, the one we were looking for . . ."

My breathing was coming so quickly I felt like I might pass out, so I focused on the tiny flowers on her dress, at the ironed pleats in the front, splatters of what must have once been blood across the pale fabric. A sob caught in my throat.

But then it hit me: This *was* my grandmother.

Abuela was here, in front of me.

The woman who took care of me every summer, made sure I knew I had a family, that *she* was my family. Who left me her home, her money, giving me a future. I should have been horrified, but I found I was no longer afraid.

As if Abuela could sense this, she moved then, dragging herself closer, and I didn't recoil.

"Raquel! No!" Luna grabbed my arm and tried to tug me away, but I wouldn't let her. After a few seconds, she gave up, and scrambled into the shadowed corner of the living room.

I looked back at Abuela. She balanced herself on one arm, lifting the other toward her nonexistent head. I noticed details like the delicate silver watch on her wrist, the cinnamon spatter of age spots across the papery skin of her hand. Yes. This was her.

"Abuela?" I whispered.

The gnarled fingers grasped the rosary and pulled up, working it over the severed stump of her neck, a scrap of flesh catching on the beads for a second before she pulled it free.

I knew the scene was grotesque, but the horror had bled from it. All I wanted was a few more minutes with Abuela, even like this.

My eyes filled as I watched her shuffle, struggling to move her destroyed body closer to mine. She stopped right in front of me, and underneath the rot and earth I could smell the faint scent of alcoholado, the spicy bay rum she used to rub into her aching limbs at night. She lifted the rosary up to my face and stopped. I knew what she wanted, and I lowered my head.

I felt the weight of the rosary fall on my shoulders, the silver beads cool and heavy against my skin. I looked down and let out a breath. It was the last piece of my grandmother, something that sat against her chest my whole life, against her heart. *Her* way of communicating with God. I held the crucifix that dangled at the end and brought it to my mouth to kiss.

When I finally looked up, I saw her hands clasped before her, as if she, too, was admiring the sight of her beloved rosary around my neck, even though she had no eyes. "Gracias, Abuela," I whispered, tears streaming down.

Then my abuela raised her hand again and lifted it to my face. It didn't even occur to me to pull away. When she reached me, I expected a caress, but her fingers gripped the meat of my cheek and pinched, hard. She gave me a playful slap, turned around, and began to drag herself back the way she'd come, following the trail of mud and leaves she'd left in her wake.

I scrambled to my feet just as Abuela reached the door. I ran after her to . . . what? Ask her to join us for some tres leches cake before she left? But when I reached the doorway, I didn't see anything. I ran out and looked around the driveway, into the greenery, toward the road. Nothing.

She was gone.

"R-raquel . . . are you okay?" Luna asked with a shaky voice from the open doorway. I looked back to see her clutching the door frame as if she needed it to ground her. I couldn't blame her.

I fingered the rosary around my neck. "Yes. I am now." I walked over and pulled my friend into a hug. We stood in silence for a bit, arms around each other, the coquíes having resumed their song in the trees outside. After a few minutes we walked back into the house, and I locked the door behind us.

"Do you think she'll be back tomorrow night?" Luna asked.

I felt a sadness spread in my chest. "No. I think she did what she came to do."

"What are you going to do now? Go back to New York City?"

"Nope." I'd decided that just as I said it. Why would I? And I didn't know, but I was pretty sure, I'd just gotten the blessing of my abuela.

"Where do you think she went? To look for her missing parts?" Luna whispered as I sat her on the couch and handed her a glass of water.

"I don't know." I sat down beside my friend. I *didn't* know, but there was one thing I knew for certain: I had found mine.

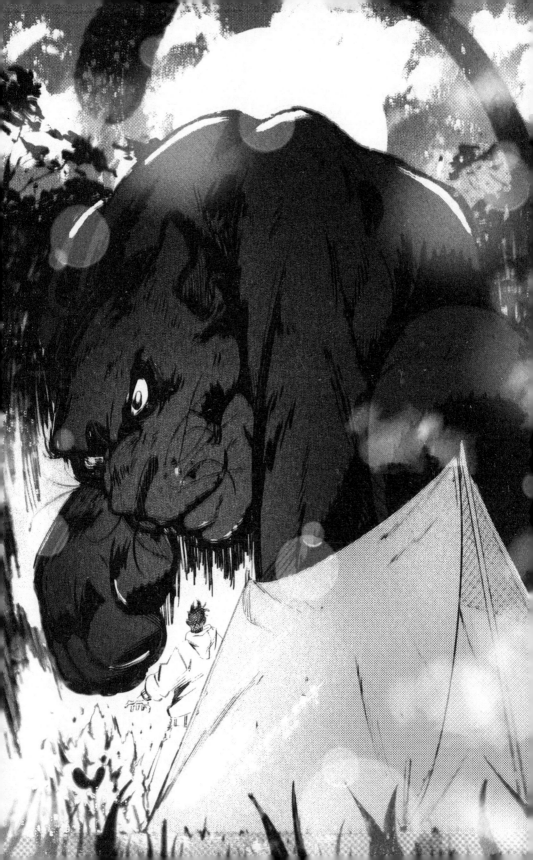

Blood Kin

Ari Tison

It is the first day of the deer hunting opener in Wisconsin, and my brother and I bike home from school wearing orange mesh safety vests. Before we get to the attached garage, we hear our mother crying through the screen door. We drop our bikes and find her in the kitchen leaning over her phone. Mateo touches my hand as he peeks around my shoulder to see her. She is weeping so hard she doesn't look to us.

"Mateo, can you go upstairs?" I ask as I unzip the orange vest. It feels more like peeling off a target than protection. I've seen my mother cry plenty before, usually after we have a fight, but even this looks serious. Mateo listens to me, swings his backpack over his shoulder, and starts up the stairs—the bonus of him being the obedient child. I may have five years on him at sixteen, but I cannot live up to his good spirit. I am never the one to leave a scene. After Mateo reaches the final step, I go to my mother and hold her shoulder. WhatsApp is open on her phone. She lifts a shaky hand and scrolls backward so I can read. She's received messages from my tía on our reservation in Costa Rica.

Dad was found in the forest. Almost everything is missing.

What is Tía talking about? I see my mother asking my questions and Tía responding. I hold my mother's body a little closer. My chest tightens as I read onward.

He didn't come home last night. Everything is missing but his head. It's horrific. I don't know what happened, but there have been a few threats from some removed settlers these past weeks toward his council. Everyone was walking together most places from what they told me. But he was found a few miles away from the trail. It looks like it could be an animal or something worse.

The air is heavy. Mom continues to shake in my arms.

I am always late on emotional responses. I never seem to find the right words and my fight instincts kick in before everything else. Even now, I want to fight more than cry because I don't believe it was an animal.

To only leave his head. A gruesome detail that to me reads intentional. A warning.

I already know the thought of it would give Mateo nightmares. But I am not afraid of death. They tell me my father was from the people of the undertakers whose traditional job was to tend to the dead before burial. Tara, my now passed grandfather, told us that from his side we are descended from ancient warriors, the Namawak, the Panther Clan. The clan which is also the root of my namesake. Nama.

Sometimes I wish I could be as fierce as our people, but the distance is hard while I live here in the States. Two years ago, my grandfather's friend, a fellow elder and land advocate, was found shot to death in his house after being terrorized and threatened by settlers who were building homes over our clear territory lines, known and allotted by the government. Despite the Costa Rican president saying she'd do everything to find the perpetrators, the government has never found anyone responsible, shelving the case almost instantaneously. I fear that they will not try for justice for my grandfather either.

My mother is still crying, and my arms have become limp around her. I ask, "Are we having a funeral?"

"Sí. We will have to have one soon."

"Will we all go? Even Aaron?" Her husband. The one that planted the seed in my mother to leave our people.

"I don't know if he'll get the time off." She holds her hands, and inside them a thinned, blotted napkin.

"Who do you think did it?" I ask.

My mother looks at me, her dark brows drawn together in a face that says I should have never asked that question. "How would I know?"

"I bet it was someone in the land dispute." Contemporary settlers are always trying to occupy the edges of our territory. Every so often our elder council has to go to San José to have the government notified with proof of our territorial maps and demand the land be repossessed.

"Mija, sometimes freak accidents happen. The rainforest is not always safe. We have pythons and jaguars and who knows what else."

"It could be one of the governments. They all want our oil. Or even the US military working with—"

"Why do you hate the military so much? After everything Aaron has taught you?"

I shake my head. Mom acts as if Aaron's service makes him an expert on all the things the American military does.

"I don't trust them." I push my long hair behind my shoulder.

Mom rubs her forehead. "Why does everything have to turn into an argument with you, Nama? Your grandfather is dead. Aren't you sad?"

"I want to know what happened."

"It was an accident." She throws her arms up. "Nothing more, mija. Send Mateo down and don't tell him the details."

How can she not want to know what happened? Grandpa was in our elder council most recently fighting for land repossession. But he had protested against the damming of our rivers, and five years ago against an oil company who had a spill and poisoned our water. A *scar*, Grandpa had called it.

I go upstairs and knock on Mateo's door.

"Yes?"

"Mom wants to talk to you about something serious."

"Did I do something?" He opens the door.

"No. Don't worry." I hug him. "We'll be okay. And we're going to figure out what happened." I tousle his cowlick. He is so young for all of this terror and why sixteen feels so much braver, I don't know. But in our stories, it is the women who are strong; it is their spirits bound to the ocean, cacao, the butterflies, the land itself, and even the Panther Queen.

I think through our annual return to Costa Rica and how many of my conversations with Grandpa were about our connection to the land. "Our land is part of our very bodies. We were planted there by the Creator, corn to soil to people." I feel it drumming in me even if no one else understands.

Fifteen minutes later, Mateo is in my room sitting on my rug. Crying. I look over at a photo on my wall of Grandpa and me. His face. I am grateful in a dark way it is his face that remains. In the photo, he smiles into the camera with a big wide grin. His hair is pulled back in a braid and resting over one of his shoulders. He wears a soccer jersey. Costa Rica made it to the World Cup semifinals that year, and the whole country cheered. We'll never get to take another photo together. His warmth has been taken, swallowed by whatever is beyond. My own sadness sinks in, and soon Mateo takes my hand to comfort me.

Aaron comes home late, and I hear him talking to my mother. He says he's sorry for her loss. He says that he wishes he was here when she found out. I can imagine him puffing up his chest. "I'd kill whatever did that to him." Aaron's family are hunting fanatics. A generation back they were traveling on safaris, shooting the Big Five or whatever they call them. He came home late tonight because he had spent his entire day deer hunting, taking tags from the neighbors for extra shots.

I have to put the bikes away. We'd left them in the front of the house. I know Aaron so well that I could already hear him chewing me out for leaving them there. I don't think he would try it today, but I figure I better do it anyway. I hate going into Aaron's garage. I put on a big loose sweatshirt on and start down the hallway.

"I'll get the bikes," I say as I come down the stairs.

"I'll help you walk them out. I was going to grab them for

you myself anyway," he says in a silky voice it almost surprises me. Mom smiles through her tears.

He has two deer strung up in the garage already. Their doe eyes and long unblinking lashes almost take my breath away. I love venison as much as anyone, but *two* feels excessive to me. We don't need two to feed a house of four. Aaron has lit a cigarette on the way and leans back on the garage frame as I put the bikes on the rack.

"I'm sorry about your grandfather," he says, sounding like a decent person for once.

"You going to the funeral?" I ask.

"Yes. I got work off. I'm going to conduct a few meetings there, so my company is going to pay for our travel and treat us to a nice dinner."

My posture tightens, but I try to hide my suspicion. "For what?"

I think he realizes quickly he shouldn't have mentioned work. "Never mind." He flicks his cigarette.

It's oil. After he retired from the navy, he went to work for a company that drills in South Dakota. If I know anything about oil drillers, it is that they all brag about knowing where all the oil is across the world. I don't respond and head back to the house feeling his eyes on my back.

Aaron and my mother met when the US sent the navy to give boxes of medicine and food to our territory after a hurricane when I was eight. I remember my grandfather rejecting them and staring down the helicopters. "This was hardly a serious hurricane, Nama," he had said. I felt his concern even if I didn't understand it all. Something about the way they expected we couldn't take care of ourselves. Something about the way the men looked at the women. I was protective of my little brother and my widowed mother. Especially when Aaron spent time with her and offered up all his own forms of "aid." He spoke Spanish that the US had paid for to woo her. Then came the promises: safety, an education for us, and a whole house with everything American.

Aaron is a whole other type of hurricane. This one, dangerous. Over the years, he's convinced my mom to buy so much of the land that belonged to other family members on our reservation with his money. When the Costa Rican government pushed for a new road through our territory, there were whispers between Aaron and Mom about selling it. I told my grandfather about it and swore that I would lay myself down on our mountains and they'd have to roll over me to get through.

"You might have to someday," my grandfather teased. He got me.

"I would do it," I said. "No doubt."

"I know you would." The earth beat inside my grandfather, too.

"But, also, Tara, if I'm American enough, they might listen."

"They might."

He gave a somber smile. My heart sank, but he hugged me, my Tara. My grandfather.

Three days later, Mom, Mateo, and I fly into San José. Aaron tells us he will follow behind the next day to finish a few calls and meetings. We begin our trip from the capital to the ocean-side town of Cahuita on a bus. The ride is rainforest, mountains. It is huge blue morpho butterflies lopping by trickling water-falls alongside the winding roads. The beauty almost hurts. Columbus supposedly called our land Costa Rica hundreds of years ago after seeing our rich land and people wearing gold. It's a name that invites others to take advantage. But I recall what my grandfather told me—our people have always resisted. We survived and kept our language and traditions. But death has been here also. The taking of life, the most painful tool wielded against us. I swallow realizing Grandpa is now among those taken.

We spend a night in Cahuita with my mother's best friend before taking a bus to Bribri, the first town in our reservation. From Bribri, it is another bus to the river, and then a boat across. On the boat, I feel everything as if Grandpa were sitting next to me. When the slim yellow-and-white butterflies swirl over the rocks, I think of Sibö the Creator, who turned spirits into butterflies after seeing how much they enjoyed the water. He transformed them to their truer forms.

Then, I look at the mountains. One called Kamu. There, the stories tell of two giant panthers who protected us when a tribe from across the Big River tried to take our land. The attackers kidnapped a young woman and leader from our tribe and killed them. But the Creator would not let their deaths be for nothing. Sibö transformed them into panthers who pushed the attacking tribe back. Afterward, the panthers are said to have settled in the mountains. The Panther Queen is in Kamu where she is said to watch over our people. My grandfather said you can still see the lemon groves she tends to on her mountain. But these are just stories.

Mateo is taking in everything on the boat. Last time we were here, Grandpa told me, "The land speaks of ferocity and beauty." I whisper the same to my brother. Mom looks tired, her arms crossed. An occasional hand goes to wipe her eyes.

When we get to the other side of the river, we take another bus to our grandfather's house. The house is traditional: wood, a woven palm roof, and stilted to shelter animals and to provide safety from the hurricanes and floods. Tía is there, and she is cooking a soup for us in the elevated kitchen, open to the elements except for the roof and support beams. When we climb up the stairs, she comes over to greet us. She has tears in her eyes. She gives us hugs.

"Ìs be' shkěna?" she asks us.

"Ye' shkěna bua'ë," I say almost reflexively. I am good. But am I really bua'ë? How long has it been since I've had to use another word? I don't remember.

We sit around the kitchen and talk while she cooks. Mom and Tía discuss Grandpa's funeral plans. They just need a date. Grandpa had been part of the local church, too, so they know that he will have something of a traditional but also Christian funeral. They will bury him right here on his property. Tía tells us that this house is to be kept for my cousins, Mateo, and me. Something Grandpa had wanted to pass down to the next generation. We eat and Tía even makes Mateo's favorite, fire-roasted plantains. The sweetness is so good it aches. The sun is going down, and the stars appear. The moon nears full, which means it will be a good time for harvest soon, as the phases of the moon signal our rainfall cycle. At the full moon, the land is neither too wet nor dry for reaping. We hear gritty wailing. Mateo's breathing sounds nervous. "Howler monkeys," I remind him. He nods his head like he knows, but they are loud and harrowing.

Tía gives a sharp eye to the forest. "Nama, you need to be careful. Someone found big paw prints around here. I saw some smaller ones a while ago. I thought it was just a cat or something. But just be careful, okay?"

Mom looks at her. "Don't talk about those things with Mateo around, please?"

"I'm just saying. Dad wouldn't want them being careless," Tía says with her lower lip sticking out in disagreement.

"I'm not scared of a panther, Tía," I say. "Besides, they don't often attack people."

Tía puts a ladle of chicken soup in my bowl and widens her eyes. "Mateo, you hear that? Your sister is fearsome. You'll be okay."

They laugh, and Mateo slips his hand into mine. I shoulder him and lift my eyebrows like I'm something to be scared of.

Mom and Tía want to talk privately in the kitchen, so I take Mateo to the central room and we fill up our small air beds and Mom's, too. We put up our nets because the mosquitos are unbearable when you aren't used to them.

I lean against the door to where Mom and Tía are talking and turn my back to Mateo so he can change and get ready for bed. I plan to stay up longer, listen in, hoping to find out who I can ask tomorrow about what could have happened to Grandpa. I hear Tía saying, "Apparently the same thing happened to a petroleum geologist who was out here looking for oil deposits just days after Dad was found. Though they didn't find his head. Just bloody scraps and shredded clothes. The whole tenting camp over there are having issues. I think it's one of the American oil companies."

"How awful," Mom says. "Maybe I should tell Aaron to stay home?"

"Why?"

"Well, that's dangerous for him."

"I still don't understand what you see in that man. Dad didn't like these people, Marcella. They aren't trying to help us. We don't need their help."

"You haven't lived in the States. You don't understand what life can be like. No more of these rickety houses and kitchens outside. I mean, I have my own kitchen *inside*."

I shake my head at my mom. Everyone knows that a palm-roofed kitchen lasts a whole lot longer than any shingle roof.

"Dad would not be proud of you right now," Tía says.

"Dad was never proud of me. He never came to visit. We always had to come here."

My heart sinks. It's painful hearing Mom talking about Grandpa like this so soon.

"Marcella, you know how hard visas are to get to come visit you. And he was so involved with the council. And if you didn't know, I've been thinking about joining, too. I've taken online law classes, and I'm committed. I had hoped his death might wake you up to his vision. For all we know, he died to protect exactly where you are sitting."

"I am just never good enough. We've bought so much land here. I'm keeping it in the family *for us*." I can hear in Mom's voice she is starting to cry again, but to me her words fall short. Buying up other tribal members' land isn't the same as protecting those with lands on the borders who are continually threatened. "I gave up everything so Nama and Mateo could have a good education. And I don't know. Maybe someday they'll be the ones to come back and help make this place better. But I didn't want them turning into their father, drunk and dead in a river."

I hear a shuffle and turn around. Mateo is staring at the door. He heard her.

"Don't give it any thought," I say, trying to let myself breathe. "You won't be like any of these men. You're going to be like Grandpa. Brave and amazing."

"But he's dead, too."

My shoulders fall. There is no good response. The monkeys howl again.

"Want to sleep next to me?" I offer.

Mateo nods. We put our sleeping pads next to each other.

Grief must make people tired because we fall asleep quickly. In the middle of the night, I dream of mountains and the lemon tree grove on Kamu Mountain. "She still lives up there," Grandpa says in the dream. "The Panther Queen. You know, she hadn't known who she would be. But when the time was right, she knew what to do." But then I turn around and see his head lying on the ground. Pale gray lips. A sharp pain in my chest, and I snap awake.

Mateo's eyes are like the moon on me. "I have to go to the bathroom. What should I do?"

"Can't you just pee off the edge?"

"I have to go more than that. Is there a bowl anywhere?"

I sigh. "Mateo, no. The toilet isn't that far from here."

"Can you come with me?"

"Of course." I breathe out, trying to shake the dream.

We tiptoe past Tía and Mom asleep on the floor. I see Grandpa's machete. I take it with me. An ōs feather on the hilt.

"See? We're going to be okay?" I let the machete glint in the starlight. "And look at the moon. It's here to help us see, too," I say as we walk downstairs.

The stars are brighter than anything I've seen in Wisconsin. The smoky dust of the galaxies is visible. We head down a trail in the backyard clearing.

Mateo walks ahead of me while my eyes adjust to the darkness. The rainforest is quiet besides the buzzing of bugs. Mateo goes into a small bath house with a tin roof top.

I lean against one of the outside walls and face the rainforest. My eyes still adjusting, grasping more starlight, I stare into the trees. It is quiet for a moment, but then I hear the crunching of leaves. A thud. The hair on my arms raises. I see a darkness shift from one tree to another. I stop breathing and lift my machete. I take a few steps forward, and then my foot slips into an indentation. I look down.

The paw print is bigger than what Tía had said. And with claws.

This is no cat.

A deep grumble comes from the forest, and I raise my machete. I whisper, "Mateo, stay in there."

My eyes adjust again, and then I see it.

The outline of a man. He's translucent like the floating spiders that I'd sometimes see in the shower. Iridescent, light blue, and pink. I lower my machete for a moment, and then I see his face. The one from my dream.

"Tara?" I whisper. Grandfather. I don't believe it.

"Nama." It's his soft voice.

All our stories—the ones I wanted to believe but couldn't quite put my hope into—promised me this. According to our stories, we've become less and less spirit with the time away from our original creation. At death, our spirits need to travel to the other side to regain their wholeness. But here he is. Like how I'd imagine the spirits of the butterflies before they were transformed, a silky spiritual substance.

"How are you still here?" I ask.

He smiles faintly. "I don't think I would be except for these men, Nama. They are hungry for everything."

"What happened?"

"I was watching them. Attempting to document everything I saw, and they ambushed me. They must have been following me after I made a trip to the capital with the council's most recent demands to stop a highway. But it was over so quickly. Some of those men are trained well."

I shiver. They are killing machines and smart planners—made it look like an animal attack. The bathhouse's door closes, and I turn. Mateo stands frozen behind me. Instant tears come down his face.

He rushes to my side. "Tara!"

Grandpa's eyes get soft again. Mateo runs up to him and tries to hug him, but his arms go through. "It's okay," Grandpa says to comfort his disappointment. "Still here in a way."

Grandpa's returned presence feels like a new kind of sorrow. My heart broke when he died, and it now feels mended but not fully.

"Grandpa," I say. "I must find who did this to you. Our tribe deserves to know."

"Sibö has his reasons for me to even appear to you. You

cannot tell the others." His looks toward his home where Mom and Tía are sleeping. I can tell he wishes he could tell them.

"We will not tell anyone," I say, and put my hand on Mateo's shoulder.

"What have you been doing?" Mateo asks.

Grandpa grins at Mateo. "Want to see?"

Mateo nods. I step back.

Grandpa's body disappears. For a moment, I wonder if I've been dreaming. But then he returns. His limbs snap in strange directions and his forearms and legs thicken. I cover Mateo's eyes, but he pulls my hands off. Grandpa's neck snaps back, and then a growl, darkness . . . fur. Black that glints rainbows in the moonlight. And then two big eyes, Grandpa's dark eyes, stare back at us. He is huge. A great panther. Larger than any I'd seen, larger than the bathhouse. His whole body radiates heat of only that which is fully living.

Mateo reaches out and puts his hand onto Tara's chest. He looks back at me and starts sobbing though smiles. Tara is beautiful. All his ferocity, his kindness and fury, are balanced perfectly in his new body. Our land must not have been able to allow him to pass. It needed him. The first Panther King returned to his tribe, and my grandfather must do as the first.

"MATEO! NAMA!" Mom calls out from the deck.

Tara looks into my eyes, and I repeat. "I must find out who did this to you." I am aware of my own duty. "We better go back," I say.

Tara presses his head against Mateo's forehead and then shoves him forward like a bossy cat. "Tomorrow," I say to Tara, and I sense affirmation in his eyes. Then Tara turns and leaps into the darkness. A thick tail and claws flashing. Huge prints behind him.

"MATEO! NAMA!" This time, it's Tía calling. They are down on the ground.

I turn and tell Mateo, "We can't say anything." Mateo nods in agreement as if he knew that already.

He sprints back to them, and I jog behind with the machete and tell them that we are fine. That Mateo just had to go to the bathroom. They give us hugs and kisses. We all go back to bed, but I hear a quiet roar before I fall asleep, and my heart burns with purpose.

Aaron arrives the next morning to say hello before going to go check on the oil company camp my tía mentioned. Mom warns him to be careful, but he brushes her off. He has his cargo pants on, the large machete he keeps at a family friend's house in Cahuita is already on his hip. It looks like he got his high and tight hair cut even tighter before he left. I am relieved we had time to just be together with Tía without him. "So many vets move to Costa Rica after serving," he tells strangers without anyone asking. "Most beautiful place on earth. They don't have bears, but there are plenty of other things to hunt. Boar, deer, tapir, big cats, snakes, you name it."

I let ten minutes pass before I lie to Mom and say I want to go to the store on the other side of the river to buy new boots for Mateo and me. She agrees and hands me colónes for the shoes and travel. Mateo agrees to stay and plays games on Mom's phone with his solar charger. I change into tan pants and a green top, and then I empty all of my other clothes and toiletries out of my backpack into Grandpa's closet and place the money there, as well. I find a number of Grandpa's knives. They are painted and some have bird feathers on them. I place two of them in his old holster. I loosen the band to fit across my hips, and I snap it on. Today, I will find out who murdered my grandfather and what other horrors they must be planning if they are willing to kill for them. I will build my own case. This is what I can do.

And pray that Grandpa will help me.

I thank Sibö I charged my cell phone with the solar panel the day before because I plan to capture anything I can on video.

I cannot follow Aaron. He would catch me in a second. But Grandpa has to know where this camp must be. I tousle Mateo's hair before I go. He doesn't look up, but I can see his smug little smile.

I sit where we saw Tara the night before. "Tara," I whisper, "if you're there, please let me help." I wait for fifteen minutes in the rainforest smelling like bug spray and clean clothes.

"Are you sure?" It's Grandpa. His spirit sits on a fallen tree trunk. The leaf cutter ants run through his translucent legs.

"Are you just showing off now?" I laugh, though it pains me.

"The ants have their work to do. We have ours."

"I want to do my part," I say. "I want to follow Aaron and see where the oil company is. I want to know what is going on. And I want to find the man who took your life."

He breathes, and I can tell his spirit is sad. I thought we both understood that I would lay myself down for our people, for our land. For him. For Mateo. For us all. But he looks like he might say no.

"I want to, Tara. I have no interest in doing nothing. I'm not my mother."

"Your mother's spirit is broken. I think she'll find her way back."

I bite my lip. He is right. Even in pain, we must hope that better will come.

"Please let me help."

Grandpa remains sad, but he nods and disappears. Then in a moment, here he is again in all of his huge panther glory. He seems even bigger somehow. I remembered the story, the first Great Panther grew and grew after he had been murdered by another tribe. He had been born out of the blood fallen from his beheading. I shiver in the light rain remembering that the oil company had beheaded my grandfather, leaving nothing else.

As I climb onto his shoulders, Tara has the warmth of the living. I lean into him, and he runs faster than a vehicle. In the speed, my hair almost camouflages me against his fur. Black on black. I sense his heart beating, heavy, thick, alive with blood. I breathe against him; danger, sacrifice even, for the sake of love feels like the deepest honor. I don't know what will happen when we get to the camp, but I intend to do everything I can because they've already tried to take my grandfather from me. I won't let them take more.

We arrive, and it rains harder.

I slide off his back, and he nods toward the campsite of brown tents. I can already tell we have beaten Aaron to his own meeting. Tara rests next to me. His big cat head up on the log. I put my hand on his front leg, and finally, I look at his paws. They are larger than anything I've ever seen, even the Wisconsin grizzly bears that are taxidermized and placed in bars and big houses.

Four men walk around the camp with XPLORATION written over the back of their rain jackets. Tara's eyes narrow at the oldest one and a growl comes from his belly. I get down behind the giant log, and I look at him. Is that the one? Another growl, and I know it is true.

I breathe. The heat of my own anger flushes. What they must have done to his body. It must be here somewhere, too. What would they do to me? I lean over to touch the knives in my waistband though I hope not to use them. My hair falls in my eyes, and I realize it's tangled and wet. I take two binders from my backpack in the front pocket with the first aid kit. I put my hair in our traditional way. Two braids. Ready.

I spot Aaron trotting in from the direction of the last bus stop. He rubs rainwater off his face, and his wet shirt sticks to his frame, which is strong but unnatural. Supplements and targeted weight training for visuals. A strength unlike a tía's arms from grinding corn or my legs from hiking.

He walks toward the brown tents and gives a little shout. Tara's ears flicker. The older man goes over to Aaron, and the two grip arms like they know each other. The man gestures at Aaron's shoulders as if he is measuring them. Then they look up at the sky and head into a different tent. I put my bag in the hollow of the fallen tree. I grab my phone, open my camera app, and start recording. Then I slip my phone into my sports bra. I touch Tara's shoulder before I circle half the perimeter of the camp to get closest to the tent Aaron went into with the man who murdered my grandfather. I soft foot from one to the next. A few of the Xploration men are snoring, and then one says, "Is that the box with the electrolytes?"

"Yeah, that's it." A small tearing. I think about the pipa trees that are all around their camp. A pipa could hydrate anyone in need. But they wouldn't know that, that this land already gives much more than they know.

I move again to the next tent, then the next, careful to make sure no one sees me. The rain covers my sound, but there are enough palms overhead I can find some respite. There are whispers. I close my eyes for a second and pray I won't be heard. I hope whatever I hear will prove to Mom these men are not to be trusted and that her own husband knows her father's murderer. I let myself hope. Finally, I am at the right tent.

"What a place you have here, Aaron! This plot is beautiful and exactly what you said. Full of oil. And quite a family you have. I saw pictures on Facebook. Really pretty wife. You met her here, right?" The man's voice is deep and cheerful in that comrade sense. I hate it.

"Yes, sir. We met when I was helping with the navy. We brought some medical personnel to the reservation after a hurricane." I pull my phone out and lean over so the rain doesn't quiet the recording too much.

"How great. She likes American life?"

"Loves it."

"I'm glad you're here, Aaron. And thank you again for the permission to be here. We couldn't do this without you."

"I'm glad to be of assistance."

"We've needed you and your Spanish out here. Without you, folks have been working against us. You are the bridge between us and the Indigenous. We need them to understand that pulling this oil will help the economy of Costa Rica. There's so much potential here. But it's a sensitive topic. I get that. We don't want much, just to frack it and get out of here. Our tools have improved, too. The last spill was a lesson that will not be repeated. But we've had some resistance and it turned violent, unfortunately, if you understand what I am saying."

My fists tighten. Does Aaron know what happened?

"Self-defense is necessary," Aaron says. His words are laced with another meaning. He knows what they did. "It's my money that bought this land anyway," Aaron continues. He can never stop bragging, but this time I'm thankful because I'm recording all of it.

"We were trying to be civil with the council, but that went nowhere. You know all this is such serious stuff," the man explains. "It's jungle law. You're like any other animal fighting for its life. And now, you know, we've got this damn tiger or whatever the hell it is. Damn cat has managed to destroy machinery. I had to get big guns to keep it back because the thing is indestructible."

I see Aaron's shadow. He takes the drink and straightens. I begin to wonder about his marriage to my mother and what it really is about. The thing about all oil businesses is that they are greedy but also patient. I cannot imagine what kind of payment he must have been given for this. I know now, he wasn't just in North Dakota on his month-long work trips. He was here.

"Well, just let me know when to give you the cash," the man says.

"In your own time," Aaron says. His shadow moves to get up, and I realize I'm too late to hide. I look around to see where I can go. I return my phone down my bra and quietly step back, and back, and then I step into a deep puddle. The splash freezes my body. Aaron's and the man's shadow turn toward me. I swear under my breath. They've heard me. I start to run to the forest where Tara was.

"Someone is here!" A person yells.

A roar. Tara.

Then shooting.

I pray that Tara cannot die twice because the gunfire is heavy.

"Stop, Nama!" It's Aaron yelling. He's seen me. I weave through the tents of people getting out with guns. Huge guns.

"I know what you've been doing," I shout back.

I hear more shooting. I lower my head, and I look over to where Tara was. But my foot clips a tent peg, and I fall. Aaron is over me in a moment. "What do you mean you know what I've been doing?" His eyes glower at me, and he picks me up by the arm.

"Don't lie to me, Aaron. I know who you are. I can see right through you." I try to pull one of the knives out of my holster.

He grips my arm tighter. "You don't want to do that, Nama. No knives."

"You're using us. And that man killed my grandfather, and you're working for him." I reach for the knife with my other hand, but he takes me by both arms.

"You do realize, Nama, that I could have already killed you in five different ways, and no one would know what happened?"

"You shouldn't have said that."

He pulls me up closer to him, and he sees my phone through my tank top. His eyes tighten, and he reaches down to pull it from my bra. I bite his hand, and he yells out in pain. I kick my foot between his legs, and I run and run and run. Then I see the fallen trunk. I slide my phone in its cavern and keep running.

Aaron's footsteps thunder behind me. He grabs me again, and he looks almost annoyed that I have gotten this far. I scratch at his face, trying to go for his eyes.

But then I feel his cold hands move around my neck.

Calculating.

Then *crack*.

My body falls. And then a roar—my grandfather is on him. The sounds of tearing and crunching of bones.

Blood starts pooling from my nose, and I realize that I no longer am.

I crack this neck back. It feels like sinking into water. I am spirit and from here everything turns with my will. I am the Panther Queen descending. Somehow Sibö has seen this as right, though I wish it were not so. Claws, tooth, a glistening black coat with whispers of spots, and I look back at Aaron. His eyes are horrified, and he begins to pull himself away, half mauled. But I have no doubt what to do.

No doubt to finish. To let my ever-present fire pour on him. I tear him apart. Limb by limb until he is no more.

I hear men shouting and shooting. Tara and I look at each other, and we run back with a strength that feels right because this is the only way. The men flee. Escaping to their choppers, hauling their gear, some shooting at us. But the bullets do nothing.

Death is not an option. We send them all running. Some to the beyond. Grandpa's murderer among them. Tara and I destroy their machines and crush every bit of equipment. We shred their tents to ribbons. I am the Panther Queen and Tara is my grandfather, the tribal leader, hundreds of years later. We are descendants of the first.

When there is no one left, I know I will go to Mateo in the night. I will tell him to send someone for my body. I don't want him to see me. I will tell him that my phone with the recording of everything that happened to me and our grandfather is inside the dead tree truck. I ache at the thought of never hugging Mateo again, of what could have been ahead if these men hadn't taken our land, our lives. I think about the lemon trees on the mountain Grandpa and I will return to after we finish this journey. I have found the truth. And those who know the truth, who fight in law, who write the stories, those who protect our land—it is in them that our ferocity still lives.

La Boca del Lobo

M. García Peña

Cuando era pequeña, I stepped into the darkness and almost
didn't come back.

The *almost* is the most important part for my family, where
everything tangles with hope, and light defeats the dark.

"Casi la perdimos," my mother would say, emphasizing how
I could've died in the thick of the mountains of Jayuya, a place
dense with trees and history both painful and resilient. I don't
like the way she tells it, like a scary story shared before a fire,
a warning; a held gaze over the dinner table as I finish my last
bite.

A child wakes in the night—I wake, groggy—*bathed in darkness
and walks*—stumble, feet caked in dirt—*into the thick of mango
and ceiba trees. When we woke we could not find her*—the path
is so clear, clearer than it had been that morning—*we shouted,
woke up the whole neighborhood*—all I can hear is the coquíes and
a song that sounds just like my name—*it took hours to find her*—
something curls around me, like wings. Something pulled up
by the roots, by the wind and rain, and days of only night—*we*

cried thinking we had lost her—keeping me warm, sinking into my skin—*the sun was rising*—asking me to stay and I say—*and that's when we saw her*—yes.

Acuérdate, it says, telling me to be careful, to shrink, but what would Mami say if I told her the warning hadn't worked?

That I still cling to the memories of that night, all jumbled, and hidden inside me; the feeling of being cradled, of being found, broken then rebuilt, only to be let go in the end.

That I've been waiting since that moment to return.

There are new cracks along the walls of Tía Eugenia's house—of *our* house, she reminds me. The cracks reach up to the sky. We will plaster them this week. They are not *foundational issues*, my father says, and were there before the earthquakes and hurricanes. Just the house shifting with time.

Like me.

"Pero se ve feísimo," my mother says, making a note to buy the plaster and yellow paint. They're in the living room while I've escaped to the porch, rocking in my hammock hypnotized by shadow and light playing with each other and me. "You'll see how nice everything will look once we're done."

There's a list of things to do, that's why we're here, they say, but I know it's not true. They missed the house, yes, even my father noted over the years how odd it was we no longer visited, but deep down I told myself it was for me. Whether it was the fight or something else, I knew we were here for *me*.

The moment I stepped foot on this mountain something shifted inside me, starting up again. I know my mother felt it, too.

I caught her watching me on the way here. But maybe not. Maybe it had nothing to do with the growing anger in my belly, and the feeling I was missing something, something big I never finished.

"We'll need to go down the mountain for a few of these things," Papi says.

"I can stay here," I say, my voice distant. I stretch my foot until I touch one particularly long shadow. It's warm, warm like the sun as it starts to coil around my toe and—I pull back, almost falling off the hammock, sending my whole body in a panic.

Just a trick. Calma.

"I promise not to disappear again," I say, curling back up in the hammock, and eyeing the shadow.

I don't need to look up to know my mother has rolled her eyes and is exchanging glances with Papi.

Which is fair. I haven't given them many opportunities to trust me lately, but Andrés—class valedictorian and all-around secret creep—deserved to be punched (repeatedly) in his stupid little face, and I will not apologize, school suspension or not.

"I'll stay with Magda," Mami says. "Eugenia, you should go down to make sure we get anything extra you may need."

Magda.

I look over my shoulder, searching for the voice; there's nothing but trees swaying to the wind and the rhythmic screech of nearby crickets.

"I'm fine by myself," I insist.

My father starts to say something, but with a quick touch from my mother he stops, shoulders dropping.

My mother shakes her head. "It's not safe."

I'm sure the last two missing posters plastered all over the news are flashing through her mind. But we're supposed to be up here—it's meant to be. I can feel it. It's like nerves and exhilaration rolled up into one.

Like a dare.

I stumble out of the hammock and through the doorway that leads from the porch to the living area, where I take my seat at the table.

"¿Algo más?" My dad pauses, examining the list as my mother sets his dinner plate in front of him.

"I don't think so," my mother replies. My father captures her hand and gives it a quick peck.

His plate is overflowing with rice, the beans soaking into the grains and forming a small pool of sauce underneath. On top is a bistec encebollado that looks bigger than humanly possible but thin enough that he'll finish it in a few bites. The sautéed onions are piled on top of the meat, a plume of steam rising from it that I swear is angling toward me in a comically tempting fashion. My mother finishes it off with slices of avocado from Tía's backyard.

My father's eyes bulge a bit, and he protests it's too much, but we know he'll eat every last bite, marveling at my mother's talent and thanking the skies for his luck.

"Bueno," Tía Eugenia says, "it's so good to have you all back. We've missed having you here."

"Me too," I say locking eyes with Tía Eugenia, feeling a swell of emotions rush up my throat. I shove a forkful of food down so fast Mami doesn't have time to tell me I'm going to choke on it.

As we eat, the conversation flows, a soothing reminder of how time can't fade our bonds.

After dinner, it's almost truly dark.

It gets dark in San Juan. Especially when our streetlamps break, and they aren't fixed for months, pockets of night in between, nestled under trees, hiding, waiting to be found. But this . . . this is different.

I feel the sun dim and the sky settle down to my bones, like a blanket placed around me.

Magda.

My skin itches. If I only I could slip it off.

Soon.

The sound of coquíes against the crickets is so loud, so constant, the static loosens the knots along my shoulder until my focus . . . my focus . . .

We're waiting.

I don't know when I moved, but I'm not in the kitchen. Mami and Tía Eugenia sit on the weathered sofa, laughing, and catching up. Next to them, in a chair far more comfortable than it looks, is my father, slipping easily into a post-food power nap.

I'm just tired.

On the porch I watch the night take shape, forming hands and teeth and fur. Shaking its hide, fur on ends, stretching into itself.

Off in the distance there's a song, traveling to me through the dark.

Ven.

It's all in my head, it always is. *Overactive imagination* written into the margins of every report card, but still my spine wants to mirror, move, bend, join.

My feet tingle, and there's no other way to explain it but my consciousness settles, until I lock onto a spot in the distance, like an opening in the night sky and see . . . myself.

I blink and reality drapes back to where it was.

I shiver, grounding myself by focusing on the physical—*my* physical. Toes, ankles, earth, no . . . knees, thighs, sweat, blood, and meat, rotting flesh . . . I can feel it thick at the back of my tongue like chocolate.

The thought is so vivid, I jump, almost colliding into my mother.

"Mira a ésta," she says. The flash of worry on her face there and gone before anyone else would see, but I know it so well. I'm so tired of putting it there, but I can't seem to stop.

My father laughs. "Don't go running off again." It's a joke, but my mother slaps his shoulder. They retreat into the kitchen, leaving Tía Eugenia and me alone.

"Don't mind them," she says. "I don't think they've ever recovered from that night."

"I'm here, though," I say, but I'm not sure I believe it; the smell of decay seems permanently lodged up my nose.

"Sabes, my grandmother, your bisabuela, disappeared in these woods, too."

What?

I turn to Eugenia. She nods. She's got me and she knows it.

"She was maybe a year older than you when you went missing," Eugenia continues. No mention of why no one has never spoken of this before. "Gone for days."

Days? Where had she gone? "Did they look for her?"

"Of course."

The rustle of leaves builds like a wave from deep within the forest, and when it reaches me, I swear it sounds like a laugh.

"And then they found her."

Eugenia doesn't answer, and the chuckling trees have yet to be quiet.

"No." It's Mami who answers, lips pursed, coming back to sit beside me; the warmth of her body the kind of grounding I desperately need. I lean against her, finally shutting everything else out. "They did not find her."

"But—" We're clearly here. Alive.

"One day she was just there again." My mother shrugs, attempting a lightness that does not reach her eyes.

"Did she say what happened?"

"In her own way." Mami wraps her arm around me. "Abuelita Karaya was interesting to say the least."

"Our mother told us to ignore her, which I thought was a bit unkind." Eugenia sighs. "She—our mother—didn't like us talking about it much. But Abuelita Karaya told the best stories."

"Can you tell me one?"

"Haven't I before?" When I shake my head, my mother leans back, turning to Eugenia. They share smiles that speak volumes I hope to read one day. "Well then, there was the one where she grew wings and flew over the land dropping flamboyán seeds, and that's why the trees dart along the mountain."

"Karaya was always going on adventures," Eugenia says.

That night, I dream of soil pulling me forward, of my feet walking in pools of infinite possibilities, sticking to me like blood, making the paths I would take as muscles coil beneath my skin. Around me there are faces in the dark, I recognize them as my own, today and past. When I turn, my family is there, they lift a hand and smile. My mother guides me, holding me in an embrace until something passes between us. On my shoulder a cut appears—twin to the one already there—it bleeds down my back and legs, soaking into the earth. My back breaks and I curve down, hugging my legs, which are bent the wrong way, thick, covered in fur coated in blood.

The next morning with the dream still fresh on my skin like dew, I bound out the door for fresh air and race to my second favorite spot on this mountain: a boulder just at the start of the forest path. I called it my looking rock though it was barely three feet off the ground. At its base are four deep cuts—I used to pretend they were made by dragons, me being the dragon, of course. They're hidden, half-buried in the ground, smoothed by time and obscured by the overgrown grass. My fingers follow them with ease.

Today they feel different, like a code for which I've lost the key. I've been here longer than I wanted, but I can't seem to leave. I stare at the curved marks so long, I can still see them when I close my eyes against the heat. My shoulders begin to ache and with each trace it feels like I'm drawing along my own skin.

"Magda," my mother calls out, holding onto that last syllable.

"Hmm?" I roll my shoulders until the ache eases.

"Want to get some fresh bread? There's a panadería not far. We can walk around a bit and eat too much pan sobao." She pats her belly as she says this, and I can't help but laugh.

That would be good, I think, my fingers absentmindedly tracing the markings again before I pull my hand away.

Yes, that would be good.

The smell of fresh bread hits before we arrive. We park down by the makeshift lot that's just a semi-even patch of land.

We buy three loaves of bread and before we leave the store we attack one of them with a deep hunger that echoes in the both of us. Next to the panadería, a lady sells fresh pastelillos stuffed with morcilla. My mother's favorite.

"I'm going to walk a bit," I yell, already past the kiosko. "Clear my head."

"Don't go far, ¿me oyes?" my mother says. I wave her away and point to where I'll be, just down the road. She nods, returning to the pastelillos. "¿Quieres una?"

I shake my head, though the smell of morcilla is more enticing than usual, my nose picking out the tang of cooked blood like a sweet treat.

The bread is soft and I'm halfway through the piece, savoring the crust and pillowy interior.

I'm humming along before I notice the bite of the sun has left and I'm hidden under a canopy of trees—the sensation like a drink of cold water. As I shove a far too large piece of bread into my mouth, a branch snaps behind me.

"What—" I choke on the bread. I heave, spitting it out.

From behind me comes another burst of sound like something galloping through the tall grass. But all I see is the lush textures of the forest, a pattern of greens to brown and curves of vines, bushes, and . . .

Eyes.

No.

Sí.

No.

Déjate de estupideces. You're imagining things, I think, and know I'm lying.

I can hear it breathing. Or is that me?

Those same eyes, not eyes, but eyes still, a tilt to the side that I mirror, and an almost tail.

We stare at each other. I'm too scared to blink. It could disappear, it could change, it could move. It could hurt me, but it had its chance when I almost died on pan sobao.

"No, I don't think you will . . ."

Will Mami let me keep it? Such a silly thought.

It expands like a pupil, before pulsing back into itself.

Shadow, textured, expanding, plucking the patterns of light peeking through trees to shape and fool.

I'm so close.

We blink at the same time; my eyes water at the sight of a shadow folding and opening.

I kneel, sitting back on my legs, placing the piece of bread between us. I reach, letting my hand hang, waiting for the swing of a tail, or the casual grin of a jaw.

Anything familiar. Anything of this reality.

Something reaches forward, pushing aside the offering, and coiling around my hand, the gentle graze of teeth that feels—

"You lost, mamita?"

I turn, pulling my hand out—catching it somewhere—skin like fabric on a broken nail. Pain flairs and I curl my fist behind me.

A man in a too-large T-shirt that hides his frame and beat-up Jeep idles on the side of the road.

"No."

"You need a ride?" He smiles easily, casually motioning to the back of the car. He turns down the music, the better to hear my heartbeat. "Hop on."

I'm cold even in the heat. I tuck my injured hand under my arm. "No gracias," I say.

His smile drops for a second, looking over my body like maybe he made a mistake, maybe I made a mistake. It's always like this. Stuck here while they look at me. Why don't I move?

Can my mother see me? Have I walked too far down the bend? If I look away, will I miss the moment when he moves toward me?

"It'll be fun."

I wonder if he truly believes that, or if he knew the chill that shot up my back, or if he noticed how I tensed.

Do they ever notice?

I bet they do.

His fingers linger on the keys, he'll hop out at any moment, my mind can't help but play it out, a hand on my arms, a pull, my mouth covered, pressure, and lost screams. Always the same eyes and smile echoing in time and space.

Always the same screams echoing, until I break.

The rage is familiar and then warm.

But the sound of the brake—old and rusted—cuts right through it; my eyes shoot up as I take a step back.

I could break now into a thousand pieces and disappear. My heart pulses until I am sound and blood and rush of noise that says, *Yes, break, but do not disappear.*

"Déjanos entrar," a voice whispers. "Déjate salir."

And I agree.

A stabbing pain juts into my back reaching out through my hands, my feet, my mouth. My body arches forward, raising me up to my tiptoes, I feel the crack of each individual finger breaking, shaping, growing. I open my mouth wide until I can no longer breathe as a tooth tumbles to the ground, bloody and white on the road.

And I snap my mouth shut.

He stops, hand on the wheel, his foot frozen inches above the ground.

We stare down at the tooth, his brow furrowing before it twists into disgust.

I laugh, blood dribbling down my chin.

It feels like a pit of fire, spreading so fast it could burn down a village. My fingers stretching the better to . . .

"Olvídalo," he says.

My mind focuses like a knife. What needs to be done, what has to be done.

Let it happen, it whispers, *you are the shadow.*

I grin and the smile is impossibly large, but I feel impossible now. I don't have to look at myself to know it.

His foot hovers for a moment before he guns it.

I follow the car until it's around the bend. The need to hunt slips off me like a passing cloud, and I gather back to what I was. A sweaty mess with thighs that rub together and hair stuck to my neck.

But that was me, too, no? Untethered. Unbound.

"Magda?" My mother's cries get closer, and I need to hurry.

"¡Voy!"

I pick up the tooth, slipping it into my pocket, running my tongue along my teeth, searching for the empty space; there is none. I desperately search for something to wipe my face with, eventually finding my father's handkerchief. I clean off the blood and run to meet my mother. I don't look back at the void between the leaves, for fear of what is watching, for fear that I'm still there.

In the car, I'm humming. My skin feels vibrant, new, traded in for pure electricity, but fragile, sensitive to the world around me. My mother's eyes bounce between my fidgeting and the road. But that's fine, everything feels fine, and I know this high will end soon and my brain will try and make sense of shit, but this is now.

I smile at my mother, content when I remember—

The gash along my palm beats with its own pulse. There is no blood, just space—a slice of black so pure I can tell it holds the universe—and when I touch it, my finger disappears like a rabbit through a top hat.

I am simultaneously freaking out and delighted.

Was there something in the bread?

"¿Qué es eso?"

"¿Qué?" I close my hand, but she's not looking there.

"You have blood on your shirt," my mother says as we exit the car. She reaches for me, touching the stain, forehead crinkling in worry, searching for the source of the blood.

I look down, a thin line of red right smack dab in the middle of my chest, which is very much there, and not in my head.

"¿Qué pasó?"

"Nosebleed."

"Nosebleed?" With her hand, she tilts my chin up to get a better look, but I slip away, giving her a closed-lip smile.

"I'm fine."

Shoving my hand in my pocket, I quickly find the tooth, still slick between my fingers.

"I know I haven't been . . . receptive. I know, okay? Pero you can talk to me." She's trying. I see it. I should try, too, maybe? But it's too much and I need to keep it to myself for now, I need to keep it. "Magda, ¿estás bien?"

I open my palm. There's no cut, no slice of the universe, just flesh, just me.

I can't help but giggle.

"Bien."

I try and sit still, but it's impossible. I'm one giggle away from a total loss of control. I watch my mother and aunt as they chat in hushed tones, eyes flicking to me, to my shirt, before returning to their conversation.

So I leave.

There's still sunlight, it's not like I'm stepping out at night, I think, but I'm so far from caring if this is reckless, if they'll yell at me.

I need to move and maybe after a walk, things will start to make more sense.

The path is clearer than it was years ago, barely a stone to kick, or twig to pick up and sword fight with. The dust swells up around me, a brown that reveals tones of red and orange as it dries.

There are two mango trees along the ceibas near the house that are incredibly easy to find. All you have to do is follow the trail of half-eaten and rotting fruit.

When I reach the tree, my body collapses against the trunk seeking balance, grounding, normalcy. Instead, I laugh again.

Boisterous, loud, tears brimming. I laugh, shaking, until I can't anymore.

I stretch my spine along the length of the tree, a part of me reaching out for something, anything to root into until reality stops spinning. The grass tickles, and on more than one occasion ants try their luck along my thighs.

I've been pressing my finger into my palm this whole way willing the galaxy to open back up, but all I have is pain. I stare at the very real lines along my hand following them like a trail to my wrist, then the hairs along my arm, grounding in the reality of my own body, until—

The tooth.

Still in my pocket, as real as the fingers that roll it back and forth. Again I search for the gap, but nothing, yet the taste of blood is just as fresh.

There is a rustle above me. I wait for the sound of mangoes tumbling through the brush, landing with a thud, but it doesn't come.

Instead, the hairs along my arms rise, my whole body feels like a tuning fork.

I'm not far from the house, but the trees are so thick I could be miles away.

Should I run? I don't want to.

I press my thumb against my palm and it pulses. My body thrums, humming with something that's been building up for days—no years—and I need to see it through. For better or worse.

A speck of starlight lands on my skin, sending sparks up and down my back, each light brightening until the world is overexposed. And there below my skin, a shadow like ink; another me, another life, my body transparent for a breath, allowing us to see each other. We tangle like snakes, sinew and muscle and air and shadow, and a deep yearning of recognition that breaks me.

"Todavía," a woman's voice behind me says.

I am off the ground in a breath, thrust back into my flesh with the ache of loss cutting through me like a knife. *Not again.* I double over for a moment before turning toward the voice. A woman steps out below the shade of a nearby tree.

"Calma," she says, hand up.

"I'm sorry," I reply quickly, brushing the dust off my jeans, and stepping out from beneath the tree. "Did I walk too far?"

"Don't worry," she replies, easing the gnawing in my belly.

Her smile makes the deep grooves in her warm face lift at the sides. Her hair is tied back in a loose bun, like mine, it barely keeps it at bay. She holds a bundle of plátano leaves in one hand and a machete tied to her belt.

"You are where you're supposed to be."

Her eyes look so much like mine it's unsettling, but I'm being silly, right? Many people have deep-set brown eyes . . . I notice scars along her arms obscured by her blouse, but it's the four long cuts on her shoulder that catch my attention.

I know them.

I motion to my own shoulder, mirroring where her scars are. "From the machete?"

She shakes her head, again with the smile. She motions to the smaller cuts along her hands and arms. "These are the machete. It takes and gives, ya sabes." She chuckles. Then she traces the four scars on her shoulder and chest. "These are a gift." My hand mirrors the movements before I tuck it behind me. The longer I stare, the more my own skin remembers the cut of flesh and fastening of claws as dark as shadows.

My shoulder itches, making me want to dig my nails into my flesh and rip my skin off like a too-warm coat.

"Does it feel good to be back, Magda?"

I nod, then freeze. How does she know I'd been here before? How does she know my name?

"I was there that night," she answers. "I'm happy you're back. The path is not as easy as it looks."

"I didn't think I would remember it so well."

"You remember it and it remembers you," she says. "You will walk this path more than once and each time it will be different. Trust it, as it trusts you."

"I—"

She stares above me, to the tree behind me, and nods. "Ahora te dejo. We'll meet again soon—I'm never far."

I whip my head back. Had she seen what I'd seen? Was it still there waiting?

But no, nothing but ordinary shadows.

When I turn, she's vanished. I have barely a breath to spare before there's a quick burst of sound, and I reach out to catch the fruit as it falls.

"A heads-up would be good, ¿sabes?" Tía Eugenia says when I get back. "I covered for you so she wouldn't freak out. You know better."

Do I, though? If anything, this trip has taught me so far is that I 100 percent do not know better.

"Perdón." I drop the mangoes on the table. "I needed to walk, and there was this lady with a machete—I KNOW—maybe a neighbor? She said I remembered the paths well."

"You're turning into one of Abuelita Karaya's tales." She motions for me to pass her the mangoes and inspects them. "Pretty good."

"Which one?"

"Hmm?" Eugenia's hand hovers over the fruit before tossing them in the nearest bowl.

"Which one of her stories?"

"Ah. Maybe el río que corre . . . No, not that one. How did it go again?" Eugenia stares at the mangoes as if they held the secrets. "It's about trails or paths . . . no sé. Pero Abuelita always said she was never lost a day in her life, but she was late to everything, so who knows?"

"She knew the paths better than they knew themselves."

Eugenia stops, turning to me. "She'd say the same thing."

Something hangs in the air between us. I want to pull on it and unravel all the secrets, but what if it makes them all disappear? So I shift.

"Can I get a machete?"

"For like everyday or a special occasion machete?" she asks with a hint of a smile.

"Everyday."

"Ah, bueno, maybe when you're old enough not to cut your hand off." She passes me a knife, pointing to the mangoes. We fall into an easy rhythm, scoring the quarters, pushing up the golden flesh to reveal uneven chunks.

"Are you happy I'm back?"

"¿Yo?" She takes a bite of the mango, using the back of her hand to wipe the juice from her chin. "Claro. ¿Y tú?"

There's a gust and the screen door swings open. Far in the horizon storm clouds gather, sending goose bumps along my spine. I wonder if I'd ever been truly gone.

"Sí."

Tonight I sleep deeper than I ever have with dreams so vivid they could be memories. I sink but do not drown, suspended, held until I open my mouth to swallow, and gulp the dark around me.

It surges in.

I extend my arms and see them reshape to form something new.

Along my back . . . the crisp sting of a third cut.

In the morning my body aches, my nails feel tender, like they grew anew overnight.

There is a bit of cold remaining in the tile floor, and I ease my feet down on it, flexing my toes and pressing until my knuckles crack. It ripples up and up until I stretch each and every part of me.

The skin along my shoulder burns, and when I take my shirt off, I gasp.

My years-old scar is the bright purple of a recently healed

one, and below it are two faint echoes of the first, skin pucker-
ing, rising, as if they'd been cut from the inside.

"Magda, ¿estás despierta?" I scramble for an oversize shirt
and shorts, careful to avoid the tender skin. Tying my loose
waves into a messy ponytail.

In the kitchen I pile my plate high with eggs and a fresh
tostada under the watchful eyes of my mother and aunt. My
father is oblivious (which is both helpful and infuriating), por-
ing over the list of things to do today.

Later my parents ride into town for cement and a few more
supplies. I spend my morning with Eugenia cleaning up the yard.

We work in silence clearing out broken branches and sweeping up leaves. A heaviness settles along my shoulders and a tingle travels up my spine begging me to close my eyes for just a
moment.

When I open them, my brain feels like I've dipped it in
honey and there's a hole in the trees deep, deep, deeper than
should be allowed. A memory echoes in my mind just out of
reach.

And a calling.

Eugenia taps me in the shoulder with her shovel. "You're
watching the mountains like you've never seen a tree before.
I know for a fact they have them in San Juan, in between the
concrete."

"It feels different, I feel—"

"Different?"

The word feels too small.

When I don't answer, she sits next to me. "I didn't say this
earlier . . . pero I'm proud of you. Well, I'm always proud of you,
but I know my sister didn't approve of your method."

"Punching someone."

"Yes, that."

I arch a brow. "So you approve?" Both my parents had been more concerned with my reaction than what caused it, at least that's what it felt like.

She smiles, now choosing her words carefully in case it gets back to my mom. "I don't disapprove. Do you want to talk about it?"

Yes. No. I don't know. My stomach is a mess of emotions, but one thought is clear and it worries me.

"I did want to hurt him," I say, thinking back to that day in school, to yesterday by the side of the road. "I wanted him to feel what I felt."

"Which was?"

"Fear," I say. "Then it didn't matter. Then it was just me and what I could do, what I wanted to do."

"Which is?"

"Devour them."

"Intense." Eugenia replies, careful. "How do you feel now?"

I quiet the world around me. Imagining myself a mass of shadow and sinew twisting around myself, opening jaws, letting the tips of my teeth graze along skin until they slip through.

"Like I'm not sorry."

Eugenia doesn't respond, but when I look at her, I don't feel judgment, just peace, and that's enough.

"How long has our family been here?"

"Longer than many of us remember," Eugenia says. "Do you want another story?"

"Tell me about the rock."

I know Eugenia is looking at me, her eyes follow me to the

rock, the one with the marks that look like the scars along my back.

"It must have a story."

We all do, something whispers.

We both sit in the heaviness of the secret.

Eugenia takes a breath. "Don't tell your mother."

"Why?" I say.

"No sé. I feel like she doesn't like these too much."

"Why?" Because of me? *Vain, Magda. Not everything is about you.* But still, something nags at me.

"Mami didn't like them. She thought that they were better off forgotten and maybe too much of that rubbed off on *your* mami. Pero you know what? Maybe you *should* ask her?"

Eugenia doesn't say more. Any other questions I had would be for another day. "A story, then?"

"Bueno . . . Tu bisabuela—Abuelita Karaya—said they marked a change."

"Like?"

"Escucha y entiende, she'd say. Each cut marks acceptance of body, understanding of mind, and release of soul. It sounded more fantastical when she said it. The first is how we meet—" Eugenia stops, looking like she's trying to solve a calculus problem. "The first is how we meet . . . Oh God, I'm getting so old, how does that go again? Something something . . . and with the fourth the world is shed, and me and I are wed."

"Ew."

Eugenia laughs. "I don't think she was talking marriage. Kayita was not traditional. I used to play there, too, you know, imagine my hands cutting through the stone." She holds out her hand to me and I take it. "I used to dream things so real, I thought I'd lived them."

I freeze, her hand warm in mine. "Did you?"

Her eyes are soft as she looks away. "Maybe we did."

I lean against her shoulder, closing my eyes once again. I wake to the coquíes singing the sun to bed, welcoming the full moon.

"Magda," Eugenia says, holding her hand out to me. "Es tiempo."

Yes, *it's time, it's time*. My heart repeats.

It's time. Let it come.

I eat more than I have all week, my hunger insatiable. I smile sheepishly when my mother watches me serve myself a third plate of carne guisá, but I can't help it. My father laughs, bellowing, "She got her appetite from me!"

Before bed, Mami hugs me so deeply I think she will consume me. She stares into my eyes. I don't know what she finds, but she kisses my forehead and says, "Okay."

I'm alone in my room, surrounded by the gentle whirring of the air conditioner blowing tepid air.

Between my body humming with unspent energy, the AC clinging to life, and the memory of my mother's kiss burning into my skin like a beacon—a blessing—it's not long before I can't stand being in bed.

I stretch to turn off the AC and the coquíes' song floods around me, eager to take center stage.

Light streams in through the crack at the bottom of the door, hitting my eyes. I hide under the blankets before they become too stifling and toss them off of me, steam rising.

I am sticky with sweat, and everything in this room is too much. I have a fever, I tell myself, but the pressure that builds in the back of my head cannot and will not let itself be called a fever. I toss and turn, stretching out my legs, curling in and out, all the while the coquíes get louder and louder and my head pounds and pounds until it explodes like a transmitter.

It's gone—the gentle whir of electricity, the light, the coquíes.

Gone.

I touch my ears, pressing on the skin like a reset.

I sit up, my feet against the cold floor, back to the metal windows shaking the feeling there's something right behind the white metal frames, when I sense the trickles flowing down my back like sweat. I don't have to see them to know it's blood. The ache along my shoulders is the sting of a fresh wound.

I need to leave this room as soon as possible.

I am up and out of the house where the world is a wash of black, paused like a breath not yet taken. With my first step, the coquíes resume.

Now is the time.

Before me is nothing and everything. I lift a hand outlined by moonlight and run it across the sky like water, setting the stars dancing.

I want to sit back and float in the depths of it all, removing skin and bones until I am nothing but expanse, and I know deep down, after tonight, it is possible.

I don't hear generators. I don't see lights. I know our neighbors have them. I know we have them. My heart hitches. A wind kicks up, strong at my back. A cry—a whine telling me to stop stalling. Out in the night, feet away, then out in the distance again.

"Magda." Her voice is a whisper, and when I turn, Mami's frame is barely visible. She stands at the doorway a million miles away. "Where are you going?"

"No sé, pero sé," I say. "I have to go."

"Can I walk with you?" Her voice cracks.

I catch my breath, tears streaming down my face as I nod. With a few steps, my mother laces her hand in mine, and we walk.

The ground is cold and gives beneath my feet, soaked in the dew of night. But the trail down the valley is easier. My mother follows, letting me guide.

"Did you know Eugenia and I used to run into the woods after my grandmother? We loved her stories. Soaked up every word. We waited to be called," she says, squeezing my hand. "And when I wasn't, my heart broke. Either I wasn't worthy, or the stories weren't real. So, like my mother, I chose the latter."

I want to wrap my mother in my arms and cry with her, but we have to keep walking, we have to. I sense the trees long before I see them, when I stumble on a root and laugh, I hear it echo back at me.

"She stopped sharing, or I stopped listening. I can't remember which came first."

Somewhere between my aunt's plátano crop and the dense vegetation, I've been here before, lost here before, found in a sca of black, thick with life.

I can see the stars like I hang among them; waiting for them, to sprinkle down like sparks from a broken transformer.

"Nothing could prepare me for that night when it called you. For the anger, the jealousy, the fear . . ."

We walk in and in, deeper.

The memory of branches brushing against my legs is as fresh as it was that night, as it is every night. "Perdón." Her breath catches and we're both crying.

There are figures in the dark, shadows, but my body sings in recognition. Eugenia, Abuela Claudia, and the woman from the woods. "Abuelita," Mami gasps, crying even harder. *Karaya*, I think. Of course. "Okay, Okay. No more." She holds me as I am, one last time. "In her stories—in her life—Karaya was always alone, but you are not, ¿me entiendes? I'll be better. Aquí te espero."

I step away, knowing she'll wait for me, will walk with me no matter the path.

I don't have to turn to know it's behind me. The air shifts as it moves closer, a dance around and around, heat against my fingers, until a cold wet nose presses against my hand.

"Tan oscuro," I say, stepping forward, feeling it brush against my leg. I almost stumble from the weight and the sudden scent of soil and rain.

A breath puffs in my face. My heart skips when it moves, hands suddenly without.

No, I say before I notice, reach my hands up and out until I find it again. *There.*

Como la boca de un lobo.

I count the teeth, shivering. I press my fingers along the tips—*blood*—but my skin remains unblemished.

I pull its mouth closed around me, feeling the teeth—my teeth—as they cut me open and I slip in. Another skin, my skin.

And me and I are wed.

Swallowing the stars, the bite, filling my belly, stretching me out as the night.

And then—

I am above gliding with thin black wings, blanketing, watching, waiting.

I am below, running, panting, not bitten but the bite.

I am shadows and sharp claws, the tallest mountains, and thickest heat.

I shake the gathered dew of starlight off my fur and pause, focusing on a sound in the distance, the rumble of an engine, the crank of a car break, and a voice saying, "You lost, mamita?"

My growl travels down the mountain in search of dinner.

And I am full.

Bloodstained Hands
Like Yours

Gabriela Martins

This is what freedom looks like to Olivia: watching her own spit go down the Túnel da Conceição until it hits a car waiting for the light to turn green.

Beside her, with a smirk of her own, Jenny says, "Dad number four-five-seven would call that unladylike."

Olivia nods slowly, still looking at the car. It's a bronze sedan. She's learned from the last family who rejected her that this type of color makes cars more expensive. It was one of the many things Dad #457 prided himself on asserting. Not that there were 456 dads before him, but it sure felt that way, going back and forth to and from the orphanage until she turned eighteen and the orphanage was done with her, too.

The traffic light turns green, and the car speeds off, carrying her spit into the wild.

"Screw that guy," Olivia decides. "I'm a lady."

"That you are, my friend. That you are," Jenny says. She turns around, looking up at the sky. The sun is almost done with them, too, setting in the horizon, behind the hospital across the street. They'll have to leave soon. Downtown Porto Alegre can get dangerous when it's dark.

Olivia offers her best friend a small smile and then elbows her. The second time she does it, Jenny protests with a fake whimper and laughter, and Olivia's face lights up. "I'm just saying, okay? But I'm glad you have a home now."

Jenny rolls her eyes, but she's hiding a smile. "Whatever."

They met four years ago, when Jenny's mom finally decided to leave her for good. The system came for her in Vila Cruzeiro and dragged her, kicking and screaming, to the orphanage near Tristeza. Olivia had been there since she learned that she existed.

Jenny's always dreamed of being adopted and finding a new family. She had plans, like finishing school and going to college and working a cool job, and these things took support that only a family could offer.

"I mean it," Olivia says. "If anyone deserves to have a nice home to go back to, it's you. And they're not going to kick you out. It's been, what? A year now?" There's an air of teasing in her voice, but they both know what that really means—that Olivia's happier for Jenny than she could ever be for herself.

"Seven months, but yeah." Jenny nods.

They're in silence for another beat, looking down at the tunnel. The cars keep passing, oblivious to the two orphans (or an orphan and a former orphan) above them. Olivia spits once more, just because she can. No more adults to tell her what she can or can't do, or that if she does this or that she'll be more or less desirable.

It's late August, and the wind is strong, cutting through their jackets. Their legs are nervous, jiggling around, as if to try to bring about some more energy and warmth. But they never get too close to each other. It's the rules.

After the pause, Jenny says, "Happy eighteenth birthday, Olivia."

Olivia just nods.

Happy fucking birthday.

By daylight, Praça da Matriz is one of the most visited places by tourists in Porto Alegre. Surrounded by imposing old buildings and the circular monument in the center, the floor is colored in red-and-black tiles, and the trees ring the block with green.

At night, it's an all right place to sleep.

After she's said goodbye to Jenny, Olivia needs a place to crash. It is only natural that she'd come back to Praça da Matriz. Ten years prior, that had been where they'd found her, taken her into the system with a number and an empty promise of finding her a family. They'd asked if she remembered anything about her past life; parents, friends, any relatives—no, she didn't. All she remembered was the streets. All she remembered was emptiness.

She hadn't known anyone who stayed at Praça da Matriz now, but it didn't take her long to get acquainted. A month in, and it was like she'd never left. New people, but in a way, they were all the same. Even the ones she didn't remember. Even the ones who worked for the system. New names and faces, but the same people.

Late winter like this, rich people sometimes bring hot coffee and cacetinhos, and all the Matrizeiros eat so much bread they'll feel satisfied for days. But tonight's too cold for any van to pull up to the curb, with their phone cameras geared toward hungry mouths, so instead Olivia just cozies up to Carioca, the only person here she trusts. The girl and the middle-aged woman hold on to each other at the bottom of the stairs of the central monument, a thick green blanket around them.

"Did you meet your friend?" Carioca asks, her southeastern accent strong, making her sound like she's singing. Olivia nods, resting her head on the woman's shoulder. "Did you ask to stay with her?"

Olivia chuckles. "Don't get up in my business, old woman."

Even though she smells like cachaça and asa, there's a reason Olivia doesn't talk to any of the other people who stay at Praça da Matriz. Carioca's just out of her mind enough that the other Matrizeiros are afraid of her. No man comes messing with Olivia because they don't know what Carioca would do if that happened. The night Olivia came there, Carioca was clawing at a man's face for having tried to steal her blanket. It was so vicious that onlookers started gathering. When she noticed them, Carioca quickly retreated—they all know what outside attention means. They call the cops. And when the cops come, all their belongings are trashed, and they have to go somewhere else.

Carioca had let Olivia stay with her that first night—maybe she reminded the old woman of someone lost—and then all the nights that followed. Took pity. But to Olivia their relationship is transactional; Carioca is a warm shoulder, owns a blanket, and keeps the others away.

"You should leave this place while you can," Carioca mumbles.

It still puzzles her, even after their time together, that Carioca would think she could *just leave*. No matter how nice of a family she'd be placed with, they would eventually get tired of her. They'd say she was unnerving, had something in her eye that didn't sit well with them. That and all the swearing, the rebelling, the way she couldn't deal well with authority, especially one imposed.

It surprised her a little that Jenny had found a family. Jenny wasn't much different from Olivia in terms of behavior . . . but she didn't have that look about her that made people uncomfortable.

In some deep and intrinsic way, Olivia knew she was unlovable.

Olivia clutches the blanket on her side. "Shut up and go to sleep."

She winks at Carioca, sure that she'll get an earful, but Carioca doesn't seem to have heard her. She shakes her head a bit, looking past the trees that engulf the square, and says, "Zeca never came back."

That gives Olivia pause.

She looks around for Zeca.

He's not great company by any means. He's a skinny man who steals food from other Matrizeiros. In a group of twenty-seven people sleeping in the same place, you don't want that kind of reputation. Even though nobody seemed to really like Zeca, he still carried himself like he was going to be famous one day. It was one of the things that made him stand out, other than his absurd thinness and shaky fingers.

On a cold night like this, he'd probably beg someone to let him stay close, but the groups are scattered around, familiar faces that Olivia has grown to know and avoid. None of them have Zeca's weirdly optimistic teeth-missing smile.

"Maybe he's . . . found a job or something," Olivia tries.

Carioca glares at her, but Olivia wasn't mocking Zeca. She just didn't want to focus on the more likely option: that he was caught by the police. Nothing good would ever come of that.

A dark shadow falls over Carioca's expression. She blinks a few times, her eyes watering, her nostrils flaring. She breathes out in chunks, and then says, like it physically pains her, "He's the seventh this year."

"The seventh what? Disappearance?" Olivia asks.

Carioca nods solemnly. "Corpo-seco caught them all." Olivia starts shaking her head, but Carioca holds her face with both her hands, rough and dirty and full of purpose. "Listen to me, child: I have seen that man. A man so evil that when he died, hell didn't want him, and the earth spat him back. I've seen him stealing our people, ripping them apart, into so many pieces there's no more body to find."

Olivia's throat feels dry. She coughs, trying to loosen the grip Carioca has on her face, but the old woman only holds her more tightly.

"Go get yourself a real life. I don't want you to be the eighth."

A shiver runs up her spine, leaving her speechless for a moment.

Slowly, Olivia nods, but her eyes venture down the silent sleeping streets.

She makes a silent challenge: *If you are real, come for me, then. Nobody will miss me. I can take you.* Between gritted teeth, she whispers his name, like a warning and a summoning at once, "Corpo-seco."

It's not the first time Olivia has come to Jenny's new home, and it's not the first she does it in the middle of the night. It is the first time, though, that as she sneaks past the Centro Histórico neighborhood, climbing up old sets of stairs and dropping lightly near fire escapes, she feels watched.

In the orphanage, the other kids used to joke that she was a cat. Nobody could see her coming. But tonight, someone seems to know.

For a second, she thinks that Corpo-seco could have heard her challenge last night and be following her now, but she doubts that even a monster took notice of her. She just keeps going, ignoring the goose bumps when the breeze turns a little colder.

Jenny lives not too far away from the iconic Andradas Street. It's a small two-story house so slim, it looks shoved in there by accident. As Olivia easily climbs to the second floor, finding her footing between old window panes, she feels it again: Something breezes past her, making the hairs in the back of her neck stand.

She looks over her shoulder, but the street is silent. No cars, no people, nothing. Just her.

Ignoring the feeling once more, she knocks on the window. Seconds later, it opens, revealing Jenny in her oversize T-shirt and shorts, with a bright smile. "Took you long enough."

Beautiful Jenny, the only one who's always seen beauty in Olivia, too. Where everyone smelled trouble and glares, Jenny saw past all that and, from the beginning, coaxed warmth and smiles from Olivia. Just being in her presence makes Olivia feel a bit more at ease, despite her reservations.

She never wants to be *at ease*. Being alert is far more sensible.

Used to being invisible, neither of them make a noise. In Jenny's small room, she tells Olivia how her new family thinks she could go to college next year, maybe, if she studied really hard. But she's looking at job prospects. She could be a cashier in a market downtown, owned by friends of her new mom. It's surreal, to hear Jenny talk about her future like this. Like she has one.

It's not that Olivia feels jealous, only disconnected. Here is all this proof that Jenny belongs in this house while Olivia is still sharing a blanket with Carioca.

The truth of the matter is that she isn't envious, but that she's unimportant.

It makes her chest heavy with regret. Somehow it must be her fault that Jenny was adopted at the last minute and she wasn't. Olivia graduated the system and became a nobody in an official way. She was left behind, purposeless.

Well, not entirely. Not now.

There is something she could do.

Out of nowhere, she blurts out, "I'm going to find Corpo-seco and kill him."

Jenny stops dead in her tracks, tilting her head to the side slowly, as if she hadn't heard that right. "You—you what?"

Olivia's chest swells with a little pride. She lifts her chin and smirks. "You know who I'm talking about, right?"

"We've all heard the stories." Jenny lowers her eyes. "You shouldn't say stuff like that. You shouldn't joke about it."

"I'm not joking," Olivia says, but chuckles immediately after. She shifts on Jenny's bed, her legs uncomfortable on the mattress. "The place where I'm staying . . . Well, people are disappearing. Folks have been saying it's him. I'll make that stop."

Jenny meets her eyes coldly. "Nobody can kill Corpo-seco. You'll just be another body." Olivia starts to contradict her, but Jenny stops her before she can go on. "Are you ever going to tell me where you're staying?"

"It doesn't matter." Olivia shakes her head. "I'll find a way. You always said I was smart."

Jenny touches her knee lightly, then pulls away. After a sigh, she says, "You are smart. The smartest person I know, Olivia. I just don't want you getting involved with stuff like that. It's . . ."

Olivia smirks, catching her hand again. "Are you scared for me?"

Jenny nods without missing a beat. "Always."

Time freezes. Olivia's heart hurts more, her chest too tight for all the emotions she can't name or properly express. Jenny keeps looking at her, like she wishes she could protect Olivia, like she wishes there was *something*, anything, that she could do that would prevent what's already happened. The two of them, going their separate ways.

If they're running on borrowed time, if they're going to keep drifting apart until there's nothing that holds them together, then maybe . . . maybe Olivia should shoot her shot. Maybe she should just abbreviate the inevitable, knowing she did everything in her power to stop it.

Holding her breath, she balls her fists so her hands stop shaking. And then she leans closer to Jenny, until there are only a few inches between their faces. She blinks nervously, and Jenny frowns slightly, but her hand comes to touch the side of Olivia's face.

It's the warmest and gentlest touch. Olivia has never been touched like this.

And then comes the shriek from downstairs, so loud and terrified that it shocks them both out of the moment, each jumping to their feet.

Jenny's face pales, and she mouths, "Mom."

Olivia nods, takes her hand, and they both rush downstairs.

The middle-aged Black woman is on her knees in the small living room. She's wearing a camisole, her dark braids loose. From the top of the stairs, Olivia sees the woman's back, and the blood that expands around in front of her.

The woman whimpers, and Jenny lets go of Olivia's hand.

Olivia watches the scene play like she's not even there.

"Mom," Jenny says, her voice shaky, each step tentative, until she's right behind her, touching her shoulder, and then Jenny sees what's in front of them and gasps.

She screams, too.

Olivia doesn't move. She knows without knowing.

How stupid of her to come here. How stupid of her to ignore the feeling that she was being followed. She'd never been followed before. She'd never felt watched before. Not really. Not like this.

Jenny pulls her mom into a hug, but her eyes are frozen on the blood on the floor. Slowly, very slowly, like Olivia could undo it if she never sees it, she takes the few steps toward the blood.

The family dog, a white-and-gray mutt, is dead on the floor, his throat slit, the blood pooling around him, making his fur dark red.

Olivia feels the bile rise to her mouth, but she hangs back, while both Jenny and her mom cry.

Jenny's mom is nice enough. Even shaking to the bone, she senses that for Jenny to let a stranger through her window in the eerie hours, there must be something special there. Between sobs, she insists on taking Olivia home. But the girls are both crying and shaking, so it's easy to convince the woman to just call Olivia an Uber to drop her at the train station.

There's no one else at Mercado Station. Dumbstruck, Olivia sits on the bench facing the rails and thinks about all that blood in the living room. Olivia had a fake mother once, who shouted at her for days for dropping a glass of Coke on the carpet. She had said it would leave a stain. Olivia would bet blood leaves a stain, too.

Alone on the platform, she relaxes against the cold hard metal of the bench and considers sleeping there tonight. Maybe it'll be all right when she wakes up. Maybe it won't have been her fault.

Don't come looking for me if you aren't ready.

Her eyes snap open.

The light above her flickers, and the air turns heavier. More humid somehow.

Smells . . . dirtier. It makes her sick.

She's brave enough. Nostrils flared and fists balled, Olivia stands up from the bench, ignoring the rotten smell under her nose, and the goose bumps on her skin.

"As the legend goes," she speaks, voice firm and loud, all alone or maybe not. "Corpo-seco was once a man. And that means he must've had a weak spot."

Dry laughter echoes in the train station, and the light flickers once more. Then it turns off. In complete darkness, Olivia feels every muscle of her body rigid with fear, but she won't back down. Jaw set, she waits for the monster to attack.

But he doesn't. He doesn't do a thing.

She feels him watching her, but he doesn't approach.

After a long minute, the light turns on again, and she knows she's alone.

Olivia's mind is a whirlwind and her body is a sack of bones. She roams the streets back to her home—Carioca's blanket—and though not once she feels true fear again, not once does she stop shaking, either. Hence the sack of bones. It's like she can hear the way her body won't stop being afraid. Like her own bones rattle with the same noise as the monster's laughter, making fun of her and her pursuit to kill him.

But she did mean what she said. He'd been a man once.

All men have weaknesses. All men can be ended.

Carioca doesn't greet her with a smile or hello or a hug, but with aggressive barking. She must've been drinking or smoking crack; either way, Olivia's used to her moods. She sits down next to her, her back stiff against the hard cold stone of an angel monument, and she feels blessed, just a little, because she isn't completely alone.

Maybe because Carioca's just out of it enough, Olivia tells her, "The monster followed me tonight. Killed my friend's dog. I thought he'd kill me, too, but he didn't."

Carioca sniffs, blinking nervously, then offers her a mostly toothless smile.

Olivia breathes out as slowly as she can. "I don't know why he didn't kill me."

"Did you want him to?" Carioca asks.

This surprises her, not because of the sudden soberness of Carioca's tone, but because Olivia doesn't know how to answer it. She decides the exhaustion will crush her if she keeps thinking about it. She scoots closer to the woman, and Carioca's jumpy body eventually settles next to her into an easy semi-hug. Semi-normal.

Everything is white behind Olivia's eyelids, and that's how she knows she's dreaming. A woman with full hair and a beautiful smile holds a baby, and she knows immediately, without a doubt in her heart, that she is the baby.

It's the first time she's seen her mother, but she knows it's her. Something breaks.

There's a monster lurking around. A shapeless evil that torments the woman. And then Olivia is alone. The little baby, in a pool of blood. And Olivia doesn't know—can't tell for *sure*—but she thinks he's killed Mommy.

She wakes up choking in sobs, overwhelmed by a heavy smell she couldn't identify at first. She touches her face, and it's slick, but . . . not with tears. Her fingers come away red.

Panic rises in her throat as she turns to warn Carioca. But Carioca sits next to her, eyes snapped open, lips slightly ajar, a few drops of blood up her face, but mostly soaking down her body. Her throat has been slashed. Her chest is bathed in blood, and so is Olivia.

Olivia tastes bile again and gets to her feet, shaking and screaming. She can sense the movement, the whispering, the growing chatter that becomes panic.

"Why *her?!*" she screams, stomping her feet. She's not hurt, but it feels as if she's bleeding, too. *"Why won't you kill me?!"*

For the first time, Olivia sees him and his shiny eyes. A tall man hunched over and made of rotten skin. He has very long nails. He smiles with sharp teeth, like he's proud of what he's doing. His reply echoes in her head: *For some people, there's nothing worse than the end. But for you and me, for our kind . . . to keep going is the punishment, daughter.*

The police come with SAMU to remove the body, but they don't really care about what happened to Carioca. Some of the people Olivia could swear she was almost friends with think that Olivia's the killer, and they tell the police, who pretend to take notes. They pretend to listen. But they definitely don't pretend to care. They're only there because there's blood.

Olivia watches from two streets above until they bag Carioca's body and the sirens stop making noise. Then she stares down at her own bloody hands and wills herself out of the shock. Her protector is dead. And the killer, the monster—the monster is her father.

He was a man once. Before.

Think, Olivia, think. He's not done yet.

But she can't think. There's evil in her. She's evil, too. Her blood is rotten, like his, destined for the worst. Is she already a monster or is she headed that way? The smell of Carioca is starting to make her nauseous. She needs to wash her hands. She needs to do something. Anything. But the sun's almost rising, and she's never heard of the shadows acting up when there's no darkness, so maybe she can cozy up in this park just around Sarmento Leite Street, and sleep for a bit.

"Mom? Is the lady dead?"

"Don't look at her. She could be dangerous."

Olivia wishes she could sleep longer. Part of her wishes she *were* dead. Or at least dangerous. Instead, she wakes up to find out that she stinks like death but is very much alive. Her T-shirt is soaked with dried blood that isn't hers.

The child jumps when Olivia opens her eyes, and the woman pulls him away fast, as if Olivia were an animal. If only.

She sits up on the park bench, taking in the sunset and the events from last night. Carioca dead. Corpo-seco killed her mother. She is half him. Carioca is dead. Carioca is . . . *dead.* And he isn't done.

Choked up, she stares up at the orange sky. She knows who his next target is.

No bus driver in their right mind would let her hitchhike her way through Porto Alegre in a shirt like this, so she steals new clothes drying on a second-floor balcony and ditches her old ones. It's a dress that's too big for her, but it does the trick. A begging smile at a bus driver later, she's on the fast track to Jenny's house, her leg bouncing nervously as she watches the sky turn dark and her vision turn red.

But she knows he'd rather wait for her to get there.

Jenny's mother isn't home, and for a second Olivia thinks Jenny might not be either. But then Jenny opens her window and frowns, asking, "What happened?" and she knows there's no turning back.

"I'm . . . cursed."

That's not what she'd meant to say. She'd meant to say: *Run. Hide.* Or maybe, *He's coming for* you *because of* me. *The second he knew I cared about you, that's the moment I cursed you, too.* But she doesn't know where the words went. When her eyes set on Jenny and her beautiful face, Olivia collapses. Her body fails, and she falls into Jenny's arms like she never knew how to stand. Jenny hugs her close, not minding the sweat and the blood, not knowing this dress isn't hers. She hugs her so tightly that Olivia feels it might squeeze the doom out of her.

Crying, she tells Jenny everything. About her blood and her homelessness, and how the monster had been watching her and not the other way around. She doesn't find it in her to say that Jenny's next, because how do you tell someone they're going to die?

Instead, she says, "We have to find a way to kill him, Jen."

She doesn't know how long she stays in her best friend's embrace. When they pull apart, Jenny's holding her close, looking into her eyes and crying, too. She nods, forehead touching hers, and softly, she says, "Mom has a gun."

It's romantic.

They hold shaking hands as they make their way to the office. There's a safe in there, and Olivia watches the window with her heart in her throat as Jenny punches numbers to release the weapon, without any hesitation. All Olivia can think of is that Jenny has truly found a family, someone that will give her the numbers to the safe. She has truly found a home, and Olivia had to come with her love and ruin everything.

"I am so sorry," she whispers. "This is all my fault."

Jenny doesn't respond. Olivia's still staring out the window, her lips trembling, afraid that if the truth comes out now, it'll be too dirty to have any meaning. It's not like in the movies. It should be better than this.

Standing in front of the wooden desk and chair, Olivia's hand touches the cold glass of the window.

"I should have realized . . . that I'm no good. And you are."

When Jenny doesn't respond, Olivia knows she believes it, too. Eyes brimming with tears, Olivia turns toward her friend and realizes they're not alone.

Corpo-seco is in the room with them, holding Jenny by the neck.

Olivia gasps.

He's taller than them by a foot. He doesn't have any skin this time, and he smells of putrefaction and sin. Olivia was a selfish fool to not have noticed the change in the atmosphere, to not smell him over someone else's dress and Carioca's blood. His hands are claws, the bones breaking out of the muscles, the nails curling down like an animal's. He still smiles. He's proud.

Jenny's still holding the gun, thrashing in his arms.

His claw presses to her neck.

For the first time, he speaks outside of Olivia's head. His voice is deep and low. "You never stood a chance." He licks his yellow teeth. "You're made of the same blood as me."

Olivia's frozen.

Is that why she wanted freedom? To see her world fall apart and stand motionless as it all crumbles down? But she can't

move. She can't even breathe. The air is too toxic. It hurts her
nostrils and her throat.

"Jenny," she whispers.

Please hang on. I have to—I have to find a way.

It's not a good plan, but it's the only one that occurs to her.
She grabs the wooden chair. Jenny knows to duck, and the
shock of the abrupt movement is enough to catch Corpo-seco
off guard. Jenny breaks free when he's hit, rushing to grab the
gun, and with shaky hands, she fires twice.

Boom boom. Boom boom.

Almost like the opposite of a heartbeat.

It's so loud Olivia's eardrums vibrate. She's disoriented,
searching for Jenny's hand, because maybe they've defeated It.
The evil. Her father. What Olivia is also made of. But when the
smoke clears and her blurry vision goes away, he still stands tall.

Corpo-seco grins. "Hilarious," he mocks. And advances.

Olivia thinks: *This is it. This is how we die. But at least, if
anything, we go together.*

She thinks of saying *I'm sorry* again, but instead—stronger
than that, more powerful than that, the only thing she says is "I
love you."

Though she still cries, Jenny smiles, too.

"I love you," she replies. Sure of herself. Like somehow, this
is worth it, because it got them to say it.

And it's like time stills for them.

A little treat. *Here, have this.*

Olivia's not sure what she was expecting. Nothing, perhaps.
But it wasn't to be loved back. It wasn't to have a home in someone's heart. It wasn't to feel bigger and higher and stronger than
she's ever felt before.

Letting go of Jenny's hand, she decides not to make a sacrifice but a statement. In her head, she says all that needs to be said. *I am not like you. Blood means nothing. I will never be like you.*

And you better face me before you touch her.

Together, father and daughter explode.

The monster and human run toward each other and there's light and darkness, so much fire that Jenny's pushed to a corner, on her knees, the destruction too bright for her to see.

But there's only one standing in the end.

Breathless and covered in blood, Olivia opens her eyes, searching the room for Jenny. When their eyes meet, she feels love again—but without fear, this time.

This is what freedom looks like to Olivia: hands intertwined with her girlfriend as she watches the cars in the grocery store's parking lot.

"Shift's starting soon," Jenny complains, head resting on Olivia's shoulder.

Olivia feels lightheaded and warm. She doesn't mind Jenny complaining about her work. She's grown accustomed to that, and hopes she can be hired as a part-timer to help with the cleaning soon, too. She reaches out and kisses Jenny.

Jenny looks up at her with a small smile. "What was that for?

Olivia shrugs. "Because I can."

Jenny looks at her, and then kisses her properly.

She's seen.

That's freedom.

The Boy from Hell

Amparo Ortiz

Hell is a pretty face with bad intentions.

That's what Abuela always says about los fríos. When it comes to Puerto Rican vampires, that woman has more dirt than a monster truck arena. According to her, our country used to be a haven for the Meléndez family—beautiful bloodsuckers who once fed on farm animals and dwelled in the coldest corners of our mountains. Specifically, in the northwestern town of Moca, where alleged sightings of giant black bats during the seventies took the country by storm.

Los fríos never grow old. Their dark brown skin is blessed with an insulting lack of spots and breakouts. Abuela swears they're smoother than a silk handkerchief.

"Diem, they always have something white on," she says, "and it's usually hideous."

Abuela has dedicated her life to training me in the art of killing vampires, which mostly consists of driving a machete through their hearts or cutting off their heads. I have a theory they'll burst into flames if I play them my favorite K-pop songs, but that's still to be determined.

I've spent my whole life—sixteen long years—on the lookout for white hideousness. I punched out Daniel Gutiérrez in sixth grade because he wore a white suit to graduation. I cracked Isabela Rosario's nose because I heard her say she'd only wear white if she could. Osvaldo Cruz never wore white, but his lips were always red, so I kicked him through a glass window at his thirteenth birthday party. Turns out he loved drinking fruit punch.

These days, my modus operandi has focused more on locating the white rose. Sixty years ago, the Meléndez vampires ventured out of the mountains, enchanting the locals to believe they'd seen a black bat at night. But the eldest son—Félix Meléndez—picked a girl in my hometown of Canóvanas and left a white rose at her doorstep. Three nights later, the rose was still there. Rejected.

On the fourth night, El Vampiro de Moca replaced it with her mother's severed head.

He didn't stop there. He sunk his nails into her family and ripped it into nothing. Spinal cords hung from streetlights. Rib cages sat on the plaza's benches. Broken bones and scalps lay scattered on the pavement.

Her dead family was the last thing she saw before she disappeared. To most people in Canóvanas, that girl is a cold case. A stain my hometown has tried to wash away yet lives on in blurry newspaper clippings, in the frightened whispers of children before their parents turn off the lights. Kidnapped, they suppose, by a serial killer. Abuela tells a different story. She believes a gorgeous boy made of sulfur and cravings chose a bride who refused him.

I've never seen Félix.

But there's a white rose on my bedroom desk.

"Diem, please don't take this the wrong way, but you're the weirdest person I know. If anyone can help me, it's you."

Pablo Cárdenas sits across from me, his leg bouncing in that jittery way it does when we have a pop quiz in calculus. It's 3:15 a.m. on a Wednesday, which would be an inconvenience for people with a normal sleep schedule. Pablo is lucky, though. I'd already been awake an hour when he knocked on my bedroom window—that pop quiz isn't going to ace itself.

I shouldn't be surprised. He's the latest in a string of classmates reaching out for confirmation of paranormal activity. They either mock me for believing in vampires (and mistaking painfully ordinary people for them), or they ask me to validate their suspicions. Pablo strikes me as the latter. Why else would someone who's never spoken to me be in my room?

I bite into my cherry Twizzler. "What do you need?" I keep my voice low in case Abuela is having trouble sleeping. She's been waking up in the middle of the night for the past week.

Pablo points to the white rose. "That was on my little sister's windowsill."

"And?" It's important to let people reveal their suspicions first. Otherwise, I'm setting myself up for either ridicule or incessant questioning. It's distracting to be called psycho on the way to Spanish class.

"Don't act innocent. I know you know what that means. My

grandpa and your grandma . . . they used to date in high school, didn't they?"

"I believe he cheated on her with your grandmother, yes."

Pablo rolls his eyes. "Whatever. The point is, when I saw the rose, I remembered that serial killer case from sixty years ago. My grandpa mentioned something your grandma had told him. He says she used to talk about the murderer like he wasn't . . . human."

I take another bite of my Twizzler, then offer my pack to Pablo.

He waves the candy away. "I mean, I don't believe in that stuff, but . . ." He checks the door, even though it's locked. "I was playing guitar when my little sister barged into my room all flustered. She told me there was something outside her window. So I checked, bracing myself. I assumed it was an iguana, but I found that rose instead."

"Maybe it fell from a nearby tree?" I offer.

He cocks an eyebrow. "There are no trees around my house, Diem."

"But you live in Luxe Paradise Gardens. I mean, I'm all the way down here in the heart of town, so forgive me if I'm unfamiliar with your surroundings."

"We're pretty far removed from vegetation." Pablo squirms like he always does at the slightest reference to his gated neighborhood. He's one of the very few wealthy students at our public high school. "Anyway, there's also this." He pulls out his phone. The lock screen is a picture of his family. The sister in question, Irene, is the brunette with rosy cheeks. She looks like his twin. He unlocks the phone and opens a photo. "Somebody left it on the hood of my car."

I can't make out what "it" is—there's enough blood to even freak Dracula out. The thing is much smaller than a person and bigger than most rodents. It lies on the silver Audi's hood, its chest up, facing the morning sun. I squint harder.

Feathers. And they belong to a pigeon.

Its wings have been torn off.

The bird lies in a pool of its own blood, spilled out from where the wings used to be.

I swallow the bile down. One, two, three, four breaths, but the queasiness still lingers. This is not another animal's fault. I check the rest of the photo. There are no signs of anything white in the perimeter. No sign of a lingering, beautiful boy, either.

This could still be him.

"What happened first?" I ask. "The rose or the pigeon?"

"The rose was last night. The pigeon was this morning."

If this is Félix, Irene has two nights left. "Has your sister mentioned a boy she's interested in? Or a boy who's bothering her?"

Pablo shakes his head, sighing. "She doesn't even know I'm here tonight."

"Any police yet?"

"No. Mami wanted to call, but I kept telling her it was probably my boys on the basketball team pranking me again. I'm trying real hard not to freak either of them out. The divorce has been hell, so . . . ." Pablo puts his phone on the desk. He rubs his red-rimmed eyes. "I was hoping your grandma could help us. What if this is the same serial killer from sixty years ago? Or a copycat? If she knows something, I need to know it, too."

I nod. Pablo deserves to know what's happening to his sister. But passing this case over to Abuela before confirming it's really Félix would be reckless. I've been wrong about los fríos too many times before. I can't afford to have my grandmother lose her faith in me, especially since she's sacrificed so much in raising me alone. It's been seven years since my mother died of breast cancer—for seven years my abuela has raised a girl whose father ran off before her birth, taken extra teaching gigs around the country so she could afford repairs to our house and old Nissan Datsun, instead of retiring to focus on vampire slaying like she always dreamed of.

I've given her so little in return. But if I found her Félix Meléndez . . . This is my chance.

"Count me in, Pablo. I'll talk to Abuela in the morning and let you know what she says."

He brightens the room with a tired smile. "You will?"

"Of course." I offer him my hand. "Happy to help."

Pablo stares at it, an eyebrow raised. This isn't the first time someone has looked at my dark skin like there's a question mark attached to its color.

"Something wrong?" I ask.

"No . . . It's just that old people close deals like this, but okay." Pablo shrugs as he takes mine. It's the quickest handshake I've ever had. "So how much do I owe you?"

"We can work out our terms later. For now, keep this to yourself."

"Not a problem, Diem. Thank you."

"You're welcome. Now get out of my house."

Abuela always scolds me when I use my laptop while eating, but the politician advocating for Puerto Rican statehood on TV has her undivided attention.

"¡Que te calles esa boca!" She flips him both middle fingers. Her obscene gesture clashes with her pink, glittery nightgown and SpongeBob slides. "You wanna live in a state, there's a whole country full of them! Pack your bags and go!"

It would be easy to change the channel. But Abuela never misses an opportunity to yell at members of the Partido Nuevo Progresista, or the PNP.

Normally, I chime in with an insult, but I'm juggling my French toast and fried eggs with Irene Cárdenas's Instagram. Bless her for making it public. She flaunts a pair of Yeezy sneakers, tickets to a Bad Bunny concert, and selfies inside her Range Rover with friends. I try not to focus on the fact that everyone is light-skinned and beautiful. I'm also ignoring the sticker on her car's rear window, which has a white palm tree on a blue background—the PNP logo.

What *does* concern me is there aren't pictures with boys. I've seen Irene hang out with a solid amount of guys in our school's parking lot (they're all light-skinned and beautiful, too), but she's more discerning when it comes to posting pictures on social media.

I'm about to click on her Stories when Abuela cusses loudly.

"Diem, este pendejo almost made me forget it's Wednesday! Get to school already!" She's rushing to the fridge and shaking her head. The chipped bobby pins in her hair are almost as silver as the Afro they're holding in place. "And I need to get this caldo de pollo to Maricarmen."

Maricarmen is Abuela's favorite coworker at CIEM, the private school in Carolina where my grandmother teaches history most of her day.

"Don't forget to pick up your new inhaler," I say. Abuela has asthma.

"Ugh! Yes, I should stop at the pharmacy before work. Gracias, mi santa."

Abuela rushes to her bedroom so she can change into publicly acceptable clothing.

I dive into Irene's Stories. There are so many white dashes at the top of the screen that they're basically just dots—this girl must have nothing better to do than document her entire life. The first couple of clips feature Irene and her friends at school. They're posing in front of vending machines, their cars, and boys. At first, I'm intrigued by the boys, but they're all light-skinned and beautiful yet again. Then the action moves to the streets. Irene's showing off a rainbow she filmed from the overpass a couple feet from our school's entrance. Chatter and laughter erupt in the background. Her pace slows as the camera pans down.

"¡Diem Rodríguez!" Abuela reaches for my plate, which is very much still unfinished. I slam my laptop shut. "Can you eat that in the next five seconds? You'll be late for your quiz!"

Arguing with her is like waiting for snow on a tropical island: futile.

I scarf down my breakfast, then I'm off. My school is a ten-minute walk away. Abuela joins me on the way to the pharmacy. She pays no mind to the people waiting for our local doctor's office to open, all of whom are staring at her. Even the kids only have eyes for Abuela.

One of them asks his mom, "Is that the crazy witch?"

"That's right! And I'm putting a hex on you! In seven days, all your toys will be *gone!*" Abuela yells in an over-the-top voice that would put Ursula from *The Little Mermaid* to shame.

The child starts crying. He looks about five or six, but wails like a newborn.

"Negra loca . . ." I catch the mom mutter.

I swerve, but Abuela yanks me forward.

"You're not going to jail for that pendeja," Abuela says firmly. She's gripping my wrist hard, as if she fears I'll decapitate the racist in front of her racist-in-training offspring.

Since that's not an option, I resort to distracting Abuela with her favorite topic. "Don't act like you wouldn't attack pendejos. You'd confront los fríos without hesitation!"

"That's different. Los fríos are dangerously devious."

"Okay, but is it just because they're vampires?" I ask. "Tell me more about them. Like, what could possibly make Félix Meléndez more dangerous than your average frío?

Abuela guides me down the sidewalk. "I only saw him once, but it was enough to remember him forever. Eugenio Cárdenas and I were out for a stroll under the stars. Félix was watching Beatriz Crespo's window the night before the killings began. He must've been waiting for her to accept the white rose on her doorstep. When I saw him, I thought he was very handsome—a brown James Dean. Do you know James Dean?"

"Yeah, his hotness is pretty legendary."

Abuela nods. "Félix looked at me, and his eyes were a dim, ash gray. They held me in place. Eugenio pulled me forward, but I couldn't move. That's what Félix did to people in Moca first—he enchanted them so they couldn't fight. I think he considered feeding on me later that night. Or chase me after he got bored with Beatriz. She called his name right then. She said, 'Félix Meléndez, leave me alone and never come back!' When he looked to her window, his magical hold on me vanished. I noticed the white pin on his shirt as I walked away."

I've heard this story hundreds of times, but it never stops creeping me out. Abuela could've been killed right there. She could've been one of the victims in the brutal aftermath of Beatriz's rejection, too. Abuela had been asleep when the massacre started. Everybody was. Abuela has never come forward with what she experienced. We live among people who hunted the Chupacabras down, but they're ill-equipped to capture such a clever predator. Instead, she committed his name to memory and found as much information on the Meléndez family as she could. But, legally, they don't exist. Their identities are nothing more than a rumor among vampire slayers in secret online forums, a whisper behind closed doors.

I don't know what compelled Félix to let her live. Whatever it was, I'm grateful.

He still needs his head cut off.

"Okay, here's the pharmacy." Abuela points to the right sidewalk. "Break a leg on that quiz, Diem. See you at training after school. Oh, and bring empanadillas!"

She's off to the pharmacy.

I turn left toward the school. Students mill about before first bell. I open Instagram on my phone and look for Irene again. When I land on the overpass clip, I pause it. There are five boys sitting on the handrail. Four of them are huddled together. The fifth boy is closer to Irene, and he's the only one with deep brown skin like mine. He's not wearing our school's uniform, a light blue polo and dark blue pants. No backpack, either. He has black hair that curls at the ends, and skin so smooth you'd think he shaves every few seconds. Even though he's seated, he appears much taller than Pablo, who's our basketball team's center. My guess is around six foot five. He's wearing a plain red T-shirt that sticks to his biceps.

I hold the phone up in case the sunlight's tricking me. He doesn't have a white pin on his shirt, but he steps down from the handrail, walking closer to Irene, his eyes stuck on her...

They're a dim, ash gray.

The next Story starts. But it's in Irene and Pablo's garage, where the former is challenging the latter to do a hundred push-ups. She cackles as he winks at the camera.

"Ugh . . ." I return to the overpass clip. The fifth boy isn't wiry-thin, but there's a tortured look on his beautiful face, and an air of risk hanging over him—like a brown James Dean.

It's him. Félix Meléndez *is* in Canóvanas.

Now I have to find his hideout.

Abuela better not realize her machete is missing.

With the newly acquired blade in my backpack, I walk past the school gates and follow the dirt path that leads below the overpass.

Cars speed past the bus stop as I approach. There's another stop across the road, where a man sells fruit out of wooden carts. He's talking to a customer next to the bananas. They pay no mind to me while I scan the grassy areas surrounding the over-pass's walls. No footprints or traces of blood anywhere. I cross the road. When the customer leaves, I smile at the vendor.

"Excuse me, sir? Have you seen a boy around my age walk through here recently? He wouldn't be in uniform like me, but he's about six foot five, deep brown skin, and curly hair?"

"Haven't seen one that tall, no. But if you like a boy, you have to let him come to *you*."

The vendor tips his head like he's just changed my life.

"Thank you. That was . . . enlightening."

I move to the plot of grass behind the vendor's cart. It's an unkempt patch big enough to serve as feeding grounds for cows and changos (their real name is the Greater Antillean grackle, which is a lot of words for such a tiny bird). The trees are bare and bend to the right, failing at blocking out the sun. Beyond the grass is a road that'll take me to the Quintas de Canóvanas neighborhood. I'll have to stake out one-story houses and a handful of businesses there—all before 3 p.m. If I'm a second late, Abuela will suspect something is wrong.

The deeper I get, the thicker the bushes are; there's barely any space for solid footing. Cows moo at me a few feet away. None have obvious bite marks, so I'm safe from being attacked by four-legged bloodsucking mammals.

Something crunches behind me. A shoe has stepped on a fallen branch.

I stop and ball my fists.

The cows aren't running in fear, but they *are* staring at whatever's approaching. Reaching for the machete will take too long.

I wheel around, ducking low. Then I kick at my attacker's legs.

"Ahh!"

I've just knocked Pablo Cárdenas down.

He falls flat on his butt, wincing in pain.

"What are you *doing* here?" I ask through gritted teeth.

"I saw you bolting away from school! I figured you'd found something, and I . . . ow . . ." He gets back up with a groan. "You didn't say anything about hunting a serial killer alone.

"You need to be in homeroom."

"And you're just going after a killer without backup? Come on. Don't be dumb."

I flinch at his insult, even though I suppose he's being protective. "That wasn't the deal. You're already in danger of being murdered. Let's not speed up the process."

Pablo pats dirt off his black jeans. "I won't let you search for this creep by yourself, Diem. Now what the hell are you doing in this low-budget mangrove? Did you find anything?"

I dig my fingernails into my scalp. He's about to ruin this. I understand he's desperate to save his sister, but his recklessness is endangering us both—what if Félix is already onto us because of his childish scream? *And* he's slowing me down. I'm about to implore him to leave again when he plows onward like Indiana Jones.

"*Pablo.*" I've never chased a boy in my life, but here I am running after one who refuses to listen. "Stop this right now!"

"Are you trying to get to Quintas?" he says, pointing at the neighborhood where Félix could potentially be hiding. "You could've just called me and asked for a ride, you dummy."

Another flinch. "I'm not a dum—"

The grass, trees, and cows vanish with a *snap!*

We're in a chamber with white marble walls. The ceiling is white, too, with an old iron chandelier hanging from its center. Five candles are placed around it, but no flames flicker on their tips. A long banquet table spreads out before me. The tablecloth is as white as the walls. Linen. Lace appliqués. Roses. The table is filled with marble trays of all shapes and sizes, but there's nothing inside. There are two high-backed chairs. One of them is in front of me; the other seat is at the opposite end. Both are unoccupied.

"Stay close," I tell Pablo as I unzip my backpack. Even though my hands are steady, there's a rumbling earthquake in my chest—Félix possesses far greater psychic abilities than I suspected. Either a slack-jawed Pablo and I have truly been teleported, or we're being fooled into thinking we're somewhere that doesn't exist.

I pull out Abuela's machete.

Pablo gasps. "You had that *in your backpack?*"

"We have more important things to worry about. Get behind me."

I raise the machete high like a sword. Pablo does as he's told, but he's pressed against the wall, leaving a few feet between us. He's almost as scared of me as he is of Félix. I suppress the urge to explain that I'm not an amateur, even though this will be my first kill. I've beheaded mannequins, sliced frozen meat in midair, and stabbed my way out of Abuela's obstacle courses, but that will never be the same as slaying El Vampiro de Moca.

Well, if Félix ever shows up.

"It's rude to keep your guests waiting!" I yell to the empty room. "You've brought us here for a reason. We deserve answers, frío, and *you* need to leave Irene Cárdenas alone."

"Should you be talking to him like that?" Pablo whispers. "Maybe be a little nicer?"

I've never spun around so fast. "You want me to be nicer to the guy who's stalking your sister and is threatening to murder us."

Pablo's a shaking, hand-wringing disaster. "I'm just trying not to piss the dude off."

"Too late," says another boy.

My veins are as dry as a desert—Félix Meléndez is now

sitting on the chair at the end of the table. He sips blood from a glass goblet.

Abuela had *not* been exaggerating about his beauty. Most vampires are gorgeous, but Félix is a diamond among the semi-precious gemstones. His curls are bouncier in person, and they frame a chiseled face that radiates an angelic glow. His ash-gray eyes are the only telltale signs of his supernatural identity. Seeing how handsome he is makes his killings harder to comprehend. How can someone this attractive rely on threats to find a mate? Especially someone who can manipulate reality like this? I've seen far too many men who behave like the Babadook with wedding rings, but this is even weirder.

"Diem . . ." Pablo's voice comes out strained, as if he's crumpled from the inside.

This boy from Hell scares me, too, but I'm not letting him do what he pleases. I won't let him touch Pablo, Irene, or anyone else. Today is his last day on Earth.

I ask, "Do you understand my terms?"

"Perfectly," Félix answers. "But you have the wrong guy."

"Of course you'd tell me that."

"I never lie." He finishes his goblet. I shouldn't have let him—he's powering up for a fight. Sure enough, he's pushing his seat back, standing with an airy grace. "Your name's Diem?"

I don't respond.

"Nice to meet you. I'm Félix. Your suspicions are correct, I am a vampire. And *that*"—he points at Pablo—"is the vampire you're looking for."

I laugh. "Blame the victim and act like one yourself? How original."

Félix nods. "Pablo is doing it right now."

"Holy shit. This guy's crazier than I thought." Pablo presses his hands together in prayer form, shaking even more. "Diem, please get us out of here, okay? I don't want any part in this!"

"Yet you're the one pulling the strings." Félix scowls at him. He steps forward, but I raise my machete even higher, and he stops. "The Cárdenas family has been trying to kill mine for centuries. They've gotten rid of most vampires here—they're vying for a throne that doesn't exist. His grandfather was El Vampiro de Moca, and Pablo's the one leaving white roses behind. He's the killer from sixty years ago."

I can't even laugh again. This is the epitome of ridiculousness.

"Why would he leave his own sister a rose?" I ask.

"I believe they planted it together. You see, I slipped up. I've been looking for the Cárdenas family ever since our last battle two years ago. They only made their social media accounts public again this month, flaunting their whereabouts so I could find them. I was so excited to see Irene that I didn't hide at the overpass. I've never fought her, but of course she'd recognize the vampire that almost killed her brother. Even with their supernatural reflexes, the Cárdenas are terrible fighters. That's where *you* come in." Félix takes another tentative step. "Pablo needs a slayer. Either he hopes to finish me off at your side or he wants you to shield him while he tries to kill me himself. People like us are disposable to him."

"Kill him, Diem!" Pablo yells louder than a cheerleader.

I almost make the mistake of turning to him, but I'm not taking my chances with Félix nearby. Still, Pablo's request is jarring. How can he go from a defenseless "get us out of here" to "kill him" in the span of twenty seconds?

Then there's Félix's last sentence.

"People like us?" I ask.

"Diem, why are you *wasting time?* He's trying to trick you into turning on me!" Pablo is standing next to me now, no longer shaking. He grabs my wrist and jabs the machete in Félix's direction. "Don't be so fucking dumb and just kill him already!"

I can't move—his grip is ice-cold.

I remember how he hesitated to touch me last night. Our handshake had been too quick for me to notice. Félix says Pablo is using me as his shield. That might be true, but his skin is his best protection. All along, the lily-white basketball player had been right under my nose.

Pablo Cárdenas is a frío. *He* is the boy made of sulfur and cravings.

The chamber is still the same, but somehow I feel the walls pushing in on me, and the air is being sucked out. There's nothing left for me to inhale.

"People . . . like us . . ." I look from Pablo's frozen hand to Félix.

He points at me, then at himself. "Brown. Black. He thinks it's his right to get rid of us. The vampires his family killed have looked like you and me. But the Cárdenas only succeeded because their victims were caught off guard. Whenever they go toe-to-toe with Los Meléndez, we overpower them. As for the girls he threatens with his roses, that's another way he feels in control. It's a game for—"

"STOP TALKING!" Pablo bares his long, sharp fangs at Félix, whose snarl also reveals his frío teeth. Pablo's eyes are crimson slits now, too—he's starving.

He grabs me and tosses me forward.

"Ahhh!" I drop the machete.

Félix catches me seconds before I split my head open on the dinner table.

"Are you okay?" he asks me.

"I—"

Pablo dashes forward, moving so fast he blurs. A loud clanging reverberates across the room.

He's taken Abuela's machete.

"You're too stupid to follow one simple order, huh? Grandpa says your grandma was the same way—that's why he dumped her ass." He smiles as he touches the machete's tip. "I mean, he also needed to skip town after Félix found us, but your grandma could've paid him to stay and he *still* would've run off. The night I went on a little hunting spree." His laugh chills me faster than his grip had. "I thought about killing her, too. Grandpa wouldn't have minded. Then I realized it was a waste of energy. Esa negra no importa."

That Black woman doesn't matter.

Pablo's grandfather married a woman who looks like him instead of Abuela. Our neighbors call Abuela a witch, a crazy Black lady, when there's a whole family of fríos walking among us. The true evil is taking math quizzes next to me in homeroom. It's voting to make our country a state every four years, buying into the lie that colonies can become well-respected members of the empire.

"I'll bleed you dry after I'm done with this punk-ass bitch." Pablo levels the machete at Félix's chin, still smiling like the undead creep he is. "It was a mistake to think I needed your help. I'm not as rusty as I was back then."

"Whatever happens," Félix whispers in my ear, "stay behind me."

Pablo rushes Félix in another blur.

Félix shoves me away before the impact. I'm launched several feet from their intense sparring, which mostly consists of ear-splitting swooshes, bared fangs, and Abuela's machete swinging at Félix's neck. He's not dodging as quickly as I expect—Pablo *is* strong enough to defeat him. He keeps trying to stab Félix instead of engaging in actual hand-to-hand combat.

He could still be a terrible fighter.

Félix lands a punch on Pablo's jaw, sending him flying across the chamber.

"Ugh!" Pablo's grip on the machete doesn't loosen. His eyes narrow even more, then he sprints toward Félix, who's coming to meet him halfway. Félix throws an uppercut.

He misses.

Pablo sinks his fangs into Félix's neck.

"NO!" I'm hurtling toward them at full speed. I can't let Pablo win.

He tears at Félix's flesh, pulling it away in slow tugs, but only because Félix is squeezing the crap out of Pablo's jaw—he's trying to crush it into dust. With his other hand, Félix holds Pablo's wrist down, forcing the machete to point toward the ground.

I sweep Pablo off his feet with a kick.

He's on his back again. Finally, he releases Abuela's weapon. I snatch it before he can move.

Félix staggers, pressing a hand against his torn, bloodied flesh. Sometimes I forget how much vampires can still bleed. "Stay . . . behind me . . ." he says through ragged breaths.

He's too weak to fight.

I shake my head, then face our true enemy. "Hey, Pablo. You can admit you didn't kill Abuela because she would've beaten you. But since she didn't get the chance . . ."

He snarls. Then he lunges for me.

I duck and roll. Once Pablo's behind me, I push myself off the ground, driving the machete into his throat. I thrust the blade up, up, up, slicing his head in half. The machete exits through his scalp in one swift, violent tug. Hair, skin, and bits of bone cling to the blood-coated weapon.

Pablo Cárdenas's body lands at my feet.

I cut off his head anyway—to honor Abuela's teachings. It rolls off like a coconut tumbling out of the palm tree on his party's flag. He died (for real) with his crimson eyes open and a mouth wide enough to suggest he was about to scream.

"I'll tell her what a little bitch you were." I'm grinning as I kick Pablo's chest. No more white roses on doorsteps. It is fulfilling to slay a vampire. But slaying a racist vampire who stalks girls and murders their loved ones holds a special place in my heart.

"You're amazing, Diem . . ." says Félix. He's still struggling to breathe, slowly dropping to his knees. "Thank . . . thank you for . . ." He can't even finish his sentence.

I stare at the frío I never thought I'd protect. Regardless of how he tried shielding me from Pablo, Félix is still a monster.

I want to save him anyway.

Abuela would be furious if she knew what I was thinking. She'd scold me for siding with a frío, accusing him of enchanting me. But I have to keep him alive—there are more Cárdenas left. After today, Félix Meléndez, his entire bloodline . . . they'll *owe* me. Abuela could be in danger once Irene and her kin find out what we've done to Pablo. I can't fight them all off alone.

So I kneel in front of a frío, offering him my exposed wrist. Félix's gaze narrows. "What?"

"You need to power up before we kill the rest of Pablo's family. We won't finish them off today, but I need to get you out of this place so we can start planning. And don't even think about drinking too much—it's only to heal a wound or two."

I've heard that Helen of Troy is the face that launched a thousand ships.

But Félix Meléndez launched a thousand lightning bolts all over me with that damn smile.

"Are you sure?" he whispers, his lips drawing near my pulsing vein.

I look away. He can smile at the side of my face, thanks. "Do it before I change my mind."

As his breath warms my skin, I picture myself beheading every remaining Cárdenas on my island. Abuela had been right. Hell is a pretty face with bad intentions.

And I'm *so* much worse.

La Patasola

Racquel Marie

Growing up as the only daughter in a house with three older brothers, I'm used to getting all the warnings. "Don't wear skirts that short!" "¡Cuidado con esos chicos!" "Don't stay out too late!" "Don't leave your drink alone at a party!"

The only warning my brothers ever received was to never, ever go camping in the forest. Or the woods. Basically anywhere with trees. Because that's where La Patasola hides. And that's where she'll find you.

The story, courtesy of Dad's adolescence in Bogotá, Colombia—near where La Patasola is actually rumored to reside—never really scared *me* because it was never really meant to. Still, as I jog toward the bus waiting to drive our senior class to the woods for our spring break trip, the story fogs my thoughts. My brothers may have said they'd grown out of their fear as they got older, but each and every one of them skipped out on their senior camping trip.

I, on the other hand, need this trip. Eddie and I both do.

He's distracted on his phone when I drop my bag and throw my arms around his neck. "Hello, hello, hello!" I sing, excited to see him after a long weekend of dodging questions about why he wouldn't be coming over for Easter at the end of break. I told my parents he had plans with his family already. The truth is, after attending nearly every one of my family's gatherings for the three years we've been together, he just said he couldn't make it. No explanation beyond that.

"You're finally here," Eddie says into my hair. One hand rests on my waist, but he lightly steps away from me. "You sure took your sweet time." His smile doesn't match his tone.

Before I can try to laugh off the comment, Eddie passes his backpack to Mr. Jiménez, who is loading the bus.

I school my face into a smile for my favorite teacher. I used to be embarrassed that I couldn't take AP Spanish until senior year because speaking casually at home didn't give me a strong enough sense of grammar to skip over the intro classes. But Mr. Jiménez's excitement over our shared Colombian ancestry squashed that on the first day of class. "Hola, Señor Jiménez, ¿cómo está?"

"Bien, Elena, gracias. Excited to keep you kids out of trouble the next few days." He winks.

"We'll be on our best behavior, scout's honor." I pick my bag off the ground, but Eddie pulls it away to hand it over himself. I clear my throat. "By the way, babe, did you pack that extra flashlight for me?"

"I said I would, didn't I?" Eddie's voice is sweeter now, but he doesn't look at me, just nods at Mr. Jiménez and heads toward the small line of students still getting on the bus.

I pick up my pace to match his. "No, I know. I was just

checking. Since Diego broke mine and my phone's flash is busted—"

He spins around so fast I almost crash into his chest. "I got it. It's in my bag."

"Well. Thank you." I reach for his hands, but he slips them into his pockets. "So, where did you want to sit? I was thinking maybe closer to the front so I don't get carsick? But I'm fine wherever!"

"I actually told Charlie I would sit with him."

"Oh." I swallow my disappointment. His phone pings. When he pulls it out, eyes scanning the screen, he has to bite down on a smile. "Is that him?"

"What?" The smile drops and his phone goes back into his pocket. "Oh, yeah. Yeah, he's pulling up now. You go ahead."

"Oh, okay." I try for a smile of my own. "Well, see you when we get there!"

"Mhm," he hums, looking away.

I step into the bus by myself, pretending not to notice the way people go quieter as I pass them. The second I spot Kelly sprawled across a seat near the back, I speed up.

"Room for another?"

"Oh, thank God." She scoots toward the window to make space for me. "I was worried I'd be stuck sitting with some weirdo. Although . . ." She arches her neck and stares behind me.

"What are you doing?"

"Looking for Eddie where he's usually attached to your hip."

"Har-har."

She leans back into her seat.

"He thought you and I could use the bonding time," I lie.

"How does it feel to have the most perfect boyfriend?"

Normally, I'd let comments like this slide. Everyone at school loves Eddie, my best friend included. He's the captain of the baseball team, top of our class, involved in student council, but just as likely to throw a party at his house. Everyone really does think he's perfect.

Which is why it's so hard to force the next words out of my mouth.

"Well . . ." I tug at the sleeves of my hoodie, which is actually Eddie's, and drop my voice to a hush. People are still glancing over at me. "He's been acting sorta weird for the past couple weeks."

"The past couple weeks? You mean since—"

"Ever since I came out," I finish for her. "I don't know, maybe I shouldn't have said anything."

"Are you sure?" she asks, frowning. As far as she knows, he's been nothing but supportive and that's the way I'd hoped to keep it. I thought maybe the weirdness was all in my head and didn't want to make a big deal out of it, but it's becoming harder to deny. "I mean, Eddie's always been cool about Gina and me. And you being queer doesn't mean you're not into him. He knows that."

"That's true." I've known I was queer since long before Eddie and I started dating. I've known basically my whole life. By the time I felt comfortable with the idea of talking about it with people, I'd just started dating Eddie, so I'd convinced myself it was pointless to mention that I was attracted to any gender when I already had him. Especially with his slight tendency for jealousy. Up until last month, Kelly was the only one outside of my family who knew, but then I read an article on upcoming Pride festivities in NorCal, and I wanted to be a part of them.

Our school is pretty diverse and I know plenty of other queer kids in our grade, Kelly and Gina included, so I didn't think my tweet would be that big of a deal. *Excited to celebrate my first Pride as an out queer woman this year!* was all it said.

But the day after I posted it, I overheard Sam and Dylan from Eddie's baseball team betting on whether or not I'd cheated on Eddie with some girl who "turned me." And Regina from homeroom just about asked me point-blank if my tweet meant we'd broken up.

I had sent Eddie the longest audio message before tweeting—explaining how much I loved him, how this part of my identity didn't change anything about us, how I'd be happy to talk about it more. I told him I knew I should have waited to tell him in person, but it felt so vulnerable. In that moment, I just wanted to get it off my chest.

But nearly the whole weekend went by before he'd replied to my message, or the countless ones that followed asking if he was okay or had any questions. By the time I received his simple thumbs-up emoji, I'd already sent the tweet.

Kelly wraps her arm around my shoulder and I lean into the needed comfort. "I'm sure everything is fine. He's probably just stressed out because you're still deciding where you're going in the fall." My heartbeat picks up at the mention of college. Eddie wants me to commit to UC Santa Cruz with him for computer science, but I'm still waiting to see if I get off Berkeley's waitlist. Even before the tweet, we'd been constantly arguing over what schools would be best for our future. "Look, I'm already bummed Gina couldn't come. We can't both be sulking the whole trip."

I sigh and sit up, noticing the girls across the row staring at Kelly and me. They look away when I make eye contact, so I try to brush away the weirdness.

"You're right." I untangled my headphones and pass her my phone. I don't think about the playlist I specifically made for Eddie and me to listen to on the drive. "Pick a podcast for us. Something scary."

And then we're off to the woods.

Daylight is precious, so everyone is immediately out of the bus and pitching their ancient, school-provided tents when we arrive at the campground.

Kelly and I make our way to the girls' side. The gendered barrier thing is pointless. Not only do we have a handful of non-binary kids in our grade, no imaginary boundary will stop students from sneaking around after lights out.

I watch Eddie and Charlie finish hammering in their last tent post while Kelly flips around our instructions. Eddie checks his phone every few minutes, smiling at whatever he reads there. Whoever is on the other end, it sure as hell isn't Charlie.

"I know longingly staring at your boyfriend is really important, but I would actually like us to have some semblance of shelter built before nightfall," Kelly says.

I shake out of my trance and start to help.

I don't want to be *that* girlfriend. The jealous one picking at flaws with her boyfriend just because he isn't showering her with attention and is sending a couple mildly suspicious texts. "Sorry, I just—"

My voice drifts off as Dylan walks past us, whispering to a girl from my chem class. Her eyes flash between me and Kelly, whose focus is still on the tent, and all I catch of her reply is "poor Eddie."

Kelly startles me as Dylan and the girl giggle away. "I get it. One bus ride without Eddie and you're already feeling lonely." I stick my tongue out at her, but it's hard to laugh after what just happened. "Go talk to him. I love you, but you're not being much help anyway."

She leans past me and cups her hands around her mouth. "Charlie!" Charlie's head pops up. "Come help me set up our tent, yeah?" He nods and slaps Eddie on the arm. Kelly pushes me forward. "Go be codependent."

Charlie and I swap spaces. Eddie pretends to not see me coming, still typing on his phone. He barely slips it into his pocket as I reach him. "You here for the flashlight?"

"Oh, well, yeah, I guess. But I—"

"I'll go grab it," he interrupts, stepping into his tent.

I sigh, alone. Their tent is closer than anyone else's to the thick trees caging our campsite. It's still mid-afternoon, but the trees crowd together so tightly over here that the shadows between them seem to transform day into night.

Eddie's taking his sweet time, so I step around his tent and walk slowly into the deep cover of the massive redwoods. My lungs fill with crisp, clean air. My family never went camping growing up. The consequences of instilling a fear of woods and forests into your sons, I guess.

Despite this, I feel at peace, basking in the fresh air, brushing my fingertips over the rough bark of the trees towering over me. I can hardly hear the camp's chatter now.

I inhale again and choke on something metallic and tangy.

Hooking my arm over my nose, I step around the closest tree and scream. The mangled corpse of a headless deer is splayed out beneath the massive trunk. Flies buzz around the bright pink flesh gleaming in a pocket of sunlight. The remainder of the neck—torn flaps of fuzzy, graying skin revealing jagged bone— sags against the bark it has stained red.

Something grabs me from behind.

I swing wildly at it, all form my brothers hammered into me disappearing as my fist makes contact.

"Shit!" Charlie grips his nose, blood trickling between his knuckles. His eyes widen as they slide to the gore behind me. "Oh my God."

Mr. Jiménez and Kelly break through the trees. I rush toward Kelly before she can see the deer. "Don't look," I tell her. She spins around while Mr. Jiménez steps past us.

He curses under his breath. "You kids go back to the tents. Send Mrs. Lang over and we'll call a park ranger to come handle this. I'm so sorry you had to see it."

Kelly leads me, shaken, and Charlie, bleeding, back to camp. Eddie emerges from their tent as we exit the trees. "Woah, what happened to you?"

"Didn't you hear Elena scream?" Charlie says. "I was on my way to get the bug spray when I heard her."

Eddie's phone lights up in his hand and I can tell it's taking all his power not to glance at it. "No, I didn't hear anything." He looks at me. "I'm sorry, babe, are you okay?"

"I'm fine. I saw a dead animal and got scared, that's all."

"You got everyone this worked up over a dead animal?" he asks, looking apologetically at our friends.

My voice comes out quiet. "It was just really gross."

Kelly and Charlie awkwardly leave to give us space and find something for his nose.

I clear my throat. "Kinda weird that Charlie heard me, but you didn't. You were closer."

"Yeah. Weird." His phone lights up again and he finally checks it. That small smile from earlier returns.

"Must've been focused on something else, then."

"Mhm," he hums again, distracted. "Must've been."

A few hours later, even with Charlie's nose bandaged and the carcass taken away by rangers, I don't feel much better. I asked the rangers what would've mutilated a deer that horrifically without eating it. "Either people scared off whatever attacked it," one of them said. "Or a person was the one who did it."

Their words haunt me.

I come back from washing my face in the bathroom for the tenth time and join Charlie and Kelly by the circle around the campfire. Charlie's bruised nose looks worse in the flickering fire's shadows.

"I'm so sorry about earlier," I say.

He shrugs it off and smiles. "No harm, no foul." The harm looks obvious, but I see the way the girls sitting behind him swoon at the thought of him heroically running to save me. When they look my way, their expressions souring, I remember Dylan earlier and face the fire. "But I'll extra forgive you if you tell that scary story your dad used to tell when we were in elementary school."

I don't need the attention on me right now, but I do love telling the story. Kelly nudges me, so I relent.

Charlie cups his hands around his mouth. "Everyone, quiet down! Elena's gonna kick off the spooky stories!" Silence wraps around us in seconds and our classmates' eyes press against me. I look at the fire instead of them.

Suddenly, it feels important I tell this story right. "It depends on who you ask, and where you're asking it, but according to my dad and his dad before him, La Patasola was once a gorgeous young woman who lived in a village bordering a forest along the Andes in Colombia." My voice is shaky, but I keep going. "Her beauty was unparalleled. So much so that men would travel for miles to court her, some from as far as northern Panama or southern Peru." I notice the blank stares of my classmates. Latin American geography wasn't hammered into everyone's heads at home, I guess. "Point is, these guys traveled *far* for her."

"Did she appreciate it?" that girl from my chemistry class shouts.

"What?" I ask, thrown off by the interruption.

"It's just so sad when girls don't appreciate everything a guy does for them," she says, eyes flickering up and down my body. Her friends beside her snicker.

I clear my throat. "Well, unfortunately for those men, she'd already fallen in love with a young man who lived in her village. Who she appreciated very, very much." I catch my angry tone and take a breath. "They'd grown up together and she trusted that he saw her for who she was, not just what she looked like. Eventually, the two got married."

"Is this a scary story or a Disney movie?" a boy shouts from off to the side, followed by a few scattered laughs. It's hard to tell in the dark, but it looks like it was Sam or Dylan who said it. As my eyes adjust, I notice Eddie standing behind them, focused on me.

"Interrupt her again and I'll give you something to be scared of!" Kelly shouts, only half joking.

Eddie stays silent. The shifting firelight hides his expression. Charlie nudges me to continue.

"But as the couple grew older, the yearning men didn't stop. Knowing others wanted what was his, the husband's love for his wife turned possessive and paranoid.

"He heard stories about other men sleeping with his wife during their courtship. Lies, of course. She loved her husband and her husband alone. But he'd seen the kindness she'd showed strangers. The type of kindness that always gets confused for flirtation when you're a pretty girl. Worrying about her leaving him, worrying about her falling for another man, and most of all, worrying he'd look like a fool in the aftermath, finally broke him.

"He accused her of adultery with those lying men backing up his claims. She denied it and begged for mercy, but he refused to listen. He and those men took her to the forest, stripped her of all her belongings, and left her to die.

"As she starved on the forest floor, her final wish was that she could one day face those men and show them who she was beyond her pretty face. The land was so overwhelmed with wishes that by the time it heard hers, she had already died.

"But the land felt the depth of her pain. And it was so sorry it hadn't helped in her time of need that it brought her back. But not as she was before."

The fire crackles. Everyone's orange-cast faces lean closer. "Her body was already rotting. One foot had been gnawed off by animals. And the kindness she'd once possessed was gone.

"In honor of her former beauty, the land shifted the light around her when she needed it to look like the woman she once was. One by one, she hunted down the lying men. While they had once dreamed of devouring her, now *she* devoured *them*. Her husband heard the whispers about these gruesome deaths. *Hungry animals*, he'd told himself. He didn't know how right he was.

"Then the day came. While hunting in the woods alone, his dead wife appeared out of nowhere, peeking out from behind a tree. She looked just as lovely as she had the day they'd married. She beckoned him closer, silently, and he obeyed. Because he was far away from home and his new wife would never need to know. Because who could fear something so beautiful. Some*thing*, not someone.

"Before she died in those woods alone, she'd realized the truth. No man had ever truly wanted her for who she was as a person. They'd hardly seen her as one. But that didn't bother her anymore. Because when he leaned in to kiss her and the scent of her blood-soaked teeth hit his nose and the light revealed her new appearance, she didn't consider herself a person either.

"She was revenge."

The circle of my classmates is silent. No one claps or laughs or makes the usual spooky "OooOo" noise.

Finally, Charlie lets out an awkward chuckle, breaking the silence. "I don't remember it quite like that, but it still scares the shit out of me."

"Yeah, watch out, Adams!" Sam shouts at Eddie, even though he's right beside him. "Better not cheat on Elena and give her a reason to go full Colombiana on you!"

He and Dylan fall onto each other laughing, a scattered few joining them again while someone else whistles. Kelly flips them off, but I look away in embarrassment. My brothers feared La Patasola their whole lives because she was gruesome and merciless, not because she was Colombian. But, of course, that's all these guys have taken away from the story.

Part of me wishes I hadn't told the story and given these white boys anything they could manipulate to validate the angry Latina stereotype. A bigger part of me wishes that I didn't have to worry that sharing my culture could do so.

Charlie saves me again. "All right, y'all, I got La Llorona from my mom's side or Kuchisake-onna from my dad's. Pick your poison."

As Charlie starts in on the latter, I notice Eddie slipping away from the group. Taking advantage of the moment, I twist off the bench and stumble my way through the dark after my boyfriend.

I try ignoring the memory of the deer as I blink against the lightless night, but flashes of its horrifically mutilated neck burst behind my eyes. I brush my feet along the floor with every step, careful not to trip over anything hidden in the darkness.

"Eddie? Where'd you go?" My stomach churns, worrying momentarily that whatever—or whoever—got the deer maybe got him. "I could really use that flashlight about now!"

My eyes adjust enough that I finally make out the shape of Eddie's tent, the light from his phone shining ghostly through the thin walls. Before I can talk myself out of it, I slip inside.

He looks up at me, then sighs and rolls his eyes. "I can't believe you really followed me all the way out here for a flashlight."

"So you heard me? And just didn't respond? While I stumbled through the darkness by myself?"

"You're actually going to pick a fight over this. Wow. *You* don't pack a flashlight for a camping trip and suddenly that makes *me* the bad guy." He clicks off his phone and shakes his head. "I literally came back here to get it for you, but you just immediately accuse me of ignoring you."

I'm annoyed with him—for not standing up for me with his friends and not answering me as I tried to find him. But maybe he's right. Here I am, trying to fix whatever's gone wrong with us, and all I'm doing is starting a fight.

"Look, I'm sorry. I really am grateful you brought me the flashlight. You've just been, I don't know, maybe it's me, I just feel like—"

"God, I hate when you do that."

"What?"

"Don't finish your sentences. You came in here to talk to me." His voice is so uninterested it stings. "So talk."

I straighten my shoulders and try my best to sound calm but stern. "I think you're upset about something and I want to know what. So we can fix it. Together."

He looks away. "Everything is fine."

"No, it's not." I try a different approach and scoot closer to him. He lets me pull his hand into mine. "Please look at me."

Finally, he lifts his green eyes. His posture softens, and I'm seeing the boy I've loved for years. The boy who always sat with my abuela at family dinners and walked me to and from every class, even if it was out of the way. The boy who made me happy and safe once upon a time, though that time feels further and further away every day.

I open my mouth to ask what's wrong again, but before the words can leave me, his lips cover mine.

He cups my cheek and lightly pulls me closer to his body. Our chests touch and I unlink my hand from his and bury it in his soft, dark hair. A small, gasping laugh escapes my mouth when he tugs me into his lap. But my joy sours to a flicker of panic when I feel his hands slip to the hem of my borrowed hoodie.

I delicately wrap my fingers around his. He holds them, squeezes once, then slips out of my grasp and reaches for the button on my jeans.

I break the kiss and lean back. "Babe, wait."

His smile falters. "Why?"

I don't know how to say it gently. That I don't want this, not right now. And not when something is still so clearly wrong between us. I don't want the type of love that uses our bodies to cover the holes in our relationship.

Before I can get the right words out, he pulls me in again, mouth hot and wet on my neck and arms wrapped around my body, pinning me to him.

I push lightly against his chest with my trapped arms. "Eddie, hold on."

He murmurs something against my skin but doesn't stop. His hands are cold against my bare back, sliding under my hoodie and shirt, fumbling to unhook my bra.

"Eddie, seriously, stop," I insist, pushing slightly harder.

He doesn't listen. I've known Eddie for years. Eddie respects me and loves me. Eddie wouldn't hurt me, not intentionally. And he's touched my body before, plenty of times.

But never like *this*.

I panic and thrash against him, forcing his front teeth to scrape along my neck. I barely register the hiss of pain, only the moment his mouth finally leaves my skin and he pulls back enough that I can shove off his chest and lap. Air knocks out of me as I fall back onto the tent floor.

"God, what is your deal?" Eddie yells as I sit up and press a hand to my neck.

"I—I told you to stop," I whisper. Adrenaline still flooding my body, I hardly register the words.

"So I can't even kiss my own girlfriend now," he scoffs. "Of course, that's just great. You know, I don't get you."

"Me?"

"Yes, you. Do you even want to be with me? Because seriously, just say the word and you can stop pretending otherwise." I wish the lantern was off so I didn't have to see the cruelty on his face. "Was it Kelly?"

"Was *what* Kelly?"

"The one who turned you."

My stomach bottoms out. "What did you just say?"

"Or was it Gina? Did you betray your best friend as well as your boyfriend? I guess I should've known. All those times you refused to come spend the night at my place when your parents were away but had no problem sharing a bed with those two."

"I—I can't believe you're saying this to me. Nothing happened between me and either of them. You're *my* boyfriend, they're *each other's* girlfriends."

"Oh, yeah, like that would stop someone like you." He barrels out of the tent. I scramble after him, desperate to contain this. Once we're both outside, he takes a few steps away before whirling back on me, a finger sharply pointed at my face. "You think I don't hear what people say in the hallways? Everyone knows you played me. I used to walk around like the king of that place until you made that tweet. Now all anyone sees is a slut and the idiot who refuses to leave her."

It's dark, but I'm aware of people watching us from the shadows. I know I have to say something to fix this, and fast.

"And that story back there? That's not the way your parents used to tell it and you know it. Trying to use your culture to bash men because you feel guilty or something? It's pathetic."

I've heard it so many times over the years. I guess I did focus on different parts than my dad would. His story felt like a warning to boys, to stay away from crazy women and beware of the ugly lurking beneath beauty. I don't quite know what my version was.

"So you're mad about the story? Or because I'm queer?"

"I'm mad because you cheated on me and you're still too cowardly to admit it. Give me any other *good* reason that after three years together, you randomly decide you like girls. That doesn't just happen." His breath singes me. "And somehow, you still want to be the victim in all of this, don't you?"

I try to shake my head, but I can hardly manage to breathe, let alone move.

"Congrats, you can be the victim. Just stay away from me, we're done."

By the time Kelly and Charlie find me crying in the tent, Eddie is long gone.

"He left his phone behind," Charlie says as he slips inside my and Kelly's tent. "It was just lying on his sleeping bag though, so I don't think it was on purpose."

It's been nearly two hours and Eddie's still not back. Curfew is in a few minutes, but anyone who already turned eighteen is volunteering to help the teachers find the golden boy of our senior class.

Everybody thinks it's my fault. They glare at me as they pass, whispering about the fight that seemingly confirmed everyone's suspicions, so Kelly and I have been hiding out in here.

I wordlessly take the phone from Charlie and try to unlock it with mine and Eddie's anniversary date—the same passcode he's used for years. I'm not terribly surprised when it fails, but that doesn't mean it doesn't hurt.

I keep trying: his birthday, his mom's birthday, the date his dog died. Finally, his jersey number repeated twice—1515—works.

Kelly and Charlie lean in.

I scroll past the countless unopened messages from people looking for him. The most recent thread that he already read is with someone whose contact name is a red heart emoji. My eyes scan the words but refuse to settle on them for longer than a brief second. From the snippets I let myself see, one thing is clear: There was a cheater in our relationship, but it wasn't me.

"Elena, I'm so sorry." Kelly rests a hand on my shoulder.

Three years of memories clash with a flood of feeling. Our tender first kiss in my backyard. Saying "I love you" on New Year's Eve as midnight struck. Holding hands in the halls and pinning boutonnieres on his suits for every school dance. Feeling seen, loved, and understood.

Pain washes over all of it, humiliation over every attempt I made to keep us together, anger over every newly broken promise we'd made to love each other forever.

But in the back of it all, almost hidden, is the subtle presence of relief; cleansing my memories of days like today, times when Eddie made me feel both useless and responsible for every problem between us. I realize I never have to endure another moment like that again.

I sigh and read the last text. Whoever this is, she asked him to sneak away and meet her in the woods.

"I have to go after him," I say. If we're truly over, I can't sit around here waiting for him to come back and decide that for us.

"We're going with you," Charlie says.

"No. I need you two to cover for me."

Kelly looks at me like I've lost it. "Elena—"

"There's no way all three of us will be able to leave unnoticed. If you lie and say I'm in the tent crying or whatever, no one will question it," I insist. Kelly starts to bite one of her already nubby nails. "Please, guys. If they think he got lost, he won't get in any trouble. But if they find him out there hooking up with some girl, he could get suspended."

"So could you! Even after—" Kelly motions to the phone. "You're willing to risk your ass for him?"

Today's been a nightmare, but at least there is this: the comfort of knowing someone else sees the way he treats me and it's no longer my responsibility to hide or deny it.

"I have to do this" is all I say in reply.

They both look unsure but nod.

"Take both phones, though," Charlie says. "And if you're not back in an hour, we're telling someone."

"Thank you." I pull them into a quick hug. "Thank you."

I head toward the bathrooms. The laughing girls in there go silent when they see me. I hold back a sigh. I can deal with them and the rumors later. Once the group is gone, I make a break for the trees, enveloping myself in their darkness.

I forgot to check the time before I left, so I have no idea how long I've been walking, though it feels like it's been forever. I rush past the hollowed shell of a massive, uprooted redwood when something scuttles inside it.

I use Eddie's phone as a flashlight. There's practically no service this far out.

"Where are you, Eddie?" I whisper to nothing. Angrily, I type a text to the heart contact, knowing it won't go through.

Where are you and my lying, cheating boyfriend at?

A roar echoes in the distance.

I spin in circles with the phone's flashlight, looking for whatever made that noise.

Something glows a few yards away.

Blood pounds in my ears, making it nearly impossible to hear anything. The glow disappears. Quickly, I type off another message.

Hello?

I hear the roar again. It's a text-tone, screaming as the glowing light comes back. Right beside them.

My eyes adjust to see the silhouette of a girl lean over Eddie. The soft, intimate sounds of lapping and whispered moaning nauseate me.

I storm over and bathe them in light. "What the hell do you think you're—"

I'm struck silent and frozen. My hand drops, the spotlight on them vanishing.

She tilts her head slowly, her joints cracking. The sliver of moonlight trickling through the trees exposes the black veins creeping up her face, the flaps of flesh rotting on her cheeks. I gag and press my sleeve against my nose when I finally smell her.

My words come out in a croak. "You're . . . It's you."

Somehow I find the strength to look down.

His body spills across her lap, neck bent at an angle that tells me there's no way he's breathing anymore. His eyes are horribly still open, cast to the sky. It's as if something burst through his chest from the inside, exposing slick, wet muscle and blood-soaked bone. In the middle of it all sits the last remaining chunks of his heart. The rest has been torn apart, one piece hanging off the side of her mouth.

La Patasola stands on one leg, and Eddie's lifeless body thumps off her to the ground in front of me.

I collapse. Scurrying backward, my hands scrape across sharp rocks and rough tree branches. Each slice stings as dirt blends with my blood, but I don't stop moving until my back slams into a tree.

She emerges from the shadows slowly, crawling across the ground on her hands and foot. As grotesque as her flesh is, her body moves fluidly. Like she learned to prowl from the very pumas whose teeth tore her to shreds.

I will die out here. Alone. Defenseless.

All it took were a few rumors to get her killed. Practically the whole school thinks I cheated on Eddie.

I close my eyes and whisper goodbye, to my parents, to my

friends, to the land surrounding me and the motherland I never got to meet.

I sense her reach me. My broken heart braces to be ripped clean from my body.

Then a hand rests gently on my chest. Nothing more.

My eyes open without instruction. Inches from my face isn't the horrific walking corpse that ripped apart my boyfriend. She's beautiful. She's young.

Her skin is smooth and brown, her black hair feathers off into the night sky. Eyes like midnight pools stare back at me. A single tear trickles from one of them. The pulse in her wrist taps against my racing heart.

A blink, and she's back to the monster she was before. Blood and flesh dribbling down her chin. The tear has turned to a drooping glob of yellow pus. Her hair is matted with dirt, a shard of Eddie's ribs caught in a dangling knot. Horrified, I watch a maggot burrow into a patch of jagged skin along her hairline.

I scream and press myself farther into the tree, begging for this to be over, praying for the death I seconds ago feared. The nightmare feels never-ending, until I dare look at her eyes.

Even with the rest of her looking like a monster again, her eyes are the same ones I saw moments before. Dark and beautiful. Kind. And still, so terribly young.

Her hand hasn't left my chest.

She blinks at me, just once, but doesn't move.

Eventually, I place my hand over hers and leave it there.

Finally, she sits back, letting go. I peel Eddie's hoodie off of me and hand it to her. She looks at the offering with wonder.

"I'm sorry," I rasp. But this time, it's not fear choking my words.

Carefully, she slips the hoodie over her head. I hold back several winces as her joints pop with every move. The sleeves peel at the graying skin on her wrists, exposing more bone and mutilated tendons. But if I squint, she doesn't look so scary. She looks a little like me.

Against all instinct, I lean forward and place a hand over her heart in return. Her eyes find mine and hold them for just a second. But it's long enough.

Slowly, she slides back into the shadows. The last thing I see before she disappears entirely is the glow of Eddie's phone from where I slipped it into his hoodie's front pocket.

The rumors won't die with him. They will likely grow.

But as I walk back to camp—leaving behind the resumed, wet sounds of tearing flesh—I don't fear the darkness surrounding me. I thank it.

The Other Side of
the Mountains

Claribel A. Ortega

A full moon doused the mountaintops in light, and so it was time to track la bruja. Yunior had been preparing for this night ever since his younger sister, Aury, was taken into the mountains, her screams like a trail of heavy smoke too thick to see beyond. The blue ribbon that had fallen from her hair was like a heartbreak you could touch.

"You cannot go," his mother had warned the night she disappeared, but Yunior, stubborn as the sun was hot, did not listen. He ventured into the mountains anyway. He was steadfast, strong, and certain he could find his sister and return her from the monster.

By lantern light, he had tracked the footprints up the path from their small home on the big hill. He'd walked for miles, always sure that his sister was just beyond another groove, or on the other side of yet another frigid brook. Yet, the strangest thing happened. Yunior had walked quickly, a sort of unbridled joy filling his heart as he reached the place where the footprints stopped, and his sister was sure to be. When he looked up, the sun obscured his vision. He threw one hand up to block the light from his eyes and when they adjusted, he was home. Yunior had walked in circles the entire night. He had ruined his shoes and bloodied his feet and was no closer to finding Aury.

"You cannot track a bruja in this way," said Bate, the old man who would shine your pots and pans for a penny and whose teeth were the color of tar.

"Then how?" Yunior had asked, angrily. Foolishly.

Bate had thrown his head back and laughed. His breath hot and putrid when he leaned in close and whispered. "You track her by the moonlight with one"—he held up one dirty finger—"hundred fireflies and four"—he raised three more dirty fingers—"drops of your blood. It is the only way. But there are terrible things on the other side of the mountain. It would be better if you did not go. Pointless, pointless. It's all backward there."

And then Bate had walked away with his mother's pot and a sack filled with tools that thunk-thunk-thunked as they bounced against his crooked back.

Yunior had spent four days walking through their town try-ing to capture one hundred fireflies, but he had only managed to trap twenty. Any time he approached a patch of the glowing bugs, they scattered as if they knew they were meant to help find a witch.

"It is impossible," he told Bate on the fifth day.

"Yes," Bate had said. One of his rotten teeth fell out and into the pot he was shining in the hot sun. Like most everyone in their town, there were terrible rumors about Bate. That he was depraved, a scoundrel, but Yunior's family paid no mind to words of clucking neighbors. Yunior knew too well how having little to do could lead to having too much to say. Bate had been friends with his father for years, had always been there for his mother, and Yunior would never turn his back on someone who was as good as family.

Days later, the full moon finally came, and it was time to find Aury. Yunior had filled a mason jar with the fireflies he could find and attached a handle to it to use as a lantern. He packed small hunting knives, many, many hunting knives, into his rucksack. Bate had even helped him shine them. Yunior was skilled at skinning animals before his mother put them in a stew, but he had never used his skills against something as big as a demon. It did not matter.

His family had already lost his father, Oscar, a few years back. He had gone to work on a farm atop the Torres Mountains, as he did every morning before the sun rose. But that night, instead of coming home, smiling and brimming with stories of his day, Yunior's father had not returned. The chair by the door, the one he sat in to take off his brown work boots, collected dust. Nobody had the heart to use it.

The neighbors whispered about this for months. They said his father had abandoned them. That he had left them for another woman. Another family. As Yunior's family's hopes for finding him died down, so did those whispers.

And now there were new whispers: La bruja had taken Aury just like she took Oscar. But Yunior would not lose his sister all so a bruja could steal more power. That was her goal of course, and every bruja's goal: to gain power by taking lives.

"This is a foolish journey, Yunior," his mother said as he laced his boots. "The mountains are being searched day and night by the guard, they will find Aury. I am certain they will.

The mountains are dangerous for a boy like you." Her face was lined with years of worry and grief, and Yunior felt terrible putting his mother through more of the same heartbreak. But he had to find his sister. For both of them.

"I am almost seventeen, Mami. I did not go and find Papi when he disappeared, and I should have. I won't make the same mistake again."

"But, Yunior," his mother pleaded, "what if it is la bruja? What if she takes you, too?"

Yunior did not have an answer for this, so instead he kissed his mother's forehead and smiled. "I won't leave you by yourself, Mami. Have faith in me."

Dolores gave her son a sad smile and a reluctant blessing as he walked out into the full moon.

"Come on, Dichoso," Yunior said to their dog. He felt a bit less alone, and a bit less afraid, with the shaggy brown mutt by his side. He used a bright red rope as a leash, and with his makeshift lantern in hand, began his journey into the deep, dark night.

The world was quiet. No birds sang, no water lapped, no people spoke. The only sounds were Yunior's footsteps against the path, the soft patter of Dichoso's paws, and a wind howling like a woman crying.

Yunior thought of the last time he saw his sister. Her brown curls in two pigtails held by those blue ribbons she always wore. He took the ribbon that had been left behind from his pocket now and held it tightly in his hand. Fear buzzed around him like mosquitos as he thought of the matching ribbon. Was it still holding his sister's hair back? Was her hair matted and tangled and dirty? Was she in pain? Was she even alive?

He shook his head and kept following the dirt path. It was no use thinking of her being hurt right now. He had to bring her home.

¿Qué buscas, Yuuuuuunior? a voice buzzed in his ear.

Dichoso howled.

Yunior swatted in the direction of the voice, but then more of them joined. They were wingless bugs, flying somehow and all asking the same question, their voices echoing like a choir in a church.

What are you looking for? What are you looking for? What are you looking for?

"I am looking for my sister, for la bruja who took her . . . Who are you?" Yunior responded, his body icy with terror despite the heat.

Wrong, wrong, wrong, the bugs responded.

Yunior whipped around, looking for the source of the voices because he did not want to believe the creatures were actually speaking. It must be a trick. More of the wingless creatures surrounded him, and no matter which way he moved, he could not get away. The creatures buzzed and hissed around his body, weaving through his curly hair, the feeling on his scalp making him retch. They seemed to come from the ground, Yunior realized, rising up in streams from the dirt, their fat, wingless bodies like dismembered flies.

He held up the mason jar and the fireflies in it swarmed, making a miniature tornado of light. But it was not enough to pierce the darkness. He swatted desperately, crying out but there were hundreds of them, thousands of them, buzzing around his body, sticking to his skin like honey. A green light flickered from the bugs' mouths, like a broken mirror of his fireflies. The weight of the creatures began to push Yunior down. He strug-gled against them, but his feet felt anchored to the dirt.

A gust of wind seemed to pull the earth out from under-neath him and send him toppling over and onto his back. Panic shot through his body, and Yunior shook with fear, his hands digging into the dirt looking for purchase but only finding more wingless creatures. The talking bugs had him pinned.

"No! No!" Yunior screamed, but it was no use. The wingless bugs covered every inch of his body. They sat on the whites of his eyes and slithered into his mouth and up his nostrils until the word, *wrong*, came from his own throat over and over again—until his throat was bloody with the word.

Dichoso howled and Yunior's eyes opened. He was not, as he had feared, dead. Nor had the wingless creatures devoured him. But it did seem, he realized upon pushing himself up, Dichoso sitting attentively on his lap, that he was in an unfamiliar part of the valley. The looming trees, the dusty road, the mountains peeking over the horizon, this was a place he knew, and yet like a dream where your house is not really your house at all, Yunior did not recognize it. Slowly, Yunior stood up, dusting himself off. Had he fallen asleep and dreamed the bugs? Had exhaustion gotten the best of him?

Looking around, Yunior realized that his surroundings did in fact look different but . . . they *were* familiar to him.

"No, not different," he said to Dichoso. "Backward."

Bate's words came back to him. *It's all backward there.*

The trees were not upside down, but the wind seemed to blow the vines of the willows in reverse. As if someone had rewound time itself and Yunior could see it.

"I probably just need water and sleep," Yunior told Dichoso. They walked toward the bank of the river, and Yunior scooped water into his hands. Before he drank, he looked down at his hands and screamed. Yunior shook his head and blinked hard, looking again and finding only red, raw muscle, no skin . . .

"Wake up!" he yelled, and slapped himself hard, his palm sticky against his face. Yunior's eyes went wide with terror. He crawled closer to the water and looked at his reflection. His face was also without the warm brown skin he had gotten from his mother. The same brown skin of his sister's face, too. It was gone and in its place was only horror. *The bugs*, his mind raced. *It was the bugs that ate your flesh.* But Yunior remembered waking up and dusting off his clothing without pain or discomfort. He remembered seeing his hands as they had always been.

This must be what Bate had meant.

This was brujería.

Yunior said a small prayer to the saints, and when he opened his eyes and looked at his face again in the moonlit water, he touched his nose and his cheeks, and his face was his own once more.

"It is brujería, Dichoso," Yunior said, somewhat relieved but still riddled with fear. "Come on. There is a doctor here at the foot of these mountains. We should find him." The doctor might be able to help Yunior continue his journey without another incident like the bugs. He needed help undoing whatever brujería had been done, if he was going to find his sister.

The dog followed him deeper into the forest.

The night had settled around them. His fireflies flitted about in their mason jar, matching the dance of their counterparts in the trees, frogs sang from their ponds, and it was like the day had been a strange dream. It was his fear getting the best of him, Yunior thought, and if he was afraid, then how must Aury feel? Dread filled Yunior but also propelled him forward. He had to find his sister.

Yunior tried to orient himself in this new, backward world. He took a path that looked familiar, only to turn around when it led to the edge of a cliff. Yunior retraced his steps in his mind and calculated where he would be by now if he hadn't been attacked by that strange dream. Or whatever it was. After an hour or so he and Dichoso reached the place where he thought the doctor's hut might be.

"It's just through here," Yunior said to the dog. Dichoso tried to head in the opposite direction, but when Yunior pulled gently on his leash, the good-natured dog pressed his nose against Yunior's knee affectionately. Yunior bent down to pat his head, and a small smile played on his lips for just a moment. He straightened up, took a deep breath, and made his way to the hut.

"Hello?" Yunior asked as he walked through the open curtain to the doctor's hut. His mother had forbidden him and Aury from ever venturing into this part of the mountains, but Yunior knew many a neighbor who came to this doctor, this . . . curandero, for help and protection.

Every few weeks he could be seen walking through their town, his bright blue hat trimmed with yellow feathers to match his robes, fake jewels on every finger glittering in the sun. He was just a helper, like Bate was, who some people had decided was terrible because he was different. Yunior knew what it felt like to be judged unfairly. He had heard the whispers of his neighbors saying he was not strong or tall enough to work in the fields, or clever and handsome enough to work in the city or find himself a good wife.

But those people didn't see the good that Yunior did. He helped his mother and looked after his sister, just like the curandero helped his neighbors. Yunior would never want to do to someone what those people did to him. He would not make up his mind based on gossip. He would see for himself.

The inside of the curandero's hut was cozy and filled with ointments and leaves and palms. Bottles were labeled with words in a language he could not understand, and a giant caldero stood over a fire in the center, bone broth bubbling inside of it.

"Un caldito," said a familiar voice in the corner.

"Bate?" asked Yunior.

Bate smiled his rotten tooth smile and continued to shine a small pot that sat between his legs.

"What are you doing here?"

"El curandero had me over for dinner. He went to town for the night, but I was too tired to go home."

Where *did* Bate live? Yunior wondered.

"Bate, do you know if there are any protection spells or items here? The forest, it's . . ."

"Terrible things. *I told you so*," Bate shook his head, then pointed to the other side of the small hut. "There, that necklace. I've seen el curandero sell those to people for protection against brujería. It will keep the bad magic away from you. It casts it, into the mountains."

Yunior nodded and went to the other side of the room. The necklace was simple: a rough cord with a jagged red crystal amulet attached. It didn't look fancy, but Yunior hoped it would work. It was better than nothing. He put it around his neck and felt an instant wave of relief and comfort. He left a few coins on the ledge where the necklace had sat and turned to Bate.

"Do you want to come with me?" he asked hopefully. Bate seemed to know a lot about everything, and maybe with his help Yunior could find Aury sooner.

Bate grunted. "I'm old and tired and full. You go. Yell if you're in trouble, I have good ears."

Yunior smiled and shook his head. "See you later, then."

Bate continued to shine his pot, not looking up as Yunior and Dichoso left the hut.

They continued farther into the mountainous woods. The moon shone bright, the trees still moving as if in reverse. The river, too, Yunior realized, ran in the wrong direction. As they walked on, uninterrupted by wingless bugs or horrifying visions, Yunior's hope grew. He touched the amulet around his neck. Perhaps the necklace could not change the strong magic around the mountains, but it would keep him and Dichoso safe.

The rumor was la bruja lived in caves. Before he set out on his journey his neighbors had told him that there was a group of caves just beyond this patch of woods. So that was where he was headed. To the caves, and hopefully, to Aury. He entered the grove and fear gripped him again. It was quieter here, darker as the trees eclipsed the moon.

"Stay close, Dichoso," he said, and the dog seemed to understand, pulling closer next to Yunior as they walked.

Everything felt still. The leaves of the trees, the wind, if the world around him seemed to go in reverse earlier, now absolutely everything felt suspended in time. Yunior grabbed a knife from his rucksack and held it up, ready to fight anything that might cross his path.

And then a figure darted across the woods. A shadow with wings. It moved so fast it was just a blur. But as the creature flew, she turned to smile at Yunior and the birdlike face became a woman's. The spread of her lips, the turn of her head, moved in slow motion.

"La bruja," Yunior said, and Dichoso howled and took off into the woods in the direction of the monster.

"No!" Yunior ran after the dog, the brambles and branches cut his face and legs as he went, and Yunior hissed with pain, but he kept following the shadow of Dichoso's fur. Yunior dropped the mason jar and with a pop, the lid flew off and his fireflies escaped.

The dog barked as he darted into a cave, and Yunior rushed in without thinking. If this was the creature's cave, he had just assured his own death.

"Is this your dog?" A voice like a songbird filled the air, and Yunior was stopped abruptly. A girl about his age stood before him, holding Dichoso by his leash. Her long black hair shone in the moonlight, which spilled into the cave. She wore a dress with delicate blue flowers, her hands were graceful, her face . . . more beautiful than anything Yunior had ever seen.

Yunior nodded yes, and the girl let go of Dichoso. He ran to Yunior's side with a whimper, but Yunior could not stop looking at the girl.

She smiled.

Her teeth were like knives.

"Is there something you need?" she asked, walking closer to Yunior.

"I . . ." Yunior tried to remember why he was even there. The girl walked even closer, close enough that her bare feet and Yunior's boots almost touched. Yunior could smell roses and dirt on her. A gentle buzz spread through his body. He had been drunk only once, on mamajuana without his parents' permission, and he'd been sick the whole day after. Everything about this girl made Yunior feel drunk. But this feeling was sweeter than that. It felt like an ocean wave taking him away on a too hot day. Dichoso whined, and it pulled Yunior out of whatever fog he was in.

"My sister," he said shaking his head. "She was taken, by . . . by you. Where is she?" Yunior had forgotten about the knife in his hand till now, but he held it up.

The girl smiled. "I do not take little girls. I am only sixteen myself. I was not the one who hurt her." She was right in front of Yunior now.

Although his hand trembled as he held his knife, he did not flinch or step back. But when the girl pushed the knife aside with a flick of her wrist, he knew that it wouldn't have helped him. He couldn't even run. The girl wrapped her hands around Yunior's neck and pulled him forward with a strength he was not expecting, his feet levitating off the ground. And then she kissed him. The knife fell with a soft thump on the dirt.

It was his very first kiss.

Yunior's eyes flew open. Smoke and wind enveloped them, like they were at the center of a rainless hurricane, and when it fell away, so did the girl's beauty. Her skin was not skin, but feathers. Her hair stringy and thin against a visible scalp, with large bulging eyes and lips sharp like a beak. Her fingernails long and twisted like claws.

"Let go," Yunior tried to choke out, but the bird . . . the thing . . . the witch held on to his neck, sucking in air through his lips. Yunior feeling weaker with every moment that passed. As she inhaled, bright red blood left Yunior's mouth and entered hers. She was killing him. Yunior struggled with all his strength, he prayed to every saint he knew the name of, but he knew he was dying. Somehow, even when his throat felt like it was moments from collapsing, Yunior screamed as loud as he could. He let out all the fear, the anger of failing to save his sister and becoming a victim instead, of losing his father, the sadness of leaving his mother alone, in that one scream.

But la bruja did not falter. She kept going. Taking, taking, taking Yunior's life as Dichoso barked helplessly, even snapping and biting at la bruja to no avail. Just when his final ounce of strength was leaving his body, la bruja's eyes went wide and she cawed, letting go of Yunior and holding her side. She turned and hissed at someone in the dark. Purple, putrid-smelling blood streamed from her wound as Bate threw Yunior's knife far from them.

"Let's go," Bate said, and the three of them ran out of la bruja's cave and into the night.

Yunior coughed as they ran; there was something wet and sticky on his face, something coming from his eyes. When he brought one hand up to his cheek and held it up to the light of the moon, he saw it was blood . . . Yunior only knew one thing: He could not run for much longer. He continued to cough, and they entered a small clearing in the woods.

"We will camp here," Bate said. "You are too weak to make it home from the backward place. You need rest."

Yunior only nodded and practically collapsed on the ground beside Dichoso. Bate got to work, getting firewood, and setting up camp. Yunior felt guilty he was not assisting the older man, so he got up to help him with dinner, grabbing a ladle from the ground. But Bate dismissed his attempts and took the utensil from his hands.

"No, no, no. Rest or you will find out why they call me Bate. Here drink, drink."

Bate handed Yunior a metal flask, and when he opened it and drank, it was not water, but morir soñando. It was ice cold and delicious, its sweet orange-and-milk flavor was Yunior's favorite. The familiar drink calmed the fast beating of his heart just a bit. As it did, Yunior felt heavy, in his limbs, his head, but especially his neck. He felt the place below his chin where la bruja's hands had touched and wondered if she had cursed him. If he would die despite escaping. The longer he laid down, the heavier his body felt, but sleep still would not come. He was too afraid. His chest was tight and hurting, like it was after his father left and Aury went missing. He was breathing in short, shallow gasps, and a sizzling sound like meat on a pan rang in his ears, but it was not Bate who was busy shining another pot. He realized then that the necklace from el brujo's hut was smoking.

It was Yunior who was burning. The necklace was boring a hole in his shirt, pushing against his chest so hard it felt more like a boulder than a gem.

Yunior yanked at the necklace, tried to pull the rough string off and around his head, but he couldn't manage. He was too weak; sleep was pulling him under. Despite the pain, he could not seem to keep his eyes open now.

"Bate, can you help me get this off?" Yunior said.

Bate was on the other side of the clearing, gathering more wood. Yunior struggled to stay awake, terrified that if he fell asleep with the necklace on, it would kill him while he dreamed.

Morir soñando—he remembered the name of the drink he'd had before and panic took hold of him again. It was irrational, not an omen like his mother or her church friends would say. It was nothing. But the pain persisted. Finally, Bate made his way back to the center of the clearing and started a fire.

"Bate," Yunior pleaded, "help me."

Dichoso wined and nuzzled Yunior, but Bate did not even look in his direction. This was another nightmare. It had to be. Or perhaps the necklace was cursed, because no matter how hard Yunior tried he could not take it off.

Bate began shining another pot. He worked so quickly, it looked like the world had picked up speed.

"Help me," Yunior said, but Bate only smiled his rotten smile.

He put the pot atop the flames.

"Para un caldito," Bate said as he opened his bag of tools and poured them into the pot. But they weren't tools at all.

They were bones.

Bate threw the bag aside, and in it, through his waning vision, Yunior could see a yellow feather trimmed hat and . . . a blue ribbon. Aury's ribbon. Yunior's eyes opened wide and he tried to scream, to run, but he could only manage to whistle once, at Dichoso, sending the dog darting into the woods, before his eyes closed.

The last thing he felt was Bate's cold hands on his neck and the edge of the blade biting into his skin. He knew then why Bate said it would be no use to go into the woods. Aury had always been dead, her bones used for soup. Just like Yunior's would be now.

Bate's laugh echoed on the other side of the mountains, as he had dinner for a second time that night.

La Madrina

Yamile Saied Méndez

The light flickered through the trees that lined the road as his car sped by. Calling me. Tempting me with its brightness, its warmth.

The right side of my face throbbed, echoing the rhythm of the revving engine. I felt my front tooth with my tongue, where he had connected the punch. It wiggled in its socket. But the worst hurt was invisible. It had started like a cavity in my heart. Instead of growing with sweetness, the rot became larger with every insult, with every scathing look. The punch opened a gaping hole in the middle of my soul. I knew nothing could ever fix it. Nothing could ever fix me.

I was done with life. Done. Heaven wouldn't want me, all ruined like this in body and soul, and I was tired of hell.

But death?

Death took all, young and old, poor and rich, happy and desolate like me, a girl desperate enough to jump from a moving car and follow la luz mala.

The wind moaned for me.

The sound of screeching wheels as the car skidded to a stop grated on my ears. The smack of my head against a rock muted the world for a few seconds. But I had no time to waste. I dragged my body toward the safety of shadows. The mossy bushes that grew only here, the Bend of Death, shielded me from his eyes.

"Suit yourself, Rocío!" he yelled. "You're nothing! Nothing!"

If he got out of the car, if he got ahold of me again, if he took me back and told the boss I'd embarrassed that big judge from the capital, I'd end up in a ditch anyway. I'd save him the trouble, and me the pain.

Quiet like a spider. Still like a rock. I waited and waited.

Finally, he left me to the frantic voices of the night. The stars pulsed furiously. The heart of the sky, the moon, wasn't there to make them shush.

"Run! Rocío, run!" they said. "Follow the light!" they urged.

I looked around the cursed road. I'd never traveled it on foot before. Crosses and shrines marked the parting spot of souls who had ended tragically in car accidents. Photos of whole families, little children, elegant people in fancy dresses, groups of friends laughing at parties witnessed my plight.

The news often blamed the fog, sleepiness, a crossing animal for the accidents. No matter the cause, the road took so many lives every year. Which way had their souls gone? There was no one to guide me, but the road sparkled with glass. I followed the crushed constellations until I reached the woods where a feeble yellow light like the glow of fireflies winked at me.

I couldn't resist its pull.

All my life I'd been warned about not following la luz mala into the woods. I always heeded that warning.

Why, then, had I ignored my mother's other advice? How

many times had she told me to steer away from men with hon-eyed lips and blazing eyes?

Too many to count. I hadn't believed her and now I had no one to blame for my ruin but myself. I should've known he was lying when he said I was pretty and talented. He'd seen me dancing with my friends on a night I was trying to for-get my mom was gone too soon, before I was ready to be on my own. My mom had said most men didn't think girls with skin dark as cinnamon, girls like me, are pretty, but his silken words wrapped around me fast and tight. Before I noticed, I was bound.

I stumbled toward the witch light. Somewhere in the bram-bles, I lost one of my shoes. Thorns tore through my soles. Blood seeped through my nylons. The earth drank it thirstily, like a payment for a grace. I wanted to lie down, close my eyes, and never wake up. But every time I was tempted to give up, the light flickered again, luring me in. The old me had died on the pavement. I had nothing else to lose.

Until . . . Hidden behind eucalyptus trees stood the shack. A single light shone from a naked bulb at the door. Large purple-and-gold moths danced around it. One noticed me and headed my way. I tried to shoo it away, but soon the others followed. They swarmed around me, their velvety wings pushing me for-ward. I was too tired to fight them.

Instead, I knocked on the door.

One. Two. Three times.

"Please open," I rasped.

"I'm coming," a woman said.

As soon as my wish was about to be granted, it soured in my stomach. I turned to run. I knew men weren't the only threat for a girl like me, alone and broken. But the moths barred my way, and the trees swayed their branches to hide the path back to the road. There was nowhere to escape. I was at the end of the world.

The door opened, and a lady of eternal beauty peered at me. The light behind her haloed her face, which was round and youthful. Her skin the same shade as mine. With a jolt, I realized I'd seen her before in her billowing black dress. A nocturnal butterfly. She smiled with tight lips as if she'd been waiting for me. Behind her I glimpsed a tidy kitchen and a large pot on the stove. The scent of puchero awoke my stomach, and it grumbled with hunger. A hunger for something other than food.

"Help me, please," I said.

I reached out to her, and she took me in her arms as if I were a baby. I burrowed my head in her long, unbound hair. It smelled of grass and homemade bread. My mother used to make the best bread in our barrio, and I was so proud of how she fed everyone.

"Shhh, you're safe, Rocío," the woman murmured, her voice like the summer breeze that heals the zonda wind wounds. "You're home, my child."

We crossed the kitchen, and I headed to a door tucked in a corner. Something in there pulled at me.

But the woman led me away from it, to another room and a bed covered with lamb's wool. She spooned honeyed tea into my mouth, the taste of yerba mate enhanced by jasmine and rose. She cleaned my skin. She washed me, and with her touch, she soothed the bruises and cuts the road and the men had inflicted on me.

The birds woke me. I was newly born.

"You're back," my savior said. A sunbeam that pierced through the window fell on her as she folded sheets and blankets beside me. "Rest, so you can heal. Then you may return to your life."

Her words floated to me like a lifesaver. I grabbed it with both hands.

"I don't want to go back."

Not to that life anyway.

"But it's not your time yet," the woman said.

"Please, señora. Let me stay. I'll earn my keep."

She nodded once. "We'll see. But don't call me señora. There is only one, the mother of us all."

"What should I call you then?"

"Call me Madrina," she said, patting my head. "All my favorites do." I never had a godmother before, but she left the room before I could tell her.

For a time I couldn't measure, I lingered in the land between sleep and consciousness. The next time I woke, Madrina was checking my bandages. She smiled, evidently satisfied with the progress of my recovery, but all I felt was dread. I couldn't remember being tended to with such care before my mother was lost, and I didn't want it to end.

"I know the warmth of the bed is irresistible," she murmured like the doves that nested outside the window. "But your body is young and strong. Go take a walk in my garden. Fresh air will be good for you."

At first, I was reluctant to leave the sanctuary of the humble room. It was sparse, but in it I felt safe. Madrina seemed to sense my fear and said, "Just for a little while, so your legs can remember what it's like to walk on the world. Then you can return."

Reassured, I followed her outside. The bright sunlight blinded me, but it wasn't harsh, and I opened my eyes. It warmed my skin while birdsong cheered me on. Soon, the blood in my veins rushed like a river of life.

"Stay here while I work," Madrina said, guiding me to a stone bench covered in moss.

All the words I wanted to say crowded on my tongue, but I couldn't string them to express my gratitude. No one did anything for free. Hadn't my mom warned me of that, too?

"How can I ever repay you?" I asked, gazing up at her serene face.

She watched me curiously, as if trying to solve a puzzle.

"I can work," I said, wanting to please her. "Honest work, I promise."

"Good, that's good," she replied before returning to the shack.

I walked around lavender, chamomile, and rue, old friends I remembered from childhood visits to my abuela's house. The other garden plants, I'd never seen before, not even when I was free to run in the sierras with my cousins. The scent of their leaves refreshed me, filled me with a buzzing energy I hadn't felt in years.

True to my promise, I got to work. I swept the trails, careful not to stray from the shack and Madrina's protection. I drew water from the well, my arms straining with the effort. I wiped the stone table, filled the birdbaths and the hummingbird feeders, and once the water was spent, I weeded the flower beds. The rosebushes tried to bar my path with their prickly thorns, but I carefully moved their branches out of my way. The sunshine played over my skin, and a splashing sound from the nearby mountain river made me smile.

When whispering voices broke the rhythm of the birdsong, I looked up and realized that little by little, I had inched closer to the kitchen window.

At first, I didn't understand the words, but I recognized the emotions. I knew what fear and desperation felt like. Hearing them in the anonymous voice made me cower and tremble, the wounds in my soul throbbing in echo.

But then Madrina broke the tense silence. "Shhh, it's only but a moment. A step and it's over, my child."

The whimper and the gasp that followed took my breath away. I braced myself for violence, but the voice said, "Gracias, gracias."

The released agony in the words of gratitude surprised me. And made me curious.

Who was Madrina speaking to? What was happening in the shack?

I peered through the window. A line of people of all ages, dressed in rags, silk and leather fineries, and everything in between, waited for Madrina. Impassive, she directed a young man in a rumpled business suit to a door of what I assumed was another room in the cottage. He seemed confused, looking around as if for a sign. "Just through there?" he asked.

Madrina nodded and the young man walked ahead.

When he opened the door, the darkness inside the room pulsed hungrily. He shuffled back like a cockroach, suddenly panicked. I wanted to tell him to run, but in a blink the door had closed, swallowing him whole.

A woman crowned in silver hair was next. She was wrapped in a colorful poncho, and she met Madrina with her chin lifted, fearlessly. Madrina kissed the woman's cheek and pointed to the door that had swallowed the man. I narrowed my eyes to catch every detail. The old woman crossed the threshold resolutely into a soft yellow light like the one that had led me to the cottage. I felt the pull of it still, but I rooted my feet in the soft dirt of the garden.

Confused, I touched my head where I'd hit it after I fell from the car last night.

Last night?

How long had I slept? My mind swirled in scraps of memory of the rooster singing, the kettle whistling, and Madrina's smiling at me as she sat at the foot of my bed.

There wasn't a bump anymore. I lifted the cotton skirt I wore to look at the cuts and scrapes on legs. They were faint and silvery, almost healed.

"Next," Madrina said inside the shack, startling me.

But she was talking to a boy, who stood at the front of the line, dressed in faded jeans and a sky-blue-and-white fútbol jersey. Instead of obeying her signal for him to head to a little door in the kitchen, he cried and begged, hugging her knees. "Don't send me back, señora, please!"

I clutched my hands at the sound of his voice. Hadn't I cried out the same way and she had let me stay?

Madrina smiled at the boy. Even from the distance I saw her eyes twinkle with unshed tears as she placed a hand over his head. Tenderly, she lifted him to his feet and, instead of leading him to the room, brought him to the front door. The scent of lemon bread now wafted from the kitchen window.

The boy nodded, resigned, and before he left, he hugged her tightly, with a furious frenzy. She urged him on with a gentle pat to his shoulder. The sound of a cheering crowd welcomed him. He looked over his shoulder at Madrina and this time, he was smiling.

On and on the line advanced. Madrina either pointed her guests back to the front door or to that other room. Sometimes, horrible sounds of torture and endless darkness came from the open door, and others, it was that yellow light. Some people resisted to cross into the room, even when the light was beautiful and peaceful, but eventually, all went where she commanded. No one stayed in the cottage.

She denied all those who asked, even when they sounded terrified.

I was so lucky she'd let me stay!

I watched the procession, until the sun went to sleep, and a hand on my shoulder made me jump in surprise.

"I thought you were earning your keep." Madrina glanced at the broom that leaned against the wall, useless.

"I'm sorry, Madrina," I said. "I heard voices, and I grew curious."

Her scowl softened. "That's good. Curiosity means life. But beware! It can be dangerous, too."

The boss had called me curious once. I'd wandered into the library at his house. And he'd been right, I was curious, but not for the things he wanted to teach. He'd lured me with promises of comfort, but in the life he gave me, I only found hunger and cold and a wish to turn back time and do everything over again.

But Madrina was different.

This was the first time my curiosity had led me to a refuge. I hadn't lived in a real home in so long. But I wasn't a lucky girl. I couldn't count on this happening again.

"I can help you," I said, desperate to stay with her. "I'll be your assistant."

"An assistant?" She rubbed her chin with her thumb. "I haven't had one for a while. I could try again, I guess. I'm old, and I work too hard."

She didn't look old, and I didn't know what her work was, or what an assistant would do, but I promised, "If you tell me what you need, I'll do it gladly."

Her dark gaze studied me for a second, and when she smiled, I knew I had passed a test. She pointed inside. The visitors waited quietly.

"Lead them where I tell them to go. Don't question, and never disobey."

I'd never disobey.

Time was liquid when we worked. The rooster crowed, and the crickets chirped. Light and shadow chased each other out the window. One time, the door of the forbidden room remained open for a few seconds. A breeze from the other side had pushed against it before the door finally slammed with a definite clap. But I still saw the snow in the meadow, although the cicadas' song made the kitchen windows vibrate. The next time the door opened for an old man in soldier's uniform, gray ocean waves and a cawing seagull flashed where the meadow once was.

I looked at Madrina for an explanation, and she shook her head slowly but firmly. I didn't ask any more questions, not even with my eyes. Sometimes the urge to peek into the doors was unbearable, but Madrina always was there, observing my every move. There was no need for her to be vigilant. I ignored my curiosity and poured myself into the work.

I helped prepare food and mate; I swept the floors. I made beds for guests that never stayed but I never questioned my madrina.

Madrina hardly ever spoke except for an occasional "It's time, my dear" or "Not yet."

I directed women, men, and children where she pointed. Some people recognized her with happiness. Others grudgingly said hello. The babies, she held tenderly, singing lullabies into their ears as she crossed the threshold into the light with them. She never returned empty-handed. Sometimes she brought back a flower. Once she held a feather and twirled it in her fingers before tucking it in her hair. One day, a line of girls covered in bruises cowered at the front door. Madrina received them with open arms. One of them ran to her and clutched her neck in a desperate embrace. When the girl walked toward the door, she saw me as I worked in the kitchen, and I recognized her bright green eyes. Guadalupe had worked with the boss, too. She was gone before I waved goodbye.

But her image remained with me for days. I wondered where Guadalupe was now. If she was safe after walking through that threshold. If she was finally happy. And the boy? He'd returned to a cheerful welcome. What had become of him once the welcome lost its luster?

One day, we had no visitors, and I was relieved. The work had made me strong, but it was also taking its toll on me. Now I cried when I saw girls like Guadalupe, and when I couldn't stop the tears, Madrina allowed me to step outside, in the garden so the sunshine and the herbs could fortify me. But she never took a break.

"Maybe today you can sit outside, Madrina," I said.

Madrina watched me and I held her gaze. "Maybe I will," she finally said. "I have missed my garden."

She stepped out back where her voice joined those of the birds worshipping the rising sun. I kept working in the kitchen, straightening plates and vases, dusting shelves and the table. The door to the forbidden room was barely ajar. I hadn't meant to, but the pull to see was too strong, and I peered inside.

At first it looked like a regular room like the one in which I slept, but without windows; the walls emanated an eerie light. There was no way out for the constant stream of people coming in.

Madrina appeared by my side.

"Where do they go?" I asked. I gripped the broom's handle to keep myself standing.

"To the beyond."

"And the others? The ones who walk out the front door?"

"Back home, some who get lost decide to return for a second chance. But eventually all my little ones cross the threshold into this room."

"Little ones? All the children?"

Madrina cupped my face with her hand like I was precious, one of the flowers from the garden that she doted on. She smiled at me with such tenderness that I had to avert my eyes. I wasn't used to this affection without a payment in return.

"You're all my little ones. Even your mother was a girl like you once."

"My mom? She passed through here, too?"

If my mother hadn't disappeared, my life wouldn't have ended up with a decision to jump from a racing car, crumbled to pieces by a roadside shrine. If my mom hadn't followed la luz mala, who knew what my life would have been like?

"How do you decide who goes back? What gives you the right?" My heart drummed in my chest. She had so much power, but she hadn't returned my mom.

"Oh, my love." Madrina didn't seem taken aback by my anger. "They started down their road with the first decision they made in this life. I just show them another door to continue. Sometimes that path doesn't end in my cottage. Sometimes I offer a refuge before they can go on."

Like me. She'd given me a refuge, but I didn't want to go on. Go where? There was no one waiting for me outside.

"And the others?" I pointed inside the empty room. "What happens to them?"

"They die," she said simply. "I only lead their souls ahead."

"Why do you do this?" I asked.

She laughed. "Someone has to! Death is a labor of love. A mother receives you into the world. A godmother ushers you out."

A knock on the door stopped my protests. Her words left me dizzy.

Madrina walked to the door herself, and she received a man in the prime of his life.

"It's time," she said.

He closed his eyes and sighed, as if relieved.

I clasped my hands over my mouth, and Madrina gave me a warning glance.

I went to the garden and sat there watching the butterflies and hummingbirds carry dust of life from bud to bud. After a while, Madrina walked out and joined me. She placed a warm hand on mine. When I finally looked at her, she smiled. She didn't judge me. She wouldn't punish the impertinence of my questions. Instead she offered me a ripe black fig. I bit into it hard, and the sweetness flooded my mouth.

She let me spend my days in the garden, and even though I worked hard, I soon got restless. Although I ate the puchero in my bowl, I was hungry. Although lamb's wool covered my shoulders, I was cold.

One morning I was in the kitchen making tea when some-one knocked on the door. Like usual, Madrina opened it herself.

"It's time," she whispered.

I turned around to see a middle-aged woman in my god-mother's arms. She had dark vivacious eyes. A curl escaped the white headband wrapping around her head, and when she walked in, she had a spring in her step.

"My life is good, Madrina. Is it really my time?"

Madrina nodded as she led the newcomer in, holding her by the elbow.

When they reached the kitchen, there was another knock at the door.

Sometimes this happened. I waited for Madrina's command to come and help.

"My assistant will show you the way," she said to the woman, glancing at me. I nodded, but inside, every part of me rebelled. I didn't want to lead someone unwilling to part.

Madrina didn't see my hesitation. She was receiving a large group of children. They crowded around her, hugging her legs.

She sang her calming lullaby, and they all joined her, matching the pitch of her voice. How did they know the words?

The woman with the vivacious eyes shifted in place, looking at the children with compassion and despair.

"Are you ready?" I asked.

The woman's legs buckled and she fell to the floor. "I can't leave them."

"Them?" I asked, crouching next to her to hear her whispers.

"My children. I love them." She clasped my hands. "Help me. Show me how! You have to know a way back."

I knew the way back. It was through the front door. Madrina said that people made the choice, and this woman wanted to rejoin life. Why didn't she let her? Why hadn't she sent the woman the way she'd come?

Madrina hadn't, but I could.

"Never disobey," Madrina had said, and the words still echoed in my mind.

The woman was crying now, her fate in my hands, and Madrina was busy with the little ones. They were hungry, and she never sent anyone ahead on an empty stomach.

"Please," the woman said again.

Without another thought, I took her calloused hand and helped her to her feet.

"Shhh, I'll show you the way," I said, leading her back to the front door.

"I'm scared," she said, running next to me.

"Hurry," I coaxed her. "Go back to them. They need you."

She didn't hesitate. She ran and I stayed outside the cottage.

When I was lost and broken, Madrina had fed me and

protected me. She'd trusted me, and I had failed her. But I didn't regret showing the woman the way back to her children.

The sun bathed me with its newborn rays, but it couldn't warm me. For the first time since I'd found the cottage, I didn't want to go back inside. I crossed my arms to stop the shivers that shook my body. I had disobeyed.

"Death was her reward for a life well-lived," Madrina said, standing next to me.

"She was good." I turned away from her, balling my hands into fists. "You never take the evil ones!"

Madrina's hand seized my arm. Her skin was still wrinkled and spotted with the sun, but it didn't look fragile as she gripped me.

I turned to her with awe. Nothing had changed in her appearance, but she exuded power and authority as the world around us seemed to vanish. Her cold, firm voice proclaimed, "You've seen my kind and healing side, but you've also seen the hungry darkness, and not only in that little room. Haven't you, Rocío? The evil ones follow la luz mala, too, and they end in that bottomless nothingness, alone with their thoughts. They follow to snatch, and I snatch them instead."

"Are you angry at me?" I asked. I could hear the anguish of the young girl I'd once been in my voice. But I knew I was much more than that now.

La Madrina held me tenderly. "Never, my child."

The stars and Madrina listened to my cries without reproach. With my tears I finally purged all the bitterness trapped inside me like bile. I didn't want it anymore.

My sorrow spent, I took a shuddering breath. Madrina lifted my chin with her index finger, and I looked her right in the eyes. "I'll lead you on, when your time comes."

It sounded like a farewell, and although I had thought I would never be ready for this moment, I wanted to go back to that road. I wanted to retrace my steps, even if I still made mistakes.

She kissed my forehead, and I closed my eyes as she murmured a blessing. Blessed by my godmother, by Death herself, I walked away.

My bare feet remembered the way I'd marked with blood. A dog howled in the distance, and the fear that had guided my actions for years made me halt. I looked around for the way back to my protector, but the shack was gone.

"Madrina!" I called, suddenly afraid to be alone.

The sounds of the night and the thunder of a car speeding ahead were the only reply. The road glittered with glass.

Madrina's home was already a memory but also a promise.

Glass bit into my skin, my face throbbed, my tooth wiggled in its socket, but I walked toward life, away from that car.

The stars sang for me.

Sugary Deaths

Lilliam Rivera

T he creases on Pinky's jeans are perfect. She spent all morning making sure they were, pressing down on the iron and producing a powerful steam that fogged up the living room windows. Her mother screamed at her to stop.

"¡Muchacha!" her mom said. "Esta no es la hora para empezar con tu bobería." But Pinky ignored her and kept doing her thing.

It's now 1 p.m. Time to make an appearance.

Pinky grabs her dull eyeliner and flicks her lighter on to soften it. She blows on the pencil to cool it down before lining her eyes dark black. Her gold name plate reads PINKY, the nickname she gave herself on her sixteenth birthday last year after she decided to dedicate her summer beating PAC-MAN at the corner pizzeria. Her parents weren't happy with the decision; they never call her Pinky. In their eyes she will always be Priscila but everyone who's good at video games has a tag and she wasn't going to be any different. Besides, Priscila is too delicate a name. Pinky is a name that can seem sweet, but the real ones know she's far from it.

Content with the way she looks, Pinky puckers her lips in the mirror and says to her reflection: "Today is the day."

She finds her father sitting at the kitchen table reading the *Daily News* and muttering to himself about los políticos.

"Hi, Papi." She gives him a peck on the cheek.

"It's 1982 and Koch thinks he's going to win with the same ol' line," he says, flicking at the newspaper. Then her father leans close to whisper at her. "Think you're going to beat your score today?"

Pinky just grins.

On all of 110th Street, no one has come close to beating the top score in PAC-MAN. Not Junior who lives across the street from the park and is always begging for quarters to play. Not this quiet white boy Brian who likes to hang with the crew. No one. The top initials on the game is PKY and that's her. It's the beginning of summer, school is out, and everyone is waiting for her to enter Delmonico's Pizza and continue her PAC-MAN supremacy.

"Stop encouraging her to spend money on esas máquinas," her mother says from the living room. "Our family didn't move here from Barceloneta para gastar dinero on robots."

It's been ten years since they left La Ciudad Industrial for another city of industry with colder temps. An uncle sent for them to come live in the building he was managing, to take over his responsibilities so he could go work at a new apartment complex en el barrio. Pinky had hated leaving her family behind, her cousins and abuelos, her beach, but she'd gained new friends and arcade games and cool clothes that she packs up and mails to her cousins back on the island when she outgrows them.

"It's not the robots, Ma," Pinky says. "It's ghosts, and I'm the best."

"We have better things to be fighting for." Her mother enters the kitchen with a load of laundry ready to be folded. Pinky looks so much like her that her family says they are gemelas. They have matching hairstyles, feathered bangs framing their olive skin with their long black hair flowing straight. Hairspray spritzed every morning to tame the flyaways. The two also display the same scorn whenever they are angry, thin eyebrows scrunched together and rose-tinged lips pressed tightly.

They mirror each other until her mother lets out a slow sigh. She hands Pinky a twenty-dollar bill.

"Bring me back quarters for the laundry," she says. "Do you hear me?"

Pinky smiles and gives her mother a kiss before rushing out. This means she can keep a roll of quarters for herself. Money for PAC-MAN and Blow Pops. It's all Pinky ever wants. A summer beating her score and sucking on sugary lollipops.

In front of the building, Pinky helps Doña Irma with her groceries until her neighbor's settled in the elevator. Then she walks farther down the unusually long driveway-like entrance. Pinky pauses and looks up at the stone gargoyles guarding the building, just ten feet above her. When they first moved in, everything about New York frightened Pinky but not the gargoyles. The stone statues reminded her of the ones sprinkled across Barceloneta, from the entrance to the Cementerio Municipal Viejo to her family's home. When she saw the stone beasts, she knew the city would not devour her. She would be safe.

The monstrous gargoyles each feature a different aspect of human life: One is cooking, another is eating from a bowl, another is stirring a pot, another appears to be telling a story, another is laughing.

"Today I'm beating my score," Pinky says in their direction.

A minute goes by and she continues to stare. Eventually, Pinky tilts her head and frowns as if she heard something she didn't like.

She crosses the street to the pizzeria.

"Ms. Pinky, what can I get you?" Mr. Delmonico, the owner of the pizzeria, asks.

"A large soda and a Blow Pop," Pinky says, handing him the crisp bill. "And quarters, please."

The video game machine is located at the far side of the pizzeria, away from the tables. There are already a handful of people crowded around it. Pinky recognizes baby Joseito from down the block. Joseito doesn't play, he just likes to watch.

"Yo, Pinky!" He runs up to her. "He just knocked your score out."

It's been exactly four months since Pinky has held the top score. Pinky slowly unwraps the cherry-flavored lollipop, and sticks the sucker into her mouth. Cool as always, she saunters over to the game to see for herself.

Gripping the joystick is a young man in a really tight shirt with hair shaved close to the sides and a braided rat tail nestling between his shoulder blades. The man presses loudly into the machine, entering his initials: BLZ.

"This is Pinky. She's the best," Joseito says, eager to introduce them.

"Not anymore."

The young man turns to Pinky and his hazel eyes do a slow

crawl from her pristine white Reeboks to the lollipop she's sucking.

"Who the hell are you?" Pinky says while glancing over to his score. She takes a step closer to him. He's only a few inches taller than her, dressed in a striped Polo shirt and cuffed blue jeans. Although he barely has a mustache, the man reminds Pinky of the singer Willie Colón in the old album her father loves to play on repeat, *El Malo*. His bushy eyebrows and brooding expression make it so you can't quite place whether he's Italian or Puerto Rican.

"I'm Blaze and I just beat your score," he says, then licks his full lips. "It's okay. I'll let you play next." He steps aside with a flourish of his hand as if he's presenting the game to her.

Pinky's never been afraid of anyone. This is *her* adopted neighborhood. Delmonico's Pizza has fed her more meals than anything, second only to her mom's Puerto Rican cooking. This newcomer isn't bringing anything to the game that she hasn't seen before, just a whole lot of bravado she ain't buying. Who cares if he's way older than her? She's got nothing to prove to him or any man.

"I play when I say I want to play," she says, making a loud smacking sound with her Blow Pop. He laughs, a kind of snicker that slowly rolls out to a deep chuckle. It dawns on her in that instance: She's heard this laugh before. His family moved into her building last week. Unlike her parents who live in a small apartment because her father works as the superintendent, Blaze's family occupies one of the largest in the building. Three bedrooms, a large living room, dining room, the works. It's only him and his parents. Pinky knows all this because her mother likes to share the current bochinche whenever she gets on the phone to speak to her sisters back on the island. Who moved in. Who is behind in rent. Who is sneaking around without their husband knowing.

"They have a twenty-three-year-old. I don't think he works. The father is a businessman," Pinky's mom said. "Gente con dinero, como siempre."

Pinky takes the lollipop out and says, "Blaze. How original."

He smiles and edges in closer, lifts her gold name plate, and mouths her name. Pinky can tell the type of guy he is: un ratón.

"You sure you don't want to play with me," Blaze says, the base of his voice dropping like a late-night radio DJ.

"Naw, I don't play with amateurs."

The restaurant's doorbell rings, and a trio of girls enters. Lourdes with her two friends, Mari and Smiley. They immediately join everyone by the machine. Blaze is quick in changing his focus to them.

"Blaze just beat Pinky's score! He was down to only one life and barely made it. Them ghosts were about to take him but he faked a turn, and . . ." Joseito gives the girls the play-by-play like he's Howard Cosell.

"Blaze," Lourdes repeats his name as if she's out of breath. Lourdes and her crew are sixteen like Pinky.

"Your slice," Delmonico calls out and Blaze saunters over to the counter. Lourdes and the other girls stare with heart eyes. Pinky shakes her head. How did they fall for Blaze so quickly? His rat tail doesn't make him unique. Besides, he's old.

Blaze sits in a booth besides Joseito. The trio of girls order slices and station themselves at a booth next to Blaze. Pinky stands in between, not joining either one, only observing.

"This is good, but we got it better in Chicago," Blaze says.

"You're from Chicago?" Lourdes asks. She has really long eyelashes. Her favorite color, green, is displayed in her eyeshadow. "I've never been to Chicago."

"You would like it. I would show you around all the spots. Take you to better restaurants than this one." Even Joseito looks ready to be escorted around by this guy. Pinky doesn't like it one bit.

"New York has the best pizza and if you don't know that, you don't know nothing," Pinky says, slamming her fist on the table and causing everyone to jump.

"You don't deserve the Delmonico special." She grabs Blaze's slice from off his paper plate and throws it in the garbage. Everyone shake their heads at her outburst, but not Blaze. He just laughs.

"I don't like girls who don't know their place." He stands and sits beside Lourdes who grins as if she won a prize.

"Tell me more about Chicago," Lourdes says, leaning in to him. Pinky's arms stay firmly across her chest.

"I'll check you guys later," Blaze eventually says.

As soon as he leaves, Pinky's friends can't stop talking about Blaze, especially Lourdes. "Did you see his beautiful eyes?"

"He ain't nothing but a vulture," Pinky scoffs.

"Pinky, you just hate him because he beat your score," Lourdes says.

It wasn't that long ago when all the girls would play video games against one another. Back then Lourdes and Pinky were tight, inseparable, roaming all over the neighborhood in their matching Lee jeans. Now Lourdes only talks about boys and making out. She likes the attention when men "mira, mami" her. Pinky curses them out each time. Video games are for kids, Lourdes said to her the other day, but now that Blaze has appeared she's changing her mind,

Pinky walks back to the game and feeds a quarter into the machine. She makes silly mistakes. It's hard to concentrate when Lourdes goes on and on about how cute Blaze is. Pinky doesn't beat Blaze's score and she soon gives up.

Two weeks later, everyone is in love with Blaze. What's not to love when Blaze appears always willing to spend money on the 110th Street crew? Food, alcohol, an unlimited supply of quarters. And when Blaze gets bored playing PAC-MAN, he eventually ushers the group to his empty apartment.

"I heard them last night," Pinky's father says. "A party that lasted till two a.m. The neighbors are not happy. I'm going to have to say something."

Pinky sits nestled in between her mother's legs as her mother does her hair in a tight French braid. It's a scorcher outside, and Pinky wears cut off denim shorts and a tank top.

"There's always a parade of young girls going in and out of that apartment," her mother says. "I don't like the way he talks, con una falta de respeto."

Her mother lets Pinky's braid fall to her back and caresses her shoulder to tell her she's done.

"I saw your friend Lourdes with him in front of the building," her mother says. "You should talk to her. Warn her. She shouldn't be hanging out with him."

Her mother turns Pinky to face her. She presses down on Pink's baby hairs and looks deeply into her eyes.

"I will," Pinky promises.

"Good. Lourdes's family took care of us when we first moved here, making sure I knew where to shop, what school to enroll you in," her mother says. "We have to protect our own."

Pinky wants to shield her friends from harm, but how can she if they won't listen? They're all being lured by Blaze's money and his fake charm. They don't see him the way Pinky and her family do.

"How many times have extranjeros shown up thinking they can do whatever they want to us?" Pinky's mother reminds her. "When I was your age, I took care of all my young cousins. No man dared to even try it, and if they did, they suffered the consequences. Now it's your turn to do the same for your friends. ¿Me entiendes?"

"Yes, Mom," she says. "I understand." Pinky knows exactly what she must do.

As the summer days go by, Pinky takes note of the way Blaze changes up who he hangs out with. It's always a new girl every time, always someone about her age. He's never seen with guys his age like the ones always heading to the block parties. The ones who are courteous to Pinky, joking with her about video games. Blaze is only ever with teenagers.

As she walks out of the building, Pinky finds Lourdes in front with tears in her eyes.

"What are you doing here?" she asks.

Lourdes angrily wipes away the wetness on her cheeks and tries to toughen up. "I'm waiting for Blaze."

"Why?" Pinky already saw him walking down the street with

a young Black girl who lives a couple blocks away. "He's not in there. He left with Tracy."

"I keep calling him, but he's not answering," Lourdes says. Her eyes still scan the streets for him. "Are the phones working?"

Pinky places her hand on Lourdes's shoulders and she starts to really sob.

"What did he do?" Pinky asks, her tone becoming angrier.

"I didn't want to do it, but he said, you know." Lourdes can't face her. Instead, she stares at her white gladiator sandals. "He said I was pretty and it's not a big deal if we did it."

"You *are* pretty, Lourdes. You don't need him to tell you that." But Lourdes is wailing. Pinky places her arm around the other girl's shoulders, lets her rest her head on her. When they were little, they used to walk around like this, shoulder to shoulder, giggling at everything and everyone. It wasn't that long ago.

"I didn't want to do it, Pinky," she says. "It hurt and now he doesn't want to speak to me like it was my fault."

"It's okay, Lourdes," Pinky says, holding her friend while the rage grows inside of her.

Blaze is PAC-MAN, gobbling up all the girls on 110th Street, using them and tossing them to the side because he can. She glances up at the stone gargoyles right above them and gives the slightest of nods. The crouched, menacing statues appear as if they are lurching forward with a grimace across their distorted monstrous faces. The grimace is almost a grin.

Pinky can smell his cologne even before she enters the pizzeria. It's a dizzying scent that can't even be masked by Delmonico's cheesy slices. The restaurant is empty save for Joseito and Blaze, who are by the machine. Joseito watches him play. Pinky nudges him out of the way.

"Hey!" Joseito says, but one look from Pinky and he knows enough to leave. "I better get home. Bye, Blaze."

"You ready to play me?" Blaze asks, not taking his eyes off the game. "Everyone says you're the best, but I haven't seen you even try."

"Naw, I don't feel like playing games," Pinky says. She caresses his hand, the one holding the joystick. "I want to do something else."

Pinky's gesture makes Blaze lose his concentration, ending his PAC-MAN life, but he doesn't seem to mind. He lets the game finish, and then he faces her. Gives his usual up and down, ogling of her body while flashing his smile. Pinky smiles back. Her lip gloss glistens.

"I don't like pushy girls," he says.

"I'm not pushy. I just know how to play," Pinky says. "But if you're not interested, well, that's on you."

She turns and exits. Across the street, the stone gargoyles on her building stand as they always have, but instead of their usual poses, one holds a handkerchief as if crying, another appears to be shouting, while another holds a spiked club.

Pinky stares at the statues and waits. She fully expects Blaze to follow her. It's only a matter of time. He's barreled through so many of her friends, including girls she doesn't even like. Each one left in shambles. The rest of the guys are aware of this, but they too seem to be seduced by his charm. "He can't be that bad if he's always buying me pizza." That's what Joseito said to her. "Those girls wanted it, didn't they?" said another. They never once think of asking why a twenty-three-year-old man only hangs out with them.

"Hey, wait up!"

Blaze joins her at the crosswalk. He places his arm around her shoulders, but she brushes his hand off and heads toward their building. In the elevator, Blaze tries to kiss her, but Pinky manages to push him away. She presses the button for the top floor.

"My apartment is on the fourth floor," he says.

"I bet you've never been to the roof. C'mon."

Blaze hesitates when the elevator door opens, but he eventually follows.

"No one is allowed up here," Pinky says as she opens the door. "But my father is the super."

"Yeah, I know that. He fixed our stuffed-up toilet the other day," he says, and stands way too close to Pinky. Her mother taught her long ago how to temper her rage, to always think before reacting. She fails sometimes, her outburst getting the best of her at times, but not today. Today, Pinky foresees each move.

Blaze twirls a strand of her hair around his finger. Pinky grins, flashes a little bit of her teeth, and takes a couple of steps away from him toward the edge of the roof.

"You ever been to Puerto Rico?" she asks. "Barceloneta is a town in Puerto Rico, on the south side of the island. Some people believe they've seen gárgolas flying in the dead of night. They say gargoyles hunt those who've caused harm on the innocent."

Blaze's eyes glaze over, obviously bored by her speech. Along the building, the stone gargoyles begin to slowly crumble, shedding their hard skin.

"On the island, we've had so many vultures taking from us and not giving back. Gobbling up everything, especially young girls," Pinky says. "But we've learned to protect our own."

Blaze walks up to Pinky again and places his arm around her waist. "You're not like the other girls," he says, nuzzling her neck.

Pinky caresses his arm. "You have no idea," she says, playfully pushing him away.

The gargoyles creep up along the building. Their talons hook on the crevices of the wall. The noises they make are masked by the city.

"Do you know why I like to play PAC-MAN?" she asks. Pinky steps farther into the dark corner of the roof. "I like it because I get to control where I want PAC-MAN to move, and I can usually anticipate a bad decision. Not everyone gets that. They go down a path that looks shiny and new, but it ends up being a dead end."

"Man, you talk too much," Blaze says.

"But I can see how things will end," she says. "Nothing shiny is ever worth it."

Blaze tugs at his belt buckle. "You gonna suck my dick or what?"

Pinky smiles, but Blaze fails to see that she, too, is transforming. Her back expands. Wings slowly protrude from in between her shoulder blades. Two horns appear along her forehead. Her nails are claws, sharp and pointy. The other gargoyles have reached the roof, but Blaze is too busy being impatient. Like her mother before her, Pinky learned to accept her role of protector, of using her rage to save those who can't save themselves, of calling on the gargoyles when needed with just a simple nod.

"You won't gobble up girls anymore," Pinky says, stepping forward in all her magnificent glory.

"What the f—"

Pinky pounces on top of him along with the other gargoyles as Blazes's words echo across the starless city sky.

Moving vans are double-parked in front of the building. A missing person's report was filed weeks ago, but no one saw or heard anything. What happened to Blaze? One minute he was there, the next, gone. Pinky steps aside as one of the movers enters. Before crossing the street, she stops to glance up at the stone gargoyles. They are back in their original spots. A cook, a joker, a storyteller.

It's early afternoon and Pinky is craving pizza. In the restaurant, she spies Lourdes sitting in a booth with her friends. They wave at Pinky, and she nods hello.

"A slice, please," Pinky says to Delmonico.

Joseito runs up to her with a Blow Pop in his hand. He hands the lollipop to Pinky.

"It's weird how Blaze stopped coming around," Joseito says. "Right?"

"Yeah, weird," Pinky says. She tucks the Blow Pop in the back of her short shorts, for later.

"You going to try to beat your score?" he asks.

"Yeah. Of course I am," Pinky says.

She inserts a shiny new quarter into the machine.

Leave No Tracks

Julia Alvarez

Hard to believe it was only yesterday when the headmistress came to our classroom door. She gestured to Ms. Halpern, our environmental studies teacher. "May I have a word with you?" A sidelong glance passed around our seminar table. One of us was in deep trouble.

We'd been discussing Rachel Carson and Bill McKibben, talking about the end of nature. You want to get really depressed? Read these prophets. I was already depressed enough, stuck in a boarding school in Massachusetts, four hours away from Mami in the Bronx, one of the few students of color.

"Guapa?" Ms. Halpern called from the door. Her voice sounded tentative, as if she had troubling news she didn't want me to know.

My father was waiting at La Guardia. He closed the glass divider in the town car. I guess he didn't want the driver to hear that Mami had died by suicide.

A hole opened in my chest. If I cried, what was left of me would pour out.

My father looked worried. "Remember to breathe," he was saying, like he was my swim-team coach.

It shouldn't have come as a total surprise. More and more my mother's midnight moods never saw sunrise. Maybe she was already making plans when she insisted that I enroll in boarding school last fall. My father had offered to pay what my swim-team scholarship didn't cover. Mami might have been getting me out of the way.

I felt guilty and angry both. Had I been living at home, I might have saved her. She always said I understood her better than anyone. Along with bad feet, I'd also inherited her dark moods. At least my heaviness lifted every time I dove into the water or went camping in the woods.

But where could Mami go for comfort and hope?

From our recent phone calls I knew my father hadn't been by in months. His wife had found out about Mami. His marriage was in trouble. He was distancing himself from us. Mami was still crazy in love with him. But I never thought she'd be crazy enough to do herself in.

"Your mother's last request was that she be taken home for burial." My father had made all the arrangements, even managing to contact my aunts. "They'll meet you at the airport in Puerto Plata."

Mami had sisters? I had aunties? Why hadn't anyone told me?

"I'm so sorry I can't go with you," my father apologized. I was ready to wither him with one of my if-looks-could-kill looks—also inherited from Mami. When was the last time he'd been there for me? But when I turned to him, what I saw was a pale middle-aged man with thinning hair, a wrinkled forehead, a drooped and surrendered spirit. I wanted to reach out and comfort him, as Mami would have done. But then I remembered, he was a big part of the reason my mother was gone.

"Your father is half of you," Mami was always reminding me. "Your artistic spirit comes from him." Supposedly, my father had dreamed of becoming a professional musician, just like I had dreamed of being a dancer. "You've only known him *after*, Guapita," she added. She told me a little of their story. My father had gone down to the Dominican Republic on some environmental music project, which involved taping birdsong. Wandering in the forest, he had caught sight of Mami. "My beautiful woodland nymph," he called her. He'd fallen madly in love with her. When he had to return to the States, Mami begged to come back with him. She was already pregnant with me.

What she didn't know was that her lover would cave to family pressure. Give up his music, his activism, go to law school, marry a classmate from a fine old family, join his father's firm. He couldn't or wouldn't get free.

Especially after I was born, we lived a life of secrecy, Mami and me. No going out openly as a family. No calling him for advice or texting him some cool news. He was good to us in many ways. We didn't lack for anything. Except him.

"Will you be okay by yourself? I can send Melanie with you," my father offered. Melanie was his executive assistant, whom Mami and I were supposed to call whenever we needed anything. Melanie was nice, but she was not a parent.

"I'm good," I said through my teeth.

"You sure?" my father asked as if he wasn't so sure.

This time I didn't lie with words, I just nodded.

Melanie would be by early tomorrow to take me to JFK. She would have all my paperwork, my tickets, anything else I might need.

My father handed me a padded envelope. "Your mother left this for you."

I recognized her handwriting. *For Guapita, from your mami.* I hugged that envelope to my chest as if it were my mother.

He pulled out his cell. "I just texted you so you have my personal number. Call me when you're ready to come back." As for school, he'd already spoken with the headmistress and my swim-team coach. "They all said you take as much time as you need."

He cleared his throat. "Believe me, Guppy" (his nickname for me I hadn't heard since I was a little kid. I used to love it, but now it was painful, recalling a simpler, happier time). "I didn't want it to end like this. I'm going to be making some changes." His voice had grown all gravelly. He glanced at the driver on the other side of the soundproof glass. "I hope to be there for you in the future."

I couldn't let myself believe in his promises. Both Mami and I had been disappointed before. Still, when he turned to me with tears in his eyes, I couldn't hold back any longer. Finally, we had something to share: we sat there and cried together.

The next morning, I pack light, just a carry-on—rejecting the whole idea that anything will make me feel better. I leave behind my favorite hoodie, my purple leggings, the asabache Mami used to pin on my diaper, which I always wear at meets for good luck—the good part of my luck has obviously run out.

I haven't yet opened Mami's envelope—I feel too alone to risk falling apart. Humpty Dumpty Guapa: Who would put me together again?

"There you go, Mami," I tuck the envelope in my backpack, as if it's a little kid I'm buckling into her car seat.

Melanie is waiting downstairs in the town car. At the airport, she has a pass so she can walk me to my gate. The flight attendant escorts me on board. She can't do enough for me. "Is there anything I can get for you, sweetie?" she keeps asking. I swear, the woman would buckle *me* into my seat if I let her.

And so at long last, I'm going home, or rather the home I would have felt at home in if Mami had ever taken me. Now it's me, taking her back, except she's riding in cargo, and I'm sobbing in coach, more alone than ever.

My ankles hurt like hell. But I can't blame it on grief or cabin pressure. I've had trouble with them all my life. Mami did, too. Something in our genes. It's why I needed an operation when I was a baby. Why I wore braces for a long while.

Of course, we all long for what we can't have. Growing up, I wanted to be a dancer. Mami enrolled me in a class, but my feet couldn't take it. The teacher came up with a solution: Had I ever considered water ballet? Less pressure on my ankles.

First time I waded in, I was in my element. I got recruited by a team. There was talk of the Olympics. I felt bad missing all that practice, letting down the team, but Coach had said not to worry, to take all the time I needed. Like forever? What was the point now?

Whenever my feet hurt, I wonder if this is what old-time convicts used to feel with a ball and chain at their ankles. What's weird is that the longer we're up here and the closer we get to our destination, they actually start feeling better. Like maybe the island is already unlocking some invisible manacles, and I will finally be released.

The woman sitting next to me on the plane has been praying the rosary nonstop.

"¿Y qué te pasa, mi'ja?" She must have seen me massaging my calves.

My Spanish is so Spanglished I'm embarrassed to speak to a native speaker. So I don't even try to explain that it's just something I was born with.

"¿Tú eres dominicana?" the woman asks tentatively.

I nod. "De cerca de Río San Juan." That's where Mami said her relatives were from the few times she spoke about them. Some rift had happened, which she never would talk about. Growing up it was hard to claim being from anyplace. Every time someone asked my nationality, I felt like saying, *I'm Rootless from the Land of Not Belonging.*

My seatmate cocks her head, checking me out: amber-color skin, jet-black hair, and eyes—I look Dominican, but I sure talk like a gringa. Off she goes in a fast-paced rattle, the cadence of her Spanish reminding me of my mother.

We hit some turbulence, and my seatmate goes back to her prayers. I try to distract myself, looking out the window. The land comes into view below: first, the turquoise sea, the white sands, then a lush green canopy like a tourist's dream of the tropics. Here and there, I notice gashes on the hills, eroded gullies, whole stretches without a single tree. Did a hurricane go through there?

"What's going on?" I ask my seatmate.

She shrugs. "Dios que sabe."

God only knows, and now, if there is an afterlife, so does Mami.

My tías—at least a half dozen—are waiting at the airport. I could have picked them out of the crowd. They all look like Mami: the soft burnished skin, the glossy black hair, pulled back into a hairnet, the eyes like deep, dark pools you can see yourself reflected in. Even the older ones can still turn heads. But their taste in clothes is a little creepy: They're all wearing long skirts like the evangelicals in our Bronx hood. I sure hope they won't start in on Jesus wanting Mami to be another angel.

"¡GUAPA!" they call out, waving wildly as I walk out of customs. Everyone was already looking at this beautiful cluster, so it's not like they're suddenly being noticed. For the first time in my life, I am no one's secret. I belong. I have a whole family to call my own.

"How did you know it was me?" I ask in my halting Spanish.

"You look just like your mother," they say, laughing, and then, we're all hugging and sobbing.

We have to leave Mami behind at the airport: Some forensic inspection and paperwork has to be completed before the body can be released. I feel a tug of mom-sickness, like my homesickness when I first went off to school. But now, I have a dozen hands to hold.

The tías aren't too happy either. But they finally agree. "Our driver will pick her up tomorrow."

The official scowls. Usually, the funeral parlor handles the remains—Mami's new name. It seems we're not abiding by some unspoken rule, or more likely, some racket going on between the airport authority and the National Morticians' Association. But Mami made it clear. Her body was to be released only to her sisters. And one thing you can't do is argue with the dead.

We set out from the airport in the van my tías hired. The driver, Leonidas, is nonstop trying to hit on the younger aunties. They give him one-word answers, looking straight ahead to avoid eye contact.

Dusk deepens, we've left civilization behind: The villages recede; the wild green countryside surrounds us. But again, I see stretches of cracked bare earth, the few trees look dead and rotting. It's especially painful to see the destruction of a country I'm just starting to claim as my own.

"What's going on?"

The tías heave a collective sigh. "The inhumans. They're ruining our home."

"The whats?"

"You know them by another name." The tías nod toward our driver. Leonidas has been smoking inside the van, then throwing his butts out the window. I want to yell at him, *HEY! THAT'S NOT OKAY!* But I still feel clumsy talking, no less hollering at someone in Spanish.

"You could start a fire," one of the younger aunts finally protests.

"Not like the fire you start in my heart, mami."

My tías and I exchange that look. I guess eye rolling is a universal language.

Up ahead by the side of the road there's an old woman sitting on a stump, surrounded by younger versions of my tías. Leonidas's eyes practically pop out like some cartoon character. He whistles. "¡Wao, cuántas curvas y yo sin frenos!"

For a second there I think something is wrong with our brakes, and I brace myself for a crash. Oh, did I mention, no seatbelts? Too wimpy, I suppose, like not smoking inside a car or littering the earth.

"Stop here," the oldest auntie orders. She seems to be the boss. Everyone calls her Tía, even the other tías.

We disembark and say our hasta luegos.

"Yo no sé," Leonidas says, looking left and right. No sign of a house or a village. I'm a little curious myself where we're headed. But I feel at home in this fortress forest, secure in the embrace of my newly found familia.

Leonidas shakes his head. "It's not safe leaving all you pretty ladies in the middle of nowhere." Surely, we need protection, not to mention help carrying my suitcase.

"No, gracias," my tías keep telling him.

Leonidas gives up on the aunties. Maybe he, too, thinks that they must be prudes in their floor-length skirts, long-sleeved blouses, hairnets, and zero interest in flirting with him. He shifts his attention to me, who, I guess, looks more promising in a short skirt and leggings and my Doc Martens. "So where do I deliver the remains?" he asks me.

I shrug. I have no idea what arrangements have been made. But instead of anxious, it's a relief to feel like I don't have to be in charge. With Mami, those last weeks I was always worrying, calling home every day, the helicopter daughter. "What did you have for breakfast? Have you gone shopping for groceries? Why not go to the salon and get your hair done?" She seemed so lost, like she was discovering she was out of her element.

The oldest tía speaks up. "Just bring her here same time tomorrow. We'll be waiting."

Leonidas looks around. "But there's nothing here. How will you move it? A coffin is heavy."

Tía aims her gaze at him. In a voice you don't want to mess with, she reminds him: "We hired you to do a job, not to ask questions."

Leonidas's eyes widen. His whole body freezes—it's like that Medusa in our mythology book just turned him to stone. "I was just trying to help," he apologizes in a small, obedient voice.

"We appreciate that," Tía says, breaking her gaze. Leonidas snaps out of his trance and hurries into his van.

"Ven, ven, ven." The aunties are pulling at my hands, one has my suitcase. "Your abuela has been waiting all day!" They undo their hairnets and toss their manes like spirited horses who will never be tamed.

I long to be that free, released from secrecy and shame. I'm not sure what all is coming down, but whatever it is, I'm game.

Abuela tries to stand, but either she can't or she's overcome by emotion. Her daughters lift her up, and she falls into my arms.

"La bendición, Abuela." What Mami taught me to say.

Abuela responds, but not with any recognizable words, more like the whistling of a songbird. Somehow, it sounds right in this forest setting.

"Hurry, hurry, it will soon be dark!" Tía looks up at the sky and then nervously at the road. She doesn't have to say what she's thinking. Leonidas might be coming back with his buddies and a bottle of rum.

We head for the woods, a thick tangle of mangrove trees hung with curtains of Spanish moss, the ground booby-trapped with exposed roots. The canopy overhead is impenetrable.

But the forest is surprisingly illuminated. Beams of light penetrate the darkness. I look around for their source. Oh my God! It's my aunties and cousins and Abuela: Their eyes glow in the dark, as if the flashlight app on my cell phone were inside their heads! Suddenly, I notice a faint beam at my feet—and it's coming from me! I'm the one who's spooked now.

Slowly, I relax. A me I didn't know was there is being released. I hear one of the tías whisper, "We're getting her back." Her voice, too, has been transformed into the same musical twitter as Abuela's. The difference is that now I can make sense of what she is saying. It sounds familiar like the nonsense ditties Mami used to sing to me when I was a little kid.

We reach the river, its waters glowing from all the firefly eyes gazing at it. One by one, the aunties and cousins undress, stepping out of their skirts; their long hair cascading like black waterfalls, covering their bodies. Oh my god, is this some sort of nudist cult?

My jaw drops; I triple blink. I guess my father's uptight Puritan genes and my New England boarding school have succeeded in colonizing me. I glance down embarrassed, but what I see is equally disturbing. Their feet are twisted weirdly, toes in back, heels in front. That must be why they all wear those long skirts, to hide their birth defects in public.

Several aunties carry Abuela to the edge of the river. I almost cry out, *Don't, don't drown her!* But once inside the water, my grandmother moves like an agile seal. This is where she belongs.

"What are you waiting for, Guapita?" my cousins call from the water.

I'm looking left and right around for my suitcase. Where did they hide it?

"You don't need a suit," my cousins remind me.

Abuela chides her granddaughters. "Don't hurry her! She has to get used to us. Remember, she's been tampered with."

Tampered with! In a fit of anger, I peel off my clothes, my leggings, my boots. They gasp when they see my corrected feet. I'm naked as the day I was born, even more naked than they are, as my hair doesn't come down past my shoulders, so I don't have their natural cover. But here's the chance I was longing for to be released from secrecy and shame. I whoop and dive in, leaping back up to the surface, hands over my head, executing one of my fancy moves. They all start spouting water from their mouths, dozens of tiny fountains, which, I learn, is their way of clapping.

At dusk the next day, a group of us wait by the side of the road. The van approaches, Leonidas driving, another guy beside him, several more peering out the windows. I get that panicky feeling like when a stranger starts following me at night on a lonely street. One of the tías emits a warning in that strange language, now not so strange. *Prepare yourselves, ciguapas!*

Leonidas pulls onto the shoulder, and three men pile out of the back of the van and reach in for my mother's coffin. "Mami," I gasp. My cousins must sense the wave of grief crashing over me. They sit me down on the stump where Abuela sat yesterday.

"We'll carry it to your casita." Leonidas is all bossy today. Too bad Tía isn't with us.

"We don't need your help." After all, only the strongest aunts and cousins were enlisted to help carry Mami's coffin.

"Of course, you do, Mamacitas." Leonidas leers. The other men mirror the predator look on his face. "Didn't I tell you they were gorgeous?"

Suddenly, there's a high-pitched bird cry. On that signal, some cousins and aunties begin unbuttoning their blouses, untying their hair, letting their skirts fall to the ground. The men's mouths drop open.

"Don't look at them!" Leonidas warns. He must be remembering the spell cast on him yesterday. But his men have sighted the promised land, and they're not about to go back to Egypt.

They dash forward, hesitating only about which beauty to nab first. My cousins and aunties leap away, the men after them, leaving my mother's coffin sitting disrespectfully in the middle of the road with a bunch of us crouched behind it.

Leonidas scrambles back into the van. "I'll be back with la policía," he calls as he roars away. But his cronies have already disappeared into the woods. I hear shouts and splashes. By the time the rest of us make it to the river, lugging Mami's heavy coffin, there isn't a sign of them anywhere.

I look around, still feeling unsafe. "Where are they?"

"They didn't look where they were going," Tía says, nodding at the river. She hands my cousins dust mops of Spanish moss. "Quick! Quick, erase their tracks!"

Several aunts open the lid of the coffin, and now it's me looking away. I don't want the last memory of my mother to be of her dead body. They fill the inside with river stones, then push the box into the water, where it sinks to the bottom.

Later that night and all the next day, we hear the search parties, accompanied by Leonidas, thrashing through the mangrove, trying to track down our whereabouts. But all the footprints lead away from the river, and the dogs can't follow our scent in the water.

Disappeared into thin air! Leonidas is convinced we were demons who seduce men by taking on the shape of beautiful women.

"Those inhumans." Abuela shakes her seaweed hair. "When will they ever learn?"

I lose track of the days. I love being here with my familia. (I love that I can say *my* family!) It's like camping full time. Every day we refresh and rebraid our tents of Spanish moss. We gather nuts and berries and harvest tubers they call víveres. We make seaweed soups, bobbing with yuca. I learn that they can stay underwater for days on end. I guess I do have their genes, or half of them anyway. Coach always said I could hold my breath the longest of anyone he'd trained.

But there is trouble in paradise; we smell the belching exhaust of trucks blowing in from the road. The sky darkens with the fires lit in the fields. Slash and burn, Ms. Halpern called it, like someone torturing the earth. We find dead fish on the shore, the clutter of plastic refuse left behind by the tide, the rotted palmas, the skeletal reefs.

"What can we do?" I keep asking.

Mami died by suicide. But this is slow suicide—slash that. It's plain and simple murder of our mother Earth.

Before it runs out of juice, I check my cell. There are several desperate texts from my father. *Are you okay? Are you ready to come back? Miss you, Guppy!*

Oh, please! I stuff the cell deep in my carry-on. My eye falls on Mami's envelope I've been avoiding.

Abuela's hand is on my shoulder, as if she knows it's time to face the loss. She's right. I can handle the pain. I'm not alone anymore.

That evening, we all sit on rocks under starlight. I open the envelope. Inside, there's a tiny recorder with a Post-it: *Por favor listen to my memo.*

I press the start button and Mami's voice floods the air. Suddenly, she is here, there, everywhere.

We are ciguapas, Guapita. Our feet are not a deformity, but nature's way to help us survive. No one has ever been able to track us down because our footprints always lead away from where we are hiding under the waters.

I was happy in my beautiful home, until I caught sight of your father wandering in the mangrove. When he saw me, he didn't chase after me. Instead he sang me a song he made up on the spot. Day after day he returned and sang it. That's when I realized not all humans are inhuman.

She sang some verses of a song she used to sing in happier times. I had no idea it had been my father's love song to her. My heart fills with longing for her . . . with a little space left over for my father, too.

We fell in love. We talked about our dreams. He wanted to be a musician. But his family did not understand, just like mine didn't understand my love for him. So, when he left, I followed. You were already inside me.

This must come as a surprise to Abuela and my tías. They look at each other puzzled and saddened by what they now know they didn't understand.

I was foolish to think I could survive away from my island home. Only your father's love made it possible. But when I lost him . . . I was like a fish too long out of the water. But I couldn't go back. Like you, I'd had the operation. I would leave footprints that would allow inhumans to track down the ciguapas. I would be endangering

*everyone I loved. I couldn't risk it. Forgive me, Guapita, this is the
only way I can go home again.*

"Play it again," Abuela says, when the recording ends.

That night, Abuela sits beside me on my special rock in the
middle of the river. The waters rush by, like one of those noise
machines with the sounds of waterfalls.

Abuela has been very quiet since listening to Mami's voice.
It's me who breaks the silence.

"I'm not going back," I tell her.

I think she'll be glad; instead she answers. "Guapita, I
know you've seen for yourself how our forests are being cut
down. Our rivers are drying up. The few that remain are full of
poisons. Many of my daughters and granddaughters are getting
sick."

"The US isn't much better!" I start quoting a bunch of facts
I learned in Ms. Halpern's class.

She nods. She knows. She is living the consequences of
these violations every day.

"But listen, Guapita. Unlike us, you have a foot in both
worlds." I can't help smiling at her choice of words, but Abuela
is dead serious. "You have the chance to get an education, to be
an advocate. You can help save us."

"What can I do? I couldn't even save Mami!"

Abuela lets me cry out my sadness before she speaks again.
"You couldn't save your mother, Guapita, but you can help save
what she loved."

She can see I'm confused because she adds, "Tell them our story. Teach the inhumans how to be human again. And remember, if you help save us, you'll always have a home to come back to."

I see her point. What good would it be to stay here and watch our home be ruined, and the family I've finally found get sick and slowly die? I can do more from the States.

But still I feel this lingering doubt. Am I making the right choice by going back? That night I lie on my back and pray to Mami to give me a sign. The stars blink, yes, no, yes, no, as if Mami herself can't decide.

Next day at the airport, I text my father. *I guess I'm ready.*

Not a minute later, he answers, *I'll be waiting at arrivals with open arms.* No mention of Melanie, the surrogate parent. *Can't wait to see you, Guppy!* This time when he says my baby name, I feel a softening in my heart.

On the flight to Nueva York, I look down at the gutted hillsides, the gashed ground. Hard as it is, I know I made the right choice. As if to confirm this, I get the sign I asked Mami for. A few miles off the north coast, the pilot announces he'll be banking so we can catch a glimpse of the humpback whales. Every year they return home to mate and nurse their newborn calves. We can make them out by the spouts of air fountaining from their blow-holes as they surface above the water.

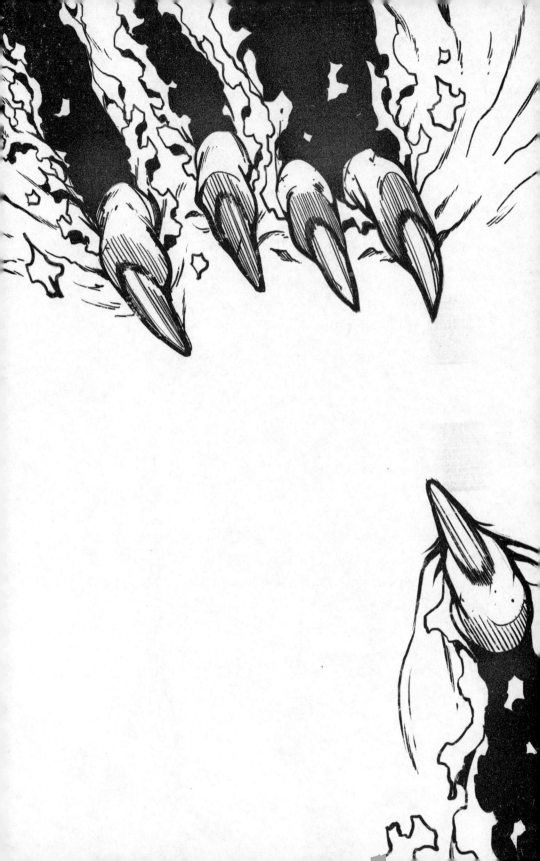

The Hour of the Wolf

Courtney Alameda

FREMONT, CALIFORNIA
OCTOBER 1968

I.

Before the theater's lights even went out, Adriana Perez knew she'd made a mistake. Maybe God had heard her lie to her mamá, or karma was rapping her across the knuckles for sneaking into the wrong theater. Either way, Adriana shouldn't have come.

The loud, rowdy boys on her left smelled like they'd had too much to drink. One of them kept trying to talk to Adriana, asking for her name, then her phone number.

Rolling her eyes, Adriana leaned toward her friend, Elena Olivares. "We can still go see *Funny Girl*," she said in Spanish. That was the movie they'd bought tickets for, after all.

"We might not get another chance to see this," Elena replied, shooting the boys a dirty look. One of them flipped her off. "It was hard enough to find this showing. Do you want me to see if someone will switch seats with us?"

"Nobody will want to sit next to these stupid drunks," Adriana replied, gesturing to the boys with a tilt of her head. It was Friday night at the new Fox Fremont Theater, and there wasn't an open seat in the house. Everyone was here to see the same movie—George Romero's *Night of the Living Dead*—the *one* movie Adriana had promised her mother she wouldn't go see. "I'd rather switch *theaters*."

"Ay, but then we'll miss out," Elena replied. "Or rather, *you* will, because I can come back tomorrow. My mamá doesn't mind if I see this."

"Hey!" Someone tossed a piece of popcorn at Elena. It bounced off her long, sleek ponytail.

Both girls turned.

Adriana's heart sank.

Katie Barnhardt and her posse of pink, pale-skinned Barbie girls sat behind Adriana and Elena. Now Adriana *knew* some cosmic force had her number; the last person she wanted to see on a Friday night was the girl who bullied her every day at school.

Katie had been kind to Adriana, once upon a time. Not anymore.

"What?" Elena snapped in English. Elena didn't attend Our Lady of Guadalupe School for Girls; she had the smooth-skinned knuckles of a public school student. And while Adriana had told her about Katie, Elena had never met her before.

"This is America," Katie said, scrunching up her nose. "We speak English here."

"Oh yeah? Well, California was a part of Mexico *first*, güera," Elena replied. "Which is why most of the cities here are named in *Spanish*." She turned around, indicating that the conversation was over.

Katie made a disgusted noise in the back of her throat. One of the girls threw another piece of popcorn, this time at Adriana, while muttering something about "those girls from Niles." The rest of them tittered and squeaked like rats.

The giggles hit Adriana like a slap, leaving her cheeks red and smarting. The Niles district was one of five townships that made up Fremont, California, and it was known for its dense population of Latino immigrants, particularly Chicanos. And the area's campesinos worked farms like the one Adriana's parents owned.

Why, Adriana had just spent most of her afternoon helping the farm's campesinos stitch eagles onto flags of red and white. The black Aztec eagle was the standard of the United Farm Workers, of La Causa, and a symbol of dignity and hope. While her parents treated their employees well, not everyone in the city did. Next Saturday, farm workers from all over the Bay Area and San Joaquin Valley were marching for higher wages, cleaner living spaces, and fairer treatment.

Depending on the day, Adriana was alternately thrilled or anxious about the event. Despite her growing sense of dignity, girls like Katie Barnhardt left Adriana searching for the courage to say ¡Viva la huelga!

Long live the strike.

Another piece of popcorn hit her shoulder. Adriana shot the girl a dark look but said nothing—she didn't want to get kicked out for causing a scene.

"Ignore them," Elena said through her teeth, switching to Spanish. "They will never understand."

Katie and her friends wouldn't understand because they didn't *want* to understand. They didn't *have* to understand.

"You sure you can handle a *scary movie*, Katie?" one of the girls said, teasing. "You've been such a baby since we went to the mission."

"Shut up, Melanie," Katie snapped. "I don't see *you* volunteering to take the wolf skull."

"You were the one who wanted it, not me," Melanie snapped back.

Wolf skull? Adriana exchanged a look with Elena but said nothing.

As the previews rolled, Katie and her friends went quiet. Maybe they would at least let Adriana enjoy the movie in peace.

To her surprise, *Night of the Living Dead* was shot in black and white. The film opened in a graveyard and spiraled quickly into chaos. It was even more shocking than people said it would be—Adriana was used to horror movies like *Psycho* or *Rosemary's Baby*, but this? Romero's film felt like a new breed.

Adriana loved every *minute* of it.

As the ghouls on-screen began to eat human remains, the boy sitting beside Adriana groaned and got to his feet, staggering a little. At first, she thought he was kidding around, pretending to be one of the film's living corpses . . .

But then he doubled over and vomited in front of her.

Adriana shrieked. The hot, stinking liquid splashed across her shoes and soaked into her knee-high stockings. It smelled like regret, like onions soaked in a warm, flat beer and sour milk, with a hint of cumin for bad measure. The scent made her eyes burn.

With a cry, she leapt out of her seat. "What's wrong with you?" she asked, shoving his shoulders with her palms. He stumbled a bit, catching himself on the tops of the chairs. Before the boy could respond, Adriana turned on her heel and fled from the theater.

In the hallway, her shoes sloshed with each step. People stared. Heat rose to her cheeks. Adriana hid her face with one hand, resting her fingertips on her temple.

That *stupid* boy and his *stupid* . . . *Ugh!*

It had been ages since Adriana had enjoyed a movie that much, and now it was ruined. Even if she was able to wash the stains from her socks, they would never dry before Mamá picked her up. Her mother would demand to know what had happened, and Adriana would be forced to lie. *Again.*

Or she could just tell her mamá the truth and be grounded for the rest of her life.

Adriana headed to the women's restroom, mortified to find it closed for cleaning. At this rate, being grounded by her mamá didn't sound so bad.

"Adriana!"

She turned her head, relieved to see Elena hurrying toward her.

"Oh my God, chica!" Elena said. "Are you okay?"

"No, not really," Adriana said, shaking her hands as if to ward off her embarrassment. "The bathroom's closed."

Elena frowned. "Can't you use the one near the concessions stand out front?"

"I'm not going to walk through the theater like this," Adriana said, gesturing at her stinking, soiled socks.

"Come on, then," Elena said, putting an arm around Adriana's shoulders. "We can go around back and slip through the front door. Do you still have your ticket?"

"Yeah," Adriana said. "But you don't have to miss the movie, too. Go back in, I'll be there in a few minutes."

"You sure?" Elena asked, her brows knitting.

"Come on, I don't want us *both* to miss out because of a drunk pendejo," Adriana said. "Go."

When Adriana stepped outside, the sky glowed as pink as a fresh burn. To the west, the sun looked like a giant, half-opened cat's eye. It made Mission Peak and the surrounding Coyote Hills gleam like gold and reflected off the cars surrounding her, blinding and bright. Her father called this time of day the hour of the wolf, the time when it was difficult to tell a dog from a wolf, a friend from a foe.

Adriana kicked off her shoes. *Stupid, stupid, stupid!* she told herself. If she'd only gone to see *Funny Girl*, none of this would be happening now. Lifting one foot, she tugged off a sock, trying to keep her fingers away from the wet, stinking splotches of vomit. Adriana couldn't stand in it for another second—she'd rather be barefoot.

As she peeled her other sock off her leg, something big darted between the cars.

Something shadowy.

Something *fast*.

Adriana paused. A strange smell tainted the air; a rottenness lurked beneath the scent of stale popcorn clinging to her cardigan and the rubbery asphalt. Adriana dropped her other sock, scanning the empty spaces between the cars. The ground felt cold and gritty beneath her feet.

It was just your imagination, she scolded herself, seeing nothing. *The movie must have scared you. How are you going to sleep tonight, huh?*

A growl rose, low and quiet. Adriana felt its reverb in her bones. *No, not a growl—stop being ridiculous!* It was the hum of a faraway motorcycle. But the hairs on the back of her neck stiffened, and she couldn't shake the sense that she was being watched. *By what?* Except for dozens of cars, the back parking lot was empty. Adriana was alone.

But she knew this feeling, the sort of fear that started as a chill in the marrow and worked into the muscles, freezing her slowly. At six years old, she'd felt it in the barn while a strange, misty little boy peeked at her from the rafters. At ten, she'd felt it while she and her brother watched a chupacabra lope through their fields. She felt it when her abuela read her tea leaves and tarot cards, too. It was her body's physical response to the presence of the otherworldly; a being her soul recognized but her mind did not.

"Hello?" Adriana called, taking a few steps forward.

Nothing moved.

Gooseflesh prickled along her arms. Heat needled her calf muscles. The impulse to run unspooled in her gut. On an instinct, Adriana glanced over her shoulder, but nothing was there.

Another growl—closer this time—turned Adriana's head.

A black dog stood between two cars, hiding in the shadows of the sunset. With the sunlight in her eyes, Adriana could barely make out its long, shaggy coat and massive paws. The creature stood taller at the withers than her father's giant German shepherds. It had black eyes that burned like coals. The stench in the air grew stronger, filling her nostrils with death and decay.

Katie's words came to her then: "My dad and I keep seeing this weird black wolf around the house . . ."

With a gasp, Adriana stepped back. Her bare heel hit a small, sharp rock, sending a bolt of pain up her leg. She stumbled, catching herself against the hood of a nearby car.

The wolf-dog lowered its head, but otherwise, it didn't move. Fear rose in Adriana's throat, burning like bile. If she made a run for it, would the wolf-dog give chase? The theater's back doors had no exterior handles—she would need to make it to the main entrance. Too far. She could scream, but Adriana doubted anyone would hear her. And she had nothing to defend herself with.

All she could do was *run*.

The back doors burst open. Katie Barnhardt came out with one arm wrapped around a boy, giggling. "I told Melanie was I leaving, she'll be *fine*. She can get a ride with—"

"Wait, Katie!" Adriana said, pointing at the theater doors. "Hold that door!"

Katie's gaze landed on Adriana, confusion spreading across her face.

The metal doors closed with a heavy *thud*.

"Adriana?" Katie asked, color springing into her cheeks. "What are you doing out here?"

"There's a wolf" —Adriana pushed herself off the car and pointed behind her— "there's . . . there's a . . ."

She turned. The wolf was gone. The last of the sunlight slipped behind the hills, leaving the sky to purple and bruise.

"A *wolf?*" Katie scoffed. "Now *you're* getting on my case about that, too?"

"No, I—I swear . . ." Adriana said, blinking hard.

"Get a life, Adriana!" Katie grabbed the boy's hand and started pulling him toward the parking lot.

Adriana grabbed her shoes and socks, watching as Katie sped away in her gleaming, candy apple red Pontiac.

A black shadow darted after Katie's car.

II.

That night, the dogs barked till dawn.

On Saturday morning, Adriana's mother stepped outside and shouted for help. Their chickens had been torn to shreds— their feathers, wings, and gory offal were scattered all across the backyard. Adriana asked her papá if he'd ever seen wolves on the farm. "No, mija," he replied. "This was probably just a feral dog, maybe even a coyote. There aren't any wolves here."

Adriana wasn't fool enough to tell him he was wrong.

On Sunday, the Filipino farmworkers complained that something had dug up and eaten their balut in the night; and the foreman spotted a black dog slinking around the farm before dawn. He and Papá took their rifles to search for it but found nothing, not even the dog's tracks.

But as night fell, Adriana heard a strange, low howling. It sounded nothing like the wolves she'd seen on television— this sound was like the keening of the wind, but a full octave lower.

Unable to sleep, Adriana wandered downstairs. She was surprised to find her abuela sitting at the kitchen table, weaving seed beads and thread into exquisite pendants and bracelets.

"You hear it, too, don't you?" her abuela asked in Spanish, without looking up. Her needle flashed as she worked. "The howling of the Tukákame."

Adriana shivered, hugging herself and crossing the room to sit at her grandmother's side. Despite the golden light in the room and the comforting scent of the spices that lingered in the air, fear nibbled on the edges of Adriana's soul.

"What is it?" She asked.

"A creature older than time itself," her abuela replied. "The Tukákame is a god of death and cruelty. At night, he comes forth from the deep places of the earth to hunt, taking the form of a wolf. But his true form is that of a skeleton, and he garbs himself in the skins and bones of his victims."

The Tukákame sounded like one of George Romero's ghouls, but Adriana knew better than to say as much. Romero's monsters were make-believe. The howling on the wind was real.

"How do we make it go away?" Adriana asked.

"One cannot shoo death away like a fly," her abuela said, but there was no malice in her tone. "We must wait for him to move on. And so, I make pendants. One for you, one for your papá, one for your mamá, and one for each of your brothers. Juanita is helping me make them for all the workers, too."

"Is that all we have to do?" Adriana asked, thinking of the wolf's burning eyes.

"No. Stay inside after sundown," her abuela replied. "Wear your pendant—I'll make you earrings, if you prefer. And beware black dogs."

Adriana paused, looking down at her lap.

"What if I've seen it?" Adriana asked in a small voice. "If I've come face-to-face with a black wolf with glowing red eyes?"

Her abuela's hands—always so industrious—stopped moving. She looked at Adriana. "The Tukákame only appears to bad people," she said slowly, studying Adriana's face. "What have you done, my child?"

"Nothing!" Adriana said, guilt gripping her heart in a vice. Yes, she'd lied to her mamá, but did that make her a bad person? It was such a small lie, a *white* lie. Adriana's guts twisted. "I—I think he was there for a girl from school—she said she stole something, and the wolf's shadow followed her car out of the parking lot."

"What did she steal?"

"I—I think it was a wolf's skull."

Her abuela frowned. "And when did you see the Tukákame?"

"Friday night."

"That is when this howling started." The creases in the old woman's forehead deepened. She put her work down, then gripped Adriana by the forearm. "You stay away from that girl, Adriana, do you hear me? If she has drawn the attention of such a creature, there is very little goodness in her heart."

I knew that much without *the Tukákame's help,* Adriana thought, but she bobbed her head and said, "Okay."

"If you have seen this thing, you will need something special," her abuela said, picking up a glimmering cobalt-and-white pendant. Her abuela regularly wove masterpieces in thread and beads, but this one was exquisite—a Huichol mandala of the sun. When she handed it to Adriana, it had a heft to it that surpassed its physical weight. It dampened Adriana's fears.

"I make beautiful things to balance out the cruelty in the world," her abuela said, closing Adriana's hand over the pendant. "Our art is like a prayer—when we make beautiful things, the gods listen. Wear this until the howling stops. It will keep you safe."

"Okay," Adriana said. "I promise."

After bidding her abuela goodnight, Adriana returned to her bed wishing she'd never stepped foot in that theater.

The next morning, Adriana went to school with her abuela's pendant tucked under her shirt. She saw no sign of the wolf, but it was *impossible* to avoid Katie Barnhardt. Adriana had three classes with her. Thankfully, Katie ignored Adriana . . . *most* of the time.

At lunch, Adriana joined her usual confederation of honors students, artists, and wannabe activists. They weren't friends, really, but there was safety in numbers.

Maggie Arden waved Adriana into the cafeteria line. "How was your weekend?" she asked as they stepped into the cafeteria, only to be smothered by the aroma of Sister Rosa's "famous" spaghetti and meatballs.

"It should've been good," Adriana answered, grabbing a tray. "Elena and I went to see *Night of the Living Dead* on Friday, but some idiot threw up on me halfway through."

Maggie took an apple from a nearby cart, making a face. "Eww, seriously? Was the movie worth it, at least?"

"I don't know," Adriana said with a little laugh, stepping into the left-hand line. "I spent part of it washing regurgitated beer out of my socks."

"That's so gross," Maggie said, joining her. "Hey, by the way, where'd you get your necklace? It's pretty."

"Oh," Adriana said, glancing down and putting a hand on her beaded pendant. She hadn't realized that it had slipped over her shirt. "My abuela—I mean, my grandmother made it for me."

"Where'd you get your necklace, *Adriana?*" someone parroted in a mocking tone. Girls on the other side of the room burst into giggles. "It's *pretty!*"

A weight dropped into Adriana's stomach, heavy and rough as a peach pit. Maggie's pale cheeks flushed red as apples.

From the other line, Katie Barnhardt cocked a hip, a smirk on her face. "I don't know if *pretty* is the word I'd use to describe *that* hippie piece of trash," she said, gesturing at Adriana's throat. Her friends giggled and whispered behind their hands, their eyes on Adriana.

Hippie.

Piece.

Of.

Trash?

Heat bubbled through Adriana's blood. When confronted, she usually wanted to melt into the floor. But this time was different—her grandmother's art was a beloved tradition, not faddish *hippie trash.*

All four lunch ladies pretended not to notice the scene in front of them, each one as white and prim as the uniforms they wore. They kept their attention on their work, dishing out wobbling mounds of spaghetti and slimy, overcooked vegetables. And as for the other students? Most of them had their heads down, too, trying not to get involved.

No one would stand up for Adriana. If she wanted change, she would have to stand up for *herself.*

"I'm not just *the girl from Niles,* Katie, and this isn't trash." Adriana gestured to the pendant she wore. Then, in Spanish, she continued: "In fact, the only piece of trash I see in this room is *you*."

Up ahead, Luci Hernandez choked down a laugh. When Katie glared at her, she cleared her throat and looked away.

"What did you just say?" Katie asked, turning to Adriana.

"Maybe if you could speak more than one language, you'd know," Adriana replied, pushing her tray down the line.

Adriana wasn't sure who threw the spaghetti first, but a wad of ground beef, sauce, and noodles soared past her and smacked into Maggie's collarbone. The wet mass slid down Maggie's starched shirtfront. Shrieking, Maggie leapt backward, tumbling into two other girls. All three went down at once. One girl, scrambling for a handhold, hit her tray and launched bowls of spaghetti, salad, and caramel pudding at the girls in the next line.

Shrieks and shouts filled the room. Katie was on Adriana in an instant. Adriana threw up her hands as Katie reached for her hair and pulled. *Hard*. Pain lit up Adriana's scalp. Grunting, Adriana knocked Katie's hand away. She jammed her heel into Katie's foot. Yelping, Katie let go.

"Girls!" someone shouted. "*Enough!*"

Putting a hand to her scalp, Adriana glanced up. Sister Eva stood at the front of the room, glaring with the sort of fury only a nun could muster. The cafeteria looked like a scene straight out of a horror movie—girls cowered under the countertops, the lunch ladies looked shell shocked, and red spaghetti sauce was spattered over the walls and floors.

Katie leapt away from Adriana, pointing a finger. "Adriana started it, Sister Eva! She said—"

"I don't care who started it, Miss Barnhardt," Sister Eva snapped, placing her hands on her hips. "To the principal's office, both of you. And, Miss Barnhardt, you'd better watch your p's and q's. I know you're behind this, and while some will turn a blind eye to it, *I* won't."

The principal's office? Adriana's heart stuttered. Mamá would be furious when she heard about this.

Adriana was so dead.

III.

When Adriana's parents heard about what happened at school, they grounded her for a week. "Stand up for yourself, mija," Mamá had said, "but you are better than your bullies! Don't stoop when you were meant to fly."

Much to Adriana's dismay, her punishment meant she wouldn't be allowed to attend the United Farm Workers protest that weekend. And no matter how Adriana begged and pleaded, her mother would not be dissuaded.

So, the following Saturday afternoon, when all her family and the campesinos headed to the Fremont Hub, Adriana found herself alone on the farm. Her mamá left her a long list of chores to keep her company. At least the work kept Adriana's mind occupied.

The sun slanted toward the horizon as Adriana finished for the day and headed home. She hadn't heard the Tukákame howl in days, but that didn't mean she wanted to linger after dark. Fremont's golden hills rose up on either side of her, peppered with California bay and oak trees. Long shadows stretched across the fields, lazy and long as cats. Birds sang, but otherwise, the land was still. Quiet. Peaceful.

In the distance, an engine rumbled. Adriana frowned. She didn't expect anyone to return until after the candlelight vigil, well after dark. Had someone come home early? She walked a little faster, worried.

As she came up over the rise, her family's home stretched out before her. Though the house was enormous, her mother called it their casita. With its white plaster walls and red tile roof, it reminded Adriana of the missions that dotted the California coastline.

A candy-apple-red Pontiac was parked in the drive.

Adriana's heart hardened to stone. Of course Katie knew where she lived; her mother often stopped by the Perez farm on church business. A light turned on in the kitchen window. Shadows—indistinct and impossible to identify—moved behind the lace curtains.

It was Katie, and she wasn't alone. Did she know that Adriana had been grounded and wasn't at the march? Were she and her friends trying to catch Adriana unawares? Or were they here to vandalize her home?

A chill wrapped its arms around Adriana's shoulders, leaving her shivering. The nearest neighbors were half a mile away. Even if she managed to get to a phone, the police would take ages to arrive. By that point, the damage would be done.

Adriana couldn't let that happen.

Mamá kept a small rifle in the barn—it wasn't much, just a pellet gun to frighten skunks and raccoons away from the house. But Adriana was willing to bet Katie and her friends wouldn't know the difference between a pellet gun and the real thing.

She sneaked around the farm's outbuildings, avoiding the windows. The shadows grew longer, too, helping to hide her from view. She took the pellet gun from the barn, then headed for the back of the house.

The mudroom door hung a few inches ajar.

Keeping the gun aimed at the ground, Adriana bumped the door with her hip. Inside, the room was empty. She stepped into the house, peering into the den. The evening gloom had crept in, greasing the window panes with blue light. Shadows clung to the furniture like funerary shrouds. The house lay silent.

Adriana paused, listening. A creak echoed from the direction of the kitchen—the sound of the dining room door swinging closed. Adriana stepped into the den. Up ahead, a dim triangle of light fell through the kitchen archway.

"Just drop it somewhere, Melanie!" someone hissed.

"We don't need to hide it" —that voice sounded like Katie's— "just leave it on the table."

Adriana frowned. *Leave* what *on the table?*

Carefully, she peered around the corner. There, through the kitchen and standing in the shadows of the dining room, was Katie Barnhardt and her posse, Hannah Eckles and Melanie Richards. The girls had their backs to Adriana.

"We need to get out of here," Hannah hissed.

"Fine." Melanie dropped something onto the dining room table, which hit with a hollow thud. It rocked a few times, grating against the wooden tabletop. Melanie glared at Hannah.

"Was that so hard? Come on, let's go." Katie turned back to the kitchen.

Adriana stepped into view, aiming the pellet gun at Katie's chest.

Katie froze, the whites of her eyes flashing. Melanie looked up and let out a cry when she saw Adriana.

"Please, don't shoot us." Hannah's lower lip wobbled. "This . . . this was Katie's idea! Not mine, I swear."

"What was Katie's idea?" Adriana asked. She kept her finger off the trigger—she wanted to scare Katie and her friends, not shoot them. A pellet gun might not kill anyone, but it could still hurt.

Katie rolled her eyes. "My mom just wanted me to drop something off—"

"You could have left it at the door." Adriana pointed the pellet gun at Hannah. She raised her voice as she said, "Hannah, *talk*."

"Please, don't," Hannah said, lifting her arms to shield her head. "It's the skull! Katie says it's cursed, so we brought it to your house to get rid of it—"

"Hannah!" Katie and Melanie gasped in unison.

"See? It's right here!" Hannah grabbed something off the dining room table and held it up. The kitchen lights gleamed off a giant wolf's skull. It was covered in swirling carvings and vibrant dyes. A sinister sort of energy leaked from the bone, one that made Adriana think it might spring to life and eat them alive.

A cold wave of fear washed over Adriana. Gooseflesh spread across the backs of her arms. The skull reminded her of a calavera, a sugar skull made to decorate ofrendas in November. But what sort of altar this skull was meant to decorate, Adriana could not say.

"Take the skull and get out," Adriana said. When the girls didn't move, she shouted, "Now!"

"You don't get to tell us what to do," Katie said with a tremor in her voice. Her gaze drifted to something behind Adriana. "You can't . . . I mean I . . ."

Katie trailed to a stop.

"Oh my God," Melanie said, pointing to the family room windows. "Is that *Erin?*"

"I told her to come inside with us!" Hannah cried.

Adriana glanced over her shoulder. Behind her, tall windows overlooked the family's fields. Outside, the last of the light slipped from the horizon. The hour of the wolf had passed and night drew its swift wings over the sky. A fourth girl—Erin Mullally—floated in the air. Her feet dangled six inches off the lawn. Her pale skin glowed like a moon in the low light.

Something twitched in the darkness. A shadow drew itself across Erin's throat, quick as a knife. She convulsed once, twice. A black waterfall flowed down her neck, pooling in the hollows of her collarbones.

"What the hell?" Katie whispered.

Erin fell lifelessly to the ground.

In the darkness left behind, two eyes burned like red coals. Adriana had seen eyes like that before, at sunset, sunken into the face of a wolf.

The other girls scattered, screaming. Melanie sprinted past Adriana. Hannah dropped the skull, which made a hollow, drumlike thump on the kitchen floor. For the space of a single heartbeat, Adriana stared at that skull, frozen. Terrified.

A crash echoed from the living room. Glass tinkled against the hardwood floors like razor-sharp bells. Melanie screamed, high and bright.

With a gasp and a skipped heartbeat, Adriana glanced over her shoulder.

The monster stood silhouetted against the windowpanes. Its figure was wasted, emaciated; its limbs stretched into strange lengths and horns corkscrewed off its head. When it moved, the bones strung from its waist chattered like maracas. The stench of death had followed it into the house—rich, meaty, and rotten.

Reaching out, the creature seized Melanie by the throat. Melanie gurgled, shuddering as the creature growled and pulled her close.

Melanie had been horrible to Adriana for years, but that didn't mean she deserved to die for it. Grabbing the skull from the floor, Adriana held it over her head.

"You want your skull back?" she shouted at the monster.

The Tukákame's fiery gaze snapped in Adriana's direction.

"Come and get it." Turning on her heel, Adriana fled into the dining room. She threw the sliding glass door open and ran out into the open yard.

A flash of white drew Adriana's attention toward the drive. Katie sprinted to her Pontiac, keys in hand, ready to abandon her friends to a monster.

Katie had brought this demon here.

She was going to take it back with her, too.

Clutching the skull in one hand and the pellet gun in the other, Adriana sprinted across the yard. Katie made it first— she wrenched her door open, stumbled in, and slammed it shut. The sound echoed across the property like a thunderclap. The engine roared. With a burst of speed, Adriana reached the passenger door. She yanked it open and tossed the skull inside, then dropped into the back seat.

"Adriana?" Katie shrieked, looking over her shoulder. "What the hell are you doing?"

"Making sure your mistakes don't get my family killed." Adriana leveled the pellet rifle at the back of Katie's head. "Drive."

"Where?" Katie cried. "That thing follows the skull wherever it goes!"

A shadow—swift and sharp—darted on the edge of Adriana's sight.

"Just go!" Adriana said, kicking Katie's seat. "Go, go, *go!*"

Katie slammed her foot onto the gas pedal. The Pontiac skidded against the gravel driveway, the car fishtailing until the tires found purchase. The car shot forward, the force plastering Adriana's guts to her spine.

As Katie pulled onto the main road, Adriana turned to look out the window. Darkness had swallowed her house. She saw no sign of the Tukákame.

"Where did you find this skull?" Adriana asked.

"Um." Katie wiped at her eyes with the sleeve of her sweatshirt. "The old mission. Not San José, you know the one near Mission Peak? I—I don't really think it's actually a mission, that's just what people call it."

"We need to take it back."

Katie glanced at Adriana in her rearview mirror. "I've already tried to *give* it to that . . . to that thing! I left it in my yard for two nights in a row. That thing never took it."

"Do you have a better idea?" Adriana snapped. "One that *doesn't* involve dumping it at a house full of innocent people?"

Katie didn't answer that, sniffling.

"Go to the mission, then," Adriana said. "Maybe if we return the skull, this thing won't kill us both."

Twenty minutes later, the Pontiac's headlights flashed over a crumbling adobe chapel. The building cowered in a valley between two towering, craggy hills. Most of the facade was over-run by vines and other creeping, growing things. Even in broad daylight, the building would have been hard to see—but maybe that was the point.

Maybe this was the sort of place that didn't want to be found.

Outside of the Pontiac's high beams, the sickled moonlight coated the edges of the world. Full night had fallen now, and the shadows looked cold and cruel.

Adriana dropped the wolf skull into the passenger seat. "Let's go."

"You're coming with me?" Katie asked, looking over her shoulder at Adriana.

"I don't have a choice," Adriana replied. "That thing's been skulking around my family's farm for the last week. It saw me touch the skull."

"That's all it takes?" Katie said, her voice no more than a hoarse whisper. "Oh God, I thought it was here for me. It already killed Erin. What if . . . what if it hurt Melanie or Hannah, too?"

Katie paused, drawing in a shaky breath. And as furious as Adriana was with Katie, anger wouldn't serve her now. She placed two fingers on the beaded pendant on her breastbone, and thought of her grandmother's sweet words: "I make beauti-ful things to balance out the cruelty in the world."

Maybe Adriana could balance out Katie's mistakes. And maybe this was a foolish plan. Adriana couldn't know, but she didn't have a better idea.

"We should go in," Adriana said. "If the monster followed us, we don't have much time."

"Okay," Katie said, wiping her sleeve under her nose. She grabbed the skull by an eye socket, took a deep breath, and said, "There's a cave behind the chapel—that's where I found the skull."

"C'mon, then," Adriana said, grabbing the pellet gun.

The girls stepped out of the car. With the sun gone, the air nipped at Adriana's cheeks, cold and sharp. The darkness around them lay dead. Unmoving. Even the stars hid their faces, and the wind didn't stir. A howl rose in the distance . . . but it sounded like a coyote, not like the unearthly wail of the Tukákame.

Katie left the Pontiac's engine running, using its headlights to flood the building with light. Heart pounding, Adriana followed Katie into the chapel. As they picked past upturned pews and ducked beneath tree limbs, the shadows danced around them. The building itself wasn't much more than four crumbling walls with a canopy of gnarled trees for a roof; and it was small, *much* smaller than any chapel Adriana had ever seen.

"How did you even find this place?" Adriana whispered.

"Hiking," Katie replied, climbing a pile of rubble to reach the chapel's altar. She pulled a lighter from her pocket, flicking it until a frail, quivering flame appeared. "I didn't want to come in here, but the boys insisted . . . I wish I hadn't listened to them."

Adriana climbed up the rubble pile. Something had torn a hole in the back wall, exposing a rocky, dark tunnel bored straight into the hill.

In the weak light, it looked like a portal to hell.

Katie lit two of the cracked, dingy glass votives on the altar. She handed one to Adriana. "Ready?" she asked.

No, Adriana thought, but "Yes" popped out of her mouth. She took the votive candle from Katie, shifting the pellet gun under an arm.

Just before they stepped into the tunnel, Katie paused and glanced over her shoulder. "You're a braver person than I am, you know that?"

Adriana frowned, confused. Katie hadn't said anything nice to her in *years.*

"Sometimes I wish . . ." Katie shook her head and headed into the tunnel. "Never mind, we should hurry."

"Yeah." Taking a deep breath, Adriana followed her in. The ground sloped down, taking them into the bowels of the earth. The light from their candles crept up the tunnel's wet walls. The air grew colder, as if they had stepped into a walk-in freezer, and the earth smelled of sulfur.

When the path leveled out, the girls found themselves in a small cavern. The light from their candles didn't reveal much: Thin, knobby stalactites hung from the ceiling, dripping water. Heaps of bones scattered across the floor, picked clean. Most of them looked old. Ancient, even. But as Adriana followed Katie into the room, their lights skirted fresher, riper animal corpses. The stench made Adriana's eyes water.

Up ahead, a rough-hewn altar emerged from the gloom, cut straight from the cavern's dark rock. Katie carried the skull to the altar. Adriana paused and set her candle atop a rocky outcropping. She needed both hands for the pellet gun, for all the good it would do against a monster the size of the Tukákame. Still, the heft of the stock against her shoulder comforted her.

Katie stepped up to the altar and lifted the wolf's skull.

On the altar's far side, something twitched.

Two points of red light opened in the darkness.

And a serrated yellow-white grin gleamed in the candle's shaking light.

Adriana felt like the air had been sucked out of the room—she could barely breathe. Before she could shout *Katie*, the Tukákame peeled itself away from the wall.

Katie looked up too late. With a screech, the Tukákame leapt up on the altar, knocking Katie to the floor. The cavern plunged into darkness. Katie screamed. The small space amplified the sound, turning it into a physical force that rattled Adriana's teeth and resonated in her bones. And in the aftermath, the wolf's skull clanged against the ground and tumbled, clattering to a stop at Adriana's feet.

The Tukákame's red eyes snapped up, focusing on Adriana. The monster snarled, still wreathed in shadows. The bones around the beast's waist chattered as it stepped toward her.

With her heart banging on her rib cage, Adriana rubbed her thumb across her abuela's pendant. For luck. For comfort. Then, grasping the pellet gun, she took aim at one of those bright red spots. A pellet gun couldn't kill a monster, no. But it could definitely put out a light.

Adriana slid her finger over the trigger and *fired*.

In the cavern, the pellet gun exploded like a cannon shot. The monster's scream was vicious, sharp, and it hit Adriana like an ax to the head. One of the Tukákame's red eyes winked out like a dying star.

With a pained cry, the creature scuttled away, bones clacking as it went. The cavern fell silent, except for Katie's soft,

339

frightened sobs. *She's alive.* The thought injected a little relief into Adriana's veins. *That's good.*

A pinprick of light appeared in the gloom. Katie's lighter. She clutched it in one hand and, with a grunt of pain, pushed herself up into a crouch. She felt around for the skull, her movements growing frantic when she realized it wasn't close. Katie turned her eyes growing wide as harvest moons. The skull sat near Adriana's feet.

"Adriana," Katie whispered. "The skull . . . but my leg, I—I don't think I can stand . . ."

Adriana shuddered at Katie's words. She would have to walk the skull to the altar. Alone. The skull was huge—she couldn't carry it *and* aim the rifle, leaving her exposed. Vulnerable. Every animal instinct in her bones told her to *run*, but in the end, a pellet gun wouldn't stop death itself, either.

Hands shaking, Adriana set the pellet gun against the rocky wall. She knelt down and threaded her fingers through the skull's eye socket.

As she rose, she said to the monster, in Spanish: "My grandmother calls you Tukákame. I don't know if that's what you are, or if you can even understand me, but I understand how an altar can be important. I'm sorry yours was desecrated. We're here to return this skull to you."

"What are you saying?" Katie half sobbed.

"I'm saying sorry," Adriana replied in English. "You should apologize, too."

"I'm sorry," Katie said. "I'm so sorry!"

Drawing a deep breath, Adriana stepped into the mire of shadows that separated her from Katie, leaving her rifle and the candle behind. She expected the Tukákame to attack again—but she saw no lights in the darkness. No bones chittered like teeth.

Adriana took another step. A bit of red light flashed on her left. She spun on one heel with a gasp. *Where is it?* She froze, breath hitching, thoughts scrambling. Adriana panicked as Katie struggled to get to her feet. *Where did that beast go?!*

Behind her, glass shattered and bones clacked.

Adriana whirled again, just in time to watch her candle's flame flicker and die on the floor. The shadows caged her in now, deep and oppressive. She backed toward the altar, holding the skull in front of her, waiting to see that telltale red light.

But it never came.

Carefully, quietly, Adriana set the skull on the altar. It chimed when it touched the stone, as if it were a bell, not bone. On instinct, she tugged her abuela's beaded pendant off her neck and placed it atop the skull.

If the Tukákame saw, it made no sign. In the distance, a coyote howled.

"Come on," Adriana said, offering Katie a hand up. "We should go."

"I—I don't know if I can stand," Katie whispered with a sob. "My leg—I think it's broken."

Adriana helped Katie to her feet. Together, they limped from the cavern, up the tunnel, and back into the ruined chapel. Outside, the Pontiac's lights glittered through the trees. She wished she could feel some measure of relief. Instead, the tension in her chest unspooled, leaving her feeling unraveled. Frayed. Exhausted.

Katie couldn't drive with a broken leg, so Adriana took the wheel. And when they reached the main road, Adriana took one last glance through the rear window. A black wolf stood just outside the Pontiac's taillights, one with a single red eye glowing in its head.

Adriana turned onto the road.

The wolf did not follow them.

Acknowledgments

My endless gratitude to Amparo Ortiz, sister and friend, for inviting me on this adventure. ¡Por muchas más! Thank you, Ricardo López Ortiz, for the beautiful cover and amazing illustrations. I ran out of adjectives to express how much I love them.

Thank you, Linda Camacho, our intrepid agent, for championing our ideas. Thank you also to the Algonquin Young Readers family: Sarah Alpert, Elise Howard, Stephanie Mendoza, Ashley Mason, Laura Williams, Stacy Lellos, and Shaelyn McDaniel.

What a wonderful honor to work with such a talented group of contributors! Gracias for trusting Amparo and me with your stories! We made a beautiful thing.

Like always, gracias totales to my family and dear friends for your support.

And thank you, reader, for walking into the shadows with us.

Yamile Saied Méndez

ACKNOWLEDGMENTS

It all started with a tweet. On May 22, 2020, I asked editors to put together an anthology featuring monsters from different Latine cultures. People asked me to edit it instead and offered to contribute their stories. Turns out, others were craving more Latine horror.

To my partner in crime, confidante, and co-editor of my dreams, the amazing Yamile Saied Méndez—going on this journey has been so much more fulfilling because of you (and your endless Maluma knowledge). Thank you so much for giving this idea its wings!

Many thanks to our superhero agent, Linda Camacho at Gallt & Zacker Literary Agency, for being our fierce advocate and a *huge* horror fan! Thank you to our family at Algonquin Young Readers, especially our other partner in crime, Sarah Alpert. Your vision for this anthology propelled it to new heights, Sarah!

Thank you to Ricardo López Ortiz for blessing us with a cover and story illustrations that will live in my heart—and my nightmares—forever.

To our dream team of contributors . . . Wow. I knew you'd blow us away, but I don't have words to describe your brilliance or the depth of my gratitude for all of you. Thank you so much for trusting us with your stories.

And to you, lovely reader, thank you for giving this book a chance. Stay awesome. <3

Amparo Ortiz

About the Authors

Chantel Acevedo has been described as a "master story-teller" by *Kirkus Reviews* and is the author of several adult novels, including *The Distant Marvels*, which was a finalist for the 2016 Andrew Carnegie Medal for Excellence in Fiction. Acevedo's middle-grade duology Muse Squad includes *The Cassandra Curse* and *The Mystery of the Tenth*. She's a professor of English at the University of Miami, where she directs the MFA program.

Courtney Alameda is a horror novelist and comic book writer. Born and raised in the San Francisco Bay Area, she now resides in the Northwest with her husband, one Welsh Corgi, two cats, three library rooms, and whatever monsters lurk in the rural darkness around her home.

Julia Alvarez has written novels, collections of poems, nonfiction, and numerous books for young readers. Best known for the novels *In the Time of the Butterflies* and *How the García Girls Lost Their Accents*, she has most recently published *Afterlife*, a novel for adults, and a new picture book for young readers, *Already a Butterfly: A Meditation Story*. The recipient of a National Medal of Arts, Alvarez is a founder of Border of Lights, a movement to promote peace and collaboration between Haiti and the Dominican Republic. She lives in Vermont.

Ann Dávila Cardinal is a novelist who feels no pressure to live up to the long line of Puerto Rican writers from whom she is descended. None at all. She is the author of the YA novels *Five Midnights* and *Category Five*, and the adult novel *The Storyteller's Death*. Ann lives in Vermont and spends her free time cycling, doing fiber arts, and preparing for the zombie apocalypse.

M. García Peña was born and raised in San Juan, Puerto Rico. She got her MFA from the New School and is the author of *Even If the Sky Falls* and *The Resolutions*. She's a founding member of the Latinx children's book artist collective Las Musas and splits her time between Puerto Rico and New York. You can find her at mgarciabooks.com.

Racquel Marie received a BA in English with an emphasis in creative writing and a minor in gender and sexuality studies from the University of California, Irvine. Racquel is the author of *Ophelia After All*, and she primarily writes YA contemporaries starring queer Latine characters like herself. You can learn more about her writing and love of books through her Twitter, @blondewithab00k.

Gabriela Martins is a Brazilian kid-lit author and linguist. Her stories feature Brazilian characters finding themselves and love. When she's not writing, she can be found cuddling with her two cats or singing loudly and off-key. Her YA romance debut is *Like a Love Song*, and her sophomore book is *Bad at Love*. Find her at gabrielawrites.com.

Maika Moulite is a Miami native and the daughter of Haitian immigrants. She loves writing: books, think pieces, journal entries, never-ending lists, you name it. When she's not scribbling every random thought into her notes app, she's sharpening her skills as a Howard University PhD student. Her research focuses on representation in media and its impact on marginalized groups. She's the eldest of four sisters and loves audiobooks, fierce female leads, and laughing.

Maritza Moulite graduated from the University of Florida with a bachelor's in women's studies and the University of Southern California with a master's in journalism. She's worked for NBC News, CNN, and *USA Today*, but her favorite roles were Head Start literacy tutor and pre-K teacher assistant. She loved working with young people so much that she is now a PhD student at the University of Pennsylvania, exploring ways to improve literacy through children's media.

Claribel A. Ortega is the *New York Times* bestselling and award-winning author of *Ghost Squad*, which is being made into a feature film; *Witchlings*; and the graphic novel *Frizzy*. Claribel is also a Marvel contributor. You can find her on Twitter, Instagram, and TikTok @Claribel_Ortega and on her website at claribelortega.com.

Lilliam Rivera is an award-winning author of the YA novels *Never Look Back* (a Pura Belpré honor book), *We Light Up the Sky*, *Dealing in Dreams*, *The Education of Margot Sanchez*, and the middle-grade Goldie Vance series. Her work has appeared in the *Washington Post*, the *New York Times*, and *Elle*, among other publications. Lilliam lives in Los Angeles.

Jenny Torres Sanchez is a full-time writer and former English teacher. She was born in Brooklyn, New York, but has lived on the border of two worlds her whole life. She lives in Orlando, Florida, with her husband and children.

Ari Tison is an award-winning Bribri (Indigenous Costa Rican) American poet and author of the YA hybrid novel *Saints of the Household*. Her poems have been published in various journals, including *POETRY*'s first issue for young people. She has her MFAC from Hamline University and teaches creative writing. You can find her on Twitter and TikTok @AriTison and online at aritison.com. "Blood Kin" was written in memory of Sergio Rojas Ortiz, a Bribri land activist who was brutally murdered in his home in March 2019. To date, not one of the perpetrators has been found and brought to justice.

Alexandra Villasante has a BFA in painting and an MA in combined media. Born in New Jersey to immigrant parents, Alex has the privilegio of dreaming in both English and Spanish. Her debut YA novel, *The Grief Keeper*, was an Indie Next pick, Indies Introduce Kids pick, and Fall 2019 Junior Library Guild Selection; was included in ALA's Rainbow Book List 2020; and is the winner of the 2020 Lambda Literary Award for LGBTQ Children's Literature/Young Adult Fiction.